BRYN GREENWOOD

ALL THE

UGLY AND

WONDERFUL

THINGS

THOMAS DUNNE BOOKS
ST. MARTIN'S GRIFFIN ☙ NEW YORK

THOMAS DUNNE BOOKS.
An imprint of St. Martin's Press.

ALL THE UGLY AND WONDERFUL THINGS. Copyright © 2016 by Bryn Greenwood. All rights reserved. Printed in the United States of America. For information, address St. Martin's Press, 175 Fifth Avenue, New York, N.Y. 10010.

www.thomasdunnebooks.com
www.stmartins.com

Designed by Anna Gorovoy

The Library of Congress has cataloged the hardcover edition as follows:

Names: Greenwood, Bryn, author.
Title: All the ugly and wonderful things : a novel / Bryn Greenwood.
Description: First edition. | New York : Thomas Dunne Books/St. Martins Press, 2016.
Identifiers: LCCN 2016002476| ISBN 9781250074133 (hardcover) |
ISBN 9781466885806 (e-book)
Subjects: LCSH: Children of drug addicts—Fiction. | Domestic fiction. | BISAC:
FICTION / Literary. | FICTION / Coming of Age.
Classification: LCC PS3607.R4695 A45 2016 | DDC 813/.6—dc23
LC record available at http://lccn.loc.gov/2016002476

ISBN 978-1-250-15396-8 (trade paperback)

Our books may be purchased in bulk for promotional, educational, or business use. Please contact your local bookseller or the Macmillan Corporate and Premium Sales Department at 1-800-221-7945, extension 5442, or by e-mail at MacmillanSpecialMarkets@macmillan.com.

First St. Martin's Griffin Edition: October 2017

Praise for *All the Ugly and Wonderful Things*

"If you're looking for a dangerous, shocking, and unexpectedly touching story, this is it. . . . This is a book that will shake you to the core."   —Bustle "31 Books Bringing the Heat this Summer"

"Captivating and smartly written from the first page, Greenwood's work is instantly absorbing. Pithy characters saunter, charge, or stumble into each scene via raw, gripping narrative. Greenwood slow-drips descriptions, never giving away everything at once. Rather, she tells her story as if lifting a cloth thread by thread, revealing heartbreaking landscapes and riveting dialogue in perfect timing. This book won't pull at heartstrings but instead yank out the entire organ and shake it about before lodging it back in an unfamiliar position."   —Christina Ledbetter, Associated Press

"This book destroyed me. I have never read anything like it. I came to the end of the novel with my mind reeling, my emotions scattered, and completely unsure exactly what I did feel about it. . . . But one thing is certain: I felt. Oh hell, I felt. I don't think I'll ever get these characters off my mind."   —Emily May, #1 worldwide most popular reviewer on Goodreads

"The title says it all. You will hold your little heart in your hands and keep blowing on it to make sure it's alive."
—*Daily News* ("The Top Ten Hottest Reads of 2016")

"This is one of those books whose story, if you heard about it on the news or glimpsed some sensationalist headline, would be horrifying, but in THIS book, with THESE characters, where you are privy to interior monologues and backstories and a hundred examples of what defines them as people, it makes sense. It's two damaged people finding something in the other that answers a need, and it's unexpectedly touching. It's so, so impressive. Vibrant. Heartbreaking. Sympathetic. Her writing is astonishing."

—Karen, #1 U.S. most popular reviewer on Goodreads

"The stirring Bryn Greenwood's *All the Ugly and Wonderful Things,* so freakishly good and dangerous that it should come with a warning label . . . The writing is direct and muscular, a snake with all the slithery danger of a coiled rattler on a hot rock. VERDICT: Greenwood (from Kansas, daughter of a 'mostly reformed drug dealer') astounds in creating a world where assorted murderers, felons, and thieves are sympathetic. Alternating narrators à la *The Sound and the Fury* create a dynamic where *Lolita* meets a dissonance of values/taboo romance like *East of Eden, Damage,* or *The Little Mermaid.*" —*Library Journal*

"Bryn Greenwood has handed readers a strange—but strangely grabbing—tale."

—Harry Levins, *St. Louis Post Dispatch* ("Best of 2016")

"Greenwood's haunting novel . . . is a story that will stay with readers long after the book is finished."

—Lisa McLendon, *The Wichita Eagle*

"[A] powerful, provocative debut . . . Intelligent, honest, and unsentimental."   —*Kirkus Reviews* (starred review)

"An emotionally resonant novel with an unlikely cast of characters you won't soon forget. Bryn Greenwood's unique voice and her understanding of human nature offer an amazing tale of family, loss, and love that's as unpredictable and inspiring as love itself."

—Brunonia Barry, *New York Times*
bestselling author of *The Lace Reader*

FOR MY SOFT-IN-THE-MIDDLE,
COOKIE-BAKING GRANDMAS

PART ONE

I

AMY

March 1975

My mother always started the story by saying, "Well, she was born in the backseat of a stranger's car," as though that explained why Wavy wasn't normal. It seemed to me that could happen to anybody. Maybe on the way to the hospital, your parents' respectable, middle-class car broke down. That was not what happened to Wavy. She was born in the backseat of a stranger's car, because Uncle Liam and Aunt Val were homeless, driving through Texas when their old beat-up van broke down. Nine months pregnant, Aunt Val hitchhiked to the next town for help. If you ever consider playing Good Samaritan to a pregnant woman, think about cleaning that up.

I learned all this from eavesdropping on Mom's Tuesday night book club. Sometimes they talked about books, but mostly they gossiped. That was where Mom first started polishing The Tragic and Edifying Story of Wavonna Quinn.

After Wavy was born, Mom didn't hear from Aunt Val for almost five years. The first news she had was that Uncle Liam had been arrested for dealing drugs, and Aunt Val needed money. Then Aunt Val got arrested for something Mom wouldn't say, leaving no one to take care of Wavy.

The day after that second phone call, Grandma visited, and argued with Mom behind closed doors about "reaping what you sow," and "blood is thicker than water." Grandma, my soft-in-the-middle, cookie-baking grandma shouted, "She's family! If you won't take her, I will!"

We took her. Mom promised Leslie and me new toys, but we were so excited about meeting our cousin that we didn't care. Wavy was our only cousin, because according to Mom, Dad's brother was *gay*. Leslie and I, at nine and going on seven, made up stories about Wavy that were pure Grimm's Fairy Tales. Starved, kept in a cage, living in the wilderness with wolves.

The day Wavy arrived, the weather suited our gloomy theories: dark and rainy, with gusting wind. Of course, it would have been more fitting if Wavy had arrived in a black limo or a horse-drawn carriage instead of the social worker's beige sedan.

Sue Enaldo was a plump woman in a blue pantsuit, but for me she was Santa Claus, bringing me a marvelous present. Before Sue could get a rain bonnet over her elaborate Dolly Parton hair, Wavy hopped out of the backseat, dangling a plastic grocery bag in one hand. She was delicate, and soaked to the skin by the time she reached the front door.

Leslie's face fell when she saw our cousin, but I wasn't disappointed. As soon as my mother opened the door, Wavy stepped in and surveyed her new home with a bottomless look I would grow to love, but that would eventually drive my mother to despair. Her eyes were dark, but not brown. Grey? Green? Blue? You couldn't really tell. Just dark and full of a long view of the world. Her eyelashes and eyebrows were translucent, to match her hair. Silver-blond, it clung to her head and ran trails of water off her shoulders onto the entryway tile.

"Wavonna, sweetie, I'm your Aunt Brenda." It was a mother I didn't recognize, the way she pitched her voice high, falsely bright, and gave Sue an anxious look. "Is she—is she okay?"

"As okay as she ever is. She didn't say a word to me on the drive over. The foster family she's been with this week, they said she was quiet as a mouse."

"Has she been to see a doctor?"

"She went, but she wouldn't let anyone touch her. She kicked two nurses and punched the doctor."

My mother's eyes went wide and Leslie took a step back.

"Okay, then," Mom cooed. "Do you have some clothes in your bag there, Wavonna? Let's get you into something dry, okay?"

She must have expected Wavy to fight her, but when she reached for the grocery bag, Wavy let it go. My mother opened it and frowned at the contents.

"Where are the rest of her clothes?"

"That's it," Sue said. "She came to us wearing a man's undershirt. Those are the clothes the foster family got together for her."

"I'm sure Amy has something she can wear for now."

Putting her hands on her knees to get to Wavy's height, Sue said, "Wavonna, I'm going to go now and you're going to stay here with your aunt. Do you understand?"

The grown-ups talked to Wavy like she was a little kid, but at five she made a very adult gesture: a curt nod to dismiss Sue.

After Sue was gone, the four of us stood in the entryway, staring. Mom, Leslie, and I at Wavy. Wavy seemed to have x-ray vision, staring through the living room wall at the Venus oil lamp that hung on the other side. How did she know it was there to stare at it?

"Well, why don't we go upstairs and get Wavonna into some dry clothes," Mom said.

In my room, Wavy stood between the two beds, dripping onto the rug. Mom looked anxious, but I was thrilled to have my real live cousin in my room.

"Here, Amy, why don't you help her unpack while I get a towel?" Mom retreated, leaving us alone.

I opened an empty drawer and "unpacked" Wavy's bag: another hand-me-down sundress as threadbare as the one she had on, two pairs of panties, an undershirt, a flannel nightgown, and a new baby doll, smelling of fresh plastic.

"This will be your dresser." I didn't want to sound like my mother, like an adult. I wanted Wavy to like me. After I put the clothes in the drawer, I held the doll out to her. "Is this your baby?"

She looked at me, really looked at me, and that's how I knew her eyes weren't brown. Her head moved left, right, back to center. No.

"Well, we can put it in here, to keep it safe," I said.

Mom returned with a towel, which she tried to put over Wavy's dripping hair. Before Mom could touch her, Wavy snatched the towel away and dried her own hair.

After a moment of stunned silence, Mom said, "Let's find something for you to wear."

She laid out panties and an undershirt on the bed. Without any embarrassment, Wavy peeled off the sundress and dropped it on the floor, before stepping out of her tennis shoes. She was almost as bony as the kids in the UNICEF ads, her ribs sticking out through the dry cotton undershirt she put on.

I offered her my favorite corduroy pants and plaid shirt, but she shook her head. With her thumb and first finger she plucked at an invisible skirt. Mom looked helpless.

"She wants her dress," I said.

"She needs something warmer."

So I went into my closet and found a Christmas party dress I hated the one time I wore it. Navy velvet with a lace collar, it was too big for Wavy, but it suited her. With her hair already drying to blond wisps, she looked like she had stepped out of an old photograph.

At lunch, Wavy sat at the table, but didn't eat anything. Same thing at dinner and breakfast the next morning.

"Please, sweetie, just try a bite." Mom looked exhausted and she'd only been a stay-at-home aunt one day.

I love my mother. She was a good mother. She did arts and crafts projects with us, baked with us, and took us to the park. Until we were practically teenagers, Mom tucked us into bed every night. Whatever Wavy needed, it wasn't that.

The first night, Mom tucked Wavy and me into bed, me with my Winnie the Pooh, and Wavy with the baby doll she said wasn't hers. As soon as Mom left the room, Wavy threw off her covers and I heard the thud of the doll hitting the floor. If something else had happened to make the room go dark—if Leslie had played a prank or the bulb had burned out—I would have screamed for Mom, but when Wavy turned off my nightlight, I shivered under my covers, afraid but excited. After she lay down again, she spoke. Her voice was small and quiet, just what you would expect from a tiny, blond elf-child.

"Cassiopeia. Cepheus. Ursa Minor. Cygnus. Perseus. Orion."

Since she had finally spoken, I grew brave enough to ask, "What does it mean?"

"Names of stars."

Until then I hadn't known the stars had names. Arm extended, finger pointing, Wavy traced out shapes above her head, as though she were guiding the movements of the stars. A conductor directing a symphony.

The next night, Wavy smiled at me as Mom crawled around looking for the unwanted doll. A minute after we were tucked in, the baby was again among the dust bunnies under the bed. Eventually that became the doll's name: Dust Bunny. If Mom failed to look for the doll at bedtime, I said, "Oh, no. I think Dust Bunny is missing again," to make Wavy smile.

While I had a growing friendship with Wavy, my mother had only anxiety.

In the first month, Mom took Wavy to the doctor three times, because she wasn't eating. The first time, a nurse tried to put a thermometer in Wavy's mouth. It didn't end well. The other two times, Wavy mounted the scale and the doctor pronounced, "She's underweight, but not dangerously so. She must be eating something."

Dad said the same thing and he had evidence to back it up. One night, he came home from work after we were all in bed, and woke us up shouting, "Oh, goddamnit! What are you doing? What are you doing?"

Wavy wasn't in her bed, so I ran downstairs alone. I found Dad in the kitchen with the trash can lid in one hand and his briefcase in the other. I'd never been in the kitchen that late. In the day it was a warm, sunny place, but behind Dad, the basement door stood open and dark, like the mouth of a monster.

"What's the matter, Daddy?"

"It's nothing. Go back to bed." He put the lid on the trash and laid his briefcase on the table.

"What's going on, Bill?" Mom came up behind me and put her hand on my shoulder.

"She was eating out of the trash."

"What? Amy, what are you—"

"Not Amy. Your niece."

Mom didn't take Wavy to the doctor again to complain about her not eating.

After failing to solve that crisis, Mom became obsessed with sewing for Wavy. The dresses you could buy hung on her like sacks and were too frilly, which Wavy hated. The first day she wore my Christmas party dress, she tore the lace collar off.

So Mom sewed dozens of dresses that Wavy unraveled, plucking at the seams until a thread came loose. From there she could unravel a dress in less than a week. Mom rehemmed her dresses each time they came through the wash. It slowed the unraveling down, which was a practical solution, but Mom didn't want a solution, she wanted a reason.

One of the book club ladies said, "Does she have toileting problems?"

Mom frowned, shook her head. "No, there's no trouble like that. She'll be six in July."

Wavy and I eavesdropped from the other side of the kitchen door. Her games all involved sneaking around and finding people's secrets, like the cigarettes my father hid in a coffee can in the garage.

"I wonder if she's acting out over some inappropriate contact," the book club lady said.

"You think she might have been molested?" another lady said, sounding shocked but excited.

That conversation led to Wavy's first visit to a therapist. She stopped unraveling her dresses and Mom went around looking triumphant. To Dad, she said: "I think we've had a breakthrough."

Then she discovered the curtains in the guest bedroom, which were what Wavy took to unraveling when she stopped doing it to her clothes.

Mom and Dad yelled at each other while Wavy stared through them.

"Why does there have to be something wrong with her?" Dad said. "Maybe she's just weird. God knows your sister's weird enough. I don't have time for you to get hysterical over everything she does. We have to wrap up the books on the fiscal year-end."

"I'm worried about her. Is that so horrible of me? She never talks. What's going to happen to her?"

"She does too talk," Leslie said. "I hear her talking at night to Amy."

Mom slowly turned to all of us, narrowed in on me. "Is that true? Does she talk to you?"

She stared into my eyes, pleading with me. I nodded.

"Well, what does she talk about?"

"It's a secret."

"There can't be secrets, Amy. If she tells you something important, you have to tell me. You want to help Vonnie, don't you?" Mom got down on her knees in front of me and I saw how it was. She would make me tell my secret. I started to cry, knowing I would tell and it wouldn't help Mom or Wavy. It would just rob me of something precious.

Wavy saved me. With her hand over her mouth, she said, "I don't want to talk about it."

My mother's eyes bulged. "I—I—I." She couldn't get a word out and even Dad looked stunned. The silent ghost girl could speak in complete sentences.

"I want you to go back to the therapist," Mom said.

"No."

Things might have gotten better after that, if it hadn't been for the other secret between Wavy and me. She liked to sneak out of the house at night, and I went with her. Breezing down the stairs on bare feet, we eased open the kitchen door and walked around the neighborhood.

Sometimes we just looked. Other times, we took things. The night of Wavy's sixth birthday, when she had left her cake uneaten, she jimmied open Mrs. NiBlack's screen door. We crept across the kitchen to the refrigerator, where Wavy pressed her finger to the lever to keep the light inside off. On the bottom shelf sat a half-eaten lemon pie, which we carried away. Crouched under the weeping willow in the Goerings' backyard, Wavy tore out a chunk of pie with her bare hand and gave me the plate. She went around the corner of the garden shed and when she came back, her piece of lemon pie was gone. No, she wasn't starving.

Some nights we gathered things. A wine bottle scavenged from the gutter. A woman's high-heeled shoe from the median of the highway, where we weren't supposed to go. An old hand mixer abandoned outside the Methodist Church's back door. We collected our treasures into a metal box stolen from the neighbor's garage, and secreted it along our back fence, behind the lilac bushes.

When autumn came, the lilacs lost their leaves, and Dad found the box of treasure, including Mrs. NiBlack's heavy glass pie plate, her name written on the bottom of it on a square of masking tape. Mom returned it to Mrs. NiBlack, who must have told her how the pie plate went missing: stolen out of her fridge on a hot July night, a trail of small dirty footprints left on the linoleum.

Or maybe something else made Mom suspicious.

As the weather got colder, I wanted to stay at home in bed, but when Wavy got up and dressed, I did, too. If I didn't go, she would go alone. Half of my fear was that something would happen to her. The other half was a fear that she would have adventures without me.

So I went with her, shivering against the cold, while my heart pounded with excitement. At the library, Wavy went up on tiptoe to reach her spindly arm into the book return. In the day, my mother would have driven us to the library to check out books, but stealing books was sweeter.

Wavy smiled and withdrew her arm to reveal treasure. The book was thin enough to pass through the return the wrong way, but it wasn't a kiddy book. *Salome*, the spine said. We leaned our heads together to consider the strangeness of an adult book with pictures. Odd pictures. The cover was worn and layered with clear tape to protect it, and the pages were heavy. It felt special.

As I reached to turn the page, a pair of headlights fell on us where we crouched beside the book deposit. Wavy darted away, but I froze when my father yelled, "Amy!" Like in a fairy tale, where knowing someone's name gives you power, my father was able to capture me.

My mother got out of the car and ran across the library parking lot. She looked so ferocious, loping toward me in her nightgown and coat, that I expected a blow. Punishment. Instead, she jerked me into her arms and pressed me to her chest.

After that, I had to tell everything. About the late night wandering. Not the stars. That was still my secret. Mom screamed and Dad yelled.

"I know you mean well, Brenda. You want to help her. I get that. But when her behavior starts endangering our children, it's time to choose. We can't keep her. She's out of control."

The police came to make a report, to get a picture, to put out a bulletin. The neighbors turned out to look for Wavy, but at dawn she returned on her own.

I woke to more yelling and screaming. That afternoon, Grandma came to get Wavy.

"It's a horrible idea. A stupid idea," Mom said. I marveled that she could talk to Grandma like that. It didn't seem possible to get away with saying something like that to your mother. "You can't keep an eye on her all the time. You can't stay up all night."

"What would be the point? I suppose she will do a little wandering. From what I remember, you and Val did some wandering when you were kids."

"That was different. We were teenagers and it was a safer time."

"Pfft," Grandma said.

"Think of your health, Helen," Dad said.

"You haven't been as strong since the chemo, Mom."

Grandma blew out a big puff of air, the same way she used to exhale cigarette smoke, and shook her head. "Tell me your solution. Foster care? Send her to live with strangers?"

"We'll keep her," Mom said.

"No, we won't." Dad stood up and blocked my view, so I'll never know what look passed between him and Mom, but when he went to the counter to pour himself more coffee, Mom nodded.

"She might as well come home with me today," Grandma said.

I sat on Wavy's bed while Grandma packed her suitcase. There wasn't much to pack. A dozen dresses that had survived the Great Unraveling. Some socks and underwear. The hairbrush that she sometimes let me run through her silky, fine hair. The last thing into the suitcase was Dust Bunny, the baby doll.

Grandma put it in the suitcase. Wavy took it out. Mom put it in. Wavy took it out. It was the only toy Wavy had. "Nothing belongs to you," she told me once when Leslie and I fought over a favorite Barbie that later disappeared.

Wavy took Dust Bunny out of the suitcase and handed it to me. A gift? Then it was time for her to go. Grandma hugged us all, while Wavy stood near the door. Mom tried to hug her, too, but she skittered away, slipping past my mother to hug me. Not close enough for our bodies to touch, she rested her hands on my shoulders, and sniffed my hair. When she released me, she ran out the front door.

"You see how it is," Mom said.

"She's her own girl. You were, too." Grandma smiled and picked up Wavy's bag.

After Thanksgiving, I found the real gift Wavy had left me in the closet under the stairs. When Mom pulled out the boxes of Christmas decorations, I crawled in to sweep up loose tinsel and a broken ornament. Tucked in the very back was the stolen book: *Salome*.

2

GRANDMA

October 1975

Irv and I raised one daughter who turned out fine. Brenda married a good man, had nice kids, kept a clean house, and worked hard. Valerie, our youngest, I don't know what happened.

I suppose nowadays, she would be diagnosed with something, but at the time, we lived with her behavior. For example, her germ problem. There was a time when she washed her hands a hundred times a day, until the skin cracked and bled. I made her wear gloves to help her feel clean. Two dozen pairs of white gloves that I washed and ironed every day.

Then her junior year in high school, she got pregnant and ran away with Liam Quinn. We didn't like him, but we'd never tried to keep her away from him. He was a troublemaker and I didn't feel he treated Valerie right. The sort of boy who thinks he's the center of the universe.

Later I found out he was worse than just a selfish boy. I found out he'd gotten her mixed up with the sorts of things that put her in prison. As for that whole mess, it wearied my heart. I hoped Brenda wouldn't hate me when she found out how much of Irv's pension I cashed out to pay for Valerie's lawyers. I'd hoped to do college money for Amy and Leslie, but there was nothing left for that.

The first day I took Wavonna home with me, she didn't speak. To be honest, she didn't talk for weeks. That's harder on your nerves than you might think, having another person in the room who won't speak. It turned me into a real chatterbox. I narrated everything I did, the way I had for Irv when he got bad at the end.

The first night, Wavonna didn't eat dinner. The next morning, no breakfast. By lunch the next day, I started to get a taste of why Brenda looked so broken. Three days of worrying, before I had the sense to count things in the fridge and cupboard to tell what she was eating. At bedtime, I had six cheese slices in cellophane, nine apricots in the crisper, thirteen saltines in the open tube. In the morning, only five cheese slices, seven apricots, ten saltines. Not enough to keep a mouse alive, but she managed on it.

The second day, I set out some new toys I'd bought her on the coffee table in the den. It had out-of-fashion pine paneling and shag carpet, but we'd used it as our family room when Irv was alive, so it was full of mostly happy memories. I spent the day piecing a quilt for a church fundraiser and watching the TV. Wavonna sat on the sofa, staring at the wall or the TV or nothing. The girl had a hundred-yard stare like Irv had when he came back from the war. Once she got up, and I thought, *Finally, she's bored. She'll do something. Play with her toys.*

She went to the powder room. The toilet flushed and the sink ran. Back she came to the couch. The Barbie, the stuffed elephant, and the Lincoln Logs stayed in their packages and eventually they disappeared.

After two weeks, I did what I should have done first. I bought some flash cards—letters, colors, shapes, numbers—the kind of thing they use in kindergarten classes. The next morning, I made her a nice bowl of oatmeal and went out of the kitchen for a good fifteen minutes. I spent the time calling the gals in my bridge club to tell them I wasn't coming that afternoon. When I went back to the kitchen, sure enough, there was less oatmeal. I cleared the table and got out the alphabet cards.

"A is for Apple." I knew she wasn't going to parrot back what I said, but at least she'd be seeing and hearing them.

I went through the whole deck that way. When I finished, Wavonna walked over to the counter and got the grocery pad. Some claptrap thing Irv built that held a roll of adding machine tape and had a hole drilled in it for a golf pencil. Wavonna rolled out some paper and started writing the alphabet. You could've knocked me over with a feather.

I reached over and put my finger on the A. "Do you know how to say that one?"

Wavonna considered my finger for a second before she said, "A."

"What about this one?"

"B."

"This one."

She sighed and said, "Abcdefghijklmnopqrstuvwxyz." Silly Grandma.

Come Monday, I enrolled her for school.

The first day, after I dropped her off at school, I took a two-hour nap. The second day, I went for some much-needed beautification. Old women need sprucing up and my hair was starting to look bedraggled. The third day, I don't remember what I did, but on the fourth day I went to bridge club. I had a martini and a lovely raucous time with the gals. They were expecting me to tell them all about Wavonna, and I pretended to be the proud grandma. *Oh, she has the finest, baby-down blond hair. She already knows her ABCs.* Nothing really about *her*.

I held Leslie in my arms after she was born. Same with Amy. They were my granddaughters, my babies. I flashed their pictures and bragged on every little accomplishment.

Wavonna, I'd never seen her until Brenda got custody of her. I know you're supposed to love the hard ones more, but most of what I felt was pity. Her wispy hair and scrawny shoulders were so sad, and then those empty looks. Leaving bridge club, though, I felt like it was going to be okay. I would learn to love Wavonna the way I loved Leslie and Amy. She would learn to love me.

When I got to the school, Wavonna didn't come out. I waited for a few minutes before I went into the front office, where I was met by the school principal and Mrs. Berry, Wavonna's teacher. I'd handed Wavonna off to her on the first day in the school office. She was a friendly woman with a big smile, but that day she was a hysterical, sobbing mess.

Wavonna had run away from school.

I cried, but mostly I remember thinking, *This is how it started with Valerie.* Of course, skipping school didn't start with Valerie until she was in high school, but all the same I had a sinking feeling I had failed.

At eight o'clock, I went home and waited to hear from the police. I held the phone on my lap as I soaked my feet. I'd walked I didn't know how many blocks, knocking on doors all around the school. I needed to call Brenda, but I couldn't bear the thought of saying, *You were right. I can't handle her.*

My doorbell rang and I didn't know what to feel. Hopeful. Terrified. With my feet wet, I went to the door. Wavonna stood on the porch alone, shivering. Once she was in the house, I locked the door, like that would keep her from escaping.

"You scared me so much! What if something had happened to you?" I knew yelling wasn't the best way to communicate with her, but I couldn't help myself. "Never, never do that again! Do you understand me?"

She nodded, but I knew that nod from Valerie. It meant, "I understand you, but that doesn't mean I'm going to do what you say."

After I called the police to tell them Wavonna was home, I made her some soup and counted out a pile of crackers. While I cried in the bathroom, she ate a few spoonfuls and two saltines. I couldn't go on like that, but I couldn't let her go into foster care. Would anyone else eye the level of soup in her bowl as carefully as I did? Would a stranger count crackers to make sure my granddaughter was eating?

I cleared the table and brewed some decaf. When I was sure I was calm, I said, "Wavonna, will you please come into the kitchen and talk to Grandma?"

She didn't sit down, but she stood waiting for me to talk.

"If you run away from school, they're going to take you away from me and make you live with strangers. I don't want that to happen. I want you to stay here with Grandma."

She didn't react to that, but I didn't expect her to. I could have had a French poodle dancing the tango with a monkey on my head and she wouldn't have reacted.

"Will you tell me what happened at school? Why did you run away? If you'll tell me, I'll try to make sure it doesn't happen again."

It was like with the alphabet. She had to prepare herself, but after a moment, she said, "The loud lady touches me."

My stomach almost gave up the coffee I'd drunk. That sweet woman? I couldn't imagine her doing something like *that* to a child. In my mind that's what bad touching was.

"Touches you?"

She stretched her arms toward me, her hands curled into menacing claws, and then brought them back tightly to her chest.

"She hugs you?" I said.

A nod.

"And you don't like that?"

She shook her head seriously. I was sick with relief, and with knowing how awful the world looked to Wavonna. Of course, she never hugged me, and whenever I touched her, she shrugged out from under my hand.

The next day, we went to school, and I did what I should have done the first day. I walked her directly to class, planning to explain everything to Mrs. Berry.

All that went out the window when I reached the classroom.

In the center of the room sat three children in wheelchairs. I don't mean to be cruel, but they were drooling vegetables. In one corner, a child flopped around on blue rubber floor mats. The school could paint the walls as bright a shade of yellow as they wanted and hang up all the pretty mobiles in the world, but it was a horrible place. I couldn't imagine Wavonna spending five minutes there, let alone the four days I'd left her there.

Mrs. Berry hurried over with a big smile and said, "Oh, Mrs. Morrison, what a relief! Wavonna, honey, you had us so worried."

That was the day I earned Wavonna's trust. Mrs. Berry swooped toward us, clearly planning to deliver an enormous, smothering hug. I spread my feet and put out my arm to block her.

"Mrs. Berry, we need to talk to someone about changing classes." She made a wounded face as we backed away from her. I had nothing against the woman, but I was too old to beat around the bush.

When I sat down with the school counselor, I took the same approach. I looked her square in the eye and said, "My granddaughter is not retarded."

"Mrs. Morrison, we don't use words like that anymore. Our concern is that her speech problems are a sign of developmental delays."

"I don't mean it to offend, but she's not stupid. Look, here. Wavonna."

She didn't look at me, but I knew she was listening.

"Give me paper and a pencil."

The counselor slid a sheet of paper and a ballpoint pen across the desk. I scooted Wavonna's chair closer and said, "Go ahead and show her. Otherwise you'll have to stay in the class with the loud lady."

As soon as I mentioned the special-education teacher, Wavonna picked up the pen and put it to the paper. First, she wrote out her name, neat as can be. Below that, she wrote her alphabet: Aa Bb Cc, and on like that. Under that she put her numbers. Then she did something I didn't even know she knew. She turned the paper over and wrote: Cassiopeia. Next to it, she drew five dots and connected them. Then seven more dots that she labeled Cepheus. She filled the paper up that way. The only ones I recognized were the Big and Little Dippers.

The way the counselor's jaw dropped down set me to giggling. I laughed right in that poor woman's face. Laughed until I cried. Before Wavonna, I'd been feeling pretty good. My cancer was in remission, and I had myself a nice retirement planned, before Wavonna moved in. After everything I'd been through in the last month, I needed a good laugh.

They put her in a regular classroom, but I told them right up front, "Don't give her a nicey-nice teacher." I spelled it out for them. Nobody could touch her. They couldn't expect her to talk, but they shouldn't assume she wasn't listening and learning. I didn't make requests and I didn't apologize.

Things weren't perfect after that, but they got better.

She lived with me for almost two years, and in all that time, she touched me twice. On what would have been Irv's and my fortieth anniversary, I had a little wine and got maudlin. Wavonna touched my hand, my wedding ring. To comfort me, I think. The second time was right before Valerie got paroled, and I hired a lawyer to help her get custody of Wavonna and the baby she'd had while she was in prison.

We drove down to Tulsa for Leslie's birthday and had a fine old time: singing, wearing silly hats, and cheering as Leslie ripped open packages. After all the big hoopla, the three girls settled into the living room to play, while Brenda and I cleaned up.

I couldn't keep putting it off, so I sat down at the kitchen table and said, "I've been talking to Valerie's lawyer about this transitional program she can get into."

"I didn't know she still had a lawyer. Are you paying for that?"

I didn't answer. I wanted it not to be her business, but maybe it was.

"Fine. So, Val's lawyer thinks she can get into some program?" Brenda cut a second slice of birthday cake. Her weight dogged her for years, because she ate when she was upset.

"It's for women with children, to help her get back on her feet so she can take care of Donal and Wavonna." I knew that would cause a ruckus and it did.

"Are you serious, Mom? Do you really think Val can take care of them? You know what Vonnie's like. That's Val's parenting skills right there. A daughter who won't speak, won't eat, and sneaks out at night."

"She's doing better."

"I know. You're doing so good with her. I—" Brenda laid her hand on my arm, and I could see she really was sorry she'd lost her temper.

"I want Wavonna to be with her mother." I wanted to want that. I wanted things to be simple and they never were.

"Do you really think that's the best thing for her?"

"Val's been getting treatment. This program will put her in an apartment, where she'll have a counselor. They'll make sure she takes her medicine, and help her take care of the kids."

"Well, what do you need to do? Is there paperwork?"

"I need you to go to her parole hearing and the custody hearing. You're going to have to do it, Brenda."

"Why?"

"Metastasized." Wavonna had crept up so quietly neither of us noticed her until she spoke.

"What does she mean?" Brenda said. "Mom?"

"She must have overheard me talking with the doctor's office. The cancer is back. It's in my lungs and my liver. Three months they think, maybe less."

Now that we were talking about hard things, Leslie and Amy stopped playing Barbies and came to stand in the doorway next to Wavonna. I tried to will Brenda to be strong, but she started shaking and crying. Amy and Leslie cried, too. They were all crying, except Wavonna. She crossed the kitchen and reached out to me. For a second, she laid her hand on my chest, touched those fake foam boobs I wore in my bra.

I loved her then, right as I was getting ready to leave her.

3

WAVY

June 1977

Aunt Brenda didn't want me to stay with Grandma at the end.

"Let Bill take her back to Tulsa. My friend Sheila is staying at the house to take care of the girls while I'm here," Aunt Brenda said.

"She's going with you soon enough. Let her stay with me," Grandma said. She held out her hand and I went to her, even though I wasn't brave enough to touch her with Aunt Brenda there to see.

"I love you, sweetie. I love you. Pretty soon I'm going to go and be with your Grandpa Irv, but God willing, you'll see me again, Wavonna. Not for a long time, but some day," she said.

For a while, Grandma slept, and Aunt Brenda went into the kitchen to make coffee, but she sat at the table and laid her head down on her arms to cry. When the big clock should have chimed three o'clock, it didn't, because no one remembered to wind it. Aunt Brenda was asleep.

"I wish I weren't afraid. It seems so silly to be afraid, but it feels like driving to a new place and not knowing where I'm going," Grandma said when she woke up. We were alone, so I held her hand.

I thought about Mr. Arsenikos, our neighbor where we lived before Mama got arrested. When Mama and Uncle Sean used to fight, Mr. Arsenikos let me hide on his back porch. He called me his "stray cat," and gave me bacon sandwiches. Sometimes they were just bacon grease spread on soft, white bread, but sometimes they had whole pieces of bacon on them. After I ate, he would sit out on the porch swing and tell me the names of stars. He used his cane to scratch them out in the dirt, so I could learn them. He was a sailor on a boat called USS *San Diego*, which is also a city in California. His boat sank in the Great War, and he knew which way to row the life raft toward land, because of the stars.

On the chenille bedspread that was stretched over Grandma's belly, I drew Ursa Minor, with his tail pointing down.

"Ursa Minor is north tonight. Little Dipper," I said, because Grandma called it that. I drew it in the palm of her hand, so she would remember. She nodded. By the time the sun came up, she was asleep again, and she didn't wake up.

Mr. Arsenikos said if you knew the constellations you would never get lost. You could always find your way home.

At Grandma's funeral, the only real thing was Grandma in a fancy box. Everything else was pretend.

Aunt Brenda pretended she wasn't mad at Mama.

"Oh, Val, I'm so glad to see you," she said.

Uncle Bill pretended, too. Before Mama came, he said, "Let's get this over with and get her out of our lives," but then he hugged her and said, "You look great, Val. You need to visit more often."

"I want us to get together for Christmas. We can't just see each other for funerals," Aunt Brenda said.

"I know! We have to keep in touch. I can't believe it's been so long since we saw each other. I've missed you so much," Mama said.

Then she brought the new baby to me.

"This is your little brother, Vonnie. This is Donal. Give him a kiss."

I didn't know why Mama wanted me to kiss him, when she was the one who said the mouth was a dirty place. In case it was a trick, I only pretended to kiss him.

After the funeral, Mama and Donal and I went to The Transitional Program.

"Everything's going to be different this time," she said.

The first two weeks at The Program, it was different. She was Good Mama and followed the rules. She washed our clothes and put them away in drawers in the new apartment. She cooked dinner. She didn't hide in her bedroom and smoke her pipe like she did before she got arrested.

Then one day she woke up Scary Mama instead of Good Mama, and I knew things weren't going to be different. I never knew which Mama she would be when she woke up.

I read the books she got from The Program. She was supposed to RECONNECT WITH YOUR FAMILY! That meant we were supposed to EAT DINNER AS A FAMILY, but every night, after Scary Mama fixed dinner, she sat on the back porch, smoking cigarettes and yelling through the screen door for me to eat. I wasn't falling for that. I knew what could happen if she caught me eating.

Even Good Mama could all of a sudden say, "Don't eat that! That's dirty!" and stick her fingers in my mouth to get the food out. Even Good Mama could pour burning Listerine on my tongue to get it clean. She always said, "Things can get into you that way." Bad things could get in through your mouth and make you sick. Just like my germs could get on other things and make them dirty.

When Megan the social worker came to check on us, Mama smiled so hard it made my stomach hurt. She wasn't going to be Good Mama.

"So, what are we cooking for dinner tonight?" Megan said.

"Oh, we're having spaghetti." That's what Mama always fixed. I had Grandma's recipe book, but Mama wouldn't let me cook. She didn't want me to make a mess.

"How is everything else?" Megan said. "You missed one of the group sessions this week."

"Oh, everything's super. I just had a little headache, that's all. Thanks for checking on us." Mama smiled and smiled, but as soon as Megan left, she said, "Fucking busybody! It's like a sitcom with a nosy neighbor always dropping in. Except you'd kill your neighbor if she dropped by the way they do on TV. Kill her! God, I don't want to be on this stupid TV show anymore!"

While Mama was yelling, Donal took her hairbrush out of her purse and put it in his mouth. Before I could take it away from him, Mama saw.

Once when I was little, I put her pipe in my mouth, just to see what it was like, since she liked it so much. Boiling and bleach could get most things clean, but not the pipe. It was so dirty after I put it in my mouth that it had to be thrown away.

Mama grabbed the hairbrush out of my hand and carried it into the kitchen. I knew she was coming back with Listerine or bleach, so I picked up Donal and carried him into the bedroom. Scary Mama dragged me out of the closet and spanked me until the brush left bloody spots on my legs, but I stopped her from putting Listerine in Donal's mouth.

After that, I took care of Donal. I fed him and bathed him, because Scary Mama, she would give baths so hot it made your skin bubble.

The Program's book also said, BE COMPLIANT ON YOUR MEDS, but Mama wasn't.

"How am I supposed to keep all these fucking pills straight?" she said, but when I tried to read the bottles, she smacked me. When she stopped taking her pills and started bringing home bottles of whiskey, she was Scary Mama all the time. One night, after the whiskey was finished, when Donal and I were supposed to be asleep, I heard Mama's keys jingle. The apartment door opened and closed.

I wasn't afraid to be alone, but Donal was too small to take care of himself. He was standing in his crib, whimpering. We were both hungry, because Mama had thrown dinner in the trash can. She said the spaghetti was dirty and the milk was sour. Even Good Mama would throw dinner away, but sometimes Scary Mama did it to be mean.

The spaghetti was sticky and still warm in the middle, and it was safer to eat it from the trash than have Mama see me eat it. After I ate, I took the jug of milk out of the trash and filled a baby bottle. Donal drank it all, and after the bottle was empty, I cleaned it and put it away, so Mama wouldn't know.

I never knew which was dirtier, my mouth or what I put in my mouth.

Liam was like that, too. He was a bad thing that could get into you. He wasn't supposed to touch me. He would get me dirty. When Mama was mad at him, she told me, "Don't you call him daddy. He's not your daddy. He's not to be trusted." She would make me say it: "Liam not to be trusted."

When she was mad at me, she said, "Don't you touch him. Don't even look at him."

I was dirtier than Liam, because I wasn't supposed to touch anyone except Mama and Donal, and sometimes not even them. I broke the rule when I touched Grandma and Amy.

The day after she left me alone with Donal, Mama called Dee and asked her to come visit. Sometimes Mama said Dee was her best friend. Sometimes she called her a dirty whore. They must have been friends that night, because Dee came and brought Mama a new pipe. They smoked and drank all night, and talked about Liam.

"He gets inside me. Like an infection. All he has to do is look at me with those eyes. I could just drown in them." The way Mama said it, I knew she wanted him to get inside her. She wanted him to infect her.

"He has beautiful eyes. Frank Sinatra eyes. Are you really going to leave him?" Dee said.

"I don't know. What should I do?" Mama was so drunk and high, she didn't even care that she drank out of the whisky bottle after Dee.

"He wants to see you. You owe him that much."

The next night, after I was in bed, Liam came. It was easy for me to listen to them talk, because my bed was against the other side of the wall.

"I can't be with you," Mama said to him. "They won't let me finish the program if I'm with you."

"The program? The fucking program? What are they going to do for you?"

"I'm getting my secretarial certificate."

"Are you kidding me? Baby, I'm here to take care of you. When we got married, I said I'd take care of you. Pack up your shit and let's go."

When Mama came into Donal's and my room, she was laughing.

"Wake up, babies. We're going with Daddy." Her hand was soft and floating when she laid it on my head. She didn't even notice that I was dressed under the covers, ready to sneak out. Donal and I lay in the backseat while Liam drove us away. I watched the stars go by out the back window.

First, we went to a motel, and Mama took the pills Liam gave her. For a few days, she was Happy Mama and said nice things.

Then Liam took us to the farmhouse that looked down on the meadow.

"Me and Butch got business to take care of," he said.

"Riding your bike and screwing around on me? That kind of *business*? I hate you. And I hate this fucking dump," Mama said. She hated the warped floors, the rust stains in the bathtub, and the way the windows rattled when the wind blew.

"Baby, don't be that way." Liam's quiet voice meant something bad could happen.

"You think you can just leave me here to wait for you? You can think again because I—"

Mama looked surprised when Liam smacked her mouth, but that always happened. While she was crying, he crept down on her, with his hand on the back of her neck, and said soft things.

Then he left, and Mama took off her pretty dress and lay in bed all day. Sad Mama didn't care when Donal cried, and he cried a lot.

"I'm so alone," she said.

Donal and I didn't count.

4

WAVY

July 1977

The first day at the farmhouse, while Liam and Mama screamed at each other, Donal and I hid in the attic. The second day, when Butch came to bring Mama pills, Donal and I hid in the cellar. The third day, I walked across the meadow to see the windmill. I thought that day was my birthday, but I didn't know, because the calendar at the farmhouse was from 1964.

Nobody looked for me in the meadow. Not Donal, who wasn't old enough to walk. Not Mama, who was sleeping while Donal cried. Not Liam, who had business to take care of.

Nobody looked for me until the Giant came at sunset.

I was walking back to the farmhouse to feed Donal, when a headlight bobbed up the road. I ran to where the meadow touched the road and stepped out to watch the motorcycle roar past. The Giant turned his head to look at me and his hair fluttered like starling wings. Gravel spit out of the wheels and then the motorcycle skidded and fell. The Giant tumbled off and the bike slid into the meadow, still rumbling, its tires spinning.

When I got to him, the Giant was lying in the road with his arms and legs spread out. I don't know why I wasn't afraid. Maybe because he was so big. Bigger than everyone who made me feel small. Maybe because the sky was purple-blue-red-orange and the moon was a tiny sliver of fingernail. I squatted beside him and touched his shoulder, where his black T-shirt was dusty. Three long scratches ran down his left arm and dripped blood on the road.

He opened his eyes and whispered, "Sweet Jesus. Are you real?"

I nodded. It was safer than talking. Words were complicated and you had to open your mouth. Things could get in you that way, too.

The Giant sat up. He cupped a hand under his elbow and winced.

"Where did you come from?" he said.

I pointed toward the farmhouse.

"You're not an angel?"

I shook my head.

He had to let go of his elbow to get up on his knees. Air hissed out between his teeth and his arm hung down limp. The Giant needed me, the way Donal did. That made me brave enough not to run away when he laid his hand on my head.

"You got leaves in your hair," he said.

He picked them out with his big, shaky hand. When he looked at me, I looked back. His eyes were so soft, I was sure he wouldn't get inside me like an infection. Not like Liam and his hard blue eyes.

Silly to think I could help a giant, but I put my arm around him, and he leaned on me. Quick, so he wouldn't catch me, I breathed him in. His oily hair smelled of mint and dirt and blood. Then he got on his feet, and I put my face close to his T-shirt to fill my nose with the rest of him. Sweat and gasoline and something delicious: bacon. Together, we shuffled toward the bike, because his ankle was hurt, too.

"Can you turn it off, get the key out?" the Giant said.

On the end of the key chain swung a little silver skull. He didn't have a hand to take it, so I tucked it into his jeans pocket. His belt buckle was big and silver with three cloudy-red stones. Like Orion's belt.

With his hand on my shoulder, we walked up the road to the house. He talked the whole way. Grandma talked too much, afraid of quiet, but he wasn't. The talking was for me, to make me feel safe.

The Giant told me about the bike. A Panhead. Seventy-four cubic inches. Custom paint job. Probably fucked all to shit. He said I surprised him, standing in the meadow with my hair blowing. Like a fairy, he said.

When I touched the big tattoo on his arm, he told me about it. Horseshoe, lucky clover.

"I tell you, I'm not feeling like a lucky motherfucker today," he said.

He asked me if I'd seen foxes in the meadow, but asking was only to leave a quiet space for me to say something if I wanted. At the stone steps that went up from the road to the house, he sat down, holding his arm tight and breathing hard.

"Can you go call somebody for me?" he said.

The phone was on the kitchen wall. I knew how it worked, but I never used it. You can't smell people on the other end of phones. And ears are openings for things to get in you.

Blood ran out of the Giant's head and his T-shirt drank it up. Something white that I thought was a bone poked out of his arm. I nodded. He told me the numbers. Then he wrote them out with his finger on my arm in streaks of blood.

"Do you know your numbers?" He thought I couldn't read, because I was small.

To show him I understood, I put my hand up to my ear to make a pretend phone. Then I thought of a problem.

"You?" I said.

"I'm Kellen. Jesse Joe Kellen."

I started to go, but he said, "Wait. What's your name?"

I'd never said it before. I tried it once without sound to see how it felt in my mouth. Then with breath: "Wavonna."

"You go call for me, Way-vonna. Tell 'em what happened."

I ran up to the house and dialed with a shaky finger, turning the little circle and waiting for it to chatter back around after each number. Ring, ring, then click and someone breathing.

"Who is this?" Liam said. A cold shiver went all over me. *Liam not to be trusted.* "Who the fuck is this?"

My throat felt so tight, I didn't know how the words would get out. I swallowed them down, over and over, until they finally came out.

"His bike wrecked. Kellen." Saying his name, I knew the Giant was worth the danger of Liam talking in my ear.

"Vonnie? Is that you? Where the fuck is Val?"

"Sleeping. Kellen wrecked. On his bike." The words hurt my throat, like a cracker going down the wrong way.

"Goddamn, I'm coming. I'll send someone."

"Fast. He's bleeding."

I hung up, grabbed the dish towel, and ran back to the Giant. Kellen. The sun had gone down while I was inside, so he was a shadow and my dress flashed white in the moonlight.

"You called?" he said.

I nodded. As gentle as I could be, I wrapped the towel around his arm. Blood soaked through the towel and dribbled into my hand. I crouched in front of him, watching his eyes go far away. He was getting lost.

"Kellen." I put my hand on his cheek and brought him back to me. When I pointed up to the North, he turned his head to look. "Cassiopeia. Andromeda. Perseus. Cepheus. Cygnus. Ursa Minor."

With the sun gone, we could see all the stars, and the planets, too. Mercury, Saturn, Jupiter, Venus, Mars, like stairs from the moon down to the meadow. I kept naming them until I heard a car coming up the road.

After Liam and Butch took Kellen away, I thought about how he left spaces for me when he talked. If I saw him again, I decided I might put words in those spaces.

5

KELLEN

August-October 1977

I woulda gone the next day to see the girl in the meadow, but the bike wreck about turned me into hamburger. I ended up with a concussion, a dislocated shoulder, three busted ribs, a twisted ankle, and my arm broken in two places with the bone poking out. After I spent a week in the hospital, it was another two months before I could do any work for Liam. Two months cooling my heels at Cutcheon's Small Engine. The old man was decent to me and I liked the work. You spend the day putting engines together, you go home feeling like you done something worthwhile.

Once I was healed up enough to be any use in a fight, I did a few runs for Liam. Me and Butch took this slicked up Monte Carlo to Des Moines, trunk full of meth. Good money.

The summer was near gone before I made it back up to the farm-house. Nobody answered when I knocked, but the door was un-locked. Soon as I walked in, the stink of dirty dishes hit me. The kitchen sink was full of them, with flies buzzing on rotten food. All these bowls and glasses with mold growing in the bottoms.

"Hello? It's Kellen, from down the hill. Anybody home?" I hollered.

Nobody answered, but in the bedroom off the front hall I heard somebody snoring, just a little louder than the fly-buzz. I poked my head around the door frame and whoever was in bed rolled over. This thin, white leg and a patch of dark hair poked out of the covers. Liam's wife? I took a step back, so I couldn't see her.

"Mrs. Quinn? I was looking for the little blond girl. Wavy?" It was fuzzy as hell in my head. More than a couple times in the hospi-tal, I thought maybe I'd dreamed it.

"She took Donal somewhere."

I didn't know who Donal was, but at least the girl was probably real, since Liam's wife didn't say, "What the hell are you talking about?"

"Do you need anything, Mrs. Quinn? You okay?"

"Who are you?" she said.

"Jesse Joe Kellen. Uh, I work for Liam."

"Fucking asshole."

"I'm gonna go. I'm sorry I bothered you."

I beat it back down the hallway, hoping real hard the whole deal wouldn't get back to Liam. Had my hand on the doorknob, on my way out, when the mess in the kitchen pulled me up short again. Was the little girl living there in that filth?

It was the end of October before I went by the house again. Every time my arm twinged, whenever I did any work on my bike, I thought about the way the girl laid her hand on my cheek and said my name.

I spent years trying to get people to stop calling me Junior, but damned if that wasn't the first time I really felt like Kellen was my name.

After I got the bike back in running order, the first place I took it was the road up to Liam's house. The gas tanks still being primer gray made me old-lady cautious, easy on the throttle going up the drive to the house. The kitchen door was unlocked again, and when I swung it open, the girl was there. She stood next to the table, her hair combed smooth, no leaves in it. There was a baby, too, clutching at her dress, and just like that I recollected the reason I'd been sent to the house the night I wrecked. A bag of groceries. Ricki had gone to the store, but she couldn't take the food up to the house, what with her being Liam's girlfriend and his wife probably not liking that. So Butch said, "Run it up there, Kellen, before the milk spoils."

Now that I could see the girl was real, I didn't know what to say. Maybe that was all I needed. She stood there, holding the little boy by his overall straps and not saying a word.

"Hey, Wavy," I said. I thought that was her name and the way she looked at me, like she was surprised I remembered; it musta been.

She straightened up and let go of the baby. "I didn't kill you?"

"Not even close. I'm as good as new. Wasn't your fault anyway." I said it real quick, not wanting her to feel bad, but she frowned. "Only I wasn't expecting to see you out there. When I hit that gravel and the front tire skidded, I over-corrected. Spilled the bike like an idiot. Not your fault. Anyway, I just wanted to say thanks for helping me."

That was what I wanted for as long as she was looking at me, but when she looked past me, what I wanted more than anything was for her to look at me again. Most people look at you like nothing, but the way she looked at me . . . it was like we were in the meadow again. Like I was important. People don't usually look at me like that.

"Is that Donal? He your brother?"

She cocked her head and frowned. Out from the road, I heard

this familiar rumble I couldn't place. I'd been just looking at her face. Her hair and her eyes. Then I looked at all of her. She was wearing a coat, with a backpack over her shoulders.

"You going somewhere?" I said.

"School."

As soon as she said it, I felt like a dope. That was the bus she'd been listening for and it was gone now.

"I can give you a ride, okay? Since I made you miss the bus."

She looked at me real serious and nodded.

You wouldn't think someone as small as her could pick up a baby that size, but Wavy heaved him up on her hip. She was stronger than she looked.

The baby set to wailing when she carried him away, and he was still going at it from somewhere in the house when she came back to the kitchen. I waited for her to say something, but she walked right out the door. I was making her late to school.

I hadn't thought at all about how her riding on the bike was gonna work, but I went at it the only way I could see. I put my hands around her waist and hoisted her up to the seat. Her back went all stiff and her eyes got wide, so I could tell I'd messed up. I let go of her like a hot potato, and she settled herself on the back of the bike.

"Hold on tight, okay?" I said, after I fired up the engine. She didn't answer and she didn't touch me. I felt like a clod, like I'd missed something important. "You ever rode on a bike before?"

I looked at her in the side view mirror. She frowned and shook her head. Figure that. Liam's kid and she'd never been on a motorcycle. Most guys as crazy for bikes as him, they take their kids riding.

"We're gonna go pretty fast, so you need to hold onto me. I don't want you to fall off," I said.

Wasn't like she could put her arms all the way around me, but she got a grip on one side of my jacket, and held onto my belt with her other hand. Out on the highway, her skirt fluttered around us, so

I reached back and tucked it between us. Doing it, my hand brushed against her knee on accident, and she pulled back from me. Her being so light made me nervous. Like having nothing on the back of the bike. I tapped the front brake to slide her closer to me, just to reassure myself she was there. Soon as I did, her hand loosened up where she was holding my jacket. For those couple seconds she wasn't touching me, my heart stopped.

"Hold on tight. Don't let go!" I yelled. She got a grip back on my belt and my jacket.

At the stoplight into town, we caught up to the bus and followed it to the school. I pulled the bike up on the front sidewalk and, as soon as I came to a stop, Wavy slid off the back. For a second, she teetered back and forth, trying to get her skirt untangled. I was worried she was about to tip over, but as I went to grab her, she rested her hand on my thigh to steady herself. Then she pushed off and ran up the sidewalk ahead of the kids coming off the bus. They all stared at me on my bike in the middle of the sidewalk.

"Hey, Wavy! What time?" I yelled.

She turned back and squinted at me.

"What time do I need to come pick you up?"

She held up three fingers. The pack of kids off the bus caught up to her. One of them knocked shoulders with her, looked to me like on purpose. Then she dropped her hand and shoved her way into the building. I rode away feeling like I'd delivered her up to the gates of Hell.

I never liked school, was always looking for excuses to stay away, but when I thought about the mess out at the farmhouse, I could see why Wavy wanted to go. All I was thinking as I rode back out there, was that I could make things a little better for her. In a stranger's house, it was easy to see what needed doing. I went in there figuring I'd just wash the dishes, but then I couldn't leave the baby crying in dirty pants. It's not my favorite thing, but I can change a diaper. I got the kid cleaned up and then I boiled a pot of oatmeal, skimming off the bugs as they floated to the top. When it cooled, I stirred in some crystallized honey and fed the kid that. He seemed to like it fine. Liked me okay, too. Patting me and smiling big while I talked to him.

Until Old Man Cutcheon took me on at the garage, I was a dish-washer at the truck stop. It's not hard, kinda nice even. Mindless. Scrubbing and rinsing. A couple things were too far gone—a burned and rusted skillet, a bowl of milk so rancid I about gagged over it. I took those out to the trash barrel behind the barn.

It tore me up a little, seeing where Wavy had been trying to make things decent. There were clean baby bottles, and she musta been the one who scrubbed the bathtub to gray. I went over it with bleach and borax, got it damn near white. Took a good hour, down on my hands and knees, scrubbing until my arm got to hurting where they put the screws in.

For lunch, I scared up a can of tomato soup with some stale sal-tines. One bite for Donal, one bite for me. No worse than what I ate as a baby. Didn't stunt my growth none.

By that point I'd been there almost four hours, and I hadn't heard a peep out of Mrs. Quinn. It spooked me, so I went to her bed-room door and called her name.

"Leave me alone," she said. The sheets on her bed were so dirty they'd turned yellow. I guess she musta got up at some point and took Wavy to enroll in school. Unless Liam or one of his girlfriends did it.

"Mrs. Quinn, are you hungry?" I said.

"Go away."

Once I had the kitchen and the bathroom cleaned, and Donal was napping, I looked around the rest of the house. Wavy's bedroom was up in the attic, squeezed into the roofline, with a long window at each end. The window over the front porch had a trellis under it. Just bare dead vines in the winter, but might could be honeysuckle come spring. Wavy hadn't made her bed up, but the sheets looked clean and she had a homemade quilt on top. There was a set of shelves with some books and the kind of junk I used to collect when I was a kid. An old purple glass bottle, a cat skull, a rock with a hole in it, a hood ornament, a mannequin's hand. Just stuff that calls out to you. Up in the joists, a couple nails had dresses hanging on them. I lifted one up, and under it was an undershirt and a pair of panties.

I lit out of there, feeling like a spy.

I got back to the school just as the empty school buses pulled into the drive. That's why Wavy gave me a funny look when I asked her what time school let out. She'd missed the bus in, but she coulda took the bus home. Except I'd said I was coming back for her. I didn't like to say that and not follow through. Too many folks do you that way.

When Wavy came out, she had a pack of kids following her. She came down the sidewalk toward me, not looking right or left. I figured them kids must be hassling her, the way she looked. Little assholes.

"Hey, Wavy," I said when she got to me. She climbed right up on the bike without any help, ready to get out of there. I put the bike in gear and roared away from them staring kids. I didn't have to tell her to hang on, either. She grabbed my jacket tight and didn't let go.

There wasn't much food at the farmhouse, so I took us through the old Biplane Drive-Thru to pick up some burgers and fries. They'd be cold from riding in the saddlebags on the trip back, but they'd still be good to eat.

When we got to the house, Wavy looked downright scared as she pushed the door open and saw the kitchen. She let go of the doorknob and stepped back far enough to bump into me.

"Mama cleaned?" she whispered.

"No, I did it. I didn't have anything else to do today and I figured you were busy at school. You know that used to be my job, doing dishes. It's good work. Kinda lets you turn your brain off. My favorite thing is plates and bowls, just making circles in them."

There I'd wanted to do something nice, and she looked like she was gonna cry. I put my hand on her shoulder, meaning to hug her, I guess, but she put her hands against my belly and shoved me away.

"I'm sorry. I didn't mean to . . ."

She shivered hard, all the way down her back, before she stepped inside. I wasn't sure if she was mad, but she looked back at me, so I followed her.

"Silverware you have to take more time washing," I said. "Because of how food gets stuck in the forks. Eggs especially are a pain in the ass once they get dried onto something."

It was easy to talk to Wavy that way. She didn't seem to care what I said, but her shoulders relaxed.

"Man, I'm hungry. I hope these burgers aren't too cold."

I made us up plates, a burger and fries on each one. She watched me do it and, when I put the plates down on the table, she got up in the chair across from me. I tucked in, wrestling with those little plastic packets of ketchup. She opened one, I figured for herself, but she squeezed it out on my plate. Then another one. The whole time I ate, she watched me, but didn't so much as touch her food. After I finished, she picked up the plate in front of her and carried it down the hall to Mrs. Quinn's room.

I fixed Wavy another plate, but when she came back she was toting Donal.

"Here, why don't I hold him, while you eat your dinner?" I said.

She put the baby up on my lap, but she didn't sit down. Instead, she went around the kitchen, one little hand running along the edge of the sink, the range, the front of the icebox, like she was testing how clean they were. When she came to the end of the countertop, she stepped behind me. I went to turn around, but then I realized she was checking me out, making sure she could trust me. My neck prickled up from her watching me.

"It hurts?" she said.

I rubbed down my hackles with the flat of my palm. Once my

hair grew back out, you wouldn't even be able to see the scar running up the back of my head. "Nah. I told you, I'm about as good as
new. It wasn't so bad, really."

Besides the road rash going up my arm, I ended up with this scar
like a centipede, the marks from the stitches coming off it like legs.
She took another step to my left and looked at it.

"That one hurts a little. They had to operate on me." I reached
around Donal to hike my sleeve up and show her how long the scar
was, just that urge to show off a good scar. The way she frowned, I
wished I hadn't.

"It wasn't your fault," I said. "I know better than to come up that
road so fast. It's lucky for me you were there. If I'd wrecked with
nobody around, I mighta died."

She shook her head. She wasn't buying that.

6

MISS DEGRASSI

September-November 1977

Her first year teaching, Lisa DeGrassi had Wavonna Quinn in her third grade class. One of fourteen names on the roster. Lisa saw them all as possibilities.

Most of the kids' parents came on the first day to meet the teacher, but Wavonna arrived alone and slipped into the desk nearest the door.

"Hi! I'm Miss DeGrassi. Are you in my class?"

The girl unzipped her backpack and handed Lisa a copy of her enrollment form. Wavonna Quinn, age eight, parents Valerie and Liam Quinn, a rural route address. The handwriting was hardly legible, and at the bottom of the form, where there was a place for parents to write comments—allergies, health restrictions—someone had scrawled two short lines. The first was "She won't talk." The second looked like "Don't try to teach her."

It unsettled Lisa. Were the Quinns backwoods antigovernment types? Opposed to the public school system, but legally required to send their child? Whatever her parents' politics, Wavonna didn't protest when Lisa moved her to a more central desk, and she eagerly filled out the math worksheet Lisa distributed after lunch.

The problem came when it was time to pass the worksheets forward, and the boy behind Wavonna tapped her shoulder. She turned in her desk and punched him in the arm, sending the worksheets flying.

"Wavonna!" Lisa stood at her desk, scrambling for something to say. "We are not allowed to hit."

In the time-out desk at the back of the room, Wavonna seemed indifferent to punishment. With nothing to do, she didn't fidget or lay her head on the desk. Given worksheets, she did them without complaint. During the planning period, while the kids were at PE, Lisa reevaluated the scrawled note on Wavonna's registration form: Don't try to *touch* her.

At the end of the day, after the kids left, Stacy, the other third grade teacher, came by to chat. She was a few years older than Lisa and the closest thing to a friend Lisa had found in Powell.

"You got the Quinn girl in your class," Stacy said.

"Do you know her?"

"Not her. She transferred here from out of state. Her mother, though. I was in the office when she came to register the little girl for school."

It was a story Lisa would hear several times in the next few weeks.

Valerie had been drunk or stoned. She slurred her words and could barely hold the pen to fill out the registration paperwork. She paid with a hundred dollar bill—registration costs were only twelve dollars for the year—and walked off without her change.

Her hair was a crazed rat's nest of knots and she'd been wearing what one person described as a nighty. With black peek-a-boo stiletto pumps.

And she stank. The assistant principal added that detail: "I mean, *really* stank. Like she hadn't bathed in weeks."

Wavonna did not stink. Her homework occasionally came back smelling of cigarettes, but there were other kids in the class with less care at home. Children who came in the same clothes three days in a row with sleep gummed in their eyes and their teeth unbrushed.

Then there was Wavonna's refusal to eat lunch. The fourth day of school, she wasn't with the rest of the class when Lisa went to escort them from the cafeteria. Wavonna sat at the teacher's table with a tray in front of her and Mrs. Norton watching her.

"Is there a problem?" Lisa said.

"I have one rule for lunch. Everyone has to try a bite of everything. She won't."

Lisa disagreed with rules like that, but in her first week of teaching, there was no way to disagree with a thirty-year veteran like Mrs. Norton.

"When will you send her back to class?" Lisa said.

"After she tries a bite of everything."

At 2:55 p.m., just before the release bell, Wavonna returned to class with a note from Mrs. Norton. Rather than try a bite of each item, she preferred to sit in the echoey cafeteria while the janitor cleaned.

PE was also a dead-end. While the other kids ran around, screaming and laughing, Wavonna sat on the bleachers and read. Take away her book and she would sit on the bleachers staring at nothing.

She was stubborn, but at least she was smart. Her reading was above grade level and she rarely scored less than 100 percent on her math worksheets. She was a problematic student, but she was less trouble than most.

Then the first cold of the season went through school, and Wavonna stayed out sick. Three days later, she returned to school with a severe-looking woman, who marched into the classroom and said, "Who's the teacher here?"

"I'm Miss DeGrassi."

"I am Valerie Quinn." The woman was tall and slender, with brown hair, but this Mrs. Quinn didn't stink or slur her words. She was dressed in a white turtleneck, white slacks, red pumps, and she wore her hair pulled back from her bare face.

"How often do you disinfect the desks?" Mrs. Quinn said.

"I'm sure the janitor does it regularly."

"You're sure? How are you sure? Do you *see* the janitor do it? Or do you just assume that he does it?"

Lisa started to say, "I trust that the janitor is doing his job," but she never got to finish.

Later, when she told the story, she found there was no way to exaggerate it for more laughs.

"It has to be every day. Every day. Say it with me: the desks have to be disinfected every day. Children are germy. They are covered in germs. These, these, these sweet little angels—" At that point in the story, Lisa swept her arm around her audience, one finger pointed accusingly at them, always aware that she would never master Valerie Quinn's contemptuous gesture. "—are disgusting disease factories. These little angels are going to the bathroom and not washing their hands. They are bringing their germs back to this classroom and smearing them over every surface."

The diatribe lasted until the cafeteria lady sent Mr. Bunder, the PE teacher, to see why Lisa's students were late to lunch. He found them in the thrall of Mrs. Quinn's unrelenting account of their hygiene failures.

Mr. Bunder was able to convince her to come down to the front office, where she unloaded on the principal and the janitor and the school nurse, too. When it was over, Mr. Bunder sacrificed his planning hour to keep Lisa's students in the gym, while Lisa went back to her room to recover. Alone, she sat at her desk and cried. When she lifted her head, she found Wavonna sitting on the bench under the coat rack, reading a book. She had been there all along, while her mother rampaged.

"Are you okay, sweetie?" Lisa said. Without looking up, Wavonna nodded. It made Lisa wish there were something worth calling Child Protective Services over. A suspicious bruise, an appearance of malnutrition, anything to get that little girl away from her crazy mother.

Mr. Bunder's take on the situation was slightly different. After having Wavy in his PE classes for two months, he suggested having a kid like that would make you bonkers. "Which came first? The crazy chicken or the crazy egg?" he said.

In November, things got better. Maybe it was the influence of Wavonna's father, who started dropping her off and picking her up most days. That was the same time she started writing Wavy on her papers instead of Wavonna.

When the crazy mother and the Hell's Angels father failed to show up for parent-teacher conferences, Lisa mailed a letter to the house. Then she called, but no one answered.

Finally, she did what she'd been too cowardly to do in the first place. At the end of the day, she walked Wavy out to where Mr. Quinn waited on his motorcycle, his hands resting on ape hanger handlebars. With his leather jacket hanging open, Lisa could see sweat stains under the arms of his greasy T-shirt. He was huge and meaty, and if Wavy hadn't been there, Lisa might have backed down from her intention to confront him.

"Hi! I'm Miss DeGrassi. I'm Wavy's teacher."

He nodded.

"I was sorry we didn't see you and Mrs. Quinn at open house, but I'd like to meet with you to talk about how Wavy's doing. I sent a letter about conferences. Maybe you didn't get it?"

"Uh, sorry," he said.

"Maybe you could come in right now? It would only take a few minutes."

He looked at Wavy, and Lisa had the weirdest feeling he was waiting for instructions. All the lights were on but nobody was home?

Wavy nodded.

"Okay," he said.

In her classroom, Lisa kept two adult chairs for parent conferences, but even they seemed too small for him. As big as he was, he hardly seemed old enough to have an eight-year-old daughter, but Lisa had learned her lesson on that subject. Grandfathers who turned out to be fathers. A mother so young, Lisa mistook her for a student's older sister. Mr. Quinn looked young, sitting across from her like a kid who'd been called to the principal's office.

"Wavonna—Wavy is already over the big hurdles in third grade: multiplication and learning to write longhand."

Lisa had kept back a sample of Wavy's penmanship to show him, a little essay she'd written about the *Voyager 1* and 2 launches. He looked at it long enough to read it, but didn't say anything.

"But she's still not participating in PE class. I was wondering if we could find a way to encourage her."

Mr. Quinn shifted in his chair and said, "What's PE?"

"Gym class. They call it Physical Education now. PE for short."

"Oh."

"The other thing that concerns me is Wavy's speech. You don't have to decide today, but I want you to think about having Wavy meet with the school's speech therapist. It won't cost anything. It's part of the district's services that are provided to all students and I really think—"

"I don't need a speech therapist," Wavy said.

Until then Lisa had heard Wavy say exactly three things: "Don't," "No," and "Asshole," which earned her a trip to the office, where the principal butted his head against her indifference to punishment.

"Oh," Lisa said.

At a look from Wavy, Mr. Quinn stood up, his wallet chain rattling against his leg.

"That it?" he said.

"Um, thank you for coming in."

After that, Lisa gave up. No wonder Wavy didn't talk. Her role models were a crazy woman who wouldn't shut up and a man who barely spoke. What could you do with a child who had that at home?

7

KELLEN

November 1977

At the bike shop in Garringer, Marilyn came around the counter with a big smile and said, "Oh my god, where did this angel come from? I didn't know you had a little girl."

"She's not my little girl," I said.

"Who is she then? Who's little angel are you? That hair is just baby fine, isn't it?"

Marilyn reached out to touch Wavy's hair, so I shifted to block her.

"She needs a helmet," I said.

Sitting there with that teacher thinking I was Liam, I realized it was plain reckless to let Wavy ride without a helmet. Never mind Liam, I wouldn't be able to forgive myself if I wrecked and got Wavy's brains scrambled.

Marilyn brought out three kids helmets. A plain black one, a blue and white striped one, and a pink one.

"I bet I know which one you'd like," Marilyn said.

Yeah, like hell Wavy wanted a pink helmet. She pointed at the black helmet, which was just a small version of a Daytona with a visor. It fit her, so that was a done deal.

While Marilyn rang up the helmet, Wavy walked down the boot aisle, running her fingertip across the toes. Her old snow boots looked cheap and worn out, so I said, "See any you like?" She nodded.

Marilyn stuck right with us, kept trying to get close to Wavy. The way Wavy looked, all sweet and blond, people were probably all the time trying to paw her. A lot of times I'd almost go to touch her hair before I remembered not to. The way I figured it, she'd let me know when it was okay.

To keep Marilyn from touching her, I had to get down on my knee to adjust the shoe sizer against Wavy's toe.

She smiled at me, her cheeks a little pink. I could see what she was thinking.

"I'm not a shoe salesman," I said.

That made her smile bigger, almost showed her teeth.

"So she's not your daughter?" Marilyn said.

"No, she's not my daughter." What was I supposed to say? *She's my bike bitch*? Not everything has a simple answer. I said, "She's a friend of mine."

Wavy picked a pair of boy's square-toed boots. Good leather to last her for a while. They were a little big, but watching her walk across the store, half strutting, half stomping, I could tell she liked them.

"You'll have room to grow," I said.

She nodded.

Wavy wore her new boots out of the store, left her ratty old ones there. She looked happy. Actually waited for me to help her up on the bike, even though she didn't need it.

"I need to put in another set of foot pegs. Put 'em up high enough for you, so you don't have to put your feet on the bike frame," I said.

She'd looked happy before, but she grinned when I mentioned the pegs. That was worth all the weird looks from Marilyn, to get not one or two smiles out of Wavy, but a smile that lasted the whole ride back from Garringer.

At the farmhouse, I figured we'd read or play games until dinner time, but no sooner did I turn off the bike than Val opened the kitchen door. It shocked the hell out of me. I'd only seen Val out of bed a couple times and there she was with her hair done, wearing clothes and shoes.

"Where have you been, Vonnie? You should have been home from school hours ago," she said.

Wavy stood on the bottom step, but she didn't move. I didn't know what to do.

"Get in here before you catch cold," Val said. "Now!"

Finally, I got off the bike and then Wavy started up the stairs. When she got to the door, Val said, "Give Kellen his helmet."

When Wavy didn't, Val took it away from her. By then, I'd come up the steps and Val handed it to me, smacking it into my palm hard enough to sting.

"She's *supposed* to ride the bus, Kellen."

If she'd gave me a few seconds, I woulda said, "It's her helmet," but before I could, Val slammed the door in my face.

8

WAVY

All winter Kellen was in charge of grocery shopping. I liked it that way, because he bought exactly what I wrote down. If I wrote "3 cans green beans," he brought back three cans of green beans. Not one, not ten, not a bag full of things Donal wouldn't eat. That was what Mama did: bring home cream of mushroom soup when I wrote down "cream of celery." Grandma's recipe book didn't have anything that called for cream of mushroom. Mama couldn't be trusted and neither could Ricki. She always lost the grocery list and Mama said she was one of Liam's dirty whores.

When Kellen brought me home from school on Wednesday, I wrote a grocery list out of Grandma's book. The recipe had Grandma's fingerprints stained in hamburger blood.

"You're making something good, I bet. What is this?" Kellen said. He propped his hands on the table, reading the list.

"Meatloaf. For you."

"Oh, hey, I wasn't fishing for an invitation."

"For you," I said.

In two weeks, school would be over for the summer, and Kellen wouldn't have a reason to come to the house, except that he liked to eat. If I cooked, he might keep coming to sit at the table with me and let me watch him eat.

While I waited for him to get groceries, I cleaned and set the table. Grandma's book had pictures showing where forks and spoons went. Water glasses, wineglasses. That's where Kellen's beer bottle went.

He came back smelling like the road and sweat. I wanted to bury my face in his shirt and smell him, the way I did when he wrecked, but I wasn't brave enough, and he was carrying bags of food and scary news.

"I saw Liam on the road in. He wanted to know what I was getting. So I told him, and he said, 'Is Val making her Mom's green olive meatloaf?'"

All the happiness crumpled up in my chest like a wad of tin foil. I shook my head. Not at Kellen, but to make it not true.

"I'm sorry. I didn't know what to tell him. He says he's coming to dinner at six."

I laid the potatoes out on the table and petted them like little animals. They were dirty, but good potatoes. Small enough for me to hold them in my hands to peel. Kellen thought of those things.

"What do you want me to do?" he said.

"Stay."

Going into Mama's room, I didn't want to touch her, but she was already awake.

"What is it, baby? Who's here?"

"Liam not to be trusted," I whispered.

"Liam's here?" Mama sat up, her hair all knots and sticking out.

"Coming."

"He's coming here? When?"

Mama looked at her alarm clock, but it only flashed twelve, because she never set it after thunderstorms.

"How long until he comes?"

I held up two fingers.

"Two hours. I can get ready. Is there shampoo? And don't be weird when he's here. Call him Daddy, okay. Just say, 'Hi, Daddy.' Okay, baby? Will you do that for Mama?"

Call him Daddy, when she was the one who said I wasn't supposed to call him that. She said he was not to be trusted.

Back in the kitchen, Kellen stood next to the table. I said, "Stay," and he stayed.

He didn't fuss like Mama. Sometimes he asked me about what I was doing, like why I put bread in the bottom of the meatloaf pan. I liked that he asked and didn't get upset if I didn't answer.

He said, "Can I do anything to help?" and he did what I asked. He fed Donal, kept him out of the way when I opened the oven door, and put him in his room before dinner. So he would be safe. Donal was two, I knew that; but I didn't know his birthday. We never had presents or cake for him, but I didn't remember having presents or cake until I went to live with Aunt Brenda. Now that Donal could walk by himself, it was harder to keep him safe. At least pretty soon he would be big enough to take care of himself. Next year.

Once the potatoes were cooked, Kellen mashed them, and he never got tired and had to rest like I did. All ten pounds of potatoes mashed at once.

While Kellen mashed, I prayed. *Let Liam not come. Make Liam stay away.* He always said he would do something and then never did it. When I was little, he said he would take me to the zoo. He never did. So let him stay away. Stay away.

Kellen turned the meatloaf out of the pan on the platter, and then he understood what the bread was for. It soaks up the grease. I laid the carrots around the meatloaf and Kellen put the potatoes in a bowl. The table looked perfect when Mama came out of the bathroom. Her hair fell in shiny brown curls over the shoulders of her silky red kimono. She was so pretty, but her face pinched up when she saw the food and Kellen.

"What's this?" she said.

"Wavy made dinner," Kellen said.

"Where's Liam? She said he was coming at six."

"It's six now. She made meatloaf."

It didn't matter how much I prayed for Liam to stay away, if Mama was going to say his name without the protection. She made him come, whistling as he walked across the porch. Smiling as he walked in without knocking.

"This looks good, Val. When Kellen said you were making your mom's special meatloaf, I said, 'I have to get some of that.'" The whole time Liam talked he was creeping down on Mama, his hand sneaking on her neck. She gave him her special smile, going softer. The way candles are softer than lightbulbs.

Liam pulled out Mama's chair for her, and then he looked around the table. Counting. Four plates.

"You staying for dinner, Kellen?"

"Yeah. She invited me."

Then Liam smiled the smile that meant he was not to be trusted.

"Oh, Kellen gives you a hand with things, does he, Val?"

Mama pouted. "You never come around. I guess I need someone to take care of things, since you can't be bothered."

"Why should I be bothered when you don't even wash your hair?"

"I washed my hair."

"First time in a long goddamn time. I almost didn't recognize you."

Mama cried while Kellen put food on the plates. Liam frowned.

He didn't like watching Kellen serve dinner. As much as I didn't like Liam eating the dinner I cooked.

"Does Val make you a lot of nice meals while I'm off taking care of the business that puts food on the table?" Liam said.

"Wavy invited me." Kellen took a bite of meatloaf.

"Oh, *Wavy* invited you?" Liam said.

Kellen finished chewing before he said, "Yeah."

For a while, nobody said anything. Kellen kept eating. Potatoes went into his mouth and the fork came out shiny. I loved the way he ate. I wanted to eat like that.

"That's a load of crap," Liam said.

"I invited Kellen." I thought the words might burn my tongue, but seeing Liam's stupid mouth hang open was worth it. Sometimes he forgot that I *didn't* talk. Not that I *couldn't* talk. He blinked and ate some meatloaf.

"This is really good, Val. You're as good a cook as your mother."

Mama smiled. She wanted any nice words, even if she didn't deserve them.

"We just about got everything ready for Myrtle Beach," Liam said.

"You're going this year?" Mama said.

"Yeah, baby. We'll take the bikes down. Take some product to sell. A little business, a little pleasure."

"I know your kind of *business*." Mama made an ugly face.

Kellen swallowed quick and said, "Which bike you riding down?"

"Eat your dinner, Vonnie," Liam said.

Safer to nod, even if it was a lie. I should have nodded, but I stared at my plate.

"I said eat your dinner."

I hated being afraid, but I picked up my fork. I moved a bite of mashed potatoes away from the mountain. Kellen bought real butter, not margarine. I could never get the lumps out, but he'd mashed the potatoes creamy smooth. They were beautiful.

"So, you're leaving tomorrow?" Kellen was talking to Liam but he sent a message to me: *Just take a bite.*

"Yeah. You're ready to go tomorrow, right?"

I tried to send Kellen a message: *Don't go.* I think he got it, because he squinted hard.

"I didn't know I was going," he said.

"Shit, yeah. I told you, buy out Old Man Cutcheon and you'll have a long line of guys wanting you to work on their bikes. You and me can do some other business that way, too. You don't want that?"

"No, yeah, I do. I just didn't know you wanted me to go to Myrtle Beach."

"You got other obligations?" Liam said.

Me. Kellen didn't say it and I let him go, so he would stop frowning. I didn't want him to be sad. I cut my carrots into neat little circles, like pennies.

"No, that's great. Just wish you'd said something sooner."

"Goddamnit, Vonnie! Eat your food and stop moving it around on your plate."

Liam smacked his hand on the table next to my plate. He had the power to steal Kellen away, but he didn't have power over me. I laid my fork on the table, but as soon as I let go of it, Liam snatched it up.

"Don't you defy me, you little bitch." He shoveled up a scoop of potatoes.

My mouth watered at the smell. I wanted to eat, but I wouldn't do it like that. Liam pressed the fork up to my mouth, so I turned my head away from him, felt the potatoes smear across my cheek. I looked at Kellen, the way his eyes went up and down, from his plate to Liam and back to his plate. He was scared.

Liam grabbed my chin, that's how mad he was. Mad enough to break Mama's rule against touching me. He jerked my head around, to keep me from looking at Kellen, so I closed my eyes. I bit my lips closed to keep the potatoes out, but Liam wouldn't quit.

"You'll fucking do what I say!" The fork stabbed my lip and knocked against my teeth. Liam squeezed my face hard, trying to make me open my mouth. And I was going to. I wasn't strong enough.

Then Liam let go of me.

The fork fell on my plate, a loud clatter in the middle of glasses falling over. I opened my eyes and saw Kellen standing up, leaning across the table. He had one hand pressed to the center of Liam's chest to push him back into his chair. That was all he needed to stop Liam, who looked small under Kellen's hand.

"Don't do that," Kellen said.

As soon as he let go, Liam sat up. All his smallness drained out and anger rushed in again.

"Are you telling me how to discipline my own kid in my house?" Liam said, but his shirt was still rumpled from Kellen's hand.

"No, but you don't need to do her that way."

Kellen sat down and smoothed the tablecloth back out.

"I'll be damned if I take orders from you, you fat fucking slob," Liam said.

"You want your kid to end up a fat fucking slob like me? Just go on doing that, forcing her to eat. It's what my pa did. Made me clean my plate whether I wanted to or not. Busted my jaw once. So, you know, think about that."

Liam laughed. He lost the fight, but everyone would have to pretend he hadn't. Mama knew how to pretend that.

"Well, damn, you're sensitive, Kellen. I'm gonna be more careful around you. I don't wanna hurt your little feelings and shit."

Kellen took another bite of meatloaf. It looked like it was hard for him to swallow, but he kept eating.

I watched him chew, wishing I could eat. Something sticky and warm dribbled down my chin. Blood. Mama watched, too soft to do anything. Kellen passed me his handkerchief under the table. When I took it, I felt how strong his hand was. I didn't understand how he could be afraid of Liam, when he was so much bigger.

Kellen's handkerchief was worn soft from being washed, and I didn't want to ruin it, but I put it against my mouth. When I took it away, my blood was bright in the middle of the whiteness.

Liam set his glass up and said, "Get me some more beer, Val."

Mama went to the fridge and took out a beer. She poured as much as would go into Liam's, and then she topped up Kellen's glass, even though it hadn't fallen over. The Giant had stopped a train, calmed a wild beast, and didn't even spill his beer.

9

WAVY

Mama was Old Val when she woke up the next morning. She shaved under her arms, between her legs, and all down them. After she curled her hair, she put on makeup and the tight clothes Liam liked. No breakfast for her, except for the pills that made her eyes sparkle and her hands float. I was waiting for her to leave the room so I could eat my oatmeal before it got cold.

"Come on," Mama said. "Get your shoes on."

No oatmeal. No school. I pulled on my boots, the good ones Kellen bought. *Room to grow*, he said.

"At least your hair's combed," Mama said.

It wasn't, but Grandma said it was so fine knots couldn't stay in it. Braids and ponytails slithered out of rubber bands like snakes.

Mama was at the door, ready to go.

"Donal," I said. I think she really forgot about him.

"Shit. I must be losing my mind."

Mama hauled him out of the playpen like that was all she had to do. I went around stuffing things into a shopping bag: diapers, a bottle, shoes. Real babies are a lot more trouble than plastic babies.

In the barn, the car wouldn't start, so Mama hiked down the gravel road to the trailers, saying swear words.

"Isn't Kellen a goddamn mechanic? Can't he make sure that car will fucking start? Donal, you weigh a ton, kid. What have you been eating?" Old Val talked fast and laughed.

In the yard outside Dee's trailer, people were loading motorcycles on trailers. I heard Kellen's voice coming from the garage, but when I stopped to look for him, Mama snapped her fingers in my ear.

"Come on, daydreamer."

I followed her up the clattery metal steps into the trailer, where the TV was on loud and something smelled sweet and cinnamony. It made my stomach growl.

Ricki and Dee were sitting in the kitchen, eating coffee cake and laughing. Dee talked with her mouth full. Mouth open for two dangerous things. Double bad. She said, "No way in hell."

"Liam was still laughing about it. He said, 'I guess Kellen's a little touchy about his weight,'" Ricki said.

"Kellen wouldn't say boo to Liam. He's a big ole cream puff."

"You didn't see him beat the crap out of that guy over at the Rusted Bucket. I think he's scary in his own lumbering retard way." Ricki always said mean things about Kellen, but she was stupid. You'd have to be stupid to like Liam and not Kellen.

Dee laughed until she saw Mama standing there, glaring.

Hate rippled off Mama and fluttered against my skin. It made my stomach hurt.

"Get up off your asses, you fucking whores. I don't stand in my own house," Mama said.

"It's not your house," Ricki said.

"The hell it isn't. Everything that's his is mine. I'm his *wife*. If I told him to, he'd kick you to the curb."

I wasn't sure Mama had that kind of power over Liam, but Ricki and Dee must have thought so, because they stood up. Mama put Donal on the floor, sat down, and lit one of their cigarettes.

"Where is he?" she said.

"Out in the lab."

"Go get him."

When he came to the trailer, Liam's smile didn't touch me and only brushed over Donal, before it burned on Mama.

"God, you look fantastic, baby," he said.

She stood up, all glowy, waiting for him to kiss her. He leaned her against the edge of the table, and his hand found the special place between her legs. There was no rule against him touching Mama there.

Mama giggled. "Are we leaving for Myrtle Beach this morning?"

"You're coming? What about the kids, Val?"

"They can go to Brenda's. It looks like you've got plenty of people sitting around doing nothing." Mama looked at Ricki and Dee in the doorway.

"Yeah, yeah. Dee, why don't you take the Charger, drive them down to her sister's?" He didn't even look at her. With Mama there, Dee was invisible like me.

10

DEE

As Dee backed out of the drive, she realized she didn't know where she was going. She looked in the rearview mirror at Liam's daughter, who was cute as could be, but creepy. Even if she knew where they were going, she wouldn't say a word to Dee. She never had.

Leaving the kids in the car, Dee walked back to the house. Liam had Val on his lap, his hand up her short skirt.

"Where am I going?" Dee said.

"To her sister's in Tulsa." Liam didn't even bother to move his hand. He was so gorgeous, all that blond hair, and tan from being out on the bike.

"I know, but what's the address?"

Her arm around Liam's neck, Val winked at Dee. "One-Four-Three-Two-Two Fawn Hill Circle. Do you think you can find that?"

They had been friends once, and Dee felt sorry for Val. She was seriously messed up, and whatever was wrong with her, it had created a chance for Dee. If Val were okay, why would Liam waste his time on Dee?

She drove Kellen's Charger, faster than she should have, and risked getting pulled over. An hour outside the city, the little boy started whining and crying. It made Dee glad she hadn't done something stupid like get knocked up. Of course, that was how Val got Liam, popping out babies for him. Popping out a son... who wouldn't stop crying.

"Can't you make him be quiet?" Dee said.

The crying didn't seem to bother Wavy, but it rattled Dee's nerves so much that she got the address turned around in her head. At 13422 Fawn Hill Circle, the man who answered the door looked confused.

"Val asked me tø drop the kids off," Dee said.

"I think you've got the wrong address."

She tried the neighbors and got the same thing. Cruising down the block, Dee felt helpless and panicked. If she didn't get back by dark, the rest of the guys would have left already and she'd be stuck at the ranch while Liam partied at Myrtle Beach. With Val.

From the backseat, Wavy said, "There."

Dee slammed on the brakes and, as she looked at the houses, Liam's daughter opened the door and stepped out of the car. She left the door open as she crossed the street and started up the walk in front of a neat yellow house. It almost made Dee sick how neat it was. Grass trimmed, white shutters, station wagon out front. The kind of thing Dee would have ended up with if she'd listened to her mother's advice.

Throwing the car into park, Dee hurried around to the open door to get Donal. If she could make the hand-off and get on the road, it would be okay.

"Who are you?" Val's sister came down the sidewalk.

"Val asked me to drop the kids off."

"What do you mean? Drop them off? For how long?"

"Probably just a week or so."

Dee shoved the baby at Val's sister, who finally held out her arms and took him. She looked stunned, but that was her problem. Let her be stunned.

Then Dee was flying down the interstate, feeling giddy and excited. Until she remembered that Val was riding behind Liam with her arms around him.

And what would Dee do? The same thing Ricki would do. Look around for whatever fun she could get that Liam wouldn't find out about. That probably meant being with one of the guys. Somebody who had as much to lose as she did if they got caught. Because Liam was jealous, unless it was his idea. If he said, "Why don't you give Vic a good time?" then that was okay. Unless he thought you'd enjoyed it too much and that'd come back to bite you.

It was still light out when Dee got back to the ranch. In the front yard, four bikes stood ready to go, with four more on a trailer behind the truck. Kellen was loading up a pair of toolboxes.

"Am I riding with you? Give me five minutes," Dee called as she stepped out of the Charger. She needed a shower, but maybe she would just grab some makeup and clean clothes so she didn't look like a piece of shit next to Val.

Kellen shrugged. He wasn't retarded, but he was definitely slow. Dee thought it was that fetus alcohol thing. That's why his eyes were slanted, too, or that was because he was an Indian. Flat-faced, too. About as homely as a mud fence.

At least he waited for her. When she came out of the trailer, he was the only one there. He jammed her pack into his saddlebag. Then he swung his leg over the bike and started it. The sound of a big engine firing up always got Dee right in her cunt and, riding behind him, who cared what Kellen looked like? She leaned into him on the highway, smoothed her hands over his belly, down to his belt buckle.

They stopped before dawn. Two of the guys bedded down in the truck, and Kellen paid for two hotel rooms. Nobody said a word about how to divvy them up, but it was four people, four beds. Butch and Liam were way old friends and Terry had rotten teeth. That left Kellen.

Alicia, one of the girls from last summer, had screwed Kellen as a favor to Liam. She said he was hung. Polite, but sweaty and awkward. Like having sex with a walrus. "You've had sex with a walrus?" Ricki had asked and they all died laughing, stoned out of their minds.

At least sex with Kellen would take Dee's mind off Liam.

Or it would if Kellen weren't so shy. Alone with her, he didn't leer when she came out of the bathroom in a too-small motel towel. He didn't even look at her, even though she stood between him and the TV. When he finally looked up, she dropped the towel.

"Are you too tired?" she said.

"Not too much, I guess."

I guess. God, she didn't ask for romance, but could he show a little enthusiasm? Not wanting the walrus experience, she pushed him back on the bed and opened his fly. As advertised, he had some equipment, what you'd expect from a guy his size. Also, he didn't try to kiss her and he lasted long enough for her to get off. She went into the bathroom to clean up and when she came out, Kellen was taking off his boots.

"Thanks," he mumbled.

It surprised her. She hadn't really thought about the fact that she was doing him a favor. She hadn't thought about him at all. Pulling back the covers on the other bed, she crawled in, relieved that she wouldn't have to sleep next to him.

"Here." He opened his wallet and counted out some money.

Dee never liked taking money for it, but she folded the bills into her purse. When she was with Liam, money wasn't a problem, but what were the odds he'd even notice her with Val there? She needed the cash.

Kellen met her gaze for a second before he looked away. "I don't mean—it's not—Liam told me to give you this."

"Oh, cool." Curling on her side away from him, Dee tried to think of something nice to say and couldn't.

Kellen was a lousy liar and he snored.

II

AMY

Mom came back to the kitchen with a crying little boy in her arms. She sat down and cried, too, rocking him back and forth on her lap. It scared me until I saw Wavy standing in the doorway with bruises on her face and a fresh scab under her lower lip. Then it all made sense.

"Oh my God," Mom said. "What am I going to do?"

By the time Dad came home from work, things were calm. Donal was napping. Mom was cooking. Leslie, Wavy, and I were upstairs playing Barbies. Or Leslie and I were playing Barbies. Wavy was playing with Ken. We never used him unless Barbie got married, but Wavy undressed him and made him trade clothes with a Barbie.

"He can't wear that," Leslie said. Everything had to be just right with her. She and I had matching rooms, right out of the JCPenney catalog. Hers pink, mine yellow. Wavy in her black leather boots didn't fit in the catalog. She tore open the catalog and made surprising things happen. Like Ken in a dress.

Dad came upstairs and stood in the doorway with a drink in his hand. He looked tired. It was the first time he'd been home before our bedtime all week. Mom stood behind him clutching her hands together.

"Hi, girls," Dad said.

"Hi, Daddy," Leslie and I said.

"Hi, Vonnie."

"Not Vonnie," Wavy said.

"Excuse me?"

"Not Vonnie. Kellen calls me Wavy."

"Who's Kellen?" Mom said.

"Jesse Joe Kellen."

We all came under the authority of the unknown Jesse Joe Kellen, because Wavy wouldn't answer to any other name. After dinner, even though it was a school night, Leslie and I got to stay up late. Wavy taught us to play poker with the money out of our piggy banks. We had to loan her money since she didn't have any. She didn't even have pajamas or a clean pair of undies.

From the bottom of the stairs, Dad yelled, "Vonnie! Come down here."

Wavy didn't move and after a minute, Mom called, "Wavy! Come down here."

When we got downstairs, Dad was saying, "For God's sake, Brenda, I thought we were done with this."

"What was I supposed to do? A complete stranger dropped off my niece and my nephew. Was I supposed to say, 'Oh, I'm sorry, my husband and I decided we were done with this'?"

Dad turned and looked at the three of us.

"Vonnie—Wavy, have you been going to school this year?"

Wavy nodded.

"What grade are you in?"

She held up three fingers.

"You see how easy that was, Brenda? Val's been sending her to school, so maybe you could cut the hysterics, okay?"

"Girls, go back upstairs," Mom said.

"Is Wavy going to stay?" I said.

Mom looked at Dad, who looked at the ceiling.

"For a while," she said. "Now, go to bed. You have school tomorrow."

Wavy and Donal stayed. Dad made Wavy promise she wouldn't sneak out at night, but it was still two magical weeks of Wavy's games and Leslie's cries of protest every time we played a prank.

On the last day of school, Wavy went with me, so everyone got to see my strange cousin who didn't eat or talk, but who wasn't afraid to pump a swing as high as it would go and jump off.

That Saturday, Aunt Val came to get them.

"She looks like a cheap hooker," Dad muttered as she came up the sidewalk.

I thought she looked beautiful, in a tight black dress that laced up the front and left her legs bare, all the way down to her tall black shoes and her red-painted toenails. She had flower tattoos on her arms and shoulders, and when she hugged me, she smelled of perfume and cigarettes.

"Val, why didn't you tell me you needed to leave the kids with us?" Mom said.

"I'm so sorry, Bren. It was a last-minute thing."

To make up, Aunt Val brought presents. Earrings for Mom, a money clip for Dad, necklaces for Leslie and me, a bracelet for Wavy, and a toy car for Donal. When he got up from his nap, she swung him around until he squealed.

After that, we had to look around and acknowledge that Wavy wasn't there.

"Where's Vonnie?" When nobody answered, Aunt Val said, "Oh, where's Wavy? Kellen started that. So where is she?"

"Amy, will you go upstairs and get your cousin?" Dad said.

I found her in my closet, reading one of my library books. I hoped she wouldn't steal it.

"Your mom wants you to come down," I said.

With a deep sigh, Wavy got up and glided past me, leaving the book on the closet floor. Downstairs, she slipped between the sofa and the lamp, so nobody could touch her.

"Hey, pretty girl. How have you been?" Aunt Val said. Wavy didn't look at her. "I brought you a present."

Aunt Val held out a jewelry box, but I was the one who delivered it to Wavy. She didn't even open the box to look at it.

"Are you staying for supper, Val?" Dad looked at his watch.

"Oh, no, Bill. Thanks, but we better get on the road before it's dark."

"Well, let's get the kids packed," Mom said.

I helped pack a bag of hand-me-down clothes from the ladies at church.

On the front porch, Mom and Aunt Val hugged.

"We don't see enough of you," Mom said.

"I know. We keep saying we'll get together, but it doesn't work out."

"What about Christmas? Even if you and Liam are busy, maybe the kids could come for Christmas."

"That'd be nice. I know Wavy would like that," Aunt Val said.

I didn't know if she would, because when they left, she walked out to the car carrying a grocery bag of clothes, and didn't even look back at me. It hurt my feelings, but when I went to bed that night, I found the bracelet Aunt Val had given Wavy under my pillow. Maybe it didn't mean anything to her, but it meant something to me.

12

KELLEN

August 1978

Most days, after school let out, I took Wavy to the shop, let her hang out while I worked. After Old Man Cutcheon showed her what the adding machine was for, she opened the folder of receipts and started adding them. She was good at math, unlike me and Cutcheon. Her deposits and receipts always added up the same. The garage was kinda run down and grease-smelling, but she seemed to like being there, even if she didn't quite belong there. Sometimes, I'd come in from the shop and find her at the desk, like walking in on a wild fawn balancing the books.

   With school out, I didn't get to see as much of her, but that afternoon, when I came back from the cemetery, she was in the office. She was kneeling in my chair, looking at the parts catalog. Seeing me come in so hot, she smiled and turned the fan on the desk toward me.

Sweat was dripping out of my hair, and my dress shirt was so wet it stuck to me as I peeled it off. For a couple minutes, I stood in front of the fan, trying to get dry enough to put on a fresh shirt. On the corner of the desk stood a pop bottle. I picked it up, still cool and half full. As soon as I tipped the bottle to my mouth, Wavy jumped out of the chair with this yelp. Startled me so bad I damn near choked on a mouthful of pop.

"Germs," she said.

"I'm sorry. I wasn't even thinking. I'll get you a new one. I know you don't want to drink after me."

She shook her head. "*My* germs. In you."

"*Your* germs? I'm not afraid of your germs." I winked at her, feeling like an idiot for making the mistake, and took another swig of her pop.

She frowned at me so hard her forehead wrinkled up. I offered her the bottle. I didn't figure she'd take a drink, but she put it up to her nose and sniffed. When she handed it back to me, she didn't have anything else to say about germs. Instead, she took my sweaty shirt and put it on the hanger I'd left lying on the desk.

"I went out to put flowers on my ma's grave. I'm the only one left around to do it. It's stupid, but I guess I always feel like I oughta dress up a little. Try to look nice when I go out there. I shoulda gone earlier, before it was a hundred goddamn degrees."

I took the shirt from her and went to hang it in my locker. While I rummaged around for a dry shirt, I could feel her watching me. When I turned around, she pointed at me and drew an X in the air.

My tattoo. There I was with my shirt off and that musta been the first time she'd seen it.

"It's a calumet. You know, a peace pipe, and the three arrows for the tribal districts. For the three Choctaw chiefs: Apuckshunnubbee, Mushulatubbee, and Pushmataha. Like my belt buckle. I got it after I left home. Went down to live with my granny on the rez. Hung around, thinking I was gonna . . . be an Indian or something. Pissed my granny off. She wanted me to stay in school."

The calumet's pipe bowl was just under my left collarbone. The three arrowheads came up and touched the right. They crossed over my chest, all the way down to the bottom of my ribs. I never thought much about it, but it kinda embarrassed me. Not the tattoo, but trying to explain it with Wavy giving me the look that meant I was important. I got to blushing with her staring, memorizing me, so I pulled on the first shirt I could lay my hand to. An old uniform shirt from four years back when I first started working for Cutcheon, *Jesse Joe* embroidered over the breast pocket and tight in the shoulders. I buttoned it on anyway, because I felt strange having my shirt off now that Wavy had seen my tattoo.

When I sat down at the desk, I saw what she was doing with the parts catalog. She'd gone through all my scribbly notes and filled out the order form. I drank up the rest of her pop while I checked it over. She didn't get annoyed about that. Like she figured I was the boss so she needed to get my okay.

Leaning on the desk next to me, Wavy ran her finger across the blotter calendar and brought it to rest on the twelfth. At some point, just doodling, I'd drawn a heart around the number.

"Yeah, today's my ma's birthday. That's why I took the flowers out." Wavy still had her finger on the day, so I knew she was waiting for more. I was afraid to say anything else for fear I'd get to crying, when I'd managed the whole day not to. "Her name was Adina. She died four years ago. In the winter, but she liked the summer better. That's why I take her flowers for her birthday."

I wiped my eyes quick and Wavy was polite enough not to look at me while I did it. She moved her finger down to the nineteenth of July and then brought it up to touch her chest.

"Is that your birthday? July nineteenth?"

Wavy nodded. That was rare, her telling me something I hadn't even asked. She was usually more interested in finding things out, like with the tattoo. When I picked up a pen, she leaned forward on her elbows, waiting to see what I was gonna do. It needed to be big, to let her know I thought it was important. In big enough letters to fill the whole square, I wrote WAVY'S BIRTHDAY. She looked so happy I went back to the date and drew a heart around the nineteen.

When I laid the pen down, she put her hand on my arm, like she trusted me. Then she stepped between my knees and slid her hand up my arm to the back of my neck. She leaned in so close, her cheek almost touched mine. I kept real still, like you would if a little bird came and landed on your finger. For half a minute, I didn't even breathe.

It wasn't like me trying to hug her on the farmhouse porch. She'd done this herself.

She pressed her chin into my shoulder, and then damned if she didn't sniff my hair. I knew I had to be rank, but she sniffed at me like I was fresh as daisies. Exhaled in my ear, and took another deep breath.

To leave her a way to escape, I only put one arm around her. She trembled so hard, I figured she was set to run away, so I loosened my arm to let her, but instead she put her other arm around my neck and pressed her bony little self against my belly. She was so small it kinda scared me.

"Hold on tight," she said, so I put both my arms around her and squeezed.

I turned my head to sniff her hair the way she did mine. Honeysuckle and what I figured the ocean must smell like—sharp and salty. She giggled, and I had the weirdest feeling she was about to say something else, but someone in the shop called, "Is Kellen around?"

Liam.

I let go of Wavy, and as soon as I pushed my chair back, she got on her knees and scrambled under the desk. Barely made it before Liam opened the office door and started in about this party he was throwing out at the ranch. Before the party, he wanted me to go out drinking with him. He never was happy having just one thing going.

"There's this girl I want you to meet out at the Rusted Bucket," he said.

It was pretty much the last thing I wanted to do, but all I cared about was getting Liam out of there without seeing Wavy. Sometimes when I'd look at that scar on her lip, I thought about killing him. Right then, I thought about the big old Colt revolver Cutcheon kept in the desk drawer. Instead, I came around the desk toward the door, so Liam had to step back into the garage.

"Well, I need a shower first. I'm filthy," I said, as I pulled the office door shut behind me.

"So go take a shower and meet me out there."

"At the Bucket?"

"Yeah. We'll have a few drinks and then take the girls out to the ranch."

Girls. By the time I showed up at the bar, Liam had these two girls in a booth with him. A pretty blonde with stripper tits and this brunette with a snake tattoo running up her arm from her hand to her shoulder. That's the one Liam wanted me to meet. I wasn't stupid. I could figure the situation easy enough. Both girls were interested in Liam and he wanted to keep them both on the hook.

Two drinks later and Snake Girl was at least pretending to be interested in me. Her name was too confusing to remember: something like Marie-Elena or Maria-Lena.

"So, you're a mechanic? Liam said you rebuilt his Harley," she said.

"Yeah."

"That's cool. What kind of bike do you ride?"

"A '56 Panhead."

"You gonna take me out on it or what?" She smiled, but she was looking over my shoulder at Liam, watching him kiss the blond girl.

"Whenever you're ready to go."

I was long past ready to leave. I couldn't hardly make small talk with a girl to save my life, but having Liam there was ten times worse. He made me nervous.

While we were on the bike, Snake Girl acted like she was happy enough to be with me. Kept her arms around me, put her head on my shoulder. Once we got to the ranch, though, she was back to staring at Liam. The trailer was packed and the stereo was up so loud it made the floor shake. I couldn't hardly hear anything Snake Girl said.

I leaned down to her and said, "Let's go outside where it's not as crowded."

She didn't stop looking at Liam, but she nodded and followed me out through the living room to the porch.

For a couple minutes we sat on the glider, not talking. Not even rocking.

"So what do you do?" I said. "Where do you work?"

"Not anywhere right now. Sandy said Liam might be looking for some people."

"Who's Sandy?"

"That blond bitch," she said. Man, she was mad about that girl.

"You wanna walk up in the meadow? It's pretty out there at night with the stars and all."

"No thanks."

I couldn't think of anything else to talk about, but when I put my arm around her, she let me. She even let me kiss her for a minute, before she turned her head. She tasted like cigarettes so I didn't really care. I gave up, and then she reached down and unbuckled my belt. I was thinking we should go somewhere more private, but she started unzipping me right there. Didn't want to kiss me or talk to me and now she had her hand on my dick? Took me long enough to sort it out. She wanted me to go away and that was how she figured to do it.

I was gonna tell her to stop, but then I decided what the hell? Being on the receiving end of that kind of brush-off was a lousy feeling, but maybe it wasn't any lousier than going home alone without a hand job.

The snake's head on the back of her hand was weird, but if I leaned my head back and closed my eyes, I could kinda forget about it. Turned out to be about as exciting as doing it myself and a lot more awkward. When it was over, she got up and went back inside. I zipped up, thinking about going out to the meadow by myself. Instead I went back inside, where the party had shifted gears. People were making out all over the place, and Liam and the blonde had disappeared. I sat down on the end of one sofa and took a few hits off a bong on the coffee table. Then I took more than a few hits.

Dee sat next to me for a while, jiggling her foot until it made the whole sofa shake. I didn't try nothing, because probably the trip to Myrtle Beach was a one-time thing. Besides, she wouldn't even kiss me.

"So, did you lose your date?" she said.

"She only came out here for Liam."

Dee's foot jiggled faster.

"Sorry," I said. I didn't guess her life was all that fun sometimes. Not that I could figure why she stuck with Liam. He was good-looking, but the way he acted was messed up. Dee shrugged and stood up.

"I knew what I was getting into with him. I wonder if that bimbo he's with does."

Later, Snake Girl wandered in and sat on the sofa next to me like we were strangers. That was alright with me. She picked up the bong and started smoking. Just like I had on the porch, I leaned my head back and closed my eyes. I wished I could go home, but I was too fucked up to ride.

"Whose little girl is this?" said some woman with a sloppy drunk voice.

I sat up and opened my eyes. Wavy stood in the trailer doorway, wearing her nightgown and looking lost.

High as a fucking kite, Dee made a beeline for the door, saying, "Wavy, baby, what are you doing here?"

Wavy dodged Dee's hand and Yvonne and Neil's legs, doing whatever they were doing on the other sofa. Before I could get on my feet, she came around the coffee table and wedged herself in beside me on the sofa.

"Hey, is everything alright?"

Wavy nodded.

"Is she okay?" Dee said.

"Yeah, she's fine."

"Should I maybe take her back home and put her to bed?"

Wavy scooted closer to me, resting her hand on my belly to steady herself. It seemed like an invitation, so I put my arm around her.

"I'll take her home," I said.

Snake Girl, who'd been crashed out on the other end of the sofa, sat up and said, "Where did she come from?"

"She's Liam's daughter," Dee said.

Wavy glared at her.

For the first time since Liam left the room, Snake Girl looked interested in something. She held her arms out and said, "Aww, she's so cute. Come here, sweetie, you wanna come sit on my lap?"

Wavy ignored Snake Girl and slid her arm around my neck. Then she laid her head on my shoulder. Her hair was wet.

"She won't come to you," Dee said. "She won't sit on anyone's lap except Kellen's. He's your boyfriend, isn't he, Wavy?"

Wavy nodded. Surprised me. So I was her boyfriend?

"How'd your hair get wet?" I said.

She pressed her cheek against mine and whispered, "Swimming."

"You want a snack or something before Kellen takes you home? We have yummy brownies," Dee said.

"Those brownies have pot in 'em." I wished Dee would shut up and let Wavy talk to me. Her coming there like that, to talk to me, it meant something.

Before anybody else could say something stupid, Wavy put her lips to my ear and said, "Come into the meadow."

It made my skin prickle all over. I'd wanted to go out to the meadow before, and I'd got myself stuck at that stupid party. I scooted forward to the edge of the sofa and said, "Saddle up."

She put her arms around my neck and I gave her my hands for stirrups. Like I was her horse, and she was a cowgirl trying to make a quick escape from some hostile Indians. Except that I was the Indian and we were both trying to escape from hostile saloon girls. It made better sense if I didn't think about it too hard, but it made me giggle.

Out in the meadow, the hay was up past my waist, ready for cutting. Bugs chattered, went quiet as I walked by, and started up again once I was past. The air was less heavy out in the open, not hot and sticky the way it was around the trailers. It felt good to be out, getting further from the lights in the yard, so that I could see the stars overhead.

I kept walking until Wavy pulled up on the reins, tugging on my T-shirt and pushing the heels of her boots into my hands. I got down on one knee to let her hop off, and when I stood back up, she took my hand. She led me past a stand of cottonwoods that made a windbreak for an old five-hundred-gallon galvanized stock tank. There was just enough breeze to make the windmill blades creak, and make the pipe dribble water. The tank looked black and bottomless at night. I wouldn't be brave enough to swim in it, but she was.

Up above the cottonwoods, there was a bluff cut into the hill. In between, there was an open patch of hay. The grass was tamped down in a circle just about her size.

It was what I wanted before: someone to lie out under the stars with me. I could see how it never woulda worked with Snake Girl. She was only interested in bikes, getting high, and Liam. Wavy, though, she smiled at me like she was inviting me into her house. I flattened a bigger section of the hay, enough room for both of us. When I spread my arms out, she laid down next to me and rested her head on my arm. I felt so weird inside my skin, like the stars were pressing me down into the earth, pressing Wavy's head down on me. Part of that was the weed, I knew, but it was the stars, too. All that light traveling from so far away.

I held my breath, kind of waiting. Usually we looked at the stars after dinner, out in front of the farmhouse, playing with Donal. Wavy would start by pointing out a few constellations, and then I'd pick out some I knew. Or thought I knew.

"Ursa Major," I said, trying to get her to start. I could always pick that one out. Big Dipper. Except I couldn't find it.

She cleared her throat, like she was scolding me, but it was just to tease.

"Cassiopeia." She lifted her hand up, drew it out for me. Five stars zigzagging.

"Cepheus." Four stars that made a triangle, plus a fifth that dropped down like a kite tail.

I couldn't keep track, but after she finished, I was pretty sure that wasn't all them.

"What about Orion? Which one's Orion?"

She turned on her side, laid her hand on my belly, and slid it down to my belt buckle. I had to grit my teeth not to squirm. She had a way of making me feel ticklish.

"Right. Orion's the one with the belt, with the three stars, but I don't see it."

"October."

"Really? It's not out 'til October? We'll have to come back in October then."

Then I saw a shooting star. I was trying to remember how that was supposed to go, to wish on it, when I saw another one and then another.

Thinking I must be imagining it, I said, "Did you see that falling star?" Right as I did another one flew across the sky.

"Perseid," Wavy said.

"Persay-what?"

"Perseid meteor shower." Another one shot past Cassiopeia like an arrow.

"Wow."

She nodded against my arm and after that, we were quiet. We didn't need to talk. We just laid there watching falling stars go streaking white through all that darkness.

PART TWO

I

KELLEN

December 1979

In high school in Oklahoma, there was this girl I liked, and one night after I went out drinking, I climbed up to her bedroom window. In bed, she let me kiss her and grope her a little, but then she told me to get lost. She really only liked my bike. Not me so much. Climbing up to her window, though, that was fun. What Old Man Cutcheon called "shenanigans."

Climbing the trellis under Wavy's window felt like shenanigans, but as soon as I knocked on the sash, I realized I was too drunk and being stupid. I shouldn't have been riding, let alone climbing up to her window.

I woulda gone back down, but Wavy opened the window before I could. I guess she'd heard the bike coming up the road. I crawled over the sill and managed to scramble into her room without busting my ass. She closed the window and stood there like a ghost in her nightgown. Waiting for me to say something. Well, yeah, since I just crawled in her bedroom window in the middle of the night.

"I brought you a present," I said.

"Not Christmas yet."

"No, not Christmas. It's a—a birthday present."

"July."

"I know your birthday's in July. I just—I don't—I'm a little drunk. It's actually my birthday. I brought you a present for my birthday."

"Today?"

"Yeah, today's my birthday. Well, yesterday. I think it's past midnight already."

Her teeth flashed in the dark and she took hold of my hand, pulled me toward the bed. It was the only place for me to sit down, but that spooked me. Made me think about climbing through that other girl's window to get in bed with her.

"No, sweetheart. I just came to bring you a present."

I'd carried it tucked flat into the back of my waistband, but when I pulled it out, I dropped it on the floor. Before I could pick it up, she pulled me another step toward the bed.

"Cold," she said.

"Yeah, you need to get back in bed. I let all the cold in opening the window."

"You."

I *was* cold. When Wavy held the covers open for me, I sat down on the edge of the bed. I shrugged outta my motorcycle jacket and kicked off my boots. Left my jeans, belt, and shirt on. Drunk as I was, that seemed okay. She was in her nightgown, but I was still dressed.

Getting under the covers was easy enough. I fluffed the quilts and tucked them around both of us, since my arms were long enough to arrange it all. She huddled up along my side, shivering, and rubbed her feet against my leg trying to warm up.

Once I got my arm around her and she laid her head on my shoulder, we were warm and comfortable, and ready to go to sleep. And that was the goddamn problem. This wasn't the same as falling asleep next to Wavy in the meadow. I was *in bed* with her. If Val came upstairs and found me there, I couldn't exactly say, "I was too comfortable to leave."

"Wavy? I better go."

She shook her head.

"I can't stay here."

She dug her chin into my arm. A nod?

"Seriously, sweetheart. I can't."

Her answer was so quiet, I wasn't sure I heard it right. I didn't want to be sure, except I needed to be sure. It felt like two dogs were playing tug-of-war with my heart. She wouldn't say it again, and it turned out I wanted to know more than I didn't want to know.

"You love me?" I said.

The sharp chin again. Twice. There weren't many things she thought were worth nodding twice for.

"I love you, too. I love you." I said it twice, to be sure she heard it. I shivered, not cold anymore but knowing that saying it out loud made it real. For a long time it was this sneaking feeling I didn't look at too closely, but now I'd said it. I laid awake for a while, feeling her breath on my arm, but finally, being warm and comfortable and drunk caught up with me, and I fell asleep.

I woke up needing to piss, with my dick hard as a rock first thing in the morning, and there I was in Wavy's bed, with her curled up next to me. When I went to get up, she held onto me.

"Present?" she mumbled.

"Yeah. Here, let me up. You think your mom'll wake up if I go down to the bathroom?"

"Window."

"Sure, I can leave the way I came."

"I won't look."

Her eyes were squeezed shut against the sun coming up, but she turned her head away, too. It was the quickest fix, so I lifted up the window sash and undid my zipper. The cold took care of my hard-on right quick. Wavy giggled at the sound of piss splattering and freezing on the metal porch roof, but she kept her face hidden until I zipped up and closed the window.

"Present." She must have been feeling brave. All that talking and the way she looked at me.

Her present was on the floor where I'd dropped it the night before. Seeing it in daylight, I was embarrassed it was something so cheap. I'd thought it was magical when I bought it and, when she took it from me, it still was. Her face lit up, so she was half angel and half little girl with sleep wrinkles on her face.

"They glow?" she said.

"Yeah, and you stick them up on your ceiling. So you can have stars even when it's cloudy like last night. So you can see Orion all year round."

"Wonderful." She said it so soft it wasn't even a whisper.

"I better go. I don't think Val would be too happy about me being up here."

Wavy shrugged. I pulled on my boots and jacket, before I opened the window again. Looking at the trellis, I couldn't believe I'd climbed up it in the middle of the night. Stupid as hell.

So the boots had to come off again and I tiptoed down the stairs behind Wavy. In the kitchen, I tugged my boots on, while Wavy waited in her bare feet. When I reached for the knob on the kitchen door, she put her hand on my arm.

"Nothing for your birthday," she said.

"Not nothing. You gave me the best present I've had in a long time."

Since she didn't step back from me, I took her face in both my hands, turned it up, so I could lean down and kiss her. On the mouth, but nothing dirty. The kind of kiss you give someone you love.

She smiled at me. A real smile, with teeth and dimples and the whole shebang.

2

AMY

After Thanksgiving, Mom started calling Aunt Val and saying, "We want the kids to come for Christmas. If you'll tell me how to find your house, I'll come get them," but Aunt Val wouldn't. Mom finally gave up, but four days before Christmas, this little bald man showed up to drop them off. He didn't even bother to take the cigarette out of his mouth to introduce himself to Mom. His name was Butch, and he was a "business associate" of Uncle Liam's, he said. He told Mom that somebody else would come pick Wavy and Donal up, but he didn't say who or when. Until then, they were all ours.

Dad made Wavy promise not to sneak out, but that didn't keep her from doing other weird things. At the rehearsal for the church Christmas pageant, Donal got cast as a shepherd and the choir director cast Wavy as an angel.

"That's probably not a good idea," said Leslie, who had been passed over as the Virgin Mary every year and twice was stuck being the Innkeeper, the jerk who makes Jesus get born in a barn. Now that she was too old to be in the pageant, she helped the choir director corral angels. She didn't want to corral Wavy.

"Why not?" the director said.

"She won't talk. Or sing," I said. In my last year in the pageant, I was the third wise man. That's the problem with the Christmas story: most of the roles are for boys. The only girl is there because men can't have babies.

"And she does *things*," Leslie said, but the choir director wasn't listening.

Wavy already wore a white dress, so for the rehearsal all she needed was a halo and a pair of wings. Even without those things, she looked like an angel.

The rehearsal went fine until we broke for our snack. When we returned to the sanctuary, the Baby Jesus was missing. Like in a crime drama, the only things left behind in the straw were his swaddling clothes.

The adults searched through piles of costumes and boxes of decorations. The church ladies accused each other.

"I put it in the manger. I always put it in the manger," said one.

"*Him!*" another lady said. "Our Lord Jesus is not an *it*."

The choir director accused the Virgin Mary, who cried, and then the Virgin Mary's mother yelled at the choir director.

In the middle of the drama, Wavy leaned close to me and whispered, "Dust Bunny."

"This isn't just some baby doll," I said. "This Baby Jesus has been in the church's Christmas pageant every year for a long time."

Wavy gave me the small, sneaky smile I knew so well.

She had Dust Bunnied the Baby Jesus.

"Let's look under the pews," I said to Leslie. So we crawled through the sanctuary, searching under the pews. The other kids started looking, too, and five minutes later, the head shepherd said, "I found it!"

I cornered Wavy on the steps to the choir loft and said, "Why did you do that?"

"Easter egg hunt."

That's what church was to Wavy: a set of games she didn't quite understand. I laughed, Wavy laughed, and the choir director yelled, "Who's giggling in the loft? And where's my third wise man? Please, can we focus?"

In Sunday School, we were supposed to make Christmas cards to deliver to church members who were too sick to come to church. Wavy cut out the wise men and the livestock, colored them in shades of purple and green, and glued them all around the edge of her card. She left Mary and Joseph and Jesus in a pile of cut out paper on the table.

Inside her card, where we were supposed to write Bible verses, Wavy wrote, "Dear Kellen."

I didn't get to read what she wrote after that and neither did anyone else. When the teacher came around to look at our cards, Wavy wouldn't let her.

"Why not, sweetie? Just let me see."

The teacher took a step closer and Wavy ran. For the rest of Sunday School she hid, and for the pageant, too. So the choir director didn't get her perfect blond angel to stand front and center and refuse to sing. After the pageant was over, as Mom was about to panic, Wavy walked out from behind the baptistery.

Back at home, Dad sat on the couch, reading his work papers, while Leslie, Donal, and I tore into our presents. Wavy had presents, too, but all she wanted for Christmas was an envelope and a stamp.

"Who's the card for?" Mom said.

Once it was safely sealed in the envelope and addressed, Wavy passed it to her.

"Jesse Joe Kellen? This is the boy who calls you Wavy?"

"Is he your boyfriend?" Leslie was in eighth grade that year and had gone completely boy-crazy, and Dad's mom was just as bad.

"What color are his eyes? Blue? Brown?" Gramma Jane said. Wavy nodded and said, "Soft."

"Soft brown eyes are very nice. Is he in your class at school?" Wavy shook her head.

"Well, is he younger than you? Or older?" Gramma Jane said. Older.

They went on asking questions about Kellen and, to my surprise, Wavy answered. He had a shy smile and Wavy got to ride on his bike.

"Mom, stop, you're embarrassing her," Dad said.

"She likes it," Gramma Jane said. "Every girl likes to talk about the boy she likes. And he likes you, too, doesn't he?"

"He loves me." Wavy followed the confession with one of her rare dimpled smiles. Mom thought it was so cute that she told the story to her book club friends when they came over for New Year's. Wasn't it sweet how her tragic ten-year-old niece had a little boyfriend who loved her?

It was sweet until Mom met Kellen.

We were in the kitchen, getting ready to leave for our music lessons, and Mom was arguing with Donal about his Christmas toys.

"Donal, we're going to come back to the house and get them, okay? You don't have to take them all with you. Wavy, will you tell him?"

Wavy shrugged, maybe because in her experience, you didn't always get to go back for your toys.

The doorbell rang and Mom sent me to answer it. On the front porch stood a huge man in jeans and a snap-front western shirt. He said, "Hey, I'm Kellen. I'm here to get Wavy and Donal."

I left him in the entryway and ran back to the kitchen.

"Who was it?" Mom said.

"Kellen. He's here to get them."

Donal dropped his toys and ran out of the kitchen, shouting, "Kellen!"

Wavy went after him.

Still in our coats, we trundled into the front hall, where Kellen swooped Donal up so high he almost knocked his head on the ceiling. Wavy smiled, while Donal talked nonstop. Now that he was talking, that was all he did. "And the Jesus baby was missing. And we crawled crawled crawled around on the floor to find it. And I wore a towel on my head. I was a shepherd. They wore towels on their heads. And Wavy was an angel. She had a halo. And . . . "

"Who is he?" Mom whispered to me.

"He said his name was Kellen."

"Is he Jesse Joe's father?"

Mom opened her purse, rattling her keys to be sure her can of mace was there.

"Excuse me," she said. "I'm Brenda Newling."

Kellen set Donal down and came toward my mother with his hand out.

"Good to meet you. I'm Jesse Joe Kellen."

I watched my mother's face as reality crowded out the story she'd invented. She had imagined little Jesse Joe as the sort of shy young man a quiet, wounded girl like Wavy could befriend. In Mom's fairy tale, they held hands and shared secrets, and would someday go away to college and have good lives, if properly encouraged by a supportive aunt.

Soft brown eyes and a shy smile, Wavy had said. His eyes were almost sleepy as he offered his hand to my mother, and a big gold cap studded the middle of his shy smile.

Behemoth was the word my mother used to describe him to her book club friends, and he was enormous. Bigger than the Incredible

Hulk on TV. Even though he wasn't green, Mom recoiled from the hand he offered. His shirtsleeves were cuffed back, revealing several tattoos, including one in a horseshoe shape. In the center of it was a four-leaf clover and the words *Lucky Motherfucker*. This was Wavy's "little boyfriend."

My mother stepped back and bumped into Leslie. Kellen still had his hand out, offering to shake, but he withdrew it and rested it on Wavy's shoulder. She didn't shake him off, like she would have with anyone else.

"Well, this is really inconvenient," Mom blurted. "No one called to say that they were leaving today. It's unreasonable for Val to expect..."

Kellen wasn't listening. He'd gone down on one knee so that he was eye-to-eye with Wavy. While he looked at her, the rest of us didn't exist.

Wavy whispered something into his ear and he answered: "I got your letter. I missed you, too." All of that was shocking enough, but then she kissed him on the cheek. Unheard of.

"Mom, I'm going to be late to my lesson," Leslie said. Only she would be upset about that. I dreamed of reasons to keep me from my violin lessons.

My mother cleared her throat and said, "Mr. Kellen, we have an appointment to go to. Perhaps you could come back this evening to discuss this."

"I guess Val forgot to call." Kellen finally took his eyes off Wavy and got to his feet.

"I guess so. If you'll excuse us, we need to leave. Come on, kids."

"Why can't I go with Kellen?" Donal said.

"Because I haven't spoken to your mother yet." My mother rattled her car keys. "Now, come on. Why don't you girls walk Mr. Kellen out, while I get the car? Don't forget to lock the front door."

I was thrilled to stand in the entryway with Kellen. He had

alarmed my mother and received a kiss from Wavy. As they parted on the front porch, Kellen reached out and ran his hand over Wavy's hair, all down her back. She turned and smiled at him.

At the music school, while Leslie was having her lesson, Mom scooted her chair next to Wavy's and whispered, "Who is that man?"

"Kellen."

"Jesse Joe Kellen? The person you sent the Christmas card to?"

Wavy nodded.

"How old is he?"

Wavy shrugged.

When Dad came home from work, he and Mom went into the den and argued for half an hour. Then Mom came out and called Aunt Val. The phone rang for ages, before Aunt Val answered. Mom's whole face clenched up and she said, "Some man came here today to pick up your children. He said his name was Kellen. I was under the impression that Jesse Joe Kellen was a very young man, since Wavy told us he was her boyfriend."

There was a long pause, as my mother wound the phone cord around her finger and then released it. Her face relaxed a little and she laughed.

"Of course, I know girls get crushes, but I am not about to hand your children over to some stranger who claims you sent him.

"Yes, not a stranger to her, but she's only ten. She can't be expected to look out for herself. It is not—"

My mother was going to have the last word until the doorbell rang. Dad answered it and the sound of Kellen introducing himself ended Mom's conversation with Aunt Val.

Donal had been playing with his cars on the floor, but he was up in an instant, running into the front hall. When Kellen stepped into the room, he had a giggling Donal slung over his shoulder. Dad shrugged at Mom and said, "Are you kids ready to go?"

For once, Wavy led the packing. As Mom watched from the doorway, Kellen held the bag for Wavy to put Donal's things in.

Next to my bed was a pile of Christmas presents that technically belonged to Wavy, including a blond Darci Cover Girl Model doll, two stuffed Smurfs, and a Mork and Mindy lunchbox. Ignoring all of that, Wavy pulled a book on constellations out of the pile. She handed it to Kellen with a smile and said, "For you."

Mom had been particularly proud of that book. Something Wavy *would* like. Obviously she did like it, if she was giving it to Kellen, but my mother acted like Wavy had spit in her face.

After they were gone, Mom called her friend Sheila and said, "I just don't know what to do about my niece." I think she only said it to be saying it, because I'd heard enough of her fights with Dad to know there were only three things we could do about Wavy. We could let her and Donal come live with us, we could call Child Protective Services, or we could "leave well enough alone." I didn't know exactly what that meant, but it was always the decision Mom and Dad came to.

3

KELLEN

August 1980

All Liam said about the pickup in Nagadoches was, "Your job is to be the biggest, scariest son of a bitch in the room." I shoulda known it wasn't gonna be that simple. What was supposed to take two days took four and when it was over, I'd done the one damn thing I'd always told Liam I wouldn't do. I killed somebody.

Driving home, I told myself it was different from Liam sending me to kill some guy on purpose. I didn't go down to Texas planning to kill them two Mexicans. They tried to kill me first. That was bad enough, but then Vic's car broke down, and there we were on the side of the road with twenty kilos of coke in the trunk. Plus the cash for the buy.

Vic drove this white '74 El Dorado Biarritz with red tufted

leather seats. The car was waxed and polished and Armor-Alled like a showroom model, but under the hood, it was a goddamn mess.

"How long has it been since you changed the fucking oil?" I said.

Stupid bastard shrugged.

I'd been trying to keep my temper under control lately, stop getting in fights, but I couldn't believe he was that stupid. I punched him.

"What the fuck?" Vic screamed, catching blood from his nose before it could drip on his shirt.

"You tell me what the fuck, you driving around in a car that doesn't run. Do you think we can just flag down the highway patrol and get a tow?"

I pushed the car off the main road, sweating through the last pair of clean clothes I had. Then I spent two hours wedged up under the car, trying to get the bitch started.

We limped it to the next town, but there was no way that car was gonna make it back to Powell. So I called Danny at the shop and said, "Bring the flatbed."

"Wouldn't it be easier to get a tow from there?" Danny was a good kid, but he smoked too much dope.

"Bring the tow truck. Tell Liam we're running late."

Six hours later, we had the car on the flatbed and got headed back to the ranch. I drove. As tired as I was, I was too pissed to put up with Danny or Vic driving. People said I was stupid, but at least I could follow some basic rules. Like don't go on a drug buy in a car that might break down.

It was past ten when we got to the ranch, and Dee smirked at me while Liam tore me a new asshole. Like it was my fault the Mexicans tried to double-deal. Like it was my fault Vic's car broke down. Goddamn, I was done with Liam Quinn. Or I woulda been done with him, if it wasn't for Wavy.

I left the flatbed there and rode the Panhead home, just to get some fresh air on me. At the house, I was through the front door, pulling off my boots before I realized the kitchen light was on. Thinking of those dead Mexicans, my guts tightened up. Those boys probably had friends who wouldn't think much of me plugging them. I walked into the kitchen and leveled my gun right in Wavy's face.

"What are you doing?" I said. The no sleep and the running on nerves caught up with me. My hands were shaking as I popped the clip. I slammed open the kitchen drawer and shoved the gun to the back.

Wavy looked as shocked as I felt. She was sitting at the table, up on two phone books, with her boots off, her bare feet dangling. The overhead light made her hair gold.

"Come on, pack your stuff up. I'll give you a ride home." The back of my shirt was filthy from lying in the dirt working on Vic's car. Her white sundress was gonna end up covered in it, but that was too bad.

I went stomping back to the front door to get my boots on, but she didn't come. When I went back to the kitchen, she was still sitting at the table, reading a magazine.

"Now. Goddamn right now. I'm not in the mood for this."

"Walk." She slid off the phone books and stood in her bare feet.

"No, you're not walking home."

"Walked here."

"Yeah, well it wasn't pitch-black out when you walked here, either."

She shrugged.

"And how'd you get in here?"

She took a key out of her dress pocket and laid it on the table. The spare from under the mat on the back porch.

Looking down at the key, I got an eyeful of the magazine she'd been reading. A skin mag from out of my nightstand. She had it open to a couple things I didn't like to think she'd looked at. A blow job on one page and some girl taking it from behind on the other.

"What are you doing looking at this fucking shit? You can't be looking at this kinda thing. And where the hell do you get off? Just coming in here and making yourself at home? This is *my* house."

I snatched that magazine off the table and rolled it up. She flinched, like she thought I was gonna hit her with it. The way you'd do a dog. Seeing her ready for me to hit her was a bucket of cold water on me. If I couldn't be any better to her than that, I didn't have any business thinking I was sticking around for her.

"It's my house, okay? You can't come in here without me."

She gave me the kinda look makes you wanna curl up and die. Just because she didn't have any titty mags for me to look at didn't mean I hadn't snooped in her bedroom. I went around the table, opened the sink cabinet, and stuffed the magazine in the trash.

"I'm sorry, but I haven't slept in two days. I'm fucking dirty and greasy and tired and I need a shower and something to eat and there isn't so much as a clean shirt in this goddamn house, because I had to leave in a hurry. So I'm sorry, but I don't have—"

I came that close to saying, "I don't have time for you." Except it wasn't just mean. It was a lie. I had all the time in the world for her. I wanted her to be there, but I was so miserable, I couldn't even talk to her like I normally would. I didn't have no business saying, *Sorry I'm in such a shitty mood, but I just killed a couple guys.*

She walked out to the breezeway, so I said, "The bike's out front, sweetheart."

She came back with a bundle of cloth in her hands. She held it out to me: a T-shirt, jeans, and a towel. Washed, dried, and folded. She did my laundry.

"Thank you. And I'm sorry. I'm just tired and I had a bad couple days."

I reached out to take the clean clothes, but she pulled them back and frowned at me. My hands were covered in grease. I followed her to the bathroom, where she laid the clean clothes on the edge of the sink and turned on the shower. She went out, closing the door after her.

In the shower, I spent a good fifteen minutes letting the hot water pound down on me, trying to be finished with the two dead Mexicans. I needed to stop playing that over in my head. It was done.

By the time I got out of the shower, Wavy was gone. I worried she'd walked home, but her backpack was still in the kitchen. Weirder, she'd emptied my wallet. It was in the center of the table with its chain coiled up beside it. Laid out next to it, like a game of solitaire, was all the stuff I kept in my wallet and my pockets. A roll of Wint-O-Green Lifesavers, my keys, a bottle of eye drops, and five shell casings standing on end. I pocketed those. I'd cleaned and tossed the gun, but forgotten to ditch the shell casings. I guess I wasn't much smarter than Vic.

I was about to put my wallet to rights, when Wavy came through the back door carrying a grocery sack from the store up the road. She dragged a chair to the counter and emptied the bag: a package of liver, an onion, a green pepper, a carton of eggs, and a box of ice cream sandwiches.

"I think I already got some ice cream sandwiches."

She shook her head.

"You ate my ice cream sandwiches?"

An embarrassed nod.

"That's okay. I'm sorry about what I said before. It's okay for you to come here."

I was so tired, I sat down at the table and drank a beer while I waited. In fifteen minutes, I had a steaming plate of liver with onions and peppers.

While I ate, she counted my change into piles and sorted through the stuff laid out on the table. She sniffed the Lifesavers and then traced her finger around the spot where the shell casings had stood.

"Those were trash," I said.

She went through all the cards as she put them back in my wallet. My driver's license, my library card, my blood donor card.

"O negative," she mouthed.

Then she hit on a card that made her frown.

She primed herself with a big breath and said it out loud: "Barfoot."

"I used to have a different name."

I put out my hand and she gave me my old tribal ID card with my
father's name on it. I was Junior when I was a kid, but after he kicked
me out, I started going by my granny's name. Tipping back in my
chair, I pitched the old card into the trash.

I finished my dinner, while Wavy watched me. I was never sure
what that meant, her watching me eat. I figured she must like it, or
she wouldn't take so much trouble to feed me.

"I'm about done in, so I better take you home before I fall asleep,"
I said.

"Mama."

It made my skin crawl the way she said it. Like you'd say, "Tornado," if one was bearing down on you.

"What about Val?"

Wavy brought her hands to her head and made her fingers stand
up, like antlers. Or flames?

"Is she acting weird? Where's Donal?"

"Sandy." Wavy came around the table behind me and rested her
hands on my shoulders. "Can I stay?"

"I don't know, that's not . . ."

I didn't even remember what I was gonna say after she tightened
her hands on my shoulders. She squeezed the spot where I'd gotten
all bunched up from the stress.

When I got down on the kitchen floor, she took off her boots and
walked on my back.

"What happened?" she said.

I knew if I didn't answer, she'd never ask again. Part of me wanted to do that, but I couldn't keep it in with her waiting to listen to me. She knew how to keep a secret.

"I killed some guys. This job Liam sent me on down in Texas. It got all fucked up and I shot these two guys."

She stopped walking her feet on either side of my spine.

"Who?" she said.

"A couple of drug dealers, so not any kinda good guys, but I guess that makes me about the same. Not any kinda good guy."

It didn't surprise me when she stepped off my back. I didn't blame her if she didn't want to be around me. I'd thought I could stick it out with Liam, to stay close to Wavy, but maybe all I was doing was turning into Liam.

"I'll take you home," I said.

"No."

She got down on her knees and slung her leg over me. There I was thinking she'd wanna leave, but she laid down on top of me, and pressed her cheek against mine. She didn't have to say anything, because I knew what that meant. She still thought I was a good guy.

I drifted off for a second and jerked awake.

Daylight was coming through the window over the sink. I'd fallen asleep on the kitchen floor and slept the whole night in a blink. When I was younger, I used to get so drunk I passed out, but I hadn't done that in years.

On the other side of the table, Wavy was working her feet into her boots.

"Hey," I said.

I was worried it would startle her, but she'd known I was awake. She stamped her feet to seat the boots and pulled on her backpack.

"Let me get myself together and I'll take you home."

I got up, stiff in weird places from sleeping facedown on the floor, but at least my back didn't hurt anymore. In my bedroom there was a rumpled spot on the bed where Wavy musta slept. Still warm when I laid my hand on it. In the bathroom, a second damp towel was hanging next to mine. So she'd had herself a shower, too. I took a piss and then splashed cold water on my face, trying to get things into focus.

In the kitchen, Wavy was standing right where I left her.

When I sat down to pull on my boots, she slid a piece of paper across the table to me.

Her school registration form. She'd filled it all out, but she needed a parent's signature and the twelve bucks to register. Nobody had registered her for school, and that morning was the first day. I couldn't pass myself off as Val, but I was getting pretty good at playing Liam.

4

WAVY

Mrs. Norton said, "I want each of you to stand up and say your name and one thing you did this summer." Whispers bubbled up all over the classroom like butter on a skillet before you pour eggs in.

We went down the rows, following the alphabet, so I was near the end. Maybe something would happen before they got to me. Maybe the fire alarm would go off. Or maybe there would be a tornado like last spring. We all went into the hallway behind the gymnasium and lots of kids cried. I liked the darkness and waiting for a tornado to tear the school away.

Nothing like that happened. It never did when you wanted it to.

The girl next to me stood up when it was her turn. Her name was

Caroline Peters and over the summer she visited her grandmother in California, where she "went to Disneyland and rode roller coasters and saw Mickey Mouse and . . ."

"That's enough, Caroline," Mrs. Norton said. "One thing."

Then it was my turn. I had things to tell. I visited my cousins. I learned to replace spark plugs on the Panhead. I watched stars with Kellen in the meadow. I taught Donal to swim. I took care of Kellen when he was tired. While he was asleep I kissed him. First on his cheek, then on his prickly sideburns. Then on his mouth, which wasn't prickly at all. Even though the mouth is a dirty place, he wasn't afraid of my germs.

"Go ahead, dear. Stand up and say your name and one thing you did this summer. Don't be shy."

Shy. That was a trick. Like the kids on the playground daring each other, saying, "What are you, chicken?" My heart was thumping inside my ears so loud, but I wasn't chicken. I just wasn't stupid enough to fall for Mrs. Norton's trick.

"Mrs. Norton," said Caroline Peters.

"You've already had your turn, Caroline."

"That's Wavy Quinn. She can't talk."

"She most certainly can talk. She chooses not to talk. And if she persists with that behavior in my classroom, it's going to earn her a mark on the board."

Mrs. Norton walked to the chalkboard and wrote "Wavonna Quinn" in the upper right corner. After recess, she wrote "Jimmy Didier." He got a mark for talking too much. You were only allowed to talk exactly as much as Mrs. Norton wanted you to.

Every day was like that. My name wasn't always the first one on the board, but it always went on the board. If it wasn't on the board before lunch, it went on after, because Mrs. Norton said I had to eat lunch. She wanted to *see* me eat lunch.

One day, I wrote my own name on the board after lunch. The

way I wrote my W was prettier, with arches on both sides and a loop in the middle. Grandma made Ws like that.

Mrs. Norton clenched her teeth and said, "You are a very disrespectful young lady." Then she erased my name. She rewrote it with a plain W and put a mark next to it. Not eating lunch. Being disrespectful.

After nine weeks, my report card had a list of every day Mrs. Norton wrote my name on the board and why.

Kellen registered me for school, so I gave him Mrs. Norton's report of bad things. After dinner he sat at the kitchen table with Donal on his lap and read the list.

He frowned so hard while he was signing Liam's name, I thought maybe he was mad at me. I put Donal to bed, and when I came back, Kellen was still scowling at my report card.

"Come here. I'm not mad at you."

I went to the table and leaned against his shoulder so he could put his arm around me. For a while, we stared at my report card.

"When I was in school, they used to paddle kids," Kellen said. "I used to get sent to the principal's office all the time. Between him and my pa, they used to whoop me so bad I couldn't sit down sometimes. They don't still paddle kids, do they?"

I didn't know, but I shook my head, so he would stop looking worried.

The next day when I came out of school, Kellen was waiting for me, but he'd put the Panhead on its kickstand.

"I wanna talk to that teacher of yours," he said.

Mama walking through the halls had been scary, her high heels clicking on the tiles, quick quick quick, going to tear somebody a new asshole. Kellen took long, slow steps that I could keep up with.

In the classroom, Mrs. Norton kept writing while Kellen waited, but she couldn't trick him into talking first. He could wait all day.

"May I help you?" she said.

"I'm here about Wavy's report card."

"I know you." Mrs. Norton squinted and made her mouth small. Kellen shrugged, but she nodded. "You're one of those Barfoot boys."

"What about it?"

"I had your brother in my class. What are you doing here?"

"I told you, I came to talk to you about Wavy's report card," Kellen said.

"I don't see how it's any of your business. If the Quinns are concerned, they're certainly welcome to come see me."

"I'm responsible for Wavy, and I wanna know what this report card means." Kellen's voice got louder, and Mrs. Norton gave him her meanest look. When she looked at me like that, I knew she wanted to do a lot worse than write my name on the board.

"It means that we have a serious behavioral problem with Wavy."

"I don't know what you mean when you write *being disrespectful*. She doesn't smart off."

"What am I to call it when she disobeys me every single day? I know the sort of young man you are. The sort of boy your brother was. You think defying authority is *cool*. I don't see that it's gotten you very far. I know it didn't get your brother very far. How long has he been in prison?"

"A while now." Kellen's jaw got tight and he wasn't looking at Mrs. Norton anymore.

Seeing how her eyes burned when she looked at his lucky tattoo, I put my hand on his arm to cover up as much of it as I could. I wanted to protect him, but he frowned.

"This ain't got nothin' to do with my brother," he said.

"*Ain't got nothin'*? Obviously you were never in my class, Mr. Barfoot. I would have cured you of that lamentable turn of phrase. One way or another."

"I just don't see why you made this whole list. You wrote down, *Didn't eat lunch* like fifty times. She's not doing it to disobey you. She just don't like eating in front of folks."

"She doesn't eat lunch because she's allowed to do as she pleases.

She's eleven years old and, from her behavior in my class, I suspect she's allowed to rule the roost. Does anyone ever say no to her?"

"How can eating lunch get graded?"

"Because it represents a serious behavioral problem that you are indulging."

Kellen's voice got too big for the classroom. "Goddamn, that's fucking bullshit."

"Mr. Barfoot! Are you in the habit of speaking that way in front of Wavy?"

"It's not like she's gonna repeat it."

"That is exactly what I mean. Perhaps she doesn't talk because you think it's funny."

Kellen hauled himself up and I wished for him to smack Mrs. Norton, the way he once smacked Danny for smoking a joint in the shop bay. Kellen slapped the side of his head, knocking the joint on the floor. Then he ground it into the greasy concrete. I wanted to see Mrs. Norton ground into the concrete.

"It's no use talking to you. You're like every teacher I ever had," Kellen said.

"Do you think Wavy will make anything of herself if you plant a hatred of school in her?"

"She doesn't hate school. She just hates you. I don't blame her."

Mrs. Norton tsk-tsked at us while we walked away. Outside, Kellen swung his leg over the bike and sat down hard.

"I'm sorry I embarrassed you. I didn't even think about that stupid tattoo. I should've covered it up like I did when I went to court. I was trying to make things better and all I did was make it worse."

I shrugged. If I was already failing sixth grade, it couldn't get much worse.

5

MISS DEGRASSI

December 1980

Lisa DeGrassi only went to the party because John Lennon was dead, and she was out of wine. Powell County was dry and she couldn't face the night sober. The party was in a double-wide trailer out in the country, where Stacy's Pinto rattled over ruts in the dirt road until Lisa thought her teeth would fall out.

Inside, the trailer was decorated like a penthouse: leather couches, glass coffee tables, and chandeliers. A trailer with chandeliers.

Walking into the party, Lisa expected the worst—bad music and people she knew. The Rolling Stones played at high volume, while people danced awkwardly. Stacy had been right about the refreshments on offer, though. There was a bar full of booze, free for the taking, and a coffee table cluttered with bongs and pipes and pills. The kind of party Lisa never went to, because she was always afraid of running into a student's parents.

"It's not even in Powell County. It's in Belton County," Stacy had said, like that made all the difference in the world. She came from a nearby town even smaller than Powell.

Lisa stood in the middle of the pounding music, downing free drinks, and when someone offered her a lit joint, she accepted. Later, when someone offered her a line of coke to snort, she thought, *Who cares if someone sees me? Who fucking cares?*

"Oops, watch that sleeve or you'll make a mess," said the man who'd cut the line of coke. He leaned over her, catching the loose sleeve of her peasant blouse so she wouldn't drag it through the fine white dust. Then he said, "You wanna go easy. That's meth, not coke."

Lisa hesitated, and instead of snorting the line, she let the rolled bill slip out of her hand onto the coffee table. She stood up, confused, to find the man smiling at her. He was blond and tanned, with bright blue eyes and perfect white teeth. Powell County's own Bo Duke. Or Belton County's?

"Hi," she said.

"Hi. I don't think I've seen you around before."

"No, I don't go out much."

"You should." He slipped his hand inside her sleeve to touch her bare arm. His fingers were warm, tracing hypnotic patterns.

She felt dizzy and nauseated. The bass line thundered in the bottom of her stomach.

"Excuse me, is there—where's the powder room?"

"Just right on down that hallway, second door on the left."

"Thank you."

Lisa was already turning to go, but the man bent over and kissed her hand with a grin. Although she never trusted those kinds of men, there was something tempting about him. A handsome stranger on a lonely night. He wasn't wearing a wedding ring.

Wobbling in her strappy sandals, Lisa worked her way through the party to the bathroom, where she broke down crying again. Mascara dribbled down her cheeks and left gray splotches on her pale blue blouse. She had to stop thinking about John Lennon bleeding to death on the sidewalk. If she'd been in Hartford, she could have taken the train into New York and laid flowers at the Dakota, or gone to the vigil in Central Park. She could have shared her grief, instead of tamping it down in some hillbilly drug dealer's bathroom. When someone rattled the door, Lisa tore off some toilet paper and cleaned up her mascara as best she could.

After giving up the bathroom to a woman in a fringed cowgirl shirt and a raccoon's mask of eye makeup, Lisa couldn't face the party again. She worked her way down the hall, using the wall as support, and ducked into the kitchen.

In the middle of the room, stood a blond woman wearing short shorts and a halter top. She looked like nothing so much as a redneck Marilyn Monroe. In her hands she held a Rubik's Cube that she was twisting furiously. Not trying to solve it, but scrambling it.

Liam Quinn sat at the kitchen table, taking a drag off a joint. So much for not running into any students' parents. If anything, he was bigger, uglier, and greasier than he had been the day Lisa met him.

"Okay, okay," the blonde said. She held out the cube and Mr. Quinn traded her the joint for it. Since he hadn't seen her yet, Lisa was about to turn around and leave but the blonde caught her by the arm and said, "Have you seen this? You have to see this. It's crazy."

The Rubik's Cube, Lisa assumed.

"My brother has one," she said. "He had to take it apart and put it back together to solve it."

"No, no, look. He can totally do it. Look!" The blonde pointed excitedly.

Lisa looked. The first thing that struck her was how ridiculously small the Rubik's Cube was in Mr. Quinn's hands. Then she realized he was actually solving the stupid thing. He had two sides done and was gaining on a third. Lisa and the blonde stood in rapt attention as he worked through it.

When he finished, he raised his head and blushed.

"Hey, Miss DeGrassi," he mumbled.

"Hi."

"Oh, you guys know each other?" the blonde said.

Lisa still hoped she could escape without being identified, but Mr. Quinn said, "This is Miss DeGrassi. She was Wavy's teacher in third grade."

"You can just call me Lisa. Since we're not in school."

The blonde giggled and said, "Oh how fun! I'm glad you came. Too bad Wavy's not here."

Presented with that horrific idea, Lisa stared at the blonde, trying to figure out if she should know her. There was no way she was Wavy's mother. All the hair bleach in the world couldn't bring about that kind of transformation.

"Okay, okay, you try it now," the blonde said. She took the cube out of Mr. Quinn's hand and gave it to Lisa.

For a moment, Lisa stared at it, feeling strangely disconnected from her own hands. Was that the marijuana? Because the blonde looked at her expectantly, Lisa turned the cube's squares into random order. When she had it as mixed up as much as she could, she put it back in Mr. Quinn's hands. It wasn't a fluke. He solved the puzzle again in just a few minutes.

"Oh my god," the blonde said. "I can't believe how you do that."

Against her natural instincts, Lisa was impressed, too. She'd spent hours on her brother's at Thanksgiving and never managed to solve more than one side at a time. Just as she reached for the Rubik's Cube, wanting to see Mr. Quinn solve it again, she heard the opening bars of "Bungalow Bill."

A second later she was crying in a stranger's kitchen.

She turned to leave, but bumped into someone in the doorway. Whoever he was caught her by the arms and said, "Hey, are you okay?"

"I just want to go home. I want to go home," she said.

Abruptly, "Bungalow Bill" cut out and was replaced by the opening bars of "Another One Bites the Dust" at full volume, for the tenth time that night.

She plunged into the party, tears pouring down her face. If Stacy was there, Lisa couldn't see her or her zebra-patterned off-the-shoulder blouse. It seemed like everyone had the same tall, frosted hair. Lisa turned a slow circle, scanning the room, until Mr. Quinn touched her elbow and said, "I'll take you home."

He held her arm all the way across the gravel drive. Two hours before, the tall strappy sandals had just been silly. Now that Lisa was drunk, high, and crying again, they were dangerous. The car he took her to was boxed in on all sides by other cars. She squeezed the bridge of her nose hard to cut off more tears.

"Damn it. I just want to go home," she whispered.

"I guess we're on the bike then."

He led her out of the maze of cars to a metal garage, where half a dozen motorcycles were parked. Lisa hesitated. She'd ridden on the back of her brother's cheap little Honda a few times, but this was something else entirely.

"Here." Mr. Quinn pulled a leather jacket off the back of the bike and held it out for her. "If you really wanna go home, this is it."

"I do." She let him help her into the jacket and zip it up to her neck. It was an unexpectedly intimate act from a near stranger, and it hinted at what it might be like putting on a bearskin coat. Heavy, warm, and permeated by a wild, musky smell.

The cold was brutal, but exhilarating, too. She clasped her hands around his waist and curled her fingers against the warmth of his belly, which was only protected from the cold by a thin layer of cotton.

"Where am I taking you?" he said over his shoulder.

"I'm on Grove and Sixth in Powell."

After that, they rode in silence. Maybe that was typical on a motorcycle, but it unnerved Lisa. She had forgotten about his impenetrable silence. He and his daughter both. Silence and worse was waiting for her at home.

"Can we stop and get a drink or something?" she said, raising her voice to be sure he could hear.

"You haven't had enough?"

"No, I'm sorry, Mr. Quinn. Just take me home."

"You know, I'm not really Liam Quinn."

Lisa stared at the white line whizzing by. Was it a joke?

"Who are you if you're not Liam Quinn?" she shouted into the rushing wind.

"I'm Jesse Joe Kellen. I work for Liam."

"Wait. What? What does that mean?"

"I do some work for him. I'm not him. You saw him there. He's the blond guy. Looks like a movie star. Wears them pointy-toed cowboy boots."

The hand-kisser who'd offered Lisa a line of meth to snort.

"Do you still want another drink? Last one, this side of Powell." He slowed the bike as a roadside tavern came into view.

"Yes," Lisa said. There was probably never going to be enough liquor, but she was willing to try.

The bar was the party once removed. The same people, the same music. As they walked in, the bouncer at the door said, "Hey, Junior. I don't want no trouble tonight."

"Just here for a drink," Mr. Quinn said. Not Mr. Quinn. Lisa didn't know what to call him.

They sat at the bar and drank old-fashioneds that were long on whiskey and short on sugar. She didn't care as long as they kept her drunk.

"So, Junior? Jesse Joe?"

"You can call me Kellen."

"Okay, Kellen. Why would you pretend to be Mr. Quinn?" At least it was something to take her mind off John.

"Somebody has to. Not like Liam or Val is gonna go talk to Wavy's teacher."

"But why you?"

It was apparently a much larger question than Lisa realized, because he had to empty his drink and order another one before he could answer.

"Because Wavy's my responsibility. I take care of her. We take care of each other."

"Even though you're not related to her?"

He laughed and drained his drink. "We're friends is all."

Lisa looked at him more closely, squinting against the pall of smoke that hung in the bar.

"How old are you?"

"I just turned twenty-four," he said.

She stared at him, feeling stupid. He wasn't old enough to be Wavy's father. He was younger than Lisa. How had she mistaken him for an adult?

They drank another round without talking. He gestured for the bartender to keep them coming.

"What got you so upset tonight?" he said when the next drink came.

"John Lennon was killed on Monday. They shot him out in front of his apartment." Lisa thought she might finally be drunk enough, because for the first time in days, thinking about it didn't make her want to bawl her head off.

"Who's that?"

"John Lennon? The Beatles?"

"Oh. Did you know him?"

"No, but—well, sort of. As a fan. I . . ."

He didn't get it, and Lisa was too drunk to explain how John had narrated her whole childhood and most of her adulthood so far. No matter where she went, John had gone with her, even to this horrible little town. Now he was dead and she was alone.

"I'm sorry," Kellen said.

To his left, a guy in a cowboy hat laid a hand on Kellen's shoulder and said, "Can I squeeze in here for a sec, Cochise?"

Kellen knocked back the rest of his drink, set the glass on the bar, and said, "You know what? Seeing as how you don't know me, why don't you just call me *sir*?"

Until then, Lisa had only considered him a curiosity: some previously undiscovered species of redneck biker Indian. At that moment, there was a menacing quality to the way he said *sir*, with the whiskey still wet on his lower lip, that also made her consider him a possible solution to one night of loneliness.

The cowboy tipped his hat with a smirk. "Whatever you say, Chief."

Kellen swung so fast that his fist whiffled the air beside Lisa's ear. When the blow landed on the cowboy's face, it was like a bomb going off. People jumped into the fight from all sides. Lisa was too stunned to do anything but put her head down over her drink and cover the back of her head with her hands.

"Goddamn it! Knock it off, you assholes!" somebody yelled, and then from that same corner of the bar came the sound of a pump shotgun being racked. The scuffle came to an immediate halt. When Lisa looked up, she saw half a dozen men clustered around Kellen. They were all bloodied and at their feet lay the cowboy, his hat trampled underfoot. Kellen's hair was mussed and someone had torn his shirt and popped open half the snaps down the front, revealing a solid-looking gut and a giant tattoo on his chest.

The man with the shotgun waded through the crowd.

"Goddamnit. Junior, what'd I tell you? You gonna get yourself banned again."

"Sorry, Glen. I was just trying to teach him some manners," Kellen said, snapping his shirt up.

"Manners, my ass. Get outta here before I call the sheriff."

"Will do." Kellen pulled a wad of bills from his pocket and tossed a hundred dollar bill on the bar. He glanced at Lisa and said, "You ready to go?"

"I think so."

She had never witnessed a bar fight, and she walked out on Kellen's arm unsure whether she had yet. She hadn't seen anything beyond the first punch, but she felt sure that was permanently imprinted on her brain. Powell in a snapshot: drunk hillbillies beating the crap out of each other.

When they pulled up in front of Lisa's house, Kellen turned off the engine. Panic engulfed her. She had not in fact invited him to spend the night, but there he was getting off the motorcycle and reaching to help her down.

"I'm fine from here," she said.

"Coulda fooled me. You couldn't walk yourself outta the bar. You're welcome to try, though."

She leaned on him all the way to the front porch and, once the door was unlocked, she remembered how empty the house was.

"Do you want to come in? I could make you some coffee."

"If you don't mind," he said, right before she kissed him. With all the whiskey, it was hard to tell where her mouth ended and his began. He pulled back after just a few seconds and said, "We should go inside."

Of course, he was right. No sense advertising her shame and desperation to the whole town. She stepped backward into the dark entry and he followed.

"Let me go put some coffee on." Turning toward the kitchen, she nearly wiped out, the floor going crooked under her. He caught her under the arms and brought her upright.

"Why don't you sit down and I'll put the coffee on."

It was ridiculous, but she nodded. He steered her to the couch, and then went into the kitchen. She slumped there, listening to him rattle around in drawers and cupboards. A few minutes later, the smell of coffee wafted out to the living room. He came in from the kitchen, carrying two mugs and handed her one of them. Then he stood there, sipping his coffee, and looked around at the dirty wineglasses, empty bottles, and record albums spread all over the rug. Having him witness the messiness of her grief embarrassed Lisa, and it seemed to bother him, too. He seemed to be thinking about cleaning it up until she set her coffee mug aside and patted the spot on the sofa next to her.

"So, where are you from?" he said as he sat down.

"Connecticut. I went to school there, too. I'd never been west of the Mississippi until I took this job. How long have you lived in Powell?"

"Forever. I was born six blocks north of here. Just across from the grain elevators."

"No offense, but I hate this town."

His only answer was a shrug.

"There's nothing to do. Nobody I have anything in common with. Stacy, the girl I came to the party with, we're only friends because everybody else our age is already married with kids. And everybody knows everybody's business. I can't even go on a date without everybody knowing about it."

Kellen leaned forward to set his mug on the coffee table. Lisa scooted closer, so that when he sat back, their arms brushed together. She turned her head up to him as a hint, but he didn't kiss her.

"Would you take some advice if I give it to you?" he said. Now that she knew how old he was, his tone of voice rankled. More paternal than he had any right to act. "You need to figure out how to live here or you need to get the hell out. I was you, I'd leave. Go on back to Connecticut."

KELLEN

Miss DeGrassi asked me to stay the night, but I could see how she'd regret it as quick as she sobered up, and I'd likely regret it sooner than that. After I left her place, I shoulda gone home, as much as I'd had to drink. I shoulda taken my own advice, and got the hell outta Powell.

Except for Wavy. She kept me there. More than that. She kept me tethered, not just to Powell, but to being alive. In the whole world, she was the only person who cared whether I lived or died. If there was anybody who remembered tonight, it was her.

When I pulled into the drive at the farmhouse, there was a light on in the kitchen. I hoped it wasn't Val, because I didn't need that kinda grief. I was doing the best I could for Wavy, and Val always treated me like garbage.

I walked through the door, not sure what I was gonna find, but there sat Wavy reading a book. On the table in front of her was a chocolate cake with candles stuck in it.

"You made me a cake," I said.

She put a finger up to her lips, so I reckoned Val and Donal must be asleep. I didn't even know what time it was. While I took off my coat and pulled out a chair to sit, Wavy went to get the box of matches off the stove.

On the way back to the table, she stopped at the chair I'd put my jacket over. Leaning down 'til her nose was almost touching the collar, she took a long whiff of it. I started to laugh, until I figured out what she was doing. Wavy wasn't sniffing my coat because it smelled like me. It musta smelled like Miss DeGrassi.

"I been down to Liam's party," I said.

She nodded and climbed up in the chair across from me. After she lit the candles, I let them burn for a while, just to look at them reflected in Wavy's eyes. When the wax started to run down to the cake I blew out the candles in one big go.

The knife was there to cut the cake, but neither of us reached for it.

"You wanna know what I wished for?"

"Won't come true if you say," she said in this husky voice.

"I don't believe that. Lean across here and I'll whisper it to you."

She got up on her knees in the chair and put her hands on the table to lean across. I put my hands on either side of the cake and met her halfway. I put my mouth up to her ear, like I was gonna whisper something, but all I did was blow a big puff of air into her hair like it was more candles. She ducked her head down against my chest and started laughing, so I kissed the only part of her I could reach: the top of her head.

"It already came true. You remembered my birthday," I said. "And I got cake."

6

KELLEN

July 1981

Wavy walked around the garage bay, looking at herself in the finish on the Barracuda. I picked the thing up cheap at an insurance auction and bought a new back end from a salvage yard down by Tulsa. For a good six months, Wavy had been watching me put it together in the evenings. I was all the time teasing her about how I was gonna paint it Moulin Rouge.

"That's a factory color," I'd say. Just to get her to roll her eyes, thinking about me driving a pink car. I ended up painting it black with metallic gray striping.

I'd planned to sell the car, but the way she looked at it once it was painted and ready to go, I wasn't sure. She looked impressed.

"Wanna take it out?" I said.

She nodded and gave me that squinty look of hers that meant, "Let's go fast." She was like me that way, kind of a speed fiend, and the Cuda was built for it. We took it easy out around the lake, taking in the view, but the damn thing was champing at the bit. So I took it out to Highway 9 and opened it up a little.

Wavy leaned back in the seat, smiling, the wind blowing her hair around. I put my foot in the gas, kicked it up to about eighty. Then we came over a hill, damn near on top of a cop sitting on the shoulder. I braked hard, got it down to somewhere around sixty, and coasted past the cop.

I held my breath, but a mile on, the cop hadn't come after us. I looked over at Wavy, who'd sat up to see why we slowed down.

"You tired?" I said.

She shook her head. She was a night owl.

"Feel like doing some drag racing?"

Hell yeah, she did. We ran the Cuda into Garringer and down to the flatlands where they drag on the weekends. It's not legal, but the cops mostly look the other way, because it keeps the draggers off the main roads. And if you're looking to sell a car like the Cuda, that's where you find buyers.

The place was nothing but hard-packed dunes and old gravel pits. Not a tree to cut the wind and just ugly. When we pulled in, there were probably thirty cars, guys talking trash and checking out the competition. I parked and got out, went around to put up the hood. Let people know I was thinking about selling. Behind me, I heard some guy say to his buddies, "Look, it's that big goddamn Indian."

That was Billy, still wearing a letter jacket for football, when he'd been outta high school longer than I had.

"What're you driving tonight?" he said.

"You're looking at it."

I didn't know him from anywhere else, but I'd seen him out there plenty of times when I had my '64 Polara. Summer before I met Wavy, I was out there nearly every weekend, dragging that old Dodge.

While Billy and his buddies checked out the Cuda, Wavy came up and slipped her hand into mine. Right away, Billy got his eye on her.

"Say, what's this little girl's mommy gonna do if you lose her in a race?"

"I ain't losing nothing tonight," I said.

"She's a little young for my taste," his buddy said, "but she'll be worth racing for in a couple years. I do like blondes."

Wavy glared at them, even though it was just a joke. Nobody ever won somebody else's girl. The drags were strictly about the money and the winning, showing your car was faster. I mean, I'd won plenty of races, and only ever took home two girls. One was done with me as soon as she sobered up. The other one went home with a different guy every week.

Billy wanted to put fifty bucks on our race, so while me and him queued up for the track, Wavy headed off to where all the spectators were.

The track was shaped like a D. A loop around the big gravel pit, then a quarter-mile straightaway. It was a good track, except for this tight spot early on. About a hundred yards from the start, the track cut into the side of a dune. It meant you had to ride close to the other car until you passed it.

As I pulled up in the line, I glanced out of the corner of my eye and caught Wavy staring up at the stars. She was the prettiest girl there easy, with her hair blowing back like a flag. Amazed me how fast she was growing up. She'd be twelve in a couple weeks and she was gonna be long-legged like Val. Every time I looked at her, the gap between the bottom of her skirt and the tops of her boots was bigger. As soon as I thought it, I got to worrying about all the other guys there looking at her and thinking the same thing. We had a minute before the flagger sent me and Billy around the loop to the straightaway, so I called her over.

"Come gimme a kiss for good luck," I said.

She walked over and rested her arm on the door panel. Leaning in through the window, she pressed her lips to the corner of my mouth, real soft. The wind whipped her hair up, and blew it all around, brushing against my face and my neck. As she straightened up, she tucked it back behind her ears.

"Thanks, sweetheart."

Then it was time for me to roll around to the start line. I watched in my side view mirror as she walked back to the spectators. She was still smiling when the flagger gave me the nod.

The trick with drags like that is not to win by too much. You wanna feel out the other guy and win by just enough. You go smoking the first couple of guys you race and pretty soon nobody wants to race you, and they sure don't wanna put any money on it.

Billy had a Trans Am, '73 I think, and for an automatic, it had some oomph, but when we came outta the squeeze between those dunes, I stepped into the Cuda and kept a car length ahead of him all the way to the finish line. He was a loudmouth, but he was a good loser. Paid up and said, "Not too shabby considering how much weight she's hauling."

"Maybe next time," I said. To remind him he pretty much always lost to me.

I raced four more guys after that. Beat a Camaro, and a Charger same year as mine, and then got my ass handed to me by this scrawny Mexican kid in a Corvette with a 427 under the hood. I knew I wasn't gonna beat him, which was why I only put twenty bucks on it, but I wasn't planning on getting smoked that bad.

I only raced him so that when I was paying him, I could give him the number for the shop.

"You bring it around, I'll give you a good deal. Make it look as nice as it rides," I said.

"It still beat you, man." He gave me this chin-up look, like we were gonna get into it.

"Yeah, well, you'd look better beating me with a new paint job."

After that race, Wavy and me took a break for a while. I sat up on the hood, watching the other races, and she sat down on the bumper while I braided her hair. She never kept braids in it, but my sister taught me how to do it a couple different ways. Just something to do with my hands.

"What is this, a hair salon?" this guy walking by said.

I shrugged him off, but a couple minutes later, he was back.

"You racing tonight?" he said.

"Yeah, I took her 'round a couple times. You wanna go?"

He didn't say nothing, but he walked around the Cuda, looking it over. When he came back around to the hood, he was grinning.

"Looks like that saying is wrong. I guess you *can* polish a turd."

"The question is whether you can beat it," I said.

"Hundred bucks."

Now I didn't have a clue what he was driving, but I didn't care. Anybody wanna walk up to me and talk that kinda shit, I'll give it a go.

I nudged Wavy and she hopped off the bumper, so I could get up.

"Hundred bucks." I stuck out my hand and we shook.

"See you up at the starting line, Chief."

"Asshole," Wavy said, not really under her breath.

"Somebody oughta wash your mouth out, little girl," he said.

"You wanna ride with me while I go beat this guy?" I said.

Wavy nodded. We were gonna show that jackass a thing or two.

We pulled up alongside him and I didn't know what to think. I leaned out my window and hollered, "What the hell is that?"

"Mazda RX-7!" the guy yelled back. Might as wella said, "Martian Armpit Smeller." Some kinda ricer car.

It looked brand new, but newness don't count for a thing. My old Polara was proof of that.

Either way, I figured if his car had any go, it'd be at the start, and I was right.

When we came off the line, he was in the lead. I did like always, hung back a little to see what he had. In the squeeze, I was half a car length back from him, but I pushed on through, and coming out the other side to the open flats, I put my foot to the floor. That Barracuda damn near redlined on rpms, the speedometer needle squeezing up past 105. Wavy was laughing out loud, when we reached the finish. Guy in his rice burner ate our dust.

We coasted down to the turn around and circled back to get our winnings.

I pulled up at the end of the row of cars and shut the engine off. Before we got back on the road, I wanted to make sure I hadn't rattled nothing loose. As soon as I popped the hood, a couple guys come over to look. They couldn't quite believe I'd hit 105 in the quarter mile.

The guy in his Mazda came barreling in while we were standing there. He threw it into park and jumped outta the car. Didn't even bother to shut the door.

"You fucking bumped me, asshole!" He grabbed my arm to turn me around, so I put my hand on his chest to make him step back.

"I didn't bump you," I said.

"You fucking bumped me in the tight spot!"

"Show me. You show me where I bumped you, because I wanna see it."

The guy stepped around me and started looking down the side of the Cuda.

Now I shoulda been trying to throttle him back, but I went and popped off with, "New car. Maybe you don't got the hang of it yet."

"You fucking bumped me, dickface!"

By then we had an audience. Some of them started looking over the cars, too, but there wasn't a mark on the Cuda. Because I hadn't bumped him. He prolly clipped that dune.

"I don't see anything," Billy said.

"Motherfucker!" The guy kicked the front quarter panel on the

Cuda. He wasn't wearing boots, just sneakers, so I figured worst he'd done was give me a scuff, but that was bullshit. I went to grab him, but he backed up, right into Wavy. She shoved him back, and he smacked her.

I grabbed the front of his jacket and slammed him into the side of the Cuda. If somebody was gonna put a dent in it, it'd be me. I punched him in the face until I was the only thing holding him up. Then I dropped him on the ground and kicked him a couple times for good measure. Next thing I knew, I had Billy on one arm and Wavy on the other, pulling me back.

"You better stay down, man," Billy called to the Mazda guy. "He's liable to stomp a mudhole in you. I seen him do it."

Before I could, a couple of guys who knew the Mazda asshole came and got him by the arms. They walked him over and sat him on the bumper of somebody's Charger. I turned around and got my head cleared enough to see Wavy standing there with a big red mark on her cheek.

Nobody stopped me when I walked across to that asshole's crap car and planted my boot in the door. I kicked it half a dozen times, stove that fucker in. If he could still drive himself home, he was gonna have to get in from the passenger side.

WAVY

I've been hit harder. The guy didn't even knock me down, but Kellen went crazy. After he kicked in the car door, he came back to me with a black cloud look on his face. He leaned down to look at my cheek, close enough I could see tiny freckles of blood on his face. Not his blood.

"Goddamnit," he said. "I'm sorry, sweetheart. I'm so sorry."

He tilted my head up and brushed his thumb over my cheek.

"We need to get some ice on that before your eye swells up."

People whispered as he opened the car door for me to get in. The guy in the Mazda was sitting on the bumper of another car. His face and his blue satin jacket were covered in blood.

"You still owe me a hundred bucks," Kellen said to him. Then he slid into the front seat next to me and started the car.

I sat in the middle and Kellen kept his arm around me while he drove. He breathed out hot and angry on top of my head.

"I'm sorry, Wavy." He apologized until I had to say something.

"Not your fault."

He kissed the top of my head five, ten, fifteen times.

At the gas station, while Kellen pumped gas, I folded my arms on the window ledge and watched him. He was calmer, but he was still under his black cloud.

He leaned down to kiss me again, and I wanted to go on being kissed, but instead he went in to pay for the gas and get some ice for me.

While he was inside, two police cars pulled into the gas station. One sheriff's deputy, one highway patrolman. The cops got out and walked over to the car, looked at the tags.

I knew what could happen when a dark cloud and the police came together, so I opened the door and got out of the car. That way, when Kellen came out of the gas station and saw the cops, I was there to take hold of his hand, where his knuckles were bloody. Even though I knew it would hurt him, I squeezed his hand hard, to hold him.

"Evening, officers." Kellen squeezed my hand back, so I knew he understood me.

"This your car, sir?"

"Yes, it is."

"We had a report you were causing trouble down at the barrens south of Garringer. Is that true?"

"No, I wouldn't say I was causing trouble."

"We had a report you assaulted somebody and vandalized his vehicle."

"I was provoked," Kellen said.

"Provoked how?"

"That son of a bitch in the Mazda hit . . . her." The hesitation was because he didn't know what to call me. A lie? Daughter, sister, niece? Or the truth?

"Is that true, young lady?"

I stepped away from Kellen, closer to the cops and their flashlights. I pushed my hair back to show them my face. I hoped it looked as bad as it felt. From the way the cops frowned, it must have.

"What was I supposed to do?" Kellen said. "Am I supposed to put up with some asshole punching her?"

"And who exactly is she? She looks a little young to be out this late," said the deputy.

"I'm taking her home now."

The patrolman almost laughed, but the deputy frowned.

"Let's see some ID," he said.

Kellen got out his, but I didn't have any.

"And who's the girl?"

"Wavy Quinn." I liked my name in Kellen's mouth.

"Does your mama know you're out with this guy?" the deputy said.

"Yeah, her folks know she's out with me."

The two cops stepped back and whispered to each other for a few minutes.

Then there was so much arguing it hurt my head. The deputy said I couldn't leave with Kellen. He said, "We need to speak to her mother," and "We're going to have to book you anyway, so why don't we just go down to the station?"

"You're seriously gonna arrest me for whooping that asshole? Because look at her, you can see he hit her. I got witnesses. So why are you riding my ass? Why aren't you out arresting him?"

"Don't you worry, sir, we're taking care of him," the patrolman said.

"How's that? I don't see you taking care of him. I see you hassling me over bullshit."

"We just want to talk to her parents, okay?"

"Okay, fine. They're gonna tell you what I'm telling you."

At the police station, when the deputy called the farmhouse, nobody answered. Mama had probably turned off the ringer. Then he called Sandy's trailer and nobody answered there either. I sat in a chair in the sheriff's empty office while the deputy took Kellen to charge him for assaulting the guy in the Mazda. It was only a misdemeanor, so Kellen got to post bail right there, but he still had to have his picture and his fingerprints taken.

He came back, wiping ink off his hands and arguing with the deputy. His name tag said Vogel.

"I'm gonna have to call Children's Protective Services," Deputy Vogel said.

"What the hell for?" Kellen's black cloud was back. Bigger.

"Because we got a minor here and not knowing who she is, I can't let her go with you."

"How about this? Why don't I go get her mama? Take me an hour to get there and an hour to get back. Think you can wait to call somebody 'til then?"

"I couldn't get CPS out here before then anyway. I just don't want to release her to somebody who doesn't have any business taking her."

Kellen's mouth got hard, but he didn't say anything to that. He ran his hand over my hair and said, "I'll be back, Wavy." He glared at the deputy. "And can you get some ice for her eye?"

After Kellen left, Deputy Vogel brought me a bottle of pop and an ice pack, but I didn't touch them.

Being in the sheriff's office was a lot like when Mama got arrested, but at least I was dressed with my boots on. When they arrested Mama, I had to sit in the police station for hours, just in my nightshirt, while strangers walked in and out and talked to me. And tried to touch me.

The deputy didn't try to touch me, but he sat at the sheriff's desk, asking me questions.

"So how do you know Mr. Kellen? Or Mr. Barfoot? That's his legal name."

I stared through him.

"Where did you two meet?"

I crossed my arms over my chest to let Deputy Vogel know he was wasting his time.

"Not at school, I'm guessing."

Ha ha ha.

"You know this isn't his first assault charge?" he said.

I knew. Kellen didn't get those scars on his knuckles from playing poker or fixing motorcycles. He got them from pulping guys in the face.

"He's got himself quite a rap sheet. Doesn't hardly seem like the kind of guy a sweet girl like you should be hanging around."

I was so sweet. Like a lemon drop.

I stared through the deputy until he had to get up and walk around the station to get away from me.

It was almost five o'clock in the morning when Kellen came back. I recognized the sound of his boots on the tiles outside the sheriff's office, but it wasn't Mama with him. Clicky heels, but too slow. I turned and looked out the window blinds. Sandy.

She looked tired but beautiful. A different kind of beautiful than Mama, who was dark. The sun was always shining on Sandy. Her hair was as blond as mine, but big and hair sprayed. She wore lots of makeup, and tight jeans and a tight T-shirt with no bra.

"Hello there, ma'am," the deputy said. He sounded surprised, and

I could tell he thought Sandy was sexy. He kept looking and looking at her. It made me wish I looked older. If I looked more like Sandy, the cops wouldn't think I was too young to be out with Kellen.

"Hi, sweetie," Sandy said to me. "You ready to go home?"

I nodded.

"Wow, that guy really did a number on you."

"Are you her mother?" the deputy said.

"Yes, I am. I'm Valerie Quinn. I'm not sure why I had to get out of bed at o'dark-thirty to come tell you that, but here I am." Sandy wasn't like me. She always sounded sweet, even when she was mad.

"I'm sorry, Mrs. Quinn, but you can see why we were concerned about her being out so late with him."

"No, I guess I don't see."

"I wasn't sure her parents knew where she was."

"Well, of course, I knew she was with him. Don't you think I'd be out looking for her if I didn't know where she was?"

"I just wanted to be sure," the deputy said.

"Is that all? Are we free to go?"

"Yes, ma'am, but can I just say? You ought to keep an eye on your girl. You shouldn't ought to let her out with a man like—"

"Thank you so very much for the advice. We're gonna go now, if that's okay?"

I got up when Sandy did, but before we could walk out, the deputy reached across the desk and handed me a piece of paper.

"If you ever need anything, Wavy Quinn, you call me," he said. That's what was written on the paper, his name—Deputy Leon Vogel—and his phone number. I stuck it in my pocket and followed Kellen outside to the car.

Sandy stretched out in the backseat and slept all the way to the ranch, snoring a little. I curled up beside Kellen and rested my head on his leg. Even though we didn't talk, I stayed awake to keep him company.

When we pulled into the yard in front of Sandy's trailer, Liam was standing on the porch, drinking a beer. Kellen got out of the car and folded the seat up so Sandy could get out of the back. Liam came down the stairs, his eyes red. If you could see into him, see what he was, his eyes would always be red. The sun was coming up when he walked across the driveway and grabbed Sandy by the arm.

"What the fuck is going on? Where you been?"

"I got into this whole dust up down by Garringer. Me and Wavy went out to the drags, I got in a fight, and a Belton County deputy gave me a rash of shit about Wavy being out so late. He wanted her folks to come get her." Kellen was talking fast, so I knew he was nervous. I scooted across the seat and swung my legs out of the car. So he wouldn't be alone.

"And what the fuck was Sandy doing out at the drags?"

"I didn't go, Liam. I went to get Wavy," she said in a soft, don't-hurt-me voice.

"What the hell does that mean?"

"Well, Val couldn't go. You know, she couldn't go. So I went, to get Wavy. I just told them I was Val and—"

"Oh, I see," Liam said. "You went and pretended to be her mama?"

"Yeah, I—"

"You went and pretended to be Val? My *wife*?"

Sandy was wringing her hands, not like Mama, who always stood up tall when Liam was getting ready to hit her.

"It was just to get Wavy. Not for—"

Pow! Liam smacked her right in the mouth. Kellen could be fast when he wanted. He yanked Liam back from Sandy so hard the beer bottle flew out of Liam's hand and landed in the gravel.

"You wanna hit somebody, you hit me. It's my fault. Sandy didn't do nothing wrong," Kellen said.

Liam's fist crunched into Kellen's jaw, hard enough to make his head snap back.

"I don't like people sneaking around behind my back," Liam said. "You know that, Sandy."

"We weren't sneaking," she whispered.

"It wasn't sneaking." Kellen had his mouth clenched up like his jaw hurt. "I didn't see no reason to wake you up. Sandy was up anyway, so—"

"And what were you doing up?" That was all Liam cared about, where Sandy was.

"I can't sleep when you're not here," she said.

"I was just next door. You know that."

"Well, we didn't wanna wake you," Kellen said. "Sandy said she'd go. And the cops were fine. They didn't hassle her. Anyway, I'm sorry. The cops were just—"

"Fucking pigs. What business is it of theirs? Like they got any business telling me what to do."

"I know." Kellen finally put his hand up to his jaw.

"You took this out to the drags? I didn't know you had it finished yet," Liam said. He leaned down to look at the polish on the Barracuda's hood.

"I finished it yesterday. That's why we took it out."

"How'd it do?"

"It's goddamn fast," Kellen said. He knew how to make Liam look the other direction. "I think it'll beat just about everything out there. Well, not one of them big-block Corvettes, but damn near anything else. We smoked a ricer, which is how I got in a fight."

Liam laughed and looked down at his empty hand. He reached over and slapped Sandy on the leg. "Go on in the house, baby, and get me and Kellen a beer."

"Okay." She hurried up the steps and slipped inside.

"How fast?" Liam said.

"I hit one-oh-five in the quarter-mile. Think she'd do one-forty out on the flats."

Sandy came back with the beers, already open. Kellen took his and drank.

"We should take it out," Liam said.

"Yeah, there's some money to be made. Plenty of guys with newer cars think they can take an old beast like this."

I touched Kellen's leg and he shifted the beer to his other hand. When he lowered his hand to his side, I slipped mine into it.

"You gotta stay outta trouble, Kellen. I got work for you to do. Can't be having the pigs hassling you on bullshit charges," Liam said.

"No, you're right."

For a few minutes, they were quiet, drinking their beers.

"Well," Kellen said. "It's late. I guess I better take Wavy on up to bed."

"Stay outta trouble."

"I will."

I scooted back in the car and Kellen got behind the wheel, with the beer bottle between his legs. At the farmhouse, he didn't turn the engine off, and he was quiet, worrying. I turned around in the seat, put my arm around his neck and laid my head on his shoulder. He sighed.

After a few minutes, he put his arm around me and kissed my hair again.

"I had fun," I said.

He laughed.

"You got punched and arrested, and you had fun?"

I nodded, careful not to bump my head against his jaw. He squeezed me tight, almost as tight as I needed. Tight enough to let me know he wasn't too afraid of Liam. Tight enough to tell me I was important to him. A little tighter and I would know I was more important than anything else. That was what I wanted.

7

WAVY

March 1982

When Donal and I came home from school, a shining red Corvette was parked in the driveway. Uncle Sean was standing in the front room, smiling and running his hands through his hair. Blond, like Liam's. Mama was dressed and pretty and smiling back at him.

"Do you remember your uncle, baby?" she said.

I remembered him. He came to stay with us after Liam got arrested. Before Mama got arrested. Uncle Sean was loud, like Liam, and sneaky. He had tricks to make you smile when you didn't want to.

To warn Donal to be careful, I pinched him, but he said, "Ow, Wavy, don't," and went right to Uncle Sean. Laughing with his mouth open, he let Uncle Sean roll him around on the rug and tickle him. Dangerous.

Then Liam came, and he and Uncle Sean slapped each other on the back. Loud thumping slaps that made my shoulders tight. I didn't want to stay there, but I didn't want to leave Donal alone with them. He was still little.

Uncle Sean tried to lift Donal up the same way Kellen did and said, "God, he's big! Are you serious he's only six?"

"He turned six back in January," Mama said.

"I thought he was born in March."

"January," Mama said. "And he's big for his age."

Liam picked Donal up, too, and said, "He's gonna be a giant."

"Like Kellen!" Donal shouted. Mama frowned when he said that, but I hoped he was right.

"Let's have dinner," she said.

She took down Grandma's cookbook and flipped through it. Nothing belongs to you. It didn't matter that Grandma gave the cookbook to me. All Mama had to do was hold it in her hands and it was hers.

"Oh, please, the good meatloaf," Sean said.

"Yeah, baby," Liam said.

Donal, too: "Meatloaf!"

"Alright, alright!" It made Mama smile, everyone asking her to feed them.

Uncle Sean went to buy groceries with the list Mama wrote, and he said, "You wanna come with me, Don? Ride in the Corvette?"

I wanted to hug Donal before he left, because what if Uncle Sean didn't bring him back? But he ran out to the car before I could.

They came back laughing and made a mess. Hamburger blood dripped off the counter onto the floor, and Mama and Liam snorted meth off the kitchen table, where it left dust under the metal edge that was so hard to keep clean.

They made so much noise. A broken plate, Liam laughing, Donal squealing. Then Uncle Sean turned on the radio and danced Mama around while the potatoes burned.

"Damn, you're gorgeous. Why don't you leave this chump and run away with me?"

Mama laughed but her eyes looked hot and scary.

"Here, now, are you trying to romance my wife right under my nose?" Liam said.

Uncle Sean laughed and twirled Mama around, while Liam set the table.

"Oh, Liam, put a plate on the table for her anyway," Mama said. Her eyes were so soft when she looked at me standing in the hallway, but I knew not to trust those eyes.

"I'm not gonna sit here with her watching us eat," Liam said.

"But your mama made the good meatloaf. You don't want any?" Uncle Sean came toward me with a green olive in his hand, but when I ducked my head, he laughed and popped the olive in his own mouth.

Pulling up chairs to the table, no one else noticed the rumble of the Panhead coming up the drive. They were too busy putting food on their plates: burned mashed potatoes and greasy meatloaf, because Mama forgot to put bread in the bottom of the pan.

"Damn, did you smell the meatloaf from down the hill?" Liam said, when Kellen walked in. "This son of a bitch can eat, in case you couldn't tell."

Uncle Sean laughed and stood up to shake hands. "Come on, pull up a chair."

"Thanks, but I just came to get Wavy." Kellen looked at me for a second, not long enough. Liam made me invisible. I needed Kellen to see me.

"Get Wavy for what?" Mama said.

"To go for a ride."

"Uh-oh, Wavy, Donal's gonna eat your meatloaf if you don't." Uncle Sean reached out with another green olive stolen from the meatloaf. Donal opened his mouth and took it.

That scared me. What if it wasn't dangerous for Donal to be with Liam and Sean, because he was one of them?

"Don't be ridiculous," Mama said. "It's dinner time, Kellen, and we've got company. She's staying here to visit with her uncle."

"Sorry, I didn't know. Maybe tomorrow, Wavy."

Kellen went out and closed the door. His boots thumped down the porch steps, but I didn't hear his bike start. He was outside waiting for me.

"Make her go up to her room," Liam said to Mama.

I thought about going after Kellen. The only question was whether to leave Donal. I slipped my fingers between the slats of his chair and pinched him hard in the side.

"Ow!" He turned around and looked at me with confused, almost-crying eyes.

"Wavy, what did you do to your brother?" Mama said.

"Nothing," Donal said.

He wasn't one of them.

I pressed my ear to the floor in my room, but all I could hear was laughing and talking. Later someone came up the stairs, slow like Kellen, but not as big. Donal.

"Mama says for me to sleep up here so Uncle Sean can have my bed," he said.

I fell asleep beside Donal and woke up to something that wasn't laughing.

"Yeah, well, I'm your brother, so I think that makes the situation special."

Was it Liam or Uncle Sean? Through the floor it was hard to tell.

"Is that the whole reason you came here? Put on this big brother act?" Liam.

"Baby, why couldn't we?" Mama.

"Stay the fuck outta this, Val. It's not your money, so shut your trap."

"It's just a loan. I guess I thought it mattered that I took care of Val after you got arrested," Sean said.

"Don't throw that in my face," Liam said.

Then it was all shouting and the sound of things breaking and someone getting hit. I couldn't tell who was who until Mama screamed. Then it was Liam who said, "You fucking whore," and Mama who said, "Don't. Don't. Please, Liam."

Deputy Vogel told me to call him if I ever needed something. It's what they taught in school, too. They said the police were there to help you, but I don't think they knew what happened when the police came to your house. Cops ruin everything. They kick in the front door, throw people on the floor and handcuff them. They break things and steal things. They lock you in a patrol car, make you spend all night in the police station wearing your nightgown, and then send you home with strangers. That's why I would never call Deputy Vogel, no matter how much Mama and Liam fought. I'd thrown away the paper with his number as soon as he gave it to me, because I remembered what happened the last time the police came to our house.

Eventually, they stopped fighting and passed out. They always did. After everyone was quiet, I opened the window and looked down at the trellis Kellen climbed up on his birthday. The stair door was locked, and I had the only key, so no one could come upstairs while I was gone. Donal was safe.

The trellis was like climbing down a ladder, and then I was free.

I cut across the fields to the north, to a house I'd never visited. Like Liam's ranch, it wasn't a real farm. No chickens in the yard and only a car in the barn. All the windows were open. I went along, tugging at the bottoms of the screens until I found one where the hook had come loose.

Always check the fridge first. The best foods are kept there. Homemade things. Also apples. And pickles. Open the jar, take out two, stuff one then the other in my mouth. Tangy and sweet on my tongue. Fried chicken, salty and firm. Nibble the wing down to bone and slip it into my pocket to throw away later. Something smooth in a bowl, but hard to tell with no light. Dip a finger in and lick it. Vanilla pudding. Chocolate was better, but vanilla was good.

Eating was most important, but once it was done, I looked at the things people think they own. I didn't take things very often, but I liked to move them. Car keys, purses, glasses, one shoe out of a pair.

The living room smelled like flowers and powder. There was a piano with pictures on top, and a candy dish on the coffee table. I lifted the lid and took a piece. Licorice. I put it back and lowered the lid. It made a tiny ching sound, but nothing worse.

"Lolene? Is that you?"

I jerked my hand away from the candy dish and took two quick steps back.

In the shadows, a woman was sitting in a chair. She had white hair in the moonlight, like Grandma.

"Do you want candy? Ma's not here to catch us. We can eat all the candy we want."

I took another step back.

"Why won't you talk to me, Lolene?"

Another step and my shoulder knocked against the piano. A picture fell over.

"Do you want me to play the piano? Ma says I play almost as well as you. Almost."

I ran, straight through the kitchen to the back door. Behind me, the woman called, "Lolene! Come back!"

When I got home, I found Cassiopeia and Cepheus and Ursa Major drawn in the gravel at the bottom of the drive, where Kellen had waited for me. He tried to draw Orion, too, but missed two stars.

I crawled back up the trellis to my room, where Donal was asleep.

Safe. In the morning, when I went downstairs to get breakfast for him, Mama and Liam were in bed naked. Uncle Sean was on the couch with a needle on the floor next to him. I picked it up and laid it on the coffee table. Safe.

8

BUTCH

April 1982

If anybody wanted to know why that kid never talked, I could've told them. That's what happens when your mom grabs you by the hair, clamps her hand over your mouth, and gives you a good shake while screaming in your face, "Don't you ever talk to people! You don't talk to anyone!"

That's what Val did to Wavy when she was about three years old. I don't know what she thought a three-year-old could tell anyone, but I guess Wavy played in the sandbox with the neighbor's kids, and the neighbor said something that made Liam nervous. More likely the neighbor noticed people going in and out of the house all hours of the day and night. Not everybody is as stupid as Liam thinks they are.

Liam and I go way back, and I owed him for keeping my name out of it when he got arrested, but watching Val rattle that kid's brain was the end of the line for me. Never mind how long we'd been in business together, I was ready to knock that crazy bitch on her ass. I didn't have to, because Liam grabbed Val's arm and said, "That's enough, baby."

I never heard another peep out of that little girl. Years later she warmed up to Jesse Joe Kellen. He was one of the local yokels we hired when we moved the operation to Powell. Not much more than a kid when Liam hired him, he was a big thug with a face like a plank. Always looked half-stoned, even though he wasn't, and didn't hardly open his mouth when he talked.

Sometimes, Kellen brought Wavy around the lab barracks when he played poker or dominos with us. She'd hang around watching the game, and bring us beers. Like a little waitress.

Kellen and her, they were cute together. She'd lean on his shoulder, look at his hand, count his chips. Him being so much bigger, it was funny how he acted with her. He talked to her like she was an adult. She always whispered in his ear, so you got the idea they were having a conversation. I don't know what she ever said to him.

One night, Kellen got up in the middle of a hand and said, "I'm gonna go up to the house for some beer."

"Let's just finish this hand," Vic said.

"She'll play for me." Kellen gave his cards to Wavy and started up the hill toward the trailers.

We laughed, but she got up in his chair, took her next card, and folded.

Scott won that hand and when he went to deal, he skipped Wavy.

"What, Scott, you don't like taking money from kids?" I said.

So he dealt her in. She lost fifty bucks on that hand, but she won the next one. Kellen had been down by almost two hundred dollars, but now he was up again. The next few hands, she won more than she lost. Her dealing left a lot to be desired since she had a hard time shuffling, but at least you knew she wasn't cheating.

Kellen came back with beer about the time Scott and Vic decided to show her how the big boys played. It pissed them off that she'd managed to win some money, so they upped the ante and put down bigger bets. Even though it was his money, Kellen stood back and watched her play. Didn't tell her what to do.

A couple hands in, Wavy apparently got some cards she liked, because she kept raising. Next thing you know, there was almost five thousand bucks on the table, and that was too rich for Vic.

Seeing she'd raised almost everything she had in front of her, Kellen reached into his pocket, and handed her a roll of bills. Big enough she could barely close her hand around it. All business, Wavy snapped the rubber band off and started counting out hundred-dollar bills.

"You do understand that's real money, little girl? This ain't Monopoly." Scott grinned and raised another two hundred.

Wavy slid the last of her chips out to see him and then the pile of cash she'd made: a thousand bucks. Raised him.

Scott looked down at the chips he had left and the roll of bills she had left. Took him a good minute before he folded. The kid had just taken us for more than a grand a piece. She went to pitch her cards in, but Scott slapped his hand on them.

"Hey, you didn't pay to see," Kellen said.

"Come on, this isn't Vegas. Just a friendly poker game, right?" I was curious.

Kellen looked at Wavy and she shrugged. Scott flipped her cards over. Pair of fours.

We busted up laughing, Vic clutching his sides and sobbing, "You do understand that's real money, little girl?" Kellen laughed so hard he laid down on the floor next to Wavy's chair and cried.

Scott, he about cried for real. Wavy watched us with this little smile on her face. She had a hell of a poker face.

Laying there like a beached whale, so weak from laughing he

couldn't get up, Kellen said, "Wavy, tomorrow we're going into town and buy you anything you want. Anything at all."

Giggling behind her hand, she put her foot on his chest and nudged him.

He took ahold of her leg and said, "First thing, I'm buying you some new boots. You got holes in these from too much walking."

Right up until that moment it was sweet and funny. Odd couple that they were, they had a real connection. Then he tugged her boot off and kissed the bottom of her bare foot. I could see him doing that kind of thing to his own kid, but she wasn't. She was somebody else's little girl.

9

WAVY

July 1982

I waited by the porch to Sandy's trailer, where the old gray cat lived. At night, the big yellow light over the garage cast shadows into my hiding place. People walked by and didn't even notice me crouched there.

Dee and Lance left, probably going to the barracks to fuck. Sandy sat on the porch smoking and crying, talking to herself: "I don't know why I put up with it." When Butch came, she went inside with him.

Danny left in the Charger and brought back beer. While he carried a case to the lab barracks, I snuck out of my hiding place and stole two cans. When Danny came back, he looked at the torn-open case in the trunk and yelled, "That's not funny, you assholes! Don't be poaching brewskies."

I started to think Kellen wouldn't come, or that he wouldn't be alone. The night he brought the snake tattoo girl on his bike, I did something reckless. I went into the trailer to get him. After that, he came to me on his own, so it had been worth the risk.

I sat down on a cinder block and slipped my boots off to bury my toes in the cool silt under the porch. I listened for the Panhead, but it never came. Finally, Old Man Cutcheon's truck pulled into the yard, groaning as Kellen stepped out.

He jingled his keys as he walked across the yard, clouds of dust kicking up around his boots. Only when he put his foot on the bottom step did I climb over the railing. Step out sooner and someone else might see me.

Kellen walked across the deck, making the floorboards thump. From inside, Butch called, "Fee fi fo fum!" Sandy giggled.

Careful to stay to the side of the front window, I stepped out of the shadows. Sometimes Kellen had business and couldn't come with me, but tonight he was waiting for me to step into the light.

"There you are. I was up to the house looking for you, but the Corvette was there, so I didn't go in," he said.

Uncle Sean was there all the time now.

"Fee fi fo no?" Butch called from inside the trailer.

Hearing that, I hurried back to my hiding place. Kellen came down the stairs while I put my boots on. When he walked around the porch, I picked up the quilt and the cans of beer, and followed him across the yard, going away from the sound of Butch and Sandy.

"Is that Kellen?" Sandy said.

"I thought so, but there's nobody out here."

In the meadow, I had Kellen all to myself. He smelled good. Sweat and motorcycle and wintergreen. No stinking weed smoke. No perfume. No sadness. He smelled like love. Between the cottonwoods and the bluff, I spread out the quilt and offered him the cans of beer.

"Dang, you even brought me beer. We need a better system. Some way for you to let me know where you are."

I liked that he wanted to know, but I also liked him not knowing. Sometimes waiting and being disappointed was good, to remind me he didn't belong to me. Nothing belonged to me. I shrugged and lay down on the quilt, which didn't smell like Grandma's house anymore, unless I closed my eyes and concentrated.

"How are these new boots treating you?" he said, as he pulled them off.

He bought me new ones every year to start school. This was the sixth pair, to get me ready for high school in August. Seventh grade was at the old middle school, the last year before they closed it. For eighth grade, I would be going to the new high school in Belton County, which was an hour each way on the bus. "You're not riding no two goddamn hours on the bus. I'm taking you," Kellen said. He didn't care that it was farther.

The boots for eighth grade had to be bought early, because I not only wore out the old ones but outgrew them, too.

I nodded, but didn't open my eyes, to test an idea. If I kept my eyes closed, would it be easier to send Kellen a message? I waited but nothing happened, except that he went on talking while he took his boots off.

"You know, I still got a whole lotta poker money burning a hole in my pocket."

"Yours." I squinted harder, making stars sparkle inside my eyelids.

"Only what I started with is mine. You won the rest. Shit, Scott isn't gonna live that down for a long time."

Smiling made it harder to send my message, but I liked winning and having Kellen kiss my foot. I crept my toes across the quilt to find Kellen's feet, which were hard as hooves. I went without socks, when I forgot to do laundry, but he didn't own any socks. Still, I liked to pet his feet with mine. Touch his hands with mine. Rub my cheek against his. I liked how we were different, but the same.

Lying back beside me, he spread his arm out to make me a pillow.

"You didn't go swimming tonight?" he said.

"Before. With Donal."

"That's nice. Is he in bed now?"

I nodded and wiggled closer so I could press my face into his armpit. Sweaty but clean.

"You need to quit squirming and lay still," he said. He was ticklish.

I swallowed a giggle and stayed where I was to tease him. He always wanted me to say the stars, and if I didn't do it soon enough, he got impatient.

"Ursa Maj—"

I poked a finger into his side to stop him and he laughed.

"What? Not Ursa Major?"

We waited, trying to trick each other. The kind of trick I liked.

"Orion?" he said.

"Noooo."

"No? Oh, right, we won't see him until October. I guess that means I can keep wearing his belt until then."

I put my hand over his mouth to make him be quiet. The message I was trying to send was, "Kiss me." He did kiss my hand before I took it away, but that wasn't what I wanted.

"I promise I'll be good," he said.

Wiggling around to get comfortable, I put my head back on his arm. Then I looked up at the sky and found my place. Looking at the stars was like opening a familiar book. I made him wait a little longer, since he didn't pay attention to my message. He must have gotten it late, because after a minute, he kissed my hair. When I turned my face to him, he kissed my lips, too.

"Cassiopeia," I said.

10

KELLEN

Waking up in the meadow was Wavy's favorite thing. She was more likely to talk first thing in the morning, too. I might get a whole dozen words out of her before the sun came up. I might even get the three I liked best.

Me, I loved falling asleep in the meadow. The hay rustling around us, the stars overhead, owls in the cottonwoods. Wavy curled up next to me so we were like two animals bedded down in the grass.

That night, I was glad I skipped the beers. I remembered things better when I was sober. Like Wavy's cheek stuck to my arm with sweat, and the wind ruffling her hair against my neck. I kissed her hand and pressed it over my heart.

"Hmmm," she said, already half asleep.

A car drove down the road to the south, going too fast. After it passed, crickets filled up the quiet. A while later, another car came down the road, scattering gravel. I was just about asleep when a squealing thud jerked me wide awake. I sat up and Wavy woke up with a whimper, clutching at me.

The car engine clunked and died.

"Somebody just wrecked up on the road. I'm gonna walk over and check it out," I said.

I wanted Wavy to stay there, but when I pulled on my boots, she did the same. We struck out across the meadow toward the road and, when we came over the rise, I could see headlights off to the southwest. The road curved there, with a fork to the north for a service road to the stock tank and windmill. There was a cattle guard across the ditch between iron gate posts. Car musta took the curve too fast.

When Wavy broke into a run, I knew she'd figured it out, same as me. Two cars driving away from the farmhouse in the middle of the night? One was probably Val.

Cutting through the hay, Wavy left me behind. When I got to the ditch, the passenger side headlight blinded me, skewing up at the wrong angle. I tripped over something and landed hard, gravel digging into my elbow. I hauled myself back up and ran like I hadn't since I played football in high school.

One of the gate posts had cut through the car's hood, ruptured the radiator, and rammed the engine right into the front seat. There was antifreeze and gas pouring onto the road, turning it to mud. The driver's side was down into the ditch, and with the engine in the way, I couldn't see any way to get to Val. She was pinned behind the wheel and covered in blood. Dead for all I knew. For all I cared really, except I didn't want Wavy to see that.

Wavy jerked open the rear passenger door, getting ready to crawl into the backseat before I caught her. She tried to pry my hand off her arm, so I grabbed her around the waist and tossed her over my shoulder. Even with her kicking and pounding on me, I didn't dare let go of her.

Headed down the road toward the ranch, with the headlights at my back, I saw what I'd tripped over coming out of the meadow. Donal, laying face down in the ditch. I set Wavy down, but when she saw her brother, she went crazy trying to get to him, so I had to drag her back.

"Don't, Wavy, don't! You can't move him. You can't."

She dug her nails into my arm where I had her around the waist, but she stopped fighting.

"If he's hurt, his back or his neck, you can't move him, okay? Promise?"

She nodded and when I let go of her, she crawled to Donal and touched his hand. I woulda checked for a pulse, but it didn't matter. If Donal was alive, we needed to get help. If Donal was dead, we needed to get help.

"You're faster than me, Wavy. You gotta run and get help."

She stood up and looked west down the road, then east. Trying to decide which was closer.

"Go down to the ranch and tell them what happened. Run as fast as you can," I said. I wanted that to be the right thing.

She ran west, toward the farmhouse.

She was gonna call 911.

The day I wrecked, I sent her to call Liam, because you don't call 911 if you wreck your bike a mile from a four-thousand-square-foot metal barn full of meth-making equipment. But when your little brother's lying in a ditch, maybe with a broken neck, things like that don't matter.

I got down on my hands and knees in the road next to Donal. I put my ear as close to his cheek as I could and held my breath. So soft I almost couldn't hear it over the wind in the hay, Donal breathed in and out. In and out. Whatever happened, Wavy made the right choice.

II

DEE

"Thank God we weren't cooking tonight," Dee said. The cops had been less than a mile from the barn. If Butch had been cooking, the cops would have smelled it, but they didn't. And nobody got killed. The cops said getting thrown out of the car probably saved Donal's life. All he ended up with was a concussion and a broken arm. If he'd had on his seatbelt, the engine would have crushed him.

The other good thing was that when the ambulance came, the only person the cops talked to was Kellen. He kept them away from the trailers.

Liam freaked out anyway. Of course, he loved Val—she was his wife—but listening to him cry and carry on pissed Dee off.

"She'll be fine," Dee said as they drove to the hospital in Garringer. She'd smoked too much crystal trying to get herself jump-started. So had Liam, because he couldn't stop talking.

"This whole deal is my fault. If I were living at the farmhouse, taking care of her like I promised, this wouldn't have happened. I've gotta fix this. I've gotta make this right."

"It's gonna be okay, baby." Dee kept saying that, because if something got fixed, it might fix her out of the picture.

At the hospital, there wasn't enough crank in the world to make Val look okay. They glimpsed her through a window, lying in a bed with tubes running in and out.

"I'm her husband," Liam said, so they let him into the room for a minute.

Dee got in with a lie: "I'm her sister."

Val was fucked up. A Frankenstein monster with stitches running across her forehead.

Liam cried for a good ten minutes after he saw Val. Dee held him, relieved. Yes, he loved Val, and he had the hots for Sandy, but Dee was there for him when there was a problem. He needed her.

People came and went all day: Sandy, Scott, Vic, Butch, Lance, Ricki. In the evening, while Liam was in the bathroom topping himself up, Kellen showed up with Wavy. They looked rough around the edges, but at least they hadn't been at the hospital all day, unlike Dee, who felt like someone had run a cheese grater over her nerves.

When Liam saw Kellen talking with Butch, he headed right for them and bailed into Kellen.

"What the hell happened?" Liam said.

"Like I was telling Butch, I was out in the meadow and heard the crash. I don't know what happened, except Val went off the road and hit that cattle gate. I'm sorry the cops came out, but it looked really bad. That's why I called 911. And the cops didn't go near the ranch."

"I mean, what happened? Why was Val out driving?"

"I don't know," Kellen said.

"How can you not know? You were at the house, weren't you?"

"No. I was in the meadow."

"Don't lie to me, you son of a bitch." Liam jabbed his finger into Kellen's chest.

It scared Dee when Liam got wild-eyed like that. As big as Kellen was, Liam would take him on when he got in that state.

"I wasn't at the house." Kellen's voice was too soft for Liam to hear when he got crazy. "I think Sean—"

"You think I don't know how you're always hanging around, trying to insinuate yourself into her bed?"

"It's not like that. I never—"

"You think she'd ever have a use for some slob like you? What? You think she's gonna divorce me and marry you?"

"What're you talking about?" Kellen said.

"Liam, don't." Butch put a hand on his arm, but Liam shoved it away.

"I oughta fucking kill you for coming around my wife even thinking that kinda shit."

Dee held her breath, waiting for it to all blow up. Kellen took a step back and brought his hands up, ready to field a punch. The nurse at the night station stood up and reached for the phone. God, if she called security, they'd have a problem. Liam couldn't back down from a fight when he was tweaking, especially if cops were involved.

"Look," Butch said. "I don't know what's going on in your head, Liam, but you need to stop and look around. Kellen isn't here for some—"

"You don't know, man. This fucking asshole's been going around my house every goddamn day, acting like he lives there."

"He brought Wavy to see her mother and her little brother. That's why he's here." Butch put his hand on Liam's arm again and turned him toward Wavy, who stood there watching in that eerie way she had. Like the little girls from *The Shining*.

"I just brought Wavy to visit. I didn't mean to cause trouble," Kellen said.

"You didn't. You're okay," Butch said. "Right, Liam? He's okay?"

"He's okay. Yeah. I'm sorry, Kellen. I'm just all turned inside out."

"It's alright. I'm gonna take Wavy home now."

"Dee, you better go spend the night with her," Butch said.

Dee glared at him. Like hell she was spending the night in an empty house with that creepy little girl while Liam was with Val.

"Wavy doesn't even talk to Dee. I'll go and sleep on the couch," Kellen said.

Butch seemed like he might keep arguing, but Kellen was already turning away. When he put his hand out to Wavy, she took it.

KELLEN

Riding down in the elevator to the parking garage, Wavy leaned against the opposite wall, staring at nothing. When the doors opened at the second-level parking, she walked ahead of me to where the truck was parked.

"Where do you want to go?" I said. "You want to stay down at the ranch with Sandy?"

Wavy turned around and took a few steps backwards so we could look at each other. She pointed at me.

"You want to stay with me? Or you want me to stay with you?"

She nodded. I knew she was gonna say that. And I knew I wouldn't sleep on the couch.

Unlike everybody else, me and Wavy had already been into the farmhouse and seen what Val did before she wrecked. Broken dishes and food all over the kitchen floor. In the living room, the coffee table was split in two like somebody had jumped on it. One of the couch legs was busted off and the cushions were cut open. Lying in the middle of that mess was a used syringe and a pair of lacy panties. Val even went into Wavy and Donal's rooms, ripped the sheets off the beds, broke toys and tore up library books.

Driving out to the farmhouse, we didn't talk about what to do. I parked the truck in the drive and we walked down into the meadow. The quilt was right where we left it, no worse for having spent the day out in the hayfield. The two cans of beer were warm, but I cracked one and drank it.

Wavy said all the stars, but we didn't make a game of it. After she fell asleep, I was still awake, listening to the quiet, thinking about what we'd have to do in the morning. While Wavy swept and mopped, I figured I'd haul the things Val had destroyed out to the trash barrel and burn them. I kept thinking about that, picturing what needed to be done, because that was as far as I could think. After we cleaned up the house, I didn't know what we'd do next.

12

DONAL

August 1982

I didn't remember Mama and me having our wreck, but I remembered Mama and Uncle Sean fighting. Just like she does with Daddy. Screaming and hitting and breaking stuff.

"I hate you!" Mama kept saying.

"Where is it? Where the fuck is it?" Uncle Sean yelled. He went stomping all around the house, tearing things up, even worse than Mama does when she's mad.

After he left, Mama said, "I'll show him."

I was hiding under the bed, but she came and dragged me out and said, "Put your fucking shoes on. We're leaving."

Then I guess we went for a ride and had our wreck, but I didn't remember that.

I got a cool cast on my arm and everybody signed it. For a while it was just Wavy and Kellen and me at the farmhouse, and I liked that. Wavy was happier, and when Kellen and me made jokes at dinner, she laughed out loud. I wanted us all to sleep together, but Kellen was too big, so he slept in Wavy's bed and she slept with me. Mostly.

Then Mama got to leave the hospital, and Daddy said, "I want you to come live with me."

I thought that would be cool because there were motorcycles and puppies and firecrackers down at the trailers. Maybe I could get a bike, too.

Plus Wavy made me eat good-for-me stuff. Oatmeal and green beans. At Daddy's house, Sandy let me eat Pop-Tarts and frozen pizzas.

Also, Mama scared me. She was different people. "Wait," Wavy said. Her rule was *Don't talk to Mama until she talks to you. Wait until you know which Mama she's going to be.* If Mama said, "Oh God, I'm so alone," it was okay for me to hug her.

If Mama said, "Worthless motherfucker. I'll show him," you better watch out. Even Kellen didn't like to come in the house when she was like that, and he was lots bigger than Daddy.

Before Mama came home from the hospital, Sandy helped me pack my stuff. We packed Wavy's clothes, too, while she sat on the bed, touching her quilt.

"We can take the quilt with us, honey." Sandy stuck her hand out, getting ready to do something stupid. Only Kellen and me got to touch Wavy. And she could hit hard. Boy, I didn't want to see that.

"Don't touch her," I said.

"Wha?" Sandy was kinda stoned so she was being silly.

Wavy stood up and Sandy started to fold her quilt.

"No," Wavy said. When Sandy didn't stop, Wavy said it loud: "NO."

"You don't want to take your quilt?"

"It's not her quilt," I said. Grandma, who I didn't remember, made the quilt for Wavy, but I knew the rule. *Nothing belongs to you.* I knew the rule, but I didn't like it. My stuff was mine, like the pocketknife Uncle Sean gave me. If somebody tried to take it, I'd sock them.

Sandy put the quilt back on the bed and took the other stuff to the car.

First thing, when we got down the hill, I showed Wavy the puppies in the garage. It was okay for animals to touch her. She petted them and let them crawl on her lap.

I wanted to light firecrackers, but it was getting hot outside, so I said, "Let's go watch TV." That was something else we didn't have at the farmhouse. Wavy had her little TV with rabbit ears, but Sandy's trailer had satellite.

Only when we went inside, Daddy and Kellen and Butch were there.

"Hey, come here, kiddo," Daddy said. Then he saw Wavy.

He yelled, "Sandy! Sandy!" until she came. She musta been in the shower, because she had a towel on her head.

"What the fuck is she doing here?" Sometimes I thought Daddy couldn't see Wavy, but he pointed at her.

"But you said you wanted the kids to move down here. You—"

"I said, 'The *kid.*' Donal. Not her."

"You—what do you want me to do?" Sandy said.

"Get her out of here. Take her back up to the farmhouse."

"I'll take her," Kellen said.

After Wavy left, I didn't want it to be fun living at Daddy's. It wasn't fair if I had fun and she didn't. But there were puppies, and then Daddy bought me a motorbike and taught me how to ride it. Anyways, Wavy didn't really want to live there, and I still got to see her. Sometimes she came with Kellen, and sometimes she snuck in to see me. Some mornings, before anybody else woke up, I went across the meadow to the farmhouse. That was the best.

13

KELLEN

Plenty of times I'd wanted to beat the crap out of Liam, but never as bad as I did when he told Wavy to get out. Her whole face went blank, and stayed that way until we walked out to the front drive. She scowled when she saw the Willys.

"The bike's at the shop," I said. "I got tired of it being dinged up. We'll have to ride in the truck for a while."

Wavy shuffled her feet, but she let me take her hand and help her up into the truck.

"You know, this is Old Man Cutcheon's truck. Good truck. Plus, it's the same age as his son. He thinks that's good luck. He sold this to me a couple years ago, when his grandkid was born, and bought himself that new Ford. He's still proud of this Willys, though. Says it's never broke down on him."

She knew all about the truck; I was only trying to fill up the quiet.

"You wouldn't want to live down at the trailers anyway. It's noisy and they smoke. Makes the place stink. You wouldn't like that."

When I turned to go up the road to the farmhouse, she said, "No."

I couldn't blame her for not wanting to go up there. Val laid up in bed, with a nurse there—some stranger. I turned around and drove the route we took around the lake on the bike, but it wasn't the same in the truck. I was sorry I'd sold the Barracuda, even though I made good money on it. Piss poor timing on my part. Once we reached the Powell city limits, there were only two options: my house or the shop.

"Is there somewhere you want to go, Wavy?"

After a second, she pointed at me.

"Yeah, we can go to my house."

"Live with you," she said.

"You can't live with me."

She pretty much had been while Val was in the hospital. That had to end now.

I didn't know what else to say, so I drove to my place and pulled into the carport. Wavy sagged back in her seat, staring out the windshield at the faded asbestos siding on the garage. She looked so small and tired, like my ma before she died.

"It's not me, Wavy. Other people wouldn't like you living with me, since I'm not your family. Maybe you could go live with your aunt. They're your family."

It made a kinda sense, but that was about the last thing I wanted. Tulsa was a long drive, and the way her aunt looked at me, it wasn't like I'd be able to visit Wavy there. But maybe things would be better for her without me. Maybe she could have a regular life with good people.

"Well, what if we . . ." I racked my brain trying figure out something. There was the spare bedroom. I could put the weight bench out in the garage. Get a bed in there. Except it didn't fix the real problem. Her living with me.

"Get married," she said. Had she heard what Liam said at the hospital? Man, I hoped she didn't believe that crap about me messing around with Val.

"If who got married?" I said.

She pointed at me and, in that slow way she had, brought her finger back to her chest.

I couldn't help it. I laughed. Not because I thought it was funny, but because I was shocked. She looked right through me, like I wasn't there. She wasn't joking, and I wished I could take it back.

"I'm not laughing at you, sweetheart. You surprised me is all. I didn't expect you to say that." She didn't make a sound. She was gonna make me answer her. "You know we can't get married."

"Why?"

"I don't think Liam would like that."

She shrugged, 'cause it was a stupid reason. Liam had kicked her out.

"I'm a good wife," she said.

"I know you'd be a good wife. I like your cooking and you clean the house and you know how to keep the books. I mean, if it was just about that, or about me wanting to be with you, sure, but you're too young to get married."

Staying out at the farmhouse with Wavy and Donal, it was something near to playing house, except Wavy didn't play at things.

"Here's the thing: in a couple weeks you start school, right? Leave the house by seven, when Val's still asleep. After school, you can go to my house or down to the shop. Stay there 'til it's time to close. Then we can have dinner, you can do your homework, watch TV, and I'll take you up to the farmhouse before bed."

Wavy didn't answer. No nod, no shrug, nothing.

"Hey," I said. "Hey."

For the first time ever, I reached over and touched her hair without waiting for some kind of invitation. Even that didn't get me a reaction. She didn't lean into me and she didn't push me away. There had to be something to make my offer stick and sitting there looking at the back door of my house, I thought of it. I started the truck and headed to the hardware store. Got there just before it closed. I came around to Wavy's side and almost spilled her on the pavement because of the way she was leaning up against the door.

"Come on, we gotta get something," I said.

She came after me, dragging the heels of her new boots. While I went looking for a clerk, she stood in the store's main aisle, staring through a display of car wax.

When I came back, she was still doing that. I had the feeling again like I'd come up on a wild animal. Only instead of a fawn, she was like a fox kit I saw once, hit by the side of the road. On its feet, but dying.

The key in my palm was hot off the grinder, smelled like graphite.

"This is for you. So you can go to my place any time you want, whether I'm there or not. Only other person got a key to my house is Old Man Cutcheon, but that's so, you know, if something ever happened to me. "

I held the key out to Wavy, but she just looked at it. If she wouldn't take it, I figured that would mean she was done with me. I wasn't ready to reach that point, so I kept talking.

"I bought that house three years ago. Mr. Cutcheon co-signed for me on the loan. If I can do a few more deals like with the Barracuda, and with the extra money coming from Liam, I figure it'll be paid off in two years. It's nothing fancy, but it's my house. Where I don't gotta put up with nobody's bullshit. That's why I'm giving you this. So it can be your house, too. So you can have a place to go. Even if you can't live with me, that other bedroom's for you. I'm gonna clean it out, so it'll be your place."

Finally she reached for the key, squeezed it tight in her fist, and then dropped it down in her boot.

Leaving the hardware store, I asked her where she wanted to go.

"Home," she said. I wished that wasn't the farmhouse, but it was.

When we got there, a strange car was parked in the drive. A '72 Buick wagon. The nurse. I turned off the engine, but before I could open my door, Wavy pulled the keys out of my hand and stuck them back in the ignition.

"You don't want me to come in?" I said.

She shook her head.

"I know you're mad, but will you at least give me a kiss?" I said.

She opened the door, got out, and walked up the porch steps without looking back. Sitting there, trying to decide what to do, I saw her answer. She'd written LIAR in the dust on the Willys dashboard.

I felt like I'd been kicked in the stomach. Not like she'd kicked me, but like life had. Kicked her, too, while it was at it.

PART THREE

I

PATTY

September 1982

There had been several home nursing assignments where Patty felt she was a member of the family, but the Quinns was the first assignment that made her feel like a patient in the asylum. When she got to the house, the only person there besides the patient was Casey, the day nurse.

"Nobody's been here. When the ambulance and I got here with Mrs. Quinn, the back door was unlocked," Casey said. She was one of those perky, up-and-at-'em people who harangued injured patients out of bed and into their physical therapy.

The house was cleaner than Patty had expected. The outside hadn't been painted in years, but the floors had been mopped and the bathroom smelled of bleach. There were fresh sheets on the bed and clean dishes in the cupboard

She knew there were children—a little boy who had been injured in the wreck and an older girl—but there was no sign of them. Mrs. Quinn's bedroom was in the front, off the parlor. The other bedroom was off the dining room. There was a full-sized bed in there. No toys or children's clothes, just some crayon marks on the wall behind the bed.

After she gave Mrs. Quinn her next dose of pain medication, Patty ventured up the narrow attic stairs. There, she found a bed with a handmade quilt on it. Only the glow-in-the-dark stars on the ceiling suggested it was a child's room.

It was dark when a vehicle pulled up outside. After a few minutes the back door opened, and Patty got to the kitchen just as a blond girl came in and slammed the door.

"Hi. I'm Patty. I'm the night nurse who's here to take care of your mommy. What's your name?"

The girl took two cautious steps into the kitchen.

"It's okay, honey. Did your daddy tell you that a nurse was coming? I'm here to make sure she takes her medication and gets better."

The girl moved around the other side of the table, and it dawned on Patty that she was planning to dash past her. The back door opened again and a large man with greasy black hair came in. He looked at Patty for an instant before his gaze went to the girl, who turned and ran up the stairs.

"Wavy. Goddamnit, Wavy!" The man started after her, yelling, "You can't just say something like that. What did I lie to you about?"

He thundered up the stairs, and Patty heard his footsteps and his voice overhead, but nothing from the girl. They were up there for nearly two hours, long past what should have been the girl's bedtime. Several times, Patty considered going up to check on them, but each time, she convinced herself it was better to wait.

Eventually, the man stomped down the stairs slowly. He seemed startled to find Patty sitting at the kitchen table with a cup of coffee in front of her. She didn't let it bother her. Sometimes she had to fend for herself. Standing up, she held out her hand.

"Hello. I'm Patty Bruce, the night nurse that Mr. Quinn hired to take care of his wife."

"Sorry about the ruckus. I hope we didn't wake her up." He shook her hand. "I'm Jesse Joe Kellen. I'm a friend of the family."

"Is that Mrs. Quinn's daughter?"

"Yeah, that's Wavy. She's a little upset."

"It's not unusual. Having a parent badly injured can be very troubling for children. They're not used to seeing their parents helpless."

He nodded and absently brought a hand to his hair to smooth down a rooster tail that stuck up on his crown.

"I'm real sorry for barging in here. Is there anything you need? I'll be back in the morning to get Wavy, so I can bring you whatever groceries you need. And Wavy did the laundry, so there's clean towels."

"Do you know when Mr. Quinn is coming?"

"Well, he—he don't actually live here. He lives down the hill. You know where you pass that other road, where there's a couple trailers?"

"Am I to understand that Wavy will be here alone tonight?"

"Not if you're here," he said.

"I don't say this to be rude, but my duties don't include childcare."

Mr. Kellen laughed. "Wavy don't need a babysitter. She'll get herself to bed, get her own breakfast. It'd be best if you didn't bother her."

"Bother her?"

"Just pretend she's not here. If you hear her get up in the middle of the night, don't come checking on her. She likes to be left alone."

Patty was so confused, she couldn't think of anything to say. She pushed her glasses up on her head and rubbed her eyes, feeling a headache coming on. While she was doing that, Mr. Kellen walked out the kitchen door. She thought of going after him, but it seemed pointless.

After she checked on Mrs. Quinn at midnight, Patty went into the living room and lay down on what looked like a new sofa. She must have dozed, because she woke to the sound of someone in the kitchen. Looking into Mrs. Quinn's room, Patty found her still asleep, or as close to sleep as the pain medication brought her.

For a moment, a light flashed in the kitchen, the fridge being opened and closed, but otherwise it was all darkness. Then a cupboard opened and a dish clinked softly on the countertop. Was the girl eating? At that hour? In the dark? Or was she sleepwalking?

Standing on the other side of the swing door, Patty was about to say the girl's name, when she remembered Mr. Kellen's cryptic warning: *if you hear her get up in the middle of the night, don't come checking on her.* Wasn't there a fairy tale with a warning like that? Beauty and the Beast? Blackbeard? After a few minutes the girl went back up the stairs and solved Patty's dilemma.

In the morning, as Casey was arriving, the girl came downstairs already dressed. Casey said, "So, this must be Wavy. Did you two meet last night?"

"After a fashion we did," Patty said.

From outside came the sound of a car horn. Again, Wavy slipped around the table, maneuvering her escape, and Casey and Patty followed her to the kitchen door. An old truck sat in the drive. Mr. Kellen rolled down the window and called, "I'm sorry! The bike's gonna take a while, okay?"

Wavy stomped down the stairs and got into the truck.

"Odd little girl," Casey said.

"You have no idea." Patty told her everything, even though it put her an hour over her shift.

She needed to compare notes with someone, and talking with Casey every day at least convinced her that she wasn't the only one who thought the family was strange.

According to Casey, there wasn't much to know about the day shift. Mrs. Quinn slept most of the first two weeks, and never said anything, except to complain about the pain she was in. And to ask where her husband and her children were.

"What am I supposed to tell her? I haven't seen her husband since he hired me, I've never seen her son, and her daughter comes home late every night with some big biker."

"And she doesn't spend the whole night here, either," Patty offered.

"Are you serious?"

"I'm sure she sneaks out at night."

"What is she? Thirteen? And she sneaks out at night?" Casey said.

"A few times she hasn't come home at all."

"Have you told anyone?"

"Well, I told Mrs. Quinn. She said, 'She's probably with Kellen.' I suppose that's good enough for her."

"Good grief. Have you thought about talking to Marjory?"

Marjory was their supervisor, and the suggestion irked Patty. Casey was eager for Patty to go to Marjory with it, but Casey wouldn't. That way if the Quinns said, "How dare you accuse our dear family friend," Patty would be the one who had made the accusation. If Patty didn't report it, and something improper *was* going on, Casey could always say, "Why didn't you tell someone?"

"So, what else have you noticed?" Casey said.

"Wavy sneaks into the kitchen at night and eats, but honestly, I've been known to do that."

Casey laughed, and Patty was glad she hadn't said the other thing she couldn't stop thinking about. The night Kellen had gone up to Wavy's room and argued with her, there was one phrase she'd overheard. "I *do* love you," he'd said, his voice rumbling through the floor. "I love you all the way." Not the sort of thing a family friend says to a thirteen-year-old girl. Now it was too late to tell Casey, who would want to know why Patty hadn't mentioned it right away.

2

WAVY

The motorcycle was beautiful, the stars sprawling over the fenders and spinning out around the gas caps on a field of deep shimmery blue, like August when the moon was dark. No matter how much he teased me, Kellen put the stars on the way they were supposed to be. Cassiopeia and Cepheus in the center and the rest of them tumbling away on the sides. Squeezed under Kellen's thigh while he rode was Orion, the three stars of his belt glinting. Every star was a tiny scrap of silver foil sealed to the gas tanks under clear enamel.

Looking at it, my heart hurt so much I almost couldn't breathe. Not because the motorcycle was beautiful, but hoping it was for me and knowing it might not be. Nothing belonged to me, but the rule didn't keep me from wanting Kellen to be for me only. I put my hand on the tank and tried to smile, but there were too many hot things trapped in my mouth.

Kellen smelled like the shop, so I knew he had just finished the bike. He had come straight to school to show it to me as soon as it was ready, and waited in the parking lot until I came out.

"Do you like it?" he said.

I nodded once, to say, "Yes, it's beautiful."

From the way he shifted on his feet, wanting to touch my hair but not doing it, I knew he thought my answer was small.

"I used that book you gave me to make sure I put them on right. Are they right?"

I nodded again.

"So, you like it, but you're still mad at me?"

Resting his hand on the seat, he leaned over and breathed on me. I loved that. His breath was warm and wintergreen-smelling. He needed me to speak, because his heart hurt, too. I didn't want to be mean, but sometimes, it was dangerous to open my mouth and let words out. Other times, my throat closed up so tight the words couldn't come out. Looking at the Panhead, at all the work he did, the words trapped in my throat weren't nice ones. They were words to say, *I don't like it, if you're going to let girls with snake tattoos ride on it.*

I knew I was breaking the rule, but I laid my hand on the seat next to his. It was a new seat, tall in back for a passenger.

"Me," I said.

"Yeah, that's your spot, Wavy. I love it when you ride with me. I'm sorry it took so long to paint, but that's . . . I don't even know how many coats of clear enamel. And I wanted it to be a surprise, but getting all those little stars right was a bitch without you to tell me where they go."

"Only me." I didn't care if it was against the rules.

"Only you?" He straightened up and sunlight fell on my hair where he had shaded me. "Oh. Oh. Come on, put your helmet on and let's ride this thing."

That was another thing I loved, the way he swung his leg over the bike, started it with one solid kick, and settled his weight on it. But the bike wasn't for me. There would be other girls. Snake tattoo girls. Perfume-wearing girls he loaned his jacket to. I wished the bike weren't so beautiful. I wished it were still primer gray, or green-and-yellow flames like the day he wrecked it. I wished it didn't feel so good to ride behind him with my arms around him. I didn't want to enjoy the way the wind spun around me and pulled at my dress. It soothed me and I didn't want to be soothed.

3

MISS HUMPHRIES

It had happened often enough in the last forty years that Miss Humphries had a well-rehearsed response. Because of the store's proximity to the County Courthouse, once or twice a month, a scruffy-looking man stepped in off the street and said, "I need to buy a wedding ring."

This one followed pattern: a big man in grease-stained jeans and engineer's boots, ham-sized forearms covered in tattoos. He looked nervous, not quite making eye contact. Sometimes, as in this instance, the man had a child with him. Perhaps a soon-to-be stepdaughter. She was too old and too blond to be his natural child.

Before they could get more than a few steps into the store, Miss Humphries offered her warmest smile, one intended to reassure.

Then she said, "You know, there's a nice little drug store on Fourteenth and Mohawk. They sell plain gold bands at a very reasonable price." She was never rude, but she considered it a kindness to dissuade people from embarrassing themselves.

"Not a band," the man said. "A real ring. A diamond ring."

"Well, we have a variety of engagement rings. In this case, I have some simple and elegant rings, starting at a quarter-carat weight."

"Come and look, sweetheart. I want you to pick it out."

The girl stepped up to the display and in the bright lights meant to make the stones sparkle, she was not what Miss Humphries had expected. Not a grubby girl, of the type who usually accompanied the scruffy-looking men. Her cheeks were scrubbed pink and her hair clung to her scalp not because it needed washing, but because it was so fine. She wore a pale blue dress with pin tucks down the front. Velazquez' Infanta Margarita in motorcycle boots.

Miss Humphries hated cleaning fingerprints off the glass cases, but the girl didn't touch the display cabinet. She stood with her hands at her sides and peered in.

"Or if you're looking for something unusual, my brother occasionally purchases estate jewelry. We have some lovely antique rings in this case."

Stepping down the counter, the girl looked into that display. Her stepfather followed, watching her, but not interfering. The scruffy men usually got uncomfortable by then, having glimpsed the occasional price tag, but he seemed more at ease now.

Miss Humphries took her cue from him and didn't say anything, but she recognized the moment the girl found something she liked. Her gaze sharpened and she leaned forward. Perhaps all women were born with that attraction to diamond rings. A magpie instinct.

"Which one do you like?" Miss Humphries said. There were a few lower priced rings in the estate case. Diamond chips in delicately scrolled ten karat Victorian settings. More than a twenty-dollar gold band from the drug store, but under two hundred dollars. The girl's father leaned over her head to look in the case.

"I see which one. What are those called, those ones that look like stars?" he said.

"Star sapphires." She knew the ring and it broke her heart that the girl had picked such a lovely ring for her mother. Something her future father wouldn't be able to afford. Normally at that point, Miss Humphries indicated the price before opening the case. That got rid of the persistent ones, who said, "That's a little more than I was looking to spend." The girl had been respectful and the afternoon was quiet, so Miss Humphries took the keys off her wrist and unlocked the display.

"It's Victorian, late nineteenth century. The diamond is natural, slightly more than one carat, E in color with no inclusions visible to the naked eye, surrounded by five natural star sapphires, each a tenth of a carat." She said it all for the pleasure of saying it, aware that neither of them understood what it meant. When she placed the ring on the velvet mat, she was careful to flip the price tag with her pinky, so that it lay exposed. The girl rose on her toes to look down at the ring. After a moment, she glanced up at the man.

"That one?" he said.

She nodded.

"That's the one we want then. You can make it fit, right?"

"Yes, of course it can be sized. Do you know what size you'll need?"

"Whatever size she wears. I don't know how you measure that."

Only when the girl held out her hand did Miss Humphries understand the ring was for her. To hide her shock, Miss Humphries turned away and retrieved the sizing rings. She fumbled with them, not sure where to begin. Usually she started with the size six. The average woman was somewhere near that, but for a child? She held out the size four, but it swallowed the girl's finger. The size three was still loose. The two, the one, and the three-quarter remained, but they were problematic.

"The dilemma here," said Miss Humphries, "is the width of the setting. I'll check with my brother, but I worry anything smaller than a three would require the setting to be curved to fit on the band. Of course, she'll grow and the setting would have to be redone to permit the band to be resized. I suppose, if we went with the four, and put in a plastic sizer, that might work. Then the plastic sizer could come out when she's a bit bigger. After that the ring would need to be resized again."

She was chattering and she couldn't stop. *The dilemma*, she wanted to say, *is that people don't buy engagement rings for children.*

"Whatever'll work," the man said. "How long will it take?"

"Oh, I should think it could be ready by Friday afternoon."

He and the girl both looked disappointed, but he nodded.

Miss Humphries wrote out the ticket in an unusually crooked hand for her, glancing up at them as she did it. They didn't touch, even by accident. The girl stood with her hands clasped behind her. He kept a thumb hooked in a belt loop and the other hand in his pocket. When Miss Humphries laid the ticket on the counter, he pulled his hand out of his pocket, removing a roll of bills held with a rubber band. He snapped the rubber band off and began counting out hundred-dollar bills. She felt corrected for having assumed he couldn't afford the ring.

"The resizing fee will be adjusted, because so much excess gold will be removed. After that's weighed, we'll refund that amount to account for it." She watched the bills pile up and when he finished, she counted them into the cash drawer. "You've given me one too many."

"That's for you, for being so nice," he said.

"I, well, that's not—"

"It'll be ready Friday?"

"Yes."

"Thanks."

A moment later, they were out the door, leaving her to stare at the hundred-dollar bill. In more than forty years behind the jewelry counter, she had never before been "tipped."

When the man and the girl returned on Friday, Clifford was at the counter. He was about to make his own less diplomatic discouragement speech, but Miss Humphries intervened.

"Ah, here you are," she said in the same bright voice she had used before to try to send them away. "Clifford, they're here for the re-sized ring with the star sapphires."

Her brother raised his eyebrow, but rose stiffly and went to the back room. He had said more than a few choice words about resizing an adult's engagement ring to fit a child.

When he returned with the ticket and the velvet presentation box, he still had his eyebrow up. Worse, he stood at Miss Humphries' elbow while she counted out the refund for the gold removed from the ring. It made her glad she hadn't mentioned the extra hundred dollars which had gone discreetly into her purse instead of the till.

"Well, shall we make sure it fits?" she said after she closed the cash drawer.

Now that the moment came to open the box, Miss Humphries didn't know how to proceed. Normally, when it was a regular ring, she laid it out on the velvet mat for the customer to try on. When it was an engagement ring, the man usually opened the box, and sometimes they had a little impromptu pre-wedding right there in the store. Miss Humphries loved those moments, when the woman got starry-eyed and the man looked thrilled and mildly terrified. It was the closest she ever got to romance outside a movie theater.

She passed the box to the man and, after a momentary hesitation, he opened it and took out the ring. It looked ridiculously small pinched between his thumb and finger. The girl didn't hesitate. She held out her hand and he slipped the ring onto her narrow finger. The setting was too large for her hand, but the plastic sizer had done the trick for the band.

It turned out to be one of those moments Miss Humphries loved. The girl looked at the ring on her finger and up at the man with sparkling eyes. He looked nervous but happy. They were not father and daughter. Romance. For better or for worse.

When the man leaned down over the girl, Miss Humphries thought he would kiss her. Instead he said, "Now you know, okay? From here on out, only you. I promise."

The girl nodded.

His gaze flicked to Miss Humphries and he blushed. "Thanks."

"Thank you. I hope she enjoys the ring. Don't forget your box, dear, and I'm sending you some jewelry cleaner, too." On impulse she reached under the counter for it. "The sapphires are delicate and they need to be cleaned properly."

After they were gone, Clifford said, "There's something very wrong there. I wish you'd talked to me before you sold them the ring."

"And what would you have done? He paid in cash."

Going to the front window, Miss Humphries looked out. Across the street, the two stood next to a motorcycle, the girl smiling as she buckled on her helmet. After she climbed on the cycle, the man ducked his head and then, then he kissed her.

4

CUTCHEON

Jesse Joe come back to the shop with Wavy, her looking happy for a
change. Girl that age ought not to have so many troubles, but she
did. Looking at it that way, them two was about made for each other.
He'd swum his share of sorrows.

That day, they was both smiling.

"Well, you're sure in a fine mood," I said. I figured she'd do what
she always did. Give me that shy smile and dart off like a spooked
cat. But no, she waltzed right over and held out her hand like she was
the Queen of England. On her finger was a diamond ring. Bigger
than the one my Paola wore for forty years.

"That is a real purty ring. Where did you get that?"

Damned if she didn't open her mouth and say, "Kellen and I are
getting married."

He got this real uneasy look on his face and said, "I don't know if you better tell people that, Wavy."

She frowned at him, so I knew they were gonna have a few words once she got him alone. Instead of going in the office, though, he changed his mind and they got back on the bike and left.

He come back an hour later by himself and went into the office. I followed him, just meaning to talk to him about the Lewiston's lawnmower, but Jesse Joe closed the door, so Roger wouldn't hear us. Then he sat down in his chair and give me a hard look. I didn't know how to feel about that, because I don't think business partners oughta give each other them kinda looks.

"Before you start in, old man, I'm not gonna marry her."

"Well, she thinks you are. Don't know if you noticed that."

"It's not what it looks like. I'm not that kinda guy."

"I didn't say a word."

"No, you just come in here and give me that look," he said.

"Now, see here, I didn't give you no look. Your business is your business."

I could see it was gonna be a while before we got to talking lawnmowers, so I parked my old bones in the other chair. Jesse Joe reached back to the ice box and pulled out two cokes, slid one across the desk to me. His way of apologizing.

"You know," I said. "I married Paola when she was fourteen. And I was twenty-six. Her parents had eleven kids and they was glad to get her settled."

"Those were different days, Mr. Cutcheon. I don't suppose you could marry a fourteen-year-old these days."

"That may be. Only thing is, why'd you buy her a ring if you ain't planning on marrying her? You go talking that way you're gonna break her heart."

Now I didn't set out to make him feel guilty, but women are sensitive about those things. Especially thirteen-year-old women.

Lord, my oldest girl, by the time she was ten you couldn't hardly tease her about nothing before she'd rear up and say, "Stop treating me like a child!"

"I love her," he said in this low voice. "I wanna take care of her."

"I can see how she trusts you. And that ain't a small thing to a girl like her."

Truth was she took care of him as much as he did her. There was a few times when he was younger that I thought to myself, *One of these days, he ain't gonna show up for work, 'cause he'll be at home with a gun in his mouth.* I had an uncle did that. Jesse Joe was a man with a deep streak of lonely, until Wavy came along.

"Nobody else looks out for her," he said. "Her folks are . . ."

Her folks were trouble. Never saw nothing to fix it in my mind as certain, but I had me a suspicion Liam Quinn was into some bad dealings.

"That's how it was for Paola. Her folks couldn't hardly feed themselves, and with the Army set to send me home, I couldn't leave her in Italy to starve. Them was dark days after the Armistice. That's why you need to watch yourself. If there's nobody else looking after that girl, she's gotta be able to count on you."

Look at the old man giving advice he ain't been asked for.

"She can count on me," Jesse Joe said.

"Then you can't be making her promises you don't intend to keep. If you don't plan to get married, why'd you tell her you was?"

"Because I love her and I want her to know I mean that. And I know, me saying I love her, that's one thing, and the ring is a whole other deal, but that's what she wanted. It's a big deal to her. To me, too. That's why I bought her a nice ring. Not some cheap piece of shit."

"How much did you spend, if you don't mind my asking?"

I thought I'd overstepped, but it was hard to tell with him. Kinda man who come to work the day of his mama's funeral and never said a word. He stood up, made me think I had gone too far, because he was a big man. He didn't shift that bulk around unless he had to. Like watching a grizzly bear heave up on his hind legs, a smart man'd think about making himself scarce. Alls Jesse Joe did was pull out his wallet, toss a receipt on the desk, and set back down. I leaned over and took a look. More'n two thousand dollars.

"Well, I don't believe I did it justice when I said it was a purty ring."

"Same as I paid for my Panhead."

"It's a good bike."

He laughed, figuring me for a superstitious old man, but it was good luck, him having a bike the same age as him.

"Didn't seem too much to pay for the ring, as happy as it made her," he said.

"It'd make you happy, too, if you'd let it. Ain't nothing wrong with thinking you're gonna marry her someday. I knew I was gonna marry Paola first time I met her, and she was only thirteen. I didn't touch her 'til we was married, but I knew." Truth was we did fool around some, but not much, 'cause Paola was a good Catholic.

"I just want Wavy to know I'm gonna be there for her. I don't think she'll grow up and wanna marry me. Why would she?"

"She could do a whole lot worse than you."

"Far as I can tell, I'm not even the kinda guy girls go home with at last call, never mind the guy they marry."

"Them's two different things entirely, son. Speaking of last call, you got any more of that bourbon in the drawer?"

Hallelujah, he did. Not that I'm big on drinking in the middle of the day, but I could do with a drop if we was gonna keep jawing about serious things. Jesse Joe give me the bottle and I tipped out a little into my coke. He didn't take none, though. His mama and daddy both was hard drinkers. They say it's the Indian blood, got a weakness for liquor. Drink and misery killed his mama dead.

"Anyway, that's all," he said. "I didn't buy her that ring planning on hanging around like a dog. When she grows up and meets a nice guy, as long as he's good to her, I'll be happy."

"And what if she grows up and wants to marry you?"

Jesse Joe laughed and damned if he didn't take out the bourbon again and add some to both our cokes.

"That ain't no way to run a business, pouring me drinks while I'm on the clock. I ain't so much as picked up a wrench to put the Lewiston's mower back together."

"It's almost time to knock off, old man. Drink up."

I could see what he meant to do, so I said, "Well? What if?"

He drained that bourbon and coke in three big swallows, and shook his head.

"Hell, if she grows up and for some crazy reason she still wants to marry me, fine. That ring is a sincere promise. If she wanted to get married, we'd go to the courthouse and do it. You know I'm not much for going to church, but if she wanted a church wedding, we'd have a church wedding, white dress, the whole deal."

"And some new boots to go with it." I said it to make him laugh, 'cause I could see it upset him. Either thinking about her wanting to marry him, or more likely thinking about her growing up and not wanting to marry him. Boy had got himself in a hell of a spot. Maybe she would outgrow the notion and he'd still be in love with her. I just hoped I'd be with my Paola before he put that gun in his mouth.

5

WAVY

October 1982

Mama kept her makeup and pills in a drawer, like secrets. Sandy spread hers out on a fancy table in her bedroom. She had lots of makeup, too, and a round plastic case with a pharmacy label on it. Real pills from a doctor.

That's what I was looking at when Sandy walked in and turned on the light.

"Oh, fuck, oh, fuck. You scared the crap out of me, Wavy. What are you doing?"

Never get caught was the rule, but sometimes I was careless at the trailers. All I was really scared of was Liam catching me, so I mostly only listened for his voice.

"Are you stealing stuff from me? Or just snooping, so you can report back to your mommy?" Sandy said.

I shook my head and showed her my empty hands. Just like that, she stopped glaring at me and smiled.

"I'm sorry, honey," she said. "You weren't taking stuff, were you? You were just looking. God, you're sneaky quiet. I didn't even hear you come in. Do you like to put on makeup?"

Sometimes Sandy talked to me like a little kid or like I was stupid. A lot of people did. Scott used to say, "She's a couple sandwiches shy of a picnic, ain't she?" Before I beat him at poker. People thinking I was stupid wasn't all bad. Sometimes they told me secrets because they knew I wouldn't repeat them.

"Do you want to try on some of my makeup? Go on and sit down," Sandy said.

I took a step toward the door, but she was in the way.

"No, don't go, honey. I'm sorry I yelled at you. You just surprised me. Don't go."

Sandy wasn't like Dee, who only talked nice to me when other people were around. Plus, she had come with Kellen to get me from the sheriff's office, even though Liam hit her for that. She walked over to the makeup table, away from the door. She wasn't going to make me stay.

"You need something pale. Pink, because you're so fair. This is a good color, this lipstick. It's called Cherub's Kiss. Do you like this one?"

She said it so singsongy, so nice, the way she talked to the cat who lived under the porch. *Kitty-kitty, do you want some of my tuna sandwich?* I put my finger on the box of brilliant blue and green eye shadow squares. It was like a set of watercolors, but more beautiful.

"That's eye shadow. You have to be careful because you're so fair. Dee wears too much eye makeup because her eyebrows and her eyelashes are pale, but that's not right. You're a natural beauty, so you don't need much makeup. But when you're older you'll have to stay out of the sun or you'll wrinkle."

We went down the table with me touching things and Sandy telling me what they were: mascara, eyeliner, lip liner, blusher, eyelash curler. I liked how she explained everything. Mama never explained anything. She just made rules and that was that.

I put my finger on the plastic case from the pharmacy.

"Oh, that's not makeup, honey. That's my pills. Are you old enough to know about where babies come from?"

I nodded. The health class textbook called it *intercourse*, but the book's drawings didn't look anything like real fucking.

"Well, those are the pills I take so I don't get pregnant. Because a lot of guys don't like to use condoms. Your daddy sure doesn't. Anyway, that's what those pills are for. Now, let's put some makeup on you. Is that okay? If I touch you?"

I shook my head. I didn't want to be mean, but there were rules. Liam touched Sandy, and if she touched me, it might be the same thing as Liam touching me.

"Well, maybe I can show you and you can put it on yourself."

Sandy showed me how to use the little wand to smudge on eye shadow. She gave me lipstick, too, but I didn't like the idea of touching the tube to my mouth.

"Well, you can rub your finger on it and put it on your lips," she said.

I did it that way, using my little finger to smooth the pink stuff on my lips.

"Don't you look pretty? Oh and your ring! Where did that come from? Are you—are you supposed to be wearing that?" Sandy frowned.

"Kellen." It was the one word that was always safe to say.

"Kellen gave you that?"

The rule was that only people Kellen knew could know about the ring. That meant Sandy was safe.

"We're getting married," I said.

Sandy giggled and clapped her hand over her mouth.

"Are you teasing me? Because that's the only thing you've ever said to me besides *no*."

To show her, I did what Kellen did: kissed the ring. My lips left behind a little smudge of pink on the diamond.

"Wow. It's gorgeous. That's your engagement ring? He must really love you if he bought you that. So you—you love him, too?"

I nodded. Sandy looked like she was going to cry, but she rubbed her nose and laughed.

"That's really sweet. You're lucky. He must love you a lot."

I was careless, listening to her and not paying attention to anything else.

"Sandy?" Liam called down the hallway.

I shook my head to warn her, but she answered: "Yeah, baby?"

He was almost outside the door, saying, "Where've you been? I gotta get on the road."

The only choice was the closet. I stepped into it, but it was so full I could only wriggle into the perfume-and-smoke-smelling clothes. I didn't even have time to close the door. I crouched down, holding my breath, and watched the bedroom door open.

Under the edge of Sandy's clothes, I saw Liam's legs. He wore jeans with creases down the fronts, and shiny red, pointy-toed cowboy boots.

"I gotta go. Kellen's waiting on me," he said.

"Where are you going?" Sandy said.

"I told you. Business."

"Yeah, but business or *business*?"

"Don't get smart with me." Liam shoved Sandy down on the edge of the bed. That was what happened if you got smart with him.

"Ow," she said.

"I don't need Kellen to help me take care of *business*."

"Asshole."

Liam grabbed her hair and pulled. He liked to pull hair, as much as Kellen liked to pet it.

"Come on, baby. Don't be that way. Why don't you do a little something for me before I go?"

"Maybe I don't want to."

He let go of her hair and put his hands on his belt.

"You don't want to or you won't? 'Cause maybe Dee will."

Sandy sat there, squeezing her hands together on her lap. Then she slid off the bed onto her knees.

"That's right, Sandy, baby. Why don't you suck it the way I like?"

I knew what cocksucking was. I'd seen it before. In Kellen's magazines. At a party. Once I saw Mama do it with a man I didn't know. It made my stomach nervous, because the mouth was a dirty place. A dangerous place. A way for people to get into you. Not safe, and Liam wasn't nice. He made Sandy gag and say, "Ow, don't, Liam. I'm doing it the way you like."

After he made her cry, Liam said nice things. He told Sandy how beautiful she was and how much he loved her. That's what he always did after he hurt you. Then he pulled up his pants and left. I listened for the sound of the door closing, for him going down the hallway. I listened for Kellen, too, but he must have been outside already.

When I crawled out of the closet, Sandy was sitting on the bed, wiping her eyes. She looked up and said, "Oh, Jesus, honey. I forgot you were here. Did you—did you see that?"

I shrugged.

Sandy sniffled. "I guess you're getting your education tonight. It's not always like that. He's good to me, but he gets in these moods."

I knew about Liam's moods.

"Oh, jeez. Stupid jerk got cum on my shirt." Sandy pulled her shirt off and under it she wore a leopard print bra. She had big tits. Bigger than Mama's and Dee's together. Looking at myself in the mirror, I put my hands on my chest. I was starting to grow there, but my dress was too loose to see anything.

"It takes time, honey. They don't grow overnight." Sandy cupped her hands over her bra. "I didn't always have these. I had to buy these. So I know a few tricks for how to make it look like you have more than you do. A lot of girls make the mistake of getting a big bra and padding it, but what you need to do is show off what you've got. Stay here, just a second."

Sandy was like Donal. When he got hurt he only cried a little and then he was happy again. She went out of the room and came back with a blue T-shirt that looked like one of Donal's. Out of the closet she pulled a fluttery blue skirt.

"Here, take off your dress. Your undershirt, too."

I usually only took off my clothes to wash or swim. Now that I was growing, there was more of me to be naked, but Sandy was smiling, so I knew it was safe, like playing dress up with Leslie and Amy when I was little.

I put on the T-shirt that was too tight and the skirt that was too loose until Sandy cinched it up around my hips. I was going to turn around and look in the mirror, but Sandy said, "No, no, take off the shirt."

Picking up a pair of scissors, she cut off the collar of Donal's shirt and made the neck of it go into a V. When I put it back on, it was still tight, but it didn't feel like it was choking me. Then Sandy let me look in the mirror.

"See?" she said. "You have cute little boobs. And this way guys can tell you have them. I'll bet Kellen would like it if you wore that for him."

Except for my hair, I didn't recognize me. My eyes looked strange with the makeup on, more grown up. I looked older.

I knew Kellen loved me. He bought me a ring, and his bike was only for me, but Sandy was right. The women in his magazines had big tits like her, and it wasn't just in the magazines. I'd seen how he looked at Sandy in her tight shorts and Dee when she went around the house in her nighty. He might look at me like that if I wore this.

"God, I don't know about you, but I need a pick-me-up," Sandy said. At least she didn't make a mess with the crystal like Mama. She had a little spoon that went into the bottle and up her nose. "No, you better not. You're definitely not old enough for this."

6

KELLEN

I knew I ought to leave. For two hours, I'd been lying on Wavy's bed, watching TV with her. The antennae could only pick up PBS, so we watched that Jimmy Stewart movie with the invisible rabbit. Then it went to something with singing and dancing. Maybe *The Lawrence Welk Show*, but it was hard to tell through the fuzz. It didn't matter. The TV was just to say, "We're watching TV," when all we were doing was lying next to each other. Sometimes talking, mostly not.

It was foggy that night, not cold yet, but we'd seen the last of September. I really wanted another night in the meadow, but the only stars out were the ones on Wavy's ceiling.

Downstairs, the night nurse was watching TV, too, and probably wondering when I was going home. I'd tried about half an hour

before and that's when Wavy showed me a crumpled up note from a
boy in her Algebra class.

It said:

Dear Wavy,
I like you a lot. Will you go to the 8th grade dance with
me? You don't have to talk to me if you don't want to. Do
you like me even a little?

Jimmy Didier

She'd answered him on his own note, with her fancy handwriting:

Jimmy,
Not even a little. And I think my fiancé would be very angry to find out you're
writing me notes like this. Please don't do it again.

Miss Wavonna Quinn

It was sad but funny. Sad that the boy got his heart broken, wad-
ded up the note and threw it back at her. Funny how Wavy answered
him. Funnier how she showed it to me, not bragging but embarrassed.

"I broke the rule," she said.

"You know, if there was a boy you liked, you could go to the dance
with him. I wouldn't be mad." I made myself say it with a smile. To be
fair to her, I didn't have no business keeping her from that kinda thing.

Her answer was to punch me in the chest, hard enough that it
stung. Then she patted the place she'd punched. I was the boy she
liked. When she held out her hand, I kissed the ring to apologize.

She wore it everywhere, including school, even though we were
still working out who could know. Teachers, no way. Cutcheon and
Roger, yes. Donal, Dee, and Sandy, and that meant Liam knew. I'd
been worried at first, but then I figured if Liam didn't like it, he
could come out and say something instead of pretending Wavy
didn't exist. Val? Who could tell what Val knew?

The only trouble I had was at the lab barracks one night when Butch said, "All I'm gonna say about this wedding ring business is there's a special place in hell for folks who hurt children."

"You don't have to tell me that." I was mostly thinking of Liam, but I knew what Butch meant.

"You know what I've heard?" Neil said. "I heard if you get a girl young enough, if you're the first guy to fuck her, it'll make her pussy so—"

We never got to find out what he heard, because I went across that poker table and grabbed the son of a bitch by the throat. Then I squeezed his windpipe hard enough to give him a taste of what going without air for the rest of his short life would be like.

Butch, who usually made peace, didn't say boo.

I liked seeing the ring on Wavy's finger. It gave me an excuse to kiss her hand and when I did, she always smiled. That's what I was doing while we watched TV, kissing her hand and petting her hair the way she liked, when I heard footsteps creeping up the stairs. My first thought was to get off the bed and quick, before the nurse got to the top of the stairs. Except I wasn't doing nothing wrong. We were just watching TV. If Patty wanted to spy on us, that's what she'd see.

It was only Donal, coming to crow about how good he was at sneaking around now that he had the cast off his arm.

"I came up the meadow all in the fog and snuck in here. The nurse didn't even hear me."

"You keep talking like that and she will," I said.

"You didn't hear me either, creeping up the stairs."

"Did," Wavy said.

"What are you guys watching?" Donal leaned over the foot of the bed, looking at the TV upside down.

"Lawrence Welk," I said.

"Let's go swimming."

Wavy sat up and nodded. Donal and her went down first, as quiet as they could. I stomped down after them, calling out, "Val,

Patty, I'm going. Have a good night." Then all three of us went out the door, across the porch and into the meadow.

Even with Donal's flashlight, we could hardly see through the fog. The windmill snuck up on us: a creaking, rusted tower coming out of a wall of white.

Donal stripped down and went into the stock tank, yelling, "It's cold!"

"What'd you expect?"

"Get in, Kellen!"

"No, I didn't bring any shorts to swim in." Beside me in the fog, Wavy was getting out of her boots and dress.

"I didn't bring any shorts either!" Donal was as loud as Wavy was quiet. He splashed over to the edge of the tank and said, "I'm totally buck naked."

"Well, I'm not getting buck naked."

"Why not?"

"Because Wavy's not my sister," I said.

"She doesn't care."

"I don't." Wavy tossed her dress over my shoulder and stepped into my arms.

"I do."

"Up," she said.

I put my hands on her waist and lifted her up to the lip of the tank, where she balanced on the balls of her feet like a tightrope walker. Holding onto her hand, I walked her around the tank's edge. Then she let go of my hand and tumbled backwards into the tank with a splash that made Donal hoot.

"Do me next!" So I balanced him on the tank edge and let him fall in.

They had so much fun, I sometimes wished I wasn't scared of water. Anyway, it was my job to keep track of Wavy's dress and Donal's flashlight, so I leaned against the tank and watched them laugh and splash around. After a while, Wavy circled back to me and held out her hand. I took it, thinking she wanted me to help her out, but she slung her other arm around my neck and tried to pull me in. There was no way she could do it, and after a second she let go and fell back in.

She hauled herself halfway out of the water, her hips against the tank edge.

"What the hell was that?" I said. Damn, she cracked me up, thinking she could pull me off my feet.

"Mermaid."

"I didn't know mermaids attacked people and tried to drown them. You're like something outta that *Friday the 13th* movie."

She grinned, and before she sank back under the water, I saw something I wished I hadn't. With her undershirt plastered to her, there was no way to avoid knowing she had tits now. I felt like an idiot for being shocked, because she was growing up and not just taller.

I figured I'd tell one of Liam's girls to take Wavy shopping and get her some bras. Except if I did, would Dee or Sandy think I was a pervert for noticing? Anyway, I got over being bothered by buying Maxi Pads for Val. For all I knew I was buying them for Wavy, too. When she wrote them on the shopping list, I didn't ask who they were for.

It couldn't be that hard to take her into a store and say, "She needs a bra." Except Wavy might think I was a pervert for noticing.

I was still worrying it over in my head, when she swam back to the edge and held out her hands.

"You can get yourself out. I'm not falling for that mermaid shit again," I said.

I guess I sounded more pissed off than worried, because she gave me a sad look and crossed her heart. Drew an X over her little tit, where her nipple stood out hard under the wet undershirt. Wasn't gonna be able to forget that either.

"Yeah, yeah, you promise." When I turned my back to her, she touched my arm.

"I'm sorry."

It wasn't her fault I felt weird, so I hauled her up on my back, dripping water all over. I tried to set her down, but she hugged me tight around my shoulders and kissed the side of my neck.

With her teeth chattering in my ear, she whispered, "I love you."

That was all I cared about.

7

WAVY

"Wavy? Your mom's a little upset. Could you come down and talk to her?" Patty said.

I liked Patty okay. She was better than Casey the day nurse, who had a big smiley voice. It was Patty's job to be there at night and listen to Mama cry and say awful things. She sounded scared.

I was getting ready to go riding with Kellen, but I went downstairs.

At least the nurses didn't let Mama lie in bed all day and not wash. I was learning their tricks. How to say, "Let's get up and brush your teeth. Little steps. Sit up first and then we'll try to stand up."

At first, Mama had been horrible to look at. Black and purple, and then green and yellow, but now she was just Mama. Crying and screaming, "Alone!"

I went into her bedroom and closed the door, trying not to be angry that she was stealing time from Kellen. I stood next to the bed, but I didn't touch her. All Mama wanted was someone to listen.

First it was Grandma. Grandma always liked Aunt Brenda better. Grandma never liked Liam. She never came to visit when Donal and I were born. But how could Grandma come visit if Mama never told her where we were?

Then Liam. Liam and his dirty whores. Liam always thinking with his dick. Liam Liam Liam. I was old enough to know there wasn't any real magic in the words *not to be trusted,* but it made my head hurt how Mama would say his name over and over without that protection. Like she wanted him to come and hurt her.

"You can't trust them, baby. As soon as they've got your pussy, they want some other girl's pussy. Liam, that's all he wants, notches in his belt. Sean, too. That's all I ever was. A score. And don't think that diamond ring means anything."

Mama grabbed my hand and glared at my ring.

"Kellen bought you that, didn't he? Liam says, 'Hell, in some countries I'd have to pay him to take her off my hands.' He thinks it's funny. And you're so stupid you think it's romantic. Let me tell you a secret, that ring doesn't mean shit."

I jerked my hand away and hid it behind my back.

"Kellen is like every other man. All he's thinking about is getting to fuck you. That's all they think about. I thought when Liam put a ring on my finger, he would love me forever, but it was a lie. You want that ring, too? I sure don't need it."

Mama tried to reach for the night table drawer, but her shoulder still hurt. She flopped back on the bed and moaned. Tears ran out of her, so much water it was like a flood that I soaked up with the corner of the sheet.

"Is everything okay?" Patty said outside.

"Baby," Mama moaned. The mean went out of her eyes and they

were only sad. "Be careful. Don't do what I did and get knocked up, because then you'll be stuck. Baby, are you listening?"

I didn't want to listen, but Mama petted my arm. So soft. Almost like Kellen when he touched my hair. I hoped it wasn't a trick.

"Make him get you on the Pill, okay? Or if he won't do it, have Dee take you. Will you do that?"

There were so many pills. The pills Sandy took so she wouldn't get pregnant. The pills she took to make her happy. The pills Mama took. I didn't want any pills.

"You can't trust him, baby. He'll get into you. You can't get clean once that happens. And then he'll break your heart, like Liam did mine. But you're special. Nobody can touch you, okay? Promise?"

Mama dug her nails into my arm.

"Promise me, baby." It was a trick. She was going to make me promise something and I didn't even know what I was supposed to promise. Not to trust Kellen? Not to let him creep into me? To take the pills? That nobody would touch me?

Mama was trying to ruin Kellen. To make him bad like Liam.

I pried her hand off my arm. I didn't even care if it hurt her. If nobody could touch me, that was her, too. When I opened the door, Patty stood outside with her eyes big. I swerved around her and ran.

8

DONAL

Wavy was lucky. She didn't have to ride the bus to school, because Kellen took her. I wished he could take me, too, but there was only room for Wavy on his bike. Other times, not for school, he let me ride, but only because I was a boy.

Ricki got really mad one night, because Daddy took Dee riding, and left her and Sandy at home. So Ricki asked Kellen to take her riding, but he said, "Sorry. Wavy's the only girl who gets to ride."

"What the hell does that mean?"

"It means Wavy is a very jealous mistress," Sandy said. She wanted to go riding, too, but she wasn't mad, because she took these special pills. I wished Mama would take some of those.

"Did you really buy her that diamond ring? There's something seriously twisted about that," Ricki said.

"Don't be such a tight-ass," Sandy said. "They're in love. It's sweet."

"No, it's fucking creepy. What is she, like ten?"

"Wavy's thirteen," I said. Ricki was bad at math.

"There's nothing wrong with me buying her a ring. She's my girl," Kellen said.

"Yeah, except for the part where you're a pedophile." Ricki wrinkled her nose up.

"That's not the only thing love means. You just got your mind in the gutter. Come on, Donal, let's go ride."

That night, I was the only one who got what I wanted, but I never got to ride to school. I had to go on the bus, because nobody ever got up early enough to take me. If I asked, Sandy would call the school to say I was sick, but if I stayed away too many days, Wavy would come down to the ranch and make me get up. Then I was in trouble.

On the weekends, it was easy to get up early, even earlier than I got up for the bus, because I could sneak up to the farmhouse and see Wavy. If I was lucky, she would let me get in bed with her, and she would talk to me.

Before Christmas something funny happened. I didn't get to see Wavy for three whole weeks because I had chicken pox and got really sick. When I went back to school, I didn't get to talk to her all week, because she was at the new high school, and then Friday night was Kellen's birthday. So I got up early, early on Saturday, and I put on my Superman costume from Halloween since she never got to see it. Then I went up the meadow to the farmhouse.

When I went in, Kellen was coming down the stairs in his bare feet, carrying his boots. He must have got in a fight on his birthday because somebody gave him a black eye. He made a funny face when he saw me, I guess because of my costume.

"Hey, Superman. You want a ride down the hill?" he said.

"I just came up the hill. To see Wavy."

"I think she's still asleep."

But why was he upstairs if she was still asleep?

Here's what I think happened: Kellen went earlier than me and got in bed with Wavy. What made me mad is that he stole all her words and didn't leave any for me, because she didn't want to talk. She let me get in bed and she hugged me, but she didn't say anything. And she was naked under the covers. I felt her boobies against my arm.

"Yuck. Where's your nightgown?" I said.

She lifted her hands over her head. I wanted her to talk to me, but she was looking at her ring. The rule was *nothing belongs to you*, but I think she was breaking the rule. If somebody tried to take that ring, she'd sock them. It was *her* ring. Kellen bought it for her so he could marry her. If it wasn't Wavy, I didn't know how he could like a girl that much. They're kinda gross.

She let the sun sparkle off the ring, so it made little rainbows on the walls and on me. I liked that almost as much as I liked her talking.

9

CASEY

December 1982

On the last Friday of Casey's duty, Wavy came home in the afternoon and took a shower. That was strange enough, but then she went up and down the stairs a few times between her bedroom and the bathroom. Casey listened to it all curiously, while she coaxed Val into doing a few exercises. Val's lassitude wore even Casey out, so they were watching TV when Wavy came downstairs.

Instead of her usual jumper, she wore a pale green dress with a fitted bodice and delicate shoulder straps. She was starting to develop, and the dress showed that off, fitted around her little breasts and her narrow hips. The outfit looked expensive, but of course, she wore big, heavy boots with it.

In one hand, she carried a matching sweater and a camera. Under her other arm, she had a wrapped package. She put the box and the camera on the coffee table and sat in the rocking chair next to the sofa, carefully, like she was worried about rumpling her dress.

"You look very pretty. Are you going to a birthday party?" Casey said.

Wavy nodded and reached up to adjust her hair.

She'd pulled it up into a chignon, but it was already slipping out. Delicate strands of blond fell around her ears, and it looked like she had sneaked some of her mother's makeup. Thirteen seemed too young to be wearing makeup, but Casey wasn't her mother, who was sitting right there on the sofa. If she thought Wavy looked too adult, she didn't say anything about it.

All Val said was, "What's in the package?"

Wavy didn't answer.

"Is Kellen coming to get you, to take you to the party?" Casey said.

He took her to school every morning and he was the one who brought her home so late or not at all, according to Patty. As for Mr. Quinn, Casey had seen him maybe half-a-dozen times in the four months she worked for him. At first, he was attentive and gentle with Val, but the last time he came, they argued. The kind of argument Casey had overheard many times.

Him saying, "You're not trying. You don't even want to get better and be with me."

Her saying, "Why should I try? Is Dee still at the ranch? Is Sandy? Is that little cunt Ricki still at the ranch? I wish you'd left me there to die on the side of the road."

"Well, you know what, baby? I wasn't the one who called 911. Kellen did that."

After that, Mr. Quinn kept paying Casey and Patty, but he didn't come back. His brother, Sean, visited occasionally and that seemed to do Val more good than her husband's visits. He got her talking, made her laugh.

On the last day of an assignment, Casey liked to "wrap things up" by offering last-minute advice and encouragement. With Val, it seemed like wasted effort. Instead of talking, they sat in front of the TV, as Casey's time there ticked away. At six o'clock, she would go home for the weekend, and on Monday, she would start a new assignment.

Normally, Wavy went outside as soon as she heard Kellen's motorcycle, but that evening she stayed in the rocking chair, smoothing her dress like she was nervous. The engine cut off and for several minutes, there was silence except for Val's TV program. Then the sound of boots on the front porch.

Casey had never seen the front door used, but that night, Kellen even rang the bell. Wavy got up and opened the door for him. He came in, looking nervous, and frowned in confusion when Wavy handed the package to him. Casey scooted forward on her seat, curious despite the fact that she might never get to tell Patty about this.

"This is for me?" he said. "You didn't need to get me anything."

The rocking chair groaned under his weight when he sat down. After he tore off the wrapping paper, he looked into the box with a blank look on his face. Then he lifted out what looked like a cast iron pot. No, a motorcycle helmet. He turned it over in his hand, forcing a smile.

"I really appreciate it, sweetheart, but you know I don't ever wear a helmet."

Frowning, Wavy slid her hand around the back of his neck and into his hair. Kellen nodded.

"Yeah, you're right. If I'd been wearing a helmet that day, I wouldn't have gotten my head so banged up. Okay. Okay. You ready to go? You look really pretty, but it's cold out there. Are you gonna be warm enough in that?"

Out of the closet she took a fleece-lined leather jacket and put it on over the sweater that matched her dress. Then the camera was remembered and the jackets came back off. Casey didn't wait to be asked. She picked up the camera and posed Wavy and Kellen, side by side. Because of the size difference, the camera had to be turned on end to make them both fit in the frame. Neither of them smiled for the picture, as awkward as high school prom dates.

10

KELLEN

For the longest time, I'd been trying to give Wavy her poker winnings, but she kept saying no. When she finally asked for some money, it was to take me out for my birthday, to this really nice steak house in Garringer. I'd been there once before with Liam and some of his friends, but they were all tweaking and made too much noise for that place. It was quiet with nice carpet and leather booths and chandeliers.

I didn't want the waiter looking down his nose at Wavy, so I got a haircut, and I wore a new pair of jeans without grease stains, with the one and only dress shirt I owned—the one I wore to my ma's funeral. That was about as dressed up as I knew how to get. I wasn't too sure about me, but Wavy looked like she belonged there. She went floating across the dining room after the hostess, that fancy dress swishing, and her neck all bare. We had a corner booth with candles on the table that made Wavy's hair like a halo around her face.

"You're so pretty," I said after the hostess was gone. I'd already told Wavy that a buncha times, but she seemed to like it. And she was beautiful. I figured her dressing up was part of my birthday present, so I ought to let her know I appreciated it.

I ordered for both of us, which I'd been told was what a gentleman was supposed to do. Then I ordered a bourbon and coke, which was probably not a gentleman's drink. After the salads came, the waiter left us alone.

"You know, this is the first time a girl ever took me on a date," I said.

That made Wavy smile. She pressed her lips together and held her breath.

"Happy birthday," she said.

"Thanks. Aren't you glad I didn't show up at your house drunk off my ass in the middle of the night this year?"

"I liked that birthday." She exhaled too fast, ended up with not enough breath to get her to the end of the sentence, so the last part didn't make any noise at all. When she reached across the table, I took her hand and turned it over so the ring picked up the candlelight and sparkled.

"So did I. I felt like such a jackass waking you up, but then you were so nice, like you were glad to see me."

Wavy was maybe getting ready to say something else, but the waiter came back before she could. He looked at our hands together on the table, but I didn't pull mine back. It wasn't none of his business.

"Are you finished with your salads?"

I was. Wavy hadn't touched hers, but the waiter took them both away when she nodded. After our dinners came, she pushed her plate off to the side to watch me eat. When the waiter came back with my third drink, he said, "Is there a problem? Is her entrée not to her liking?"

"No, it's fine. She'll just need a box."

We got to giggling after the waiter was gone. Wavy took her fork and moved the food around on her plate, and I ate a few bites to make it look better.

After I finished my steak, she scooted around the booth to sit next to me. Her dress strap was slipping down her arm so I lifted it back into place. I couldn't believe how soft the back of her neck was, where her hair was sneaking out of its pins. I'd never seen her hair up like that.

"This is a really nice birthday present. You planning it for me. Nobody ever did that for me."

She kissed my cheek, and that was when the waiter came back with the check. I didn't say a word when Wavy added up the tip and counted her money into the leather folder. I wanted to let her give me something. It was important to her.

She picked the movie. Not *Annie*, which was a kid movie, or *Porky's*, which looked dirty. *Poltergeist*. I was the one jumping in my seat at the scary parts. She laughed and squeezed my hand. After the movie, we went by the store for ice cream. She paid for that, too.

At home, I made myself another drink and, even though I knew she wouldn't eat it, I scooped up two bowls of ice cream. She carried hers out to the living room, cupped in both her hands like a prize. I turned on the TV to some old movie on PBS, and settled into my recliner. Wavy stood there, waiting for an invitation.

"Well, come on." I patted my knee.

Like I figured, she wasn't gonna eat her ice cream. She put it on the coffee table before she sat on my lap. Somewhere in the last five years, she musta been eating something, because she'd grown. There was a time when she fit all the way in my lap, but now her legs were long and her head reached my shoulder. The way she leaned into me was the same, though. She trusted me. When I pushed her dress strap up, she shivered, but then my hands were cold from the ice cream.

The movie was just background noise, while Wavy watched me eat my ice cream. Mint chocolate chip, that was what she picked.

After I set the empty bowl on the coffee table, she handed me my drink and scooted further up my legs. She leaned into me real nice, slipped her arm around my neck and put her cheek up against mine. That moment was a good birthday present by itself, just to sit with her and be happy together. During the movie, her hair had come out of the bobby pins, so I smoothed it out over her shoulder and snuck in a sniff.

When I got that first prickly heat in my crotch, I figured it was the booze. I shouldn't've had another drink. It felt so good sitting there with Wavy, her hand stroking the back of my neck, but it didn't seem right either. Even if it was just the bourbon, I had no business letting her sit on my lap when I was worked up.

"Let me up, sweetheart. I gotta step out," I said.

She made this annoyed sound, but she got up. In the bathroom, I splashed some water on my face and took a piss. That put me back to rights.

As soon as I sat down, she came right back to my lap. With the problem taken care of, I wanted her there. She brushed her cheek against mine and then she gave me a cold little kiss on the corner of my mouth. Minty.

"You finally ate some of your ice cream?"

She nodded.

"Why won't you eat it with me here?" I didn't expect an answer, because I'd asked before and never got one.

"No looking," she said.

"So, if I close my eyes, will you eat your ice cream before it melts?"

She thought hard about it, walking her fingers along the ribbing on my undershirt. When she got to my bare arm, she ran her finger over the scar from my wreck, staring at her ice cream the whole time.

"Cover them," she said.

Once I put my hands over my eyes, she picked up her bowl. Like I was her favorite chair, she stretched back against me and rested her head in the triangle my elbow made. I didn't cheat, wasn't even tempted to look, but I knew she was eating. First came the squeak of the spoon scooping up ice cream. Then the sneaky sound of the spoon going into her mouth and coming out clean. After a couple bites, she put the bowl back on the coffee table.

"Are you done? Can I open my eyes?" I said.

"No."

She shifted in my lap to straddle me, getting her knees into the gaps between my legs and the sides of the chair. Then she rested her head on my shoulder and said, "Lean back."

I took my hands off my eyes, but didn't open them. I eased the recliner back, and she settled into me with a sigh.

When she put her cheek against mine again, I turned my head, hoping for maybe one more kiss. She gave it to me, cold and soft. The next kiss was still cool, but getting warmer. Every one after that was warmer and softer, like ice cream melting, until she gave me a kiss that wasn't just a peck on the lips. Her lips were warm but her tongue was still cold.

"Hey," I said. I didn't want to startle her.

"Hey."

That wasted word surprised me, so I opened my eyes. She was looking at me. I couldn't guess what she was thinking, but deep down I knew what would happen if I closed my eyes. I did it anyway. Closed them and waited for her to kiss me. It started with both of us shy, but not too long after, her mouth was full on mine, and then her tongue slipped past my teeth to my tongue. All the while her arms got tighter around my neck.

After that, there was just one kiss that kept on going, which was what I liked. She let me play with her hair, and after a while, I petted her bare shoulders. I wondered how it felt to her with my hand being so rough and her being so soft. To me, it was like all the skin on my palms coming awake after being asleep. Same way I felt lying under the sky at night. The stars rubbing across me, making static electricity.

Until she gasped into my mouth, I didn't even know what I'd done—slid my hand down from her shoulder to cup her little tit in my palm. She leaned into me and her dress slipped down, leaving her naked in my hand. Her nipple went hard in the curve of my thumb, and she shivered. Made me shiver, too.

I tried to pull my hand back, but she pressed hers over mine to hold it there.

"Orion," she said.

She ran her fingers down my belly to my belt buckle and un-hooked it. I brushed her hand away, and I was gonna refasten the buckle, except if I sat up and did that, I figured that would be the end of her kissing me. So I pushed her hand away and kissed her some more. Her hand went right back to my belt, like a fly that won't quit buzzing around. She unthreaded the belt and opened the but-ton on my jeans.

I had to stop her.

I opened my eyes and sat up, but it only made things worse. Her eyes were thunderhead dark, her lips were red from kissing, and I'd turned her hair into a tumbled mess. She was straddling my lap with her skirt riding up. Holding her by the hips, my forearms rubbed against her bare thighs. Just short of letting go of her and dumping her on the floor, I didn't know what to do.

The zipper on my jeans came down with some help from her, but mostly from the pressure of a hard-on that had built up on me like a temperature gauge going into red.

"Wavy, you can't—"

"I want to," she said.

She kissed me until my blood pounded in my ears, like I was fixing to have a heart attack. She held the back of my neck with one hand and, with the other, she petted my dick like it was a wild animal. Real gentle at first. Then she closed her fingers around me as far as they would go, and goddamn, when she squeezed a little harder, it was far enough.

"Wavy." That was me begging, and not for her to stop.

As much as I always wanted her to kiss me, I didn't have no idea how desperate I was for her to touch me like that. I couldn't even recollect how long it was since somebody besides me had. And Wavy. Wavy. Her hand was so soft, not a callous on it. Took less than a minute to get me off. As soon as I came, I knew what I'd done. My stomach turned over and, for a second, I thought I was gonna be sick.

"Oh, Jesus, Wavy. Jesus fucking Christ. What are we doing? Get up. Get up."

She did what I said, slid off my lap awkwardlike, and staggered back a step. Standing there with the TV flickering on her face, she looked like she was worried about me. A string of cum dripped off her hand and she wiped it on the front of her skirt. I stood up, trying to get my pants fastened, but I was all thumbs, and my dick was still half-hard. Goddamn belt opened up easy enough in her hands and I couldn't hardly get it to close.

"I did it wrong?" she said.

"No—it's—oh, God, Wavy."

"You liked it with the girl at the party."

"Wha—what party? What girl?"

With the hand she'd wiped on her dress, Wavy drew a slithery line up her arm. She'd seen the girl with the snake tattoo giving me a hand job? That was the last time somebody else had touched me.

"But you, Wavy. It's not okay for you to do that." I couldn't catch my breath and my voice wouldn't stop shaking.

"Why?" she said.

"Because it's not. You—it's—it's dirty for you to do that."

She flinched like I'd slapped her.

Standing there, both of us not talking, I saw the thing I shoulda looked at first—the ring on her finger. It was my fault she didn't understand. When I told her she was too young to get married, I figured she knew I was talking about sex. But I bought her a wedding ring. I promised there wasn't gonna be other girls, and there hadn't been. I didn't even look at other women anymore. Maybe I was the one who didn't understand.

"Wavy—" As shitty as it was, I wasn't getting ready to apologize. I was so ashamed of myself, I was gonna say, "You can't tell anybody about this."

Before I could, she clamped her hands over her mouth and said, "Mama was right. I am dirty."

She was gone like a flash, leaving the kitchen door slapping in the frame.

I stood in the middle of the room, shocked as hell, wondering where she learned all that. The kissing, the other stuff? Did Liam's girls talk about sex with her?

No, that was my fault, too. Except for the one skin mag I threw away, I hadn't done anything with the other magazines in my nightstand. How many times had she been there without me and looked at those pictures?

Wherever she got those ideas, she was only thirteen. All those times I said, "I'm not that kinda guy," maybe I *was* that kinda guy. What happened hadn't just *happened*. There was that whole half hour of us making out before she unzipped my pants. I'd had plenty of time to put a stop to it, and I didn't. Because I liked kissing her. I liked all of it, no matter how messed up that was.

My pa was a crazy, mean drunk who beat the shit out of my ma and us kids. Alcohol did that. It didn't make you do what I'd just done.

As much as I wanted to, I couldn't blame the booze. I don't think I'd ever been as sober as I was right then.

I I

KELLEN

I paced up and down, until the TV played the national anthem and went to the test screen. Standing there in the quiet, I knew how bad I'd fucked up. Not just that fooling around with Wavy was illegal—considering all the other laws I'd broken, I didn't care about that—but that up 'til then, I'd never betrayed anybody I loved. Wavy trusted me, and I took advantage of her.

I got my gun out of the drawer next to the sink and pushed the clip in. When I was younger, I thought about it plenty of times. Just put the barrel in my mouth, pull the trigger, and paint the ceiling with my brains.

I used to think about it when I was lonely and miserable, but now it seemed like something I deserved. Except Wavy had said, "I'm dirty," and I couldn't stand for her to think *she* did something wrong. I didn't want her going through life thinking she was so dirty I had to kill myself after she touched me. Whatever I deserved, she didn't deserve that.

The temperature gauge at the kitchen window showed forty-two degrees. I'd let her run out into the night, wearing that skimpy dress with no coat, knowing she'd have to cross two highways and the meadow to get home.

I put the gun away and washed my hands. Then I put her coat and sweater in the saddlebag, and rode. I scanned the shoulder ahead for her as I went, but I'd waited too long.

At the farmhouse, the porch light was on, but the rest of the house was dark. I wasn't brave enough to call her name, so I stood in the kitchen and listened until I picked out two clear sounds. Splashing water and a muffled hiccup.

I tapped on the bathroom door, and there was a hiccup followed by silence. There was no latch on the door and, when I pushed it open, it thudded against something. Wavy's boots. The air burned when I sucked it into my lungs. Bleach.

I got down on my knees and crawled to the tub, saying, "I'm sorry, Wavy. I'm sorry I let that happen. That was all my fault and I'm sorry."

I put my hand down and found her crumpled up dress. I couldn't see a thing, so I reached for her, but she smacked my hand away.

"No one touches me. I'm dirty. I'll make you dirty," she said.

"You're not dirty."

"Dirty whore."

"You're not dirty and you're not a whore."

I couldn't take the scrubbing, the sound of her feeling dirty. Even knowing she wouldn't like it, I reached out to stop her.

She screamed and tried to shove me away, but I caught hold of her hands, and got the bar of soap and the washcloth away from her.

Her arms were slippery, too hard to hold. She jerked one free and managed to punch me smack in the left eye. Lit up the whole inside of my skull. I been in bar fights where I didn't get decked that hard, but once I had her tucked under my arm, she wasn't big enough to put up a real fight against me. The water running off her soaked through my jeans and made the floor slippery. She'd been washing in cold water and bleach.

When I reached for the towel I knew was hanging behind the door, something sharp—Wavy's knee—caught me in the kidney, almost doubled me over, and I slid into the wall with a thump.

"You kids quit making so much noise," Val yelled from her bedroom.

I waited for Val to open the door, turn on the light, and find me wrestling with her naked daughter, but Val didn't get up. She didn't even call again. It boiled my fucking blood.

"You stupid bitch! I could be in here raping her! And you can't even get your ass out of bed to come see what she's screaming about? What the fuck is wrong with you?"

No answer to that.

While I was yelling at Val, Wavy finally stopped fighting me, and I got the towel around her as best I could. In the dark, I carried her up the stairs, expecting more darkness, but the moon lit up her whole room. Full moon. Did that explain what I'd done?

After I got Wavy under the covers I took the towel and dried her hair. She laid there shivering and let me.

"You have to talk to me," I said. We weren't gonna solve this with charades. "You're *not* dirty. Why would Val say that?"

"Liam not to be trusted." She always said it that way, like it was his name.

"What about him?"

"Sitting on his lap."

"When?"

I knelt next to the bed, with the covers pulled tight over Wavy, but she slipped a hand out of the sheets and touched my arm. Then she found my hand and squeezed it. I squeezed back.

"Before I could read," she said. "And Mama said, 'Don't touch her. That's dirty! If you touch her you'll go to hell! No one touches her!'"

"Did Liam do something to you?" After what I'd done, I knew I didn't have no business feeling self-righteous, but this hot thing welled up in me. If Liam had messed with her, I was gonna kill him. Choke his fucking neck with my bare hands. "What did he do to you?"

"Nothing."

"What was he doing when Val told him that?"

"Reading to me."

I tried to picture Liam with Wavy on his lap, reading her a story. I couldn't manage it 'til I remembered even my pa did some nice things. Took me to a few ball games. If Jesse Joe Barfoot had a few days when he was a decent father, maybe Liam had some, too.

And Val was crazy as hell. The kind of person who could see her daughter on her husband's lap and think the worst thing. Might explain why Liam never went near Wavy. If your wife accused you of doing something nasty to your baby daughter, you might think twice before you ever touched her again.

"He didn't touch you? Not—" With her holding my hand like she still trusted me, my throat about closed up around what I wanted to ask. "Not in your private place?"

"No. She said he would, but he didn't. She said all men would."

"Wavy, I'm sorry I—"

"Now you'll go to hell and it's my fault, because I'm dirty."

"If I go to hell, it won't be because of you." I was definitely going to hell, but that wasn't her fault. "And you're not dirty."

"You said."

"I said *it* was dirty, not that *you* were dirty. You're a good girl."

My knees were killing me, so I sat down cross-legged next to the bed, keeping her hand in mine.

"Why is it dirty? You liked it," she said.

"Because you're thirteen." There were a lot of other reasons I shouldn't have been fooling around with her, but that was the big one. "You're not old enough."

"I'm old enough to like it."

She pulled more of my arm under the edge of the sheet and pressed her cold, bare little tit into my hand. I jerked it away without even thinking. For a while, she laid there quiet. Then she snaked her arm out of the covers and dropped something that clattered next to my knee.

I patted the floor and found her ring. I'd been so hell-fired against anybody turning it into something nasty, and then that's what I did.

"Wavy, this is yours. I gave you this because I love you."

She turned over, away from me, and sighed real heavy. She'd used up all her words. Maybe for months. I'd never heard her say so much. Holding that ring in my hand, I came up with three things I could do. One was really bad. One was too awful to even think about. That left me just the one option.

The radiator rattled and it got me moving. I pitched the wet towel on top of it and sat down on the bed. I held the ring on the tip of my pinky to keep track of it while I pulled off my boots and jacket. I shoved Wavy toward the wall and lifted up just the quilt, keeping the sheet between us. She was wound tight when I put my arm around her, her spine stiff against my chest.

"I love you, Wavy. I love you." I said it until she relaxed. "Now put your ring back on."

She didn't move, but when I leaned up on my elbow and reached for her hand, she didn't pull away. As I tugged on her arm to turn her towards me, I let the sheet fall back so her tits were naked in the moonlight. They were beautiful, and she trusted me enough that she'd let me touch them. She stared at the stars on the ceiling while I put the ring on her finger.

"It's not dirty," I said. "I was stupid to say that. It's not dirty if you love me as much as I love you. And I love you all the way. But we gotta go slow. We went too fast tonight."

She wiggled the ring on her finger, and I worried she was gonna take it off again.

"That night I first saw you, I was going too fast. There I was rubbernecking at you and dumped the bike. Wrecked me up. I don't want to wreck us up like that. I don't want you to get hurt."

She eased her hand up my arm to touch the scar. The ring was still on her finger and she looked at me, looked me in the eye. Real slow, like a striptease going in reverse, she pulled the sheet up to cover herself and nodded.

12

WAVY

March-June 1983

Kellen was unhappy. I could smell it on him.

I went with him when he got his hair cut, and the barber said, "Hey, this ain't your daughter, is it, Junior?"

"No." Kellen swallowed hard and said, "This is my girlfriend."

I was happy to hear that I was his anything, but the ring was heavy on my finger and I wished he'd said, "This is my fiancée."

The barber looked at me while he cut Kellen's hair. The way Kellen looked at engines, to figure out what was wrong with them.

To see what the barber saw, I looked at myself in the mirror behind the barber chairs. Too young. I tried to be more like Sandy, but I still looked like a little girl.

Opening my jacket, I pushed my shoulders back against the chair and slid my hips forward. I crossed one leg over the other so that my foot dangled. Then I rested my forearms on the chair and let my hands hang from the wrists. Slowly, I leaned my head back and made my eyes soft. The look Mama used to make Liam come to her after they fought. The limp limbs that invited, the soft eyes that promised things.

The barber would have come to me, if the invitation had been for him, but Kellen blushed and looked away. I didn't know what to do, because the things Mama and Sandy did when Liam was upset, I wasn't allowed to do those things to Kellen.

Night after night, he sat next to me on the sofa, watching TV. Never on my bed or the recliner. He held my hand, but he didn't put his arm around me or touch my hair or kiss me.

If he didn't want to touch me, I could accept that, but I wanted to touch him. That was never against the rules before, but it was now. All of December he didn't let me touch him, and then I spent winter break at Aunt Brenda's without him. Now January and February were gone, and I still wasn't allowed to touch him.

Even though he wouldn't say it, I knew what he felt. I'd felt it enough to know. Dirty. Too dirty to touch. Too dirty to be touched.

If he wouldn't touch me, that was bearable, but to have him look away from me wasn't. I needed him to see me.

On the sofa that night, after the haircut, he reached for my hand. I looked down at his jeans, the ones he wore for his birthday that got ruined by bleach. Bright white spots already going threadbare. Because of me. I pulled my hand away and said, "I'm too dirty to touch."

He jumped like a bee had stung him and leaned forward to put his elbows on his knees.

"No, sweetheart. I told you. You're not. You're beautiful. I love you, but you're only thirteen. So we can't be fooling around."

He didn't look at me when he said, "You're beautiful," so he might as well have said, "You're invisible."

"I'm sorry I made you dirty." Saying the words felt like swallowing burning cigarettes, but I had to say them.

"You didn't make me dirty. You couldn't, because you're not dirty, okay?"

"Then you're not dirty."

"Okay, I'm not," he said.

I slid my hand along his belly toward his buckle, but he shoved my hand onto my leg and pressed on it to make it stay. "Don't, Wavy."

After that my words were hot enough to burn my tongue, but I couldn't swallow them, either. They stayed in my throat, so that I almost couldn't breathe. I stood up and went into the kitchen, because I wasn't going to cry in front of him again. As quietly as I could, I pulled on my coat and slipped out the back door.

Orion was in the sky, but the clouds hid him, so there was no sense cutting through the woods, where it would be dark. I followed the safety rule—*walk facing traffic*—and made it as far as the second stoplight before the Panhead rumbled up behind me. Kellen rode ahead and turned around to pull up facing me.

"Get on. I'll take you home if that's where you want to go," he said.

I ducked my head and kept walking. After I passed him, he turned the bike around and pulled up beside me, going the wrong way down the highway, his boots dragging in the dirt of the shoulder. His arms were bare, muscles tense as he braked and clutched. He came out in his T-shirt after me, so I was guilty twice. I made him unhappy and he was cold, but walking was the only thing that kept me from crying.

"Please, Wavy. You're breaking my heart and I don't know what to do."

He was unhappy when I was there, he was unhappy if I went away, and I was miserable. Now I understood what Mama's hot, scary eyes meant when she danced with Uncle Sean. They meant everything was broken.

"I broke everything that made me happy," I tried to say, but I had to press my hands against my eyes to stop the flood.

Kellen grabbed my wrist and put my cold fingers to his warm mouth. After he kissed the ring, the worst of the words slid down my throat. He lifted me up to the gas tank in front of him and when I kissed his neck, he didn't stop me. After I kissed his neck, I kissed his cheek. After his cheek, his lips, and then he kissed me back. He loved me. If the mouth was a dirty place and he wasn't afraid to kiss mine, I wasn't too dirty.

A car honked, and Kellen said, "Get on the bike, sweetheart. It's cold out here and we're giving everybody a show."

After that we only pretended to watch TV. Slow was a game. While Kellen ate the dinners I cooked for him, I ran my hands along his shoulders until he took off his shirt to have his back rubbed. Once I rubbed his back, I could touch his bare chest and his belly. Almost to his belt buckle.

Even more than I wanted food, I wanted his flesh. I wanted to touch the places where he was hard, and the places where he was soft. He didn't like his soft places, but I wanted them the way I wanted mashed potatoes made with real butter. I had nothing on my body like the warm damp crease between his tits and belly. Nothing like the muscles that bulged in his arms when he used the pulley in the shop ceiling to hoist engines out of cars.

Kellen's slow game was different, like getting a wild rabbit to take a piece of carrot from my hand. If I tilted my head a certain way when he kissed my mouth, he might kiss my throat, too. If I reached my arms up around his neck, his hands would slide down to my waist, searching for skin to touch in the gap between my T-shirt and skirt. I had to invite him, like the stories where you have to invite the vampire in.

Sandy said, "The right outfit will make or break a date." Kellen would never take off my dress, but he would help my T-shirt creep up and up. Sandy was right about that, too. The tight shirts made me look older. They made Kellen want to touch more than my hair, and he didn't mind how small my tits were.

If I went slow enough, I was allowed to touch him almost everywhere. Almost. He said, "Slow down," so many times that even when he let me go faster, I went slow to tease him. A different game. To make him say, "Faster."

One night in the meadow, we kissed until our lips were raw, and my T-shirt was off and my panties were wet under my skirt from rubbing against his thigh. He would run his hand up my legs, but he was too nervous to touch me there. Finally, he let me unbuckle his belt and take him in my hand. I went slow, so slow, until he was breathing hard and his voice was deep in his throat when he said, "Wavy, you're driving me outta my mind."

"You said slow," I whispered in his ear.

Laughing, he squeezed my arm hard enough to hurt, and said, "Goddamn, I know I said slow, but that's not what I meant. You're gonna kill me if you keep doing it that way."

I didn't kill him, but I made him beg, sweaty and gasping. He didn't even beg for anything. He was just begging, with my name in between. "Please, Wavy, please," until his hips lifted off the quilt and he came. A strange word for it, like he was leaving somewhere else and arriving in the meadow with me.

Summer played games, too. It changed time, changed fast and slow.

Secretly, I knew, Kellen wanted to go fast. He said, "No, don't. We can't, sweetheart." Alone with me, he turned his back while I went swimming, unless I kept my T-shirt and panties on. When Donal came swimming under the full moon, though, I took off all my clothes to swim, and Kellen watched me. I came out of the tank naked and went to him, trailing water through the grass. When I put my arms around him and stamped my wet shape on his T-shirt, he didn't say, "No, don't." He said, "Oh, Wavy," in his begging voice. He ran his hands down my slippery sides to my hips, and kissed me until Donal said, "Ew, gross! No suck-face!"

Summer had so many tricks. The nights lasted longer than the days, even though the angle of the Earth's axis meant that was impossible. The night couldn't be longer, but summer made it seem that way. Summer sneaked time for me, taking a minute from February, three minutes from English class in March, ten whole minutes from a boring Thursday in April. Summer stole time to give me another hour under the stars with Kellen.

The only time summer slowed down was for the two weeks at Aunt Brenda's house. Time stolen from me instead of for me.

The night before Aunt Brenda picked us up was the Fourth of July. Kellen bought fireworks: rockets for Donal and sparklers for Sandy and me. Then we took the bike around the lake and back to Kellen's house. He let me lie on top of him on the sofa and he kissed me for so long. Nothing more than that, even though his heart pounded under my hand.

"I better take you home soon so you'll be ready when your aunt comes in the morning," he said.

"Not yet."

"Yeah, sweetheart, we better."

I pressed my leg between his, where Orion's belt kept him closed up in his jeans. I loved how kissing made me soft between my legs, but it made him hard in the same place. It was wonderful magic.

Kellen groaned and said, "You need to sleep. I need to sleep. I gotta go pick up that wrecked Knucklehead tomorrow."

I went but not before I left him a message. Once he had the bike started, I darted back into his bedroom. Going down on my knees on the linoleum tiles—so much like a classroom—I dug into his nightstand and found the magazine. I'd looked at it so many times, it opened to the page I wanted. The pleasure I wanted. I laid it on his pillow and ran back out to the bike.

Would he understand the message? Would he think it was dirty? No. He said, *if you love me as much as I love you, it's not dirty.* I loved him all the way and that meant nothing was dirty. He wasn't afraid of my germs. He wasn't scared of me sneaking inside him.

PART FOUR

I

AMY

July 1983

Everything was different that summer. Before, whenever Mom wanted Wavy and Donal to come visit, she would call Aunt Val, and Kellen would deliver them. That summer, it was Aunt Val who called and said, "Why don't Wavy and Donal come see you for a few weeks?" Mom insisted that she would pick them up, and I went with her.

After we got off the highway, we drove along narrow gravel roads, following directions Val had given Mom. When we got there, Wavy and Donal were alone in an old farmhouse surrounded by hayfields.

"Where's your mother?" Mom asked.

Wavy shrugged.

"We're supposed to tell you that she had to go to the doctor," Donal said.

"Well, she knows I'm picking you up today, right?"

Wavy pointed at the grocery bags by the kitchen door. Their luggage. She seemed so annoyed that I wished I had stayed home. In the car, Wavy dug in her book bag and pulled out a package of Magic Markers. Choosing a bright turquoise one, she leaned across the seat toward me. Just below the hem of my shorts, she started drawing what would become an elaborate peacock over the course of the drive home. I knew my mother would screech about even a fake tattoo that covered my whole thigh, but I didn't stop Wavy. Her hair tickled where it brushed against me, and it smelled like gunpowder.

That was what I loved about her. You never knew what she would do.

The first thing she did was ruin Leslie's summer. Wavy didn't even arrive until after the Fourth of July, but the ruining was retroactive.

Leslie had a crush on a lifeguard at the city pool. Miss Goody-Goody even broke the rules and drove by his house when we were supposed to go to the library. Then she ditched her one-piece swimsuit and bought a bikini so small she had to shave off most of her pubic hair. The lifeguard was a year older and more popular than Leslie, but by July, I started to think she had a chance with him. On his breaks, he let her climb up the chair ladder to bring him a can of pop.

Then Wavy came. Wavy, with her eyes that weren't any particular color except dark. Even after Mom told her to take it off, she wore eye shadow that made them look smoky. She didn't like to swim with all the people, so she sat on a lawn chair, wearing a cowboy hat, a wispy skirt, her motorcycle boots, and a tight white T-shirt with no bra. A year before it would have been a costume for a weird little girl, but that summer it seemed strangely sophisticated. Wavy relaxed in the chair and crossed her legs, swinging her foot back and forth.

When Leslie's lifeguard went on break, he climbed down and bought two cans of pop. He walked over to where she was tanning in her skimpy bikini, looked past her at Wavy and said, "Who's your friend?"

"She's my cousin," Leslie said.

"What's her name?"

"Why don't you ask her?"

Leslie should have said, "She's only thirteen." That might have worked to shut him down. What didn't work was him asking Wavy her name, because she just shook her head. A year before, it might have passed for shyness. That summer it was an alluring mystery.

"Oh, come on. You won't even tell me your name?"

Wavy looked through him.

"You want a coke?" He held out the can to her. She took it and rolled its cool, sweating surface over her arms and across the back of her neck. Then she set the can down next to her chair. Done with his offering. Done with him.

He sat on the deck chair next to hers and for the rest of his break, he sweet-talked her. In response, he got a big, fat nothing.

All he managed to do was break Leslie's heart.

He wasn't Wavy's only suitor, either. The way she strolled up and down, her skirt swishing around the tops of her boots, her narrow hips jutting out, it was like throwing chum into a pool of sharks. The old guys were the worst. Guys who had to have been twenty-five or thirty. They were more persistent, too, offering her cigarettes and beers.

"She *can* talk, right?" Leslie's lifeguard asked me one day.

"If she wants."

"How do I make her want to talk to me?"

By then, I knew the answer: "You need to be Jesse Joe Kellen." Besides being one of the few people she would talk to, Kellen was one thing Wavy would talk about.

Leslie's friend Jana came over to our house with this book, *Forever*. She got it at summer camp and she said, "Oh my god, you *have* to read it."

We read it. Jana's sister Angela even read the dirtiest parts out loud to make us laugh. Angela was pretty, with gray eyes and a dimple in her chin. She had a boyfriend, but I don't think she'd done anything but hold his hand. As for me, I thought, *I'm never doing that with a boy. Never.*

Wavy found the book worth three words: "Not like that."

"Oh, you think you know so much. I bet you've never even kissed a boy," Leslie said.

Wavy gave us the smoldering look that had stolen Leslie's lifeguard and said, "A man."

"What man?" Angela said.

"Kellen."

"You really kissed him? Like a real French kiss with your tongue?" Jana said.

"More."

"How much more?"

Wavy flicked her finger against the Judy Blume book.

"Oh, bull. You're lying," Leslie said. "I wish you guys could see him. He's huge."

Wavy grabbed at her crotch like a guy and gave Leslie a nasty smile.

"He's so disgusting. Seriously, he's fat and he has all these gross tattoos."

Jana and Angela weren't listening to Leslie. They were staring at Wavy.

"So, you really touched him?" Jana said. "You touched his—his penis? What was it like?"

"Hot. Hard. Desperate."

Leslie scowled, but Jana, Angela, and I broke up laughing. The dirty-minded Wavy was fun, but I assumed most of it was an act to upset Leslie. Ken in a dress.

"Do you really go all the way with him?" Angela said.

Wavy nodded, but Leslie said, "No, she doesn't!"

I didn't know what to believe. I was older than Wavy, but something had happened to her in the last year. She seemed a lot more grown up than I felt. She seemed more like Aunt Val, and not just her clothes, but the way she held her head, the way she walked.

"She's not even fourteen. She doesn't either go all the way," Leslie said.

Wavy shrugged and flashed her ring at us. I'd thought it was costume jewelry, but that day she let us look at it up close, so we could see it was a real ring. Not some gumball prize that would turn your finger green.

"You wouldn't! He's *so* grody," Leslie said.

Anyone else might have been offended, but Wavy wasn't. She opened her backpack and took out a photo album. In the front were pictures of Aunt Val and Donal. After that were pictures of Kellen. Playing cards with some men. Holding Donal up to feed a giraffe. Standing next to Wavy, her in a pretty green dress. The last one showed him astride a motorcycle on a sunny day with his shirt off, tattoos all over. He smiled, his gold tooth glinting.

Jana was fascinated. She came back the next day and, instead of her younger sister, she brought a friend of hers. Someone who was a lot more popular than Leslie. That was Leslie's consolation prize for losing the lifeguard.

Jana and her friend grilled Wavy about everything, which was funny since she hardly said more than a word at a time. Sometimes she didn't even need a word, like when she used me to demonstrate some sexual position that seemed completely ridiculous when I was fifteen. I couldn't imagine two grown-ups doing that with straight faces, and when I started giggling, Wavy collapsed on top of me, laughing.

They even got Donal involved. Luring him upstairs with cookies, Jana said, "Is your sister really getting married?"

"Kellen loves her. When we go swimming buck naked, he kisses her and lets her rub her boobies on him. It's gross. He says, 'Oh, Wavy.'"

Donal tried to make his voice deep and Wavy, who'd been drawing a dinosaur tattoo on his shoulder, flicked him on the back of the head.

"You go skinny-dipping with him?" Jana said.

That raised Wavy even higher in Jana's eyes, but it reminded Leslie of her swimming pool tragedy. It left me with divided loyalties. I loved Wavy, but Leslie was my sister. I was sad and relieved when the two weeks were up. Maybe Leslie could get her lifeguard back, if she still wanted him.

Mom had planned the visit the way she wanted, but there was confusion about when Wavy was going back. Wavy was furious when she found out she wasn't going home until after her birthday. Grabbing the calendar off the kitchen wall, she threw it down on the table and started counting off the days to indicate two weeks.

"Wavy, we're going back on the twentieth. Your mother and I agreed."

"You agreed. Not me," Wavy said.

"I thought you'd like to spend your birthday with us."

Wavy tapped her finger over the fourteen days again and she had a scary look in her eyes. A look that said she would do what she wanted.

"Goddamn it," Dad yelled from the den, where he was probably tired of listening to Wavy's mime-show argument. "Why not take her back tomorrow?"

"Because I don't take orders from her."

"Take her back tonight for all I care. Christ. I'm trying to work."

Wavy slammed her hand on the table to bring Mom's attention back to her.

"Don't you act that way toward me, young lady."

For a minute, she and Mom glared at each other. Then Wavy walked over and picked up the phone. I'd never seen her use one before, but she started dialing.

"Who are you calling?" Mom said.

"Kellen."

"I don't think so. You're a guest here and you'll go back when I say so."

Mom came around the table and disconnected the call. From the look on Wavy's face, I expected violence, but she won the argument with four words: "Guest? More like prisoner."

In the morning, Mom packed us all in the car, even Leslie, who whined about it.

"Why do I have to go?" she said.

"We're all going to drive up and spend Wavy's birthday with your Aunt Val. Won't that be nice? Happy birthday, Wavy." Mom was so mad she looked like flames were going to shoot off her head.

"Why doesn't Dad have to go?" Leslie said.

"Your father has to work. Do you have a job? No. You spent all summer at the pool, flirting with lifeguards. So shut up!"

Wavy and Donal didn't seem fazed by Mom yelling, which made me wonder what they were used to, that he could go on happily playing with his cars in the front seat, while Mom blew a gasket.

The whipped cream on Mom's shit sundae was that Wavy tricked her.

As we drove through Powell on our way to the farm, Wavy leaned forward and pointed for a turn.

"That's not the way to the house, is it?" Mom said.

Wavy pointed for the turn again. Mom took it and drove down the street until Wavy said, "Here."

"Cutcheon's Small Engine? What's that?"

"That's where Kellen works." Donal started to open his door, but Wavy stopped him.

"Now, look," Mom said. "I'm dropping both of you off at home. I'm not leaving you here."

Wavy slid her hand down my arm and was out of the car before Mom could drive off.

"Wavy!" Mom shouted as the door slammed. She scowled as Wavy walked toward the garage, but what could she do? Run after Wavy and force her into the car? After a minute, she drove off.

The cherry on Mom's shit sundae was that when we got to the farmhouse, nobody was there. The back door was unlocked and dirty dishes were piled in the sink. Beer bottles and a full ashtray sat on the coffee table in the living room, next to a bunch of burned pieces of tin foil.

"It's okay," Donal said, when he saw the look on Mom's face. "You can take me down to the ranch. That's where I sleep anyway."

"You don't sleep up here?"

Donal gave Wavy's it-is-what-it-is shrug.

The ranch looked like an armed compound you might see on the news. White supremacists or a religious cult. Past the gate stood two metal garages, and off in the trees a big metal barn. Clustered up by the road were four trailers, one with a deck on the front. Sitting on the deck, smoking, was a life-sized Barbie doll.

Donal jumped out of the car and ran to hug her. Then he took off toward the garages. The Barbie doll came down the porch, cigarette in her hand and said, "Hey, are you Donal's auntie? And his cousins? I'm Sandy."

We waited for an explanation of who Sandy was but she didn't offer one.

"Do you want to come in for a drink or something?"

"Do you know where Valerie is?" Mom said.

Sandy was the prettiest sad woman I'd ever seen, and for a second, she frowned, more sad than pretty. "No, but she'll be back later if you want to wait."

"It's okay to leave Donal here, with you?"

"Sure, hon. I'll get him a snack here in a while. Did Wavy come back with you?"

Mom didn't answer, so I said, "She's at Kellen's."

Sandy was pretty again, smiling.

"Oh, he'll be glad to see her. They're so sweet to each other. Yesterday he took a big cooler full of ice and drove over to Garringer. They have a Baskin Robbins there, and he bought her a scoop of every flavor of ice cream they have. You know, for her birthday. Isn't that the sweetest thing? Sure you don't wanna stop for a drink? Donal could show you his little motorbike. He's so cute on it."

"No," Mom said. She didn't even wait to say good-bye to Donal.

An hour into the drive home Mom turned down the radio we'd turned up to avoid talking, and said, "How do you think Wavy seemed?"

My sister glared. Like the girl who stole her lifeguard, that's how she seemed to Leslie.

"Happy," I said.

"She didn't seem hostile to you?"

"Only because you wanted her to stay for her birthday."

"Oh, good grief. Would it be so terrible to spend her birthday with us?"

"She wanted to spend her birthday with Kellen. He bought her a lot of ice cream." I laughed at the thought of her eating thirty-one scoops of ice cream, but nobody else did.

"I thought she'd outgrow having a crush on him. Some big, dumb motorcycle hooligan. And that filthy tattoo on his arm. I mean, do you girls think he's cute?"

"Gag me with a spoon," Leslie said.

I did a Wavy shrug, because I didn't even think Leslie's lifeguard was cute. I hadn't yet seen a boy I thought was worth having a crush on.

"Well, she's always been different," Mom said.

"I bet she's pregnant by the end of the school year," Leslie said.

"What's that supposed to mean?"

I wanted to say, "It means Leslie is a bitch," but I kept my mouth shut.

"You know she's having sex with Kellen," Leslie said.

"I most certainly do not know that." Mom tapped the brakes and looked at Leslie, who stared straight ahead.

"Well, she *is* having sex with him. Now you know."

"You don't know that," I said. I still thought it was one of Wavy's weird games.

"She said she went all the way with him," Leslie said.

"Yeah, but—"

Mom braked hard and pulled over to the shoulder.

"What do you mean she said she went all the way with him?"

Leslie sighed like she was bored. "We asked her about her wedding ring, and Jana said, 'Do you go all the way with him?' and Wavy said, 'Yes.'"

"What wedding ring?" Mom's hands shook as she put the car in park.

"That ring she was wearing with the diamond." Leslie smirked.

"Oh my God." Mom said it about ten times and then she said, "I can't believe you two have been keeping this a secret. Shame on you. Shame on you both. Tell me everything. Right now."

We told her everything. No, not everything. Neither of us was brave enough to say, "Hot. Hard. Desperate."

Mom put the car in drive and turned around. We were going back.

I felt like a traitor and I was glad the lifeguard had ditched Leslie. She deserved to lose her boyfriend for ratting Wavy out like that.

On the drive, Mom talked to herself, saying, "Oh, God, Val, how could you let this happen? You let this guy come around and you didn't ever think there was something funny going on? It didn't seem right to me. The way he touched her."

I didn't say it to my mother, but that was what struck me: Wavy let Kellen touch her.

———

Mom didn't go back to the garage. Either she didn't remember how to get there or she wasn't ready to confront Wavy. At the farmhouse, there was a car in the driveway.

"Thank God, she's home," Mom said. She parked and opened her door, but Leslie and I stayed put. "Come on, you two. You're involved in this."

"Mom!" Leslie's desire for revenge had gone to cold fear. Mom was going to make us tell Aunt Val everything.

I trudged up the stairs behind Leslie and Mom, my stomach in knots. The door stood open a couple inches. Mom knocked on the frame and called, "Val? Val? It's Brenda."

Nobody answered, so Mom pushed the door all the way open.

Beyond a certain amount of blood, your brain freezes up, like there's a limit to how much blood it can understand. There was more than that in the kitchen. Past Mom's shoulder, I saw a body lying in the doorway to the hall. A man in jeans and cowboy boots lay facedown in a puddle of blood. More blood was splattered on the wall and bathroom door.

Leslie bent over and vomited on her own shoes. That's when I saw the woman crumpled on her side on the kitchen floor, with a chair toppled next to her. I knew Aunt Val from her long, brown hair soaked in blood.

I don't know what other people would have done in that situation, but my mother walked around the table, picked up the phone and dialed 911. While she was waiting to be connected, she said, "Get your sister a cold, wet washcloth."

That was Mom's solution when someone vomited. I was supposed to step over my aunt's body, go into the bathroom, stepping over another dead body on the way, and get Leslie a cold, wet washcloth. It wasn't going to happen. Mom, she was on autopilot, trying to follow some inner guidelines for What to Do in a Crisis.

"Yes, my name is Brenda Newling and I need to report an

emergency. My sister's been—I think she's been shot." Mom started off all business, but by the end her voice was shaky.

While the 911 operator talked, Mom picked up a dish towel and turned on the kitchen faucet.

"It's off County Road 7. Near Powell. I don't know. I don't know the name of the road."

All we had were a series of landmarks and turns written on the back of an envelope. Maybe the road didn't even have a name. Mom frowned, her lip trembling, as she wrung out the towel. She held it out to me, but I was paralyzed.

"God, I don't know! It's Valerie and Liam Quinn's house. You turn off the highway after the tractor dealership and take the left. There's a silo there with a tree growing in it. I think it's four miles and—coming from Powell. What do you mean is it Belton side or Powell side? I don't know what county it's in! Amy, please."

She was waiting for me to take the towel. I made myself move, following the same route she had taken, around the table on the opposite side of Aunt Val. The towel felt good in my hand. Fresh. Cool. Not hot and sticky like the blood that was attracting flies.

A few drops of water dripped off the towel, and Mom and I watched them fall to the floor. That's why we saw it at the same time: a footprint in blood. A small one, and then another, a trail of them going toward the back door.

"Oh God, Donal."

Mom laid the phone on the counter and followed the footprints out the door. In the dirt at the foot of the porch steps, there were no more prints. The blood had dried or soaked into the ground. Mom looked toward the road, the barn, the meadow.

"Wavy," I said, because at that moment, I realized her mother was dead.

"Get in the car," Mom said.

Leslie and I stared at her.

"Now! We have to tell someone who can help. Someone who can tell the police where this is."

Mom drove down to the ranch without making us put on our seat belts. As we pulled up in front of the trailer, Sandy came down the steps. Her tanned legs seemed a mile long below her white shorts. She smiled at us. Beautiful. Something to look at that wasn't blood.

"Hey, girls."

"Where's Donal?" Mom opened the car door and got out.

"Oh, he went up the hill to see Val. She's up there now, if you want to see her."

2

BUTCH

I don't know why, but Liam had a taste for crazy women and dumb women. My ex-wife wasn't a beauty queen, but at least she had half a brain in her head. Not Sandy. She came into the lab at full tilt, running in high heels with her tits bouncing, never even looked to see if it was safe.

"It's Val. There's a problem," she said.

That wasn't news. All Val did was cause problems.

"You're going to have to take care of it, Sandy. We're busy down here. Where's Liam?"

"He took the bike out. It's serious, Butch. You have to come."

I left Vic and Scott to cook, and followed Sandy out.

When I got to Sandy's trailer, there was a woman on the porch. An older, straightlaced version of Val with housewife hair and a pink sundress showing off her chubby arms. Val's sister, Brenda. She looked shaky and the two girls sitting in the car looked freaked out.

I figured it was some bullshit problem, because people like Brenda get upset easy. Maybe they'd gone up to the house and caught Val and Liam in one of their fighting and fucking moods. Maybe Val was high. Maybe Liam had given her a taste of the back of his hand. If she'd been my wife, I would've done it more often.

"Hey, Brenda. We met once before. I'm Butch." I held out my hand but Brenda just stared at it.

"Val and Liam are dead. I think they've been murdered."

I pulled my hand back, I was that shocked. Sandy started screaming.

"Liam! You didn't say Liam! You didn't say! Oh my god! Liam!"

"Shut up, Sandy. Calm down and let me think." I wasn't some wet-behind-the-ears idiot, and the first thing I thought about was the lab.

"What happened?" I said.

"I don't know. I think they've been shot. And Donal's missing. I didn't know the address to tell Nine-One-One."

I could see if I didn't play things right, I was going to have a bunch of ruined product and the cops sniffing around. What I needed was help. Kellen could say he didn't have the stomach for dirty work, but you could've fooled me. We once went to take care of some former business associates of Liam's who backstabbed him. Kellen wouldn't pull the trigger, but he didn't blink when I did. That's what the situation called for. Somebody who wouldn't blink.

I left Brenda and Sandy on the porch and went into the trailer. I called the shop and let it ring a dozen times. Nobody answered at Kellen's house, either, and when I tried the shop again, I got a busy signal.

Brenda came in and said, "Did you give them the address?" She thought I'd called the cops.

"Yeah, they're on their way. Look, we're gonna take care of this, okay. Your girls are pretty upset, I bet."

She nodded and the first tear snuck out.

"I know, Brenda. I'm sorry. This has got to be so hard for you. Here's what we're gonna do. Sandy, get in here."

Looking like a raccoon with her makeup running all over the place, Sandy hiccupped and said, "Butch—he—he didn't even—"

"Sandy, you have to pull yourself together. We've got things to do. I'm gonna take Val's sister and her girls into town. You go down to the barn, and tell Scott to wrap things up down there. Do you understand? And tell Lance to go up to the farmhouse. To meet the cops."

"What about Donal?" Brenda said.

"Don't worry. I haven't forgotten about him. Sandy, you and Dee go up in the meadow. When you find him, bring him into town to Kellen's."

"I should go with them," Brenda said.

"No. I don't want you getting lost up there and you've got your girls to take care of. So you come into town with me." Last thing I needed was her wandering around out there, while I tried to get the lab cleaned up. Wherever Donal was, he knew how to get home.

"Why don't I drive you over in your car, Brenda? Is that okay?" I said.

That way, I was in charge, and it left the guys any vehicles they needed to haul stuff away. My plan was to go by the garage and get a key to Kellen's house. They'd be out of the way there, because I knew Kellen didn't keep any product at his house.

After we got Brenda and the girls settled, Kellen could come up to the ranch and help me figure out what to do. We'd have to call the cops, but not until we cleaned up and had a story in place.

3

AMY

Kellen's garage was the same as any other run-down mechanic shop you see in little towns. Two garage bays, both doors standing open. Lawnmowers and motorcycles in various states of disassembly. On the back wall were a window and a door. Parked there was what I knew had to be Kellen's motorcycle. The fenders were chromed and all of it was covered in stars.

"I bet he's in the office," Butch said, but when he pushed the door open, he said, "What the fuck?"

Through the open door I saw what everyone else saw, I suppose. Wavy on the desk, leaning back on her hands, completely naked, resting her bare feet on Kellen's legs. He was in the desk chair, his shirt off, his pants open. I didn't notice any blood, although later that was all anyone talked about—the blood on his desk blotter. Small amounts of blood are almost invisible when you have a puddle of blood burned on your retinas like a sunspot.

I saw what everyone else saw, except that at the moment the door swung open, I saw Wavy smiling before her eyes went wide.

Kellen stood up, and as he fastened his fly, Butch lunged at him and swung. Butch punched him in the face and all Kellen did was say, "Goddamn, Butch, let her get dressed before you come in here and try to kick my ass."

He didn't look like he'd been punched until he saw Mom, Leslie, and me.

"You son of a bitch," Mom said. "How long have you been doing this? How long?"

"Okay, ma'am, I know—I know how it looks." Kellen put his hands up, like he was surrendering, or preparing for Mom to fall on him like a hungry lioness. "But I love her. We're gonna get married."

Kellen picked up a piece of paper from his desk and held it out to her. She took it and glared down at it, her face getting redder.

"Val and Liam know, okay? I bought her a ring and Liam signed the paperwork. He signed it today and the judge says—"

"Liam can't give you permission to marry her anymore!" Mom twisted and tore at the paper until it was just a pile of scraps at her feet.

Then I understood the dead man in the hallway of the farmhouse was Uncle Liam.

While all this was going on, Wavy got dressed, pulling up her panties and tugging on her T-shirt and skirt. As she stomped into her boots, Mom stepped around Butch and reached for the phone that was lying off the hook on the filing cabinet. As she did, she looked down at the desk blotter and said, "You're going to burn for this, you fucking bastard." I'd never heard her use the F-word before.

Mom put the receiver to her ear and, for the second time that day, dialed 911. When the operator answered, she said, "I want to report a rape."

"Wait, Mrs. Newling. Just wait." Butch, not Kellen, said that.

"What's the address here?" Mom said.

Sitting back in the desk chair, with a hand to his head, Kellen gave my mother the address and she repeated it to the operator.

"My name is Brenda Newling. It's my niece. Yes, yes, I did make that earlier call. I had to leave there. I—no, this is *not* a prank. I was there and they were—" Mom's voice got louder and louder until she was silent for a moment. "They're there? You have someone at the house?"

Until then, Butch had been shaking his head, but he came around the desk and jerked the phone away.

"You dumb cunt. You called the cops out to the house? You called the cops?" he said.

"Valerie and Liam are dead! Somebody shot them! Yes, I called the police!"

"Fuck! Fuck!" Butch tossed the phone on the desk and ran out through the garage. A moment later we heard the car start and drive away. He'd left us there.

"Oh, sweetheart, I'm sorry," Kellen said.

Mom looked at Wavy and realized what she'd done: blurted it out with no warning. *I'm calling the cops on your fiancé, and by the way, your parents are dead.* Wavy started trembling. Kellen put his hands on her hips and walked her back until she was sitting on his lap. Wrapping one arm around her shoulders, he tucked her head under his chin. He kissed her hair and said, "I'm here, Wavy. I'm here."

It seemed like that would be the end of it. Mom would stop yelling and saying awful things, and Kellen would take care of Wavy. He obviously knew how.

They were still sitting like that five minutes later when a police car pulled up. Mom went outside and, when she came back, two sheriff's deputies were with her.

"Why don't you girls step outside?" the younger deputy said, while the older one went into the office.

"Come on, Junior," he said. "You're gonna have to come with us."

"Give us a couple minutes, okay?" Kellen said.

"No, you need to let go of her and stand up."

"Jesus, Delbert, she just found out her mother's dead. Give us two goddamn minutes."

The deputy stepped back and we waited. Kellen set Wavy up on the edge of the desk and for a while they hugged each other. She whispered in his ear, and then she kissed him. That didn't help the situation with the deputies, because it was a movie kiss, like when the hero and heroine are saying good-bye, and maybe they're never going to see each other again.

The older deputy said, "That's enough of that. You need to step back and put your hands on your head, Junior."

Before he did it, Kellen reached into his pockets and tossed a handful of things on the desk: keys, bolts, a pocket knife, and loose coins that rattled across the desk and tumbled to the floor. He unhooked his wallet and tossed it on the desk, too. I could tell he'd done it before, from the way he turned around and laced his hands on the back of his head. The deputy cuffed him, while Wavy sat on the desk, watching.

The deputy turned to Mom and said, "Normally, we'd get another patrol car to take her to the hospital, but things are a little crazy today. We've got a real situation up at the Quinn place."

"I know. This is their daughter. Have they found her brother yet?"

"Holy crap, ma'am. That's the Quinn girl?" The deputy blinked. "I don't know. I didn't know he was missing."

"I told Nine-One-One."

"Well, a whole lot's happened since then, so I'd better radio the sheriff and let him know."

"Delbert!" The younger deputy shouted from the far garage bay. "There's blood over here. A lot of it."

"Ma'am, I need you to get these girls out of here. If you could take them out to the drive so I can secure this place."

Mom gathered Leslie and me around her, but when she tried to bring Wavy into our huddle, Wavy refused. She put her arms around Kellen, where he stood next to the desk. Mom grabbed the back of Wavy's T-shirt and tried to pull her away.

"Miss Quinn, you need to step outside," the deputy said. Wavy didn't move.

"Wavy, it's okay." Kellen couldn't put his arms around her, but he leaned down and kissed her. "Go outside with your aunt. I love you. It's gonna be okay, sweetheart."

She looked up at him and shook her head, but she let Mom lead her away. Even though Wavy wasn't fighting anymore, Mom kept her shirt clutched in one fist as we walked out through the garage. As we passed the other deputy, we saw what he was looking at. There were a dozen quarter-sized drops of blood on the floor and on a nearby work-bench a puddle as big as a dinner plate. An hour before, I might have thought that was a lot of blood, too.

As we stood outside in the sun, I heard the younger deputy say, "Jesus, Mary, and Joseph. I got a gun over here, Delbert. There's a gun over here with blood on it."

4

WAVY

Of course Kellen said, "It's gonna be okay." He didn't want me to be scared, but Mama was dead. Not Sad Mama or Good Mama or Scary Mama ever again. Just Dead Mama. And Donal was missing. And Kellen was in handcuffs.

The cops took us to the hospital, where I saw Mr. Cutcheon in the parking lot. He waved at me, but Aunt Brenda wouldn't let me go to him. The hospital smelled like disinfectant and sadness, like when Mama and Donal had their wreck. In a white room with a maze of blue curtains, a nurse said, "How's she doing? We're going to have a private exam room for her in a few minutes. Are you her mother?"

"I'm her aunt. Her mother—" Aunt Brenda couldn't say it. Dead Mama. Always. That was how death worked. Dead Grandma. I closed my eyes and tried to remember the smell of Grandma's house. I wanted to smell something nice that wasn't sadness. I pulled my shirt up over my nose. It smelled like Kellen's sweat. Safe.

Aunt Brenda dragged me into a room with a black table covered in paper.

"Why don't I take the other girls down to the visitor's lobby? The candy stripers have magazines and stuff," another nurse said.

Leslie and Amy looked scared, and their eyes were red from crying. Dead Aunt Val for always, too.

Then Aunt Brenda and the nurse and I were alone in the little room.

"Sweetie, why don't you let your aunt help you change into this gown, okay?"

It was one of those blue hospital things with strings and no back. Aunt Brenda pulled on my T-shirt, trying to take it off, but I twisted her wrist until she let go.

"Ma'am, does she understand? Have you told her anything?" the nurse said.

"I didn't know what to tell her. Is it like a pelvic exam?"

"Yeah, like when you have your pap smear. Has she had one before?"

"I don't think so. She's only thirteen."

"Oh, sweetie. Oh, I'm so sorry," the nurse said.

I hated hearing them talk about me like I was broken. Mama was dead, but I was fine. I knew what "rape" meant and that wasn't what Kellen had done.

"You know, ma'am, we might give her a sedative. To calm her down."

"That's a good idea. She's pretty nervous about people touching her," Aunt Brenda said.

I wasn't going to take any sedative. No pills. No needles. They weren't going to put anything into me.

"I'll go get that and maybe while I'm gone you can help her change into the gown."

The nurse opened the door, and that was all I needed. I dodged around Aunt Brenda, ducked past the nurse, and into the hallway. I was free.

Where to go was the hard part. Not to the shop or Kellen's house, where the cops might catch me. At the Lutheran Church, a carnival had been set up in the parking lot, which was crowded with people. The air smelled like funnel cakes, heavy and greasy.

No one even noticed me when I sat down in one of the tents, where people were playing bingo. I stayed there all afternoon and into the evening, going from tent to tent. When it started to get dark, a woman came up to me and said, "Are your parents here? Do you need a ride home?"

I shook my head and forced myself to smile and wave as I walked away. The police were still at the shop, but at Kellen's house, they had gone. The front door and the back door were closed with yellow tape, but the window to the laundry room was open. Balancing on a trash can, I popped out the screen, and crawled inside. The cops had made a mess, dumping things out of drawers.

After I put everything away, I took a shower. All day in the heat had made me sweaty, and I felt sticky between my legs. Wrapping up in a towel, I took my dirty clothes into the laundry room and put them in the hamper. In the dryer were clean clothes, mine and Kellen's mixed together. I put on a pair of my panties and one of his T-shirts that I liked to sleep in.

When I opened the freezer, I was hoping for ice cream sandwiches, but I found something better. Thirty-one little foam cups of ice cream. On top of each plastic lid, Kellen had written a letter in black marker. Setting them out on the table, I moved them around until I solved the puzzle: HAPPY BIRTHDAY WAVY! I LOVE YOU!

He'd drawn lopsided hearts on the other four cups.

I opened the first one and took a bite. Chocolate with cherries in it.

5

AMY

After Wavy ran away from the hospital, we walked to the police station. Mom asked one of the deputies about our car, but he shook his head.

"I don't know anything about that, but I expect the DEA will impound everything on the property."

"The DEA?" Mom said.

"It's crazy up there. I went out to help with roadblocks and it's knee-deep in feds."

"Because of the murders?"

"What? No. Mrs. Newling—there's—your brother-in-law has a meth lab up there about the size of a—it's big."

Mom made all the right noises of shock, but I don't think it surprised her. After all, she knew what he'd done in the past. Did she really think he was *ranching*?

Whatever she thought, she was too tired to argue. Leslie was too tired to even whine. The three of us sat in the police station, our backsides going numb on hard plastic chairs, until the sheriff's wife took us to a motel.

She was a tiny, wiry woman, what I imagined Wavy growing into. Physically, anyway, because the sheriff's wife filled up dead air with talking. Probably she had to. Mom, Leslie, and I were like zombies, trudging into the motel room.

"Don't you worry, Mrs. Newling. We'll find your niece and nephew."

The sheriff's wife put her hand on Mom's shoulder, and that's when she fell apart. The night we found out about Grandma's cancer was the first time I saw Mom cry, but the night of Wavy's fourteenth birthday was worse. Mom let the sheriff's wife hold her, and she cried so hard it shook the bed they were sitting on. Leslie and I just watched. We were cried out. More than anything, I wanted to go home, so I was relieved when the sheriff's wife said, "Now, have you had a chance to call your husband?"

When Dad answered the phone, Mom went stiff and she didn't even say hello. She said, "Bill, I need you to come pick up the girls. Something happened with Val."

He must have said a lot more than hello, because she listened for several minutes. She got up and dragged the phone around to the other bed to sit down facing away from Leslie and me.

"Bill, I need you to drive up to Powell in the morning and pick up the girls. We're staying at the Blue Moon Motel that's on the highway into town. Room One-Oh-Seven. Bill, I don't want to talk about it on the phone. They're fine."

She was quiet again, listening, her shoulders tight.

"I don't care about your stupid meeting! Come get your daughters and take them home!" When she glanced over her shoulder at us, I could see she was getting ready to cry again. "They're safe, but they want to come home."

Mom came around the bed and held out the phone. "Tell your father that you're okay."

Leslie took the phone and said, "Hi, Daddy."

"Leslie, are you okay? Your sister's okay?" I heard my father say.

"We're okay."

"What happened? What's going on?"

"Aunt Val's dead. And Unc—"

Mom jerked the phone away from Leslie.

"Ow!" Leslie clamped her hand over her ear, and when she pulled it away there was blood on it. Mom had yanked her earring out. Not hard enough to tear the lobe, but hard enough to make it bleed.

"No. You don't need to come tonight. It'd be after midnight by the time you got here," Mom said to Dad.

It wasn't, which meant he'd sped to get there. He didn't wake us up, because we weren't sleeping. We had changed into nightgowns donated by church ladies, and crowded together in a bed that smelled of bleach and cigarette smoke. Lying in the dark, we were staring at the ceiling when he pounded on the door.

He'd come straight from work, wrinkled and tired. Pulling all three of us into his arms, he hugged us hard. Usually I hated his stale coffee breath, but that night it was familiar and comforting.

"I'm so glad you're safe," he kept saying. Sitting on the edge of the bed, with Leslie under one arm and me under the other, he listened to Mom tell what had happened. When she was done, he said, "Let's go home."

Leslie and I didn't have to be told twice. We were ready to leave that dark paneled room with the sticky carpet. We picked up the plastic bags that held our clothes and Leslie's puked-on shoes, ready to go out to Dad's car in our borrowed nightgowns. I thought of

Wavy, going from one place to another, never knowing what stranger's clothes she'd have to wear.

Mom stayed sitting on the edge of the bed.

"Come on, Brenda. We've all had a long day. You don't want to hear it, but I have to be at work in the morning. Let's go."

"I can't go."

"Yes, you can, Brenda. There's nothing you can do here. We can make the funeral arrangements from home."

"Wavy and Donal are missing. I can't go. They need me."

"I'm so sorry about Val, but your daughters need you, too." Dad jingled his car keys. "The police will find Wavy and Donal and take care of them."

"What am I supposed to do? I can't just walk away," Mom said.

"That's exactly what you can do. There's a system in place to take care of kids like Wavy and Donal. There's a reason I pay through the nose on my taxes, so that when things like this happen, we don't have to disrupt our lives. So we don't have to live in the chaos people like Val create. We keep stepping in, but let's let the system work this time."

"Are you serious? If something happened to us, is that what you'd want to happen to Leslie and Amy?" Mom stood up, not to come with us, but to fight.

I stood in my socks, on the sidewalk between the room and the car, waiting to see what Dad would do. He stepped out of the motel room and closed the door behind him, leaving Mom alone.

"Get in the car, girls."

I slept on the drive home, curled up in the front seat. I dreamed in blood that night, speeding through darkness, with Dad's hand on my back. Aunt Val's skull ruptured on the kitchen floor in a sea of creeping red. Footprints running away. A trail of blood drops across a concrete floor. A calendar blotter on a desk, with a heart drawn around the nineteenth, and a smear of blood beside it.

6

KELLEN

I knew exactly how Wavy's birthday would go. I would make her wait at the table with her eyes closed, while I set out the ice cream to spell the message I'd written on the lids. Then I would sit down across from her and say, "Okay, you can look now."

She would uncover her eyes and stare. The same way the girl at the ice cream place stared at me when I ordered. After she got over the surprise, Wavy would laugh. Stuff like that cracked her up. Then we'd eat ice cream together, even if I had to close my eyes.

After that, I was gonna take her over to the shop to see her real birthday present, the Triumph Terrier. It wasn't finished yet, but that way she could tell me how she wanted it painted. The guy who sold it to me planned to return it to mint condition, but I had my eye more on the size, only 150 cc. Now that she was fourteen, she could get her learner's permit, and the bike would let her go where she wanted, when she needed.

Then there would probably be some fooling around. Okay, there was definitely gonna be some fooling around after two weeks apart. Not too fast, but maybe not that slow. I could not stop thinking about the magazine she left on my pillow.

Eventually, I imagined we'd end up lying on the quilt in the meadow and she would name all the stars for me. Last of all, I was gonna say, "Do you really wanna marry me?"

If she said yes, I'd tell her about the conversation I had with Liam.

We were driving back from a deal, and I waited until he was all talked out about business.

"So, what do you want to do about Wavy?" I picked that question because if somebody asked me that, I had an answer.

"Do about her? Is there a problem?" Liam said.

"No, but I was thinking maybe we could make things more official."

"Didn't you buy her a ring?"

"Yeah, but I talked to Lyle Broadus. You know, my lawyer on that assault charge over in Garringer. That fight I got into at the drags?"

"Yeah, I remember. Can't believe he got you probation for turning that guy into hamburger."

"Well, it was justified. Anyway, Lyle says, once Wavy turns fourteen, we can get married, if you give us permission. It's just a piece of paper you'd have to sign with a notary, that's all."

Liam laughed and shook his head. My stomach went south and I eased up on the accelerator.

"Kellen, as a married man, let me tell you, you don't want to rush into anything. How old are you? Twenty-five or something? Why are you in such a hurry to tie yourself down? Think about that girl we met at Myrtle Beach last year. The redhead. The one with the tiny, tiny waist and the black leather dress?"

I didn't have a clue what he was talking about. I had room in my head for about five women: my ma, Wavy, Val, and maybe two of Liam's girlfriends. Beyond that, I couldn't keep them straight. I wished Liam would lay off the coke or the meth, whichever one made him talk so fast.

"So, would that be okay? If we got married? You wouldn't have to do anything except sign that form. It'd be easier for school, too. If Wavy lived with me, she'd be closer to the new high school in Belton County."

"Does she still go to school? You didn't finish school, did you?"

"No, but Wavy's a lot smarter than me."

"No offense, but that's not saying much. She's a little slow." Liam laughed. "I tried to teach her to read and never got anywhere."

"You know I'd treat her good. You wouldn't have to worry about that."

Liam fumbled around in his shirt pocket for the coke. "Can't talk you out of it, can I? You're like a—you know in those Budweiser commercials—you're like a big fucking horse with blinders on. I'm trying to expand your horizons, introduce you to girls, and you got your eye on that weird little runt. Does she even talk to you? Seriously, don't lie, now, you sad sack of shit, does she talk to you?"

"Yeah, she talks to me."

"That's something." Liam took a snort and, after he put the coke away, laid his hand on my shoulder. "Sounds like you've got it all figured out. Get me whatever paper I gotta sign and we'll get you a ball and chain. How would you feel about a honeymoon in Colorado? I need you to make a run for me next week."

I wasn't gonna tell Wavy what Liam said about her being weird or slow. I'd just say, "I talked to Liam and he signed off on the form. If you really wanna marry me, we can apply for the license tomorrow."

Honestly, I figured on her saying *yes*.

Didn't figure on spending her birthday in the county jail. When I was younger, me and the sheriff had some run-ins, but not in a while. If we saw each other on the street, I'd say, "Sheriff Grant," and the sheriff'd say, "Junior." Which was what we said to each other when he walked into the interview room. He looked about as confused as I felt, but I played by Wavy's rule: *wait.*

The sheriff sat down and lit a cigarette, held the pack out to me. I shook my head.

"Junior, we got ourselves a real situation. I don't guess I have to tell you that, but I need to know what in Hell happened today."

"Not much 'til this afternoon. Roger was sharpening a lawnmower blade and managed to cut the tip of his finger off. Mr. Cutcheon took him up to county hospital, and I stayed at the shop. After they left, Wavy showed up."

"That's the Quinn girl?"

"Yep. Her aunt dropped her off, and a couple hours later her aunt came back. That's when I found out something had happened up at Quinn's place."

"Junior, it seems to me you're leaving out a whole bunch of stuff there in the middle. The aunt told my deputy that girl was bare-ass naked on your desk."

I wanted not to blush so bad, but it came creeping up outta my collar. "Yeah, we were fooling around. But she's my fiancée. I bought her a ring, and her daddy gave me permission to marry her. Got the letter from the judge, notarized and everything."

"Don't lie to me, Junior. You don't want to go down that road. Even if I could make heads or tails of what's left of that letter, the fact is, the girl's not your wife. Age of consent's sixteen, and her aunt is real goddamn upset, talking about pressing charges. So you need to tell me exactly what you were doing."

"It went a little further than it should have. I know that. But it didn't go all the way. I wouldn't do that. We're gonna get married and all." I felt bad enough how far it did go, because I was sincere about wanting to marry her first.

"Okay. I'm glad to hear that, but the situation with the Quinn girl is the least of your worries. I've also got a gun that my deputy found in your shop. Now, we don't know for sure yet, but my suspicion is that's the gun used to kill Liam and Valerie Quinn. So you tell me, how'd the gun end up there?"

"I don't know." I knew that gun was gonna end up in front of me to explain. "After Roger and Cutcheon left, the phone in the office rang. I went in to answer it, 'cause we'd left a message for Roger's wife, thought it was her. While I was on the phone, Wavy came in. She closed the office door and the window blinds, but the garage doors stayed open. Anybody coulda walked in there."

"That puts us at nearly three hours between when her aunt says she dropped the girl off and when she made the call to dispatch from your office. You didn't leave the garage any time in those three hours?"

"No, Sheriff. I didn't even leave the office."

"Three hours is an awful lot of fooling around, even for a young man like you."

My face got hotter and hotter, and even though it was air-conditioned in there, I started sweating. The sheriff waited, looking at me.

"Well, we talked quite a bit, too," I said.

"So, that's your story? You and the girl talked. And you fooled around some, but you didn't have sex with her. And you didn't leave the office any time in there. And that's what the Quinn girl will say?"

I nodded, but it made my guts tight, thinking about the police questioning Wavy.

"Anything else you want to tell me?" the sheriff said.

"That swab they took?"

"For the gunshot residue?"

"That might come back positive."

"Damn it, Junior. What's the story?" The sheriff put out his cigarette and leaned a little closer, frowning.

"There was a possum messing in my trash this morning and I took a shot at him."

"Don't suppose you killed him?"

"I missed."

"That figures," the sheriff said. "Is that it? I'm not gonna find your prints on that gun? That Quinn girl's exam ain't gonna show there was more than a little fooling around?"

"No, sir, but what kind of exam?"

"I believe they'll do a swab for semen and look at, you know, whether she's got any injury. Like that."

"Are they going to touch her?"

"Yes, I suppose they will."

"I wish they wouldn't. She can't stand for people to touch her."

It made me sick. That I hadn't had the self-control to say, "No, Wavy." Or the goddamn good sense to close up the shop and take her to my house. I'd had this great plan and I screwed it up with plain old carelessness.

"She'll be okay," the sheriff said. "And so will you, if you're telling me the truth."

7

SHERIFF GRANT

The federal agents crawling all over the Quinn place were part of some drug task force, and apparently that meant they couldn't help look for two missing kids. We lost daylight before we found Wavy and Donal. I've had some sleepless nights as sheriff, but that was one of the worst.

By four o'clock I gave up on sleep and went back to the station. The feds had made about a dozen arrests, left me to figure out where to keep them overnight. I sent the women over to Belton County, and put Junior Barfoot in the old drunk tank in the basement. It hadn't been used in twenty years and still smelled like piss. Down there in the dark, he was this big mountain on the narrow bunk.

"You asleep, Junior?"

"Not likely." He sat up and gave a long sigh.

"I thought you might have some idea where those Quinn kids are."

"Isn't Wavy with her aunt?"

"No, your girl ran off from the hospital yesterday afternoon."

"You just now decided to tell me that?"

He was a soft-spoken man, but when he took hold of the bars in front of me, I stepped back. I'd never been afraid of him, but right then, I was glad for those bars between us. I'd seen a few men who needed a doctor when he was done with them.

"Did you look up in the meadow? Those cottonwoods? By the windmill? What about my house?" he said.

"We can check again. And your house is locked up."

"She's got a key."

"Alright, we'll start there."

"Let me know, will you, Sheriff? When you find them."

I promised I would, and went up to the desk, where Haskins was on duty.

"Have Delbert check Junior's house for the girl. I'm going up to the Quinn place," I said.

"The Rotary's coming out to volunteer come dawn," Haskins said.

"Did Barfoot tell you something?" Agent Cardoza said. I hadn't noticed him sitting at one of the desks in the squad room, and I wished he hadn't noticed me. A fireplug of a man with a bristly black mustache, he looked as rough as I felt. But he was a federal agent, so even at four in the morning, he wore a suit and tie.

"He's got an idea about where the Quinn kids might be," I said.

"You mind if I tag along?"

I did mind, but I shrugged. Cardoza seemed decent enough, but he wasn't losing any sleep over those missing kids. What was keeping him awake was the fact that his big career-making drug bust had farted and failed. With Liam Quinn dead, Cardoza and the rest of the feds were looking around to see what they could salvage.

Driving out to the ranch, he said, "I like Barfoot for the murders. Looks to me like he tried to make it look like a murder-suicide."

"If you're looking for somebody who'd plan a thing like that, he's not your man."

"In a big drug operation like this, murder is sometimes the best way to move up the ladder."

Cardoza could like Junior for the murders all he wanted, but I'd believe it when I saw the evidence.

I'd known Junior Barfoot his whole life, although I don't suppose I knew him by name until the night I drove him to the emergency room in Garringer. He was maybe ten years old and his old man broke the boy's jaw. Junior didn't even cry when they wired his mouth shut and took out a tooth to put a straw through. Coming from that, I figured he'd end up on the same path as the rest of his family. Both his folks drunk all the time, an older brother in prison for armed robbery, older sister in and out of jail, and the oldest brother shot dead in a bar fight before he was even old enough to drink.

Wasn't but four years after that trip to the emergency room, when Junior was about fourteen, we got our usual domestic disturbance call out to their house. Mrs. Barfoot was standing on the front lawn, her housedress torn and her nose bloodied. Inside, I expected to find the old man going at Junior, but for the first time it was the other way around. Junior was pounding on him and screaming, "I'll fucking kill you!" It took me, two deputies, and a volunteer fireman to pry Junior off his father. He was a big boy.

After Barfoot Senior was in the hospital, their youngest girl, who was retarded, was put in a state home, and Junior went to stay with Mrs. Barfoot's family down in Oklahoma. That's when he started going by Kellen, her maiden name. He came back two years later, and almost immediately got into trouble. I never saw anybody could tear up a bar the way he could. Furniture broken and grown men bleeding and crying, looking like they'd been hit by a train.

So I could imagine Junior killing somebody if he got angry enough, but he wouldn't waste any energy trying to plan it or cover it up.

"The rape charge is a problem for us, since the girl isn't cooperating," Cardoza said. "We'd rather get Barfoot on the murders or the meth production. Your county prosecutor isn't going to give us any trouble, is he?"

"My county prosecutor is likely to do whatever he wants. He usually does."

At the farmhouse, I headed for the windmill, with Cardoza trailing.

I panned my flashlight around the stock tank, and there sat a little boy. He was awake, huddled up in his undershorts with a pile of bloody clothes next to him, probably been there all night.

"Hey," I said. "Are you Donal?"

He looked scared, but he nodded and said, "Is Wavy okay?"

"Why are you worried about her?" Cardoza said, trying to make that one question mean something.

"She's fine, son." I hoped it wasn't a lie. "You want me to take you to her?"

"Will you piggyback me like Kellen does?"

The kid was worn out, so I wrapped him in my windbreaker and carried him up the hill to the car. Left Cardoza to gather up the bloody clothes for evidence.

Driving back to Powell, I radioed the station.

"I was just set to call you," Haskins said. "Delbert picked up the Quinn girl at Junior Barfoot's house. Looks like she spent the night there."

"Well, take her up to the motel to her aunt. I'm bringing her brother."

"I'd rather we didn't put them together just yet," Cardoza said. "He's our only eyewitness."

"Your eyewitness is seven years old. He's been up all night, and I bet he'd like to make sure his sister's okay."

"Look, I have a little boy about Donal's age. I just—"

"Bet you wouldn't think much of me interrogating your son at a time like this."

The sun was coming up when we got to the motel. Mrs. Newling was already dressed, didn't look like she'd slept either. I carried Donal into the room and put him to bed. As I was leaving, Delbert pulled up with Wavy Quinn. She stepped out of the patrol car, wearing a man's T-shirt like a dress, and a pair of motorcycle boots. She brushed past me and went straight to her brother.

Driving back to the station, Cardoza said, "I wonder what he saw yesterday that he was so worried about her. Do you think he saw Barfoot kill his parents?"

"You're barking up the wrong tree there."

"But you have to wonder if Donal brought the gun to the garage to point a finger at Barfoot," Cardoza said.

"Or maybe the garage was someplace familiar. And he knew his sister was there."

"Why bring the gun, though? And why'd he leave if he went there for his sister?"

"Your little boy, does everything he do make sense?"

I'd had enough of Cardoza, but I wasn't anywhere near getting shut of him. The feds were like a plague of cockroaches, except they didn't scatter when you turned on the lights. They were convinced somebody would roll over on Junior, but everybody they interviewed said the same thing: Junior wasn't Quinn's second-in-command. This Butch character was, and he'd lit out in Brenda Newling's car. Junior was just Quinn's mechanic, and that held some water, seeing as he had half-ownership in Cutcheon's garage. The feds took that place apart, pored over the books, and got nothing. Not a trace of meth, not a misplaced decimal point, which I could've predicted. Dan Cutcheon wouldn't put up with any nonsense.

As for the murders, the gun being on his property was the only thing to connect Junior to them. That made Cutcheon a suspect, too.

In the end it all came down to the kids' statements. The girl wouldn't talk and they had to hold her down to get fingerprints and a blood sample. That left us with her brother.

Against my better judgment, I went along with Cardoza's idea to take the boy on a walk-through of that day. Kids are tough, but Donal sure didn't want to go back to that house. I held his hand going up the drive, with half-a-dozen agents behind us, including Cardoza. Never mind that he had a boy that same age, he was looking out for his career.

"What were you doing before you went inside the house?" Cardoza said.

"I was outside," Donal said.

"Where did you come from?"

"Outside. On the porch."

I knew what Cardoza was trying for, but the kid's story started with him standing on the porch.

"I was going to see Mama. Because Sandy and me heard the car coming back."

I opened the door and, brave as can be, Donal went in. The place was mostly cleaned up, but there was a brown spot on the kitchen floor, where blood had stained the linoleum. Same in the hallway.

Donal walked us around the crime scene. Here was Daddy. Here was Mama. He pointed to where the gun had been in Mrs. Quinn's hand, before he took it.

"Kellen says you can't leave a gun lying around."

"Kellen told you that on the day you found Mommy and Daddy?" Cardoza said.

"No. Before, when he let me and Wavy try his gun. He said, 'You have to be careful. You can't leave a gun lying around.' "

"He let you shoot his gun?"

"If we were careful and only pointed at the beer cans."

"Was Kellen here to tell you to take the gun?" I don't know how

Cardoza figured to get the truth if he was going to keep feeding Donal lines.

"No, I was all by myself," Donal said, the same way he said, "I was outside." Like he'd practiced it.

"But you took the gun?"

"Because it wasn't safe to leave it lying around."

You couldn't fault the kid on his logic. Or his gun habits. When my deputy found the pistol, the safety was on.

After the house, Donal showed us the route he took that day, more than five miles of hayfields and woods, to Cutcheon's garage.

On the walk, Cardoza said to me, "He's lying about what happened up at the house." Like he was the only one could see that. "You think Barfoot threatened him?"

"Don't seem to me he's scared of Junior."

"It just kills me. I keep seeing my son, walking all this way." Cardoza seemed sincere, but he kept looking at his watch. The feds were set on proving Junior had time to go from the garage to the farmhouse and back. They didn't have any eyewitnesses for that, aside from a neighbor who *might* have heard a motorcycle, but wasn't sure what time.

It was hot and humid, like the day the Quinns were killed, and by the time we got to the garage, Cardoza and I were dripping with sweat. Junior would have been in worse shape, as much weight as he was carrying.

Donal showed us how he walked in through the open garage door and laid the gun on Junior's workbench. Instead of knocking at the office door, he looked through a gap at the bottom of the blinds. Up on his toes, resting a hand on the windowsill.

"Wavy says it's okay to watch. That's how you learn things."

"Who was in the office?" Cardoza said.

"Wavy and Kellen."

"What were they doing when you looked in?"

"Fucking. Like Daddy does to Sandy on the kitchen table. When is Sandy coming back? I miss her."

"I don't know, son." I doubted she was coming back. The feds had charged her with possession and intent to distribute.

"I'm thirsty. Can we get a pop out of Kellen's fridge?"

"Did you do that on that day?" Cardoza said.

"No. I didn't want Wavy to catch me spying."

We were all thirsty from hiking, so we went into the office and got some drinks. Cardoza sat Donal down in the chair, perched himself on the corner of the desk, and said, "What do you mean by *fucking*? What was Kellen doing to Wavy?"

"You know. On the table. Like cooking. Wavy says that's how babies are made."

"Maybe you could just tell me what you think it means."

Donal took a drink of his pop and gave Cardoza a suspicious look. Apparently the rape charge wasn't a problem for the feds anymore.

"Putting his thing in her. Making a baby. Except Daddy fucks Sandy all the time and they never make a baby. But maybe Wavy and Kellen could make one."

It would've been funny, if it wasn't so messed up. Made me think a little harder about him asking, "Is Wavy okay?" Because of what he'd seen at the garage? I planned to ask Junior about that.

"So what did you do then?" Cardoza said.

"I left the gun here. Kellen would know what to do with it. I needed to tell somebody about Mama, so I went back to the house to see if he—" The boy went pale as ashes and snapped his mouth shut. He started to shivering so hard I reached out to take the pop bottle before he dropped it.

"To see if who what?" I said. I'd been letting Cardoza take the lead, but something had just happened.

Donal brushed his hand against his shirt.

"There was dirt on me. I wanted to go swimming. To wash the

dirt off," he said. Blood, he meant, but I couldn't blame him for not wanting to think about that. He went back to the farmhouse, but when he got there, my deputies were there.

"Daddy says, stay away from the pigs, so I hid."

That was the end of the boy's story.

After we returned Donal to his aunt, Cardoza and I went for coffee.

"Goddamn it," Cardoza said. "He almost slipped and told us what he's trying to keep a secret."

"He won't make that mistake again. Now he's had a chance to practice it."

"That poor kid. He walked ten miles. One way carrying the gun that killed his parents, and back the other way knowing that lowlife was banging his sister. You still think Barfoot is innocent?"

On the one side, I had the feds trying to ram murder charges down Junior's throat and on the other side, I had Brenda Newling, who was just as eager to see him in jail. I'm not a squeamish man. I'd been sheriff for twenty-two years, and dealt with more than a few rapes, but I didn't relish having a woman sit in my office and say the word "rape" twenty times in ten minutes.

I made the mistake of suggesting that the girl was willing.

"She is barely fourteen years old and he raped her," Mrs. Newling said.

"The problem is we don't have much in the way of evidence for a rape charge. Indecent exposure might stick, since we've got you as a witness."

"The prosecutor says that the evidence from the office and Wavy's clothes is enough."

Make that the feds, Mrs. Newling, and the county prosecutor breathing down my neck, plus a mess of evidence from the two scenes.

At the farmhouse: Liam Quinn's blood in the hallway and

bathroom. Four bullets, two through his chest while he stood in the hallway, and two through his back while he crawled away. Valerie Quinn's blood in the kitchen. One bullet above her right ear. Entry wound with contact powder burns around it. Exit wound the whole left side of her head. What looked like a suicide note on the kitchen table.

> Liam, I'm done letting you make me miserable. I hope you're happy with your whores, but you're never going to fuck me again. Val.

At the garage: blood on the floor and the workbench belonged to Roger Betsworth, from his accident. The smudge of blood on the windowsill of the office belonged to Valerie Quinn. Her son transferred it from his hand, left his fingerprints behind. Left them all over the gun, too, which was covered in Valerie Quinn's blood.

Inside the office: Wavy Quinn's blood on the desk blotter and some under Junior's fingernails on his left hand. Also on the desk blotter: semen. Junior's. More of the same in Wavy Quinn's underpants, retrieved from a hamper at Junior's house.

On Junior's right hand: gunshot residue.

Valerie Quinn had GSR on her elbow and shoulder, but none on her hands. Her fingerprints were on the gun, but so were Liam Quinn's. His were also on the five shell casings ejected from the gun and nine of the bullets left in the magazine.

On the other round in the magazine: Junior's thumbprint.

Valerie Quinn didn't shoot herself in the head holding the gun with her elbow, so some unknown party staged it to look like a murder/suicide.

Who was the unknown party? Junior? His print on that one bullet and GSR on his hand. He had an answer for both. He and Quinn went target shooting together and they both had nine millimeters. Assuming the gun at the garage was Quinn's, Junior's was in his kitchen drawer. Recently fired, he claimed, at a possum. Two of the bullets in that gun had Liam Quinn's fingerprints on them. The gun also had Wavy and Donal Quinn's fingerprints on it.

Toward the end of summer, when we hadn't had rain in weeks, a farmer over in Belton County found Liam Quinn's Harley Davidson submerged in an irrigation pond. It'd likely been there since the day of the murders, but it wasn't until the water level dropped that the bike was visible. If that was the motorcycle the neighbor heard, who was riding it?

Not Junior, who was fooling around with the Quinn girl in his office when the motorcycle was ditched. I put it to him that he could have killed the Quinns and had time to get back to the garage.

"That don't even make sense," Junior said. "It's not like Wavy's aunt is gonna let us get married."

"All I have is your word that Valerie Quinn was okay with you marrying the girl. And I got these two gals, Ricki and Dee, say Mrs. Quinn didn't like you at all. The feds figure their testimony establishes motive for you killing her. And those gals are real eager to cut a deal."

"First of all, Lyle Broadus says I only needed Liam's signature. I didn't need Val to sign nothin'. And second, Val didn't like me, but she didn't give a shit about Wavy, neither. She woulda let me do anything I wanted."

"So, you were having sex with her while the Quinns were murdered?"

"No, sir. I wasn't lying. We didn't have sex." That was what Junior said, but he covered his face with his hands when he did.

"I'm looking at the report, son. I got blood. I got semen. On the desk. In the girl's underpants. Prosecutor says that's enough to prove vaginal penetration and ejaculation. Sounds like you had sex to me. And the girl won't talk to us."

"Will you let me write her a letter? Let her know it's okay to tell you what happened?"

I figured that couldn't hurt, so I got him pen and paper.

Dear Wavy,

I'm really sorry about your mama. I know you must be pretty sad, but I was glad to hear they found Donal alright. I hope you're taking care of each other. I'm sorry your birthday didn't turn out better.

You know I love you, right? I love you all the way, so I don't want you to be scared, whatever you hear. Probably I'll be in jail for a while, but you don't need to worry. I can take care of myself.

It's okay for you to tell the cops what happened on your birthday. I know it won't be easy for you to talk to them, but maybe you could write it down. You can trust Sheriff Grant, he's a good guy. Go ahead and tell him what happened, answer his questions.

I love you and I miss you a lot.

Kellen

It was a nice letter. You could tell he was concerned about her, and he wasn't coaching her on what to say.

When Mrs. Newling came in the next day, I let her read it.

"I'm not going to pass her love letters from that pedophile," she said.

"I don't see how it's a love letter, just because the man tells her he loves her."

"He raped her. I'm not giving her a letter from him that says, 'I love you all the way.'"

"You may not like it, but this situation is different than if he was a stranger. I need the girl to tell me what happened and, if this letter will help me get that, I want her to read it."

"No. I will not let the man who murdered my sister send her daughter letters."

"You can't have it both ways, ma'am. He can't be up at the house with a gun at the same time he's fooling around with your niece at the garage." I took the note back from her, before she could tear it up.

"The FBI says he had more than enough time to get back to the garage, with time to spare to assault my niece."

"That's why I need her to tell me how long they were at the garage fooling around."

"Stop saying that! They were not *fooling around*. He *raped* her."

Mrs. Newling was like a terrier. In my office every day until I asked her who in Hell was taking care of her kids. It was like putting a match to gasoline. She pounded her fist on my desk and screamed at me.

"How dare you accuse me of neglecting my children? I am trying to make sure that my niece gets justice—that my sister gets justice!"

"Then make that girl talk. And then get her out of this dog and pony show. The longer you keep her here, the more likely it is some reporter'll put her all over the front page. Is that what you want?"

Finally, I'd found something to make her listen to me. By the end of the week, she brought the girl into the station to give a deposition. In all my years as sheriff, I had a few occasions when I skirted around official police procedure. One of those occasions was the minute I spent in my office with the Quinn girl before she gave her deposition. For all I knew, she'd get in there and not say a word, and I didn't want that, so I got her away from her aunt and laid it out for her.

"Miss Quinn, is that your engagement ring? Junior Barfoot gave that to you?"

She nodded, all serious and distrustful. My wife said how cute she was, but I thought she was downright spooky. She had old eyes.

Knowing eyes. Wasn't hard to see how Junior had got himself in that situation. She looked fragile as a doll, but she wasn't.

"Now, the county prosecutor, the red-haired guy in the suit? He'd like to send Junior to prison for a long time. I don't think you want that. The thing is, you're his alibi. Do you know what that means?"

She nodded, but she wasn't any closer to trusting me.

"You're the only one who knows whether Junior left the garage that afternoon. If he was with you all afternoon, you need to tell the prosecutor that."

I'd run out of time; her aunt was coming toward my office. Years on, I don't know how to feel about what I told her. I don't believe Junior had a thing to do with the murders, but I'm not sure what effect my advice had on the girl's statement.

8

COURT REPORTER

I've recorded a few rape depositions, but Wavonna Lee Quinn's was the strangest one I've ever done.

She was an alibi witness for a guy who was suspected of murder, but he was also charged with raping her. At the same time. Basically, his story was that at the time of the murder, he was having sex with her, so he couldn't have committed the murder.

When I found out she was just fourteen, I figured it was going to be brutal. The kind of deal that would haunt me. I wasn't too far wrong, because I still can't get it out of my head. She walked into the room and sat down, not nervous at all. A thin little blond girl with big eyes, wearing a white skirt, a green T-shirt, and heavy motor-cycle boots. If it hadn't been for her breasts, I would have guessed she was even younger than fourteen, but she wore a tight shirt to show them off.

For depositions, most people start out pretty businesslike but clam up when they get to the difficult parts. She had to be prompted at first, to give her name and to tell things like dates and times and places. There was a lot of that, because she was providing an alibi.

Rape victims usually just say *he*, instead of the suspect's name. *He* did this. Then *he* did this. She called him by a nickname, even though the prosecutor kept trying to get her to say his legal name. Finally she looked at me and said, "Can you put in that Kellen is Jesse Joe Barfoot, Jr.?"

She spoke in this small, soft voice, and she had a strange way of talking. Sometimes she used big words she didn't know how to pronounce, and she inhaled and exhaled in odd places, not in between sentences, but in the middle of words.

She didn't sound upset, but even in statutory cases, the girls want to avoid details. She was happy to give them. Leaning back in her chair, she crossed her legs, swung her foot, and told the court everything.

"First we kissed. Kellen tastes like wintergreen. He kissed my mouth for a long time and then he kissed my neck. It tingled all down me. He lifted up my shirt. Slow. He slipped his hand under it and touched my tits. Held them in his hands. Rubbed his thumbs over my nipples. Kellen has beautiful hands. Big and strong. Rough from working in the garage."

It was unsettling to listen to a little girl saying things like that and she enjoyed describing it.

It didn't get really bad until she started in with the graphic details. In police reports, often victims will be asked to describe their attacker's genitals and things like that, but in depositions, there's less of that, unless the defense or prosecution hinges on some identifying feature. Miss Quinn didn't even wait for the attorneys to ask her for details.

"He still has his foreskin. He was born at home and his mother didn't have him circumcised." She stumbled on the word, inhaling in the middle of it, and looked at me. "Is that right? Circumcised?"

When I didn't answer, she went on. "My hand won't go all the way around his cock. Unless I squeeze hard. Kellen likes that." She brought her hand up to demonstrate, fingers held in a semicircle. The girl's guardian put her head in her hands and cried. Quietly at first and then louder. Almost in response, the girl let the hand she'd held up drift to her breast. Just for a moment, maybe not even aware she'd done it.

"My pussy was very wet. I was sitting on his desk, my legs open. He pushed against me, not hard. Rubbing against me. Then he slid his cock into me. It hurt a little, but he went back and forth in me. Every stroke, his cock was rubbing against my clitoris." She struggled with the word, said it three times to get it right. Or she said it three times to shock people. "That made it not hurt. It felt good."

Her guardian sobbed so loudly that the prosecutor said, "Miss Quinn, would you like to take a break?"

"No." That time there was no mistaking that she was trying to provoke a reaction. She moved her hand off the arm of the chair and pressed it between her thighs. "I wrapped my legs around him. Held on tight to him. He moved faster, going in and out of me. His cock was so hard, swollen up in me. I felt how close he was getting. I remember saying his name. Kellen. Like this: 'Harder, Kellen. Fuck me harder, Kellen.'" That came out in little breathy pants. "He did. Right as my pussy clenched up on him, he exploded."

I looked up at her, but I was the only one who did. The lawyers all had their heads bent over their legal pads, but none of them were taking notes. Why bother, when they could get a transcript of it from *Penthouse Letters*?

The girl sat back in her chair, smiling like an angel.

"Miss Quinn, would you please—" The prosecutor cleared his throat.

"He never raped me. I love him. I want to marry him."

I hesitated with my fingers over the keys.

"Type it. That's part of my statement," she said.

"Miss Quinn. Do you understand that this will be entered into the evidentiary record and legally, your signature indicates that you swear this account to be true?" the prosecutor said.

"I understand. Will Kellen see it?"

The prosecutor and the public defender swapped nervous looks.

"I want him to see it," she said.

Definitely one of the more disturbing depositions I ever took, and I didn't for a minute think her testimony would convict him. All the defense needed to do was put that girl in front of a jury and let her do her little reenactment.

9

AMY

Fall 1983

When Mom finally came home from Powell, she brought Wavy and Donal.

The whole first month, they slept together in the other twin bed in my room. They didn't have anyone else, besides us, and I wasn't sure how they felt about us.

For a while, we lived in a circus with Mom as the ringleader. In the middle of the night, I often heard her on the phone with one of her friends, or fighting with Dad. Once I woke up to Mom yelling, "Restitution is important! Wavy deserves something for what happened."

All of Val and Liam's property was tied up in the mess with the drug bust. Most of the property wasn't even in their names, and the government confiscated it all. Mom wanted to sue Kellen, but he was *indigent*, dead broke with a public defender.

All along Mom had said, "If he actually cared about her, he'd plead guilty, so she wouldn't have to testify."

He pled guilty to one count of Criminal Sexual Penetration of a Minor under Sixteen and was sentenced to ten years. Mom still wasn't satisfied.

"The S-O-B who stole her innocence gets to walk free after ten years," she told her book club. It wasn't much of a book club by then, more like Mom's personal support group.

On the day we got the news that Kellen had pled guilty, we found out what happened to his assets. There wouldn't be any restitution. No "making that bastard pay." Kellen had already signed everything over to Wavy: his house, his business, his bank account, plus half-a-dozen vehicles, including a 1956 Harley-Davidson Panhead.

It stuck in my mother's craw for a long time. She wanted revenge, but no one had to force him to do it. I think that's why she went on trying to get revenge against Wavy. Mom insisted everything had to be sold and the money put in a trust for Wavy, which Mom would control. Kellen's business partner bought out his share, Mom found a buyer for the house and some of the vehicles. She wouldn't even let Wavy go to the house and retrieve anything of Kellen's. Wavy didn't argue. *Nothing belongs to you*, she always said.

When Mom found a buyer for the motorcycles, though, Wavy put her foot down. In the middle of our driveway, as Mom tried to leave for the lawyer's office to sign the paperwork.

"Mine!" Wavy screamed it until my mother gave in. How could she do anything else, with Wavy standing in front of our house, shrieking that one word at the top of her lungs over and over, until the neighbors came out and stared? Wavy got to keep the Panhead. A mechanic from the motorcycle shop in Garringer delivered it and wheeled it into a corner of the garage. Wavy and Kellen's helmets were in the saddlebag.

Watching her run her hand over the gas tank, the mechanic said,

"Maybe she'll ride it someday," but her feet didn't even touch the ground on either side of the bike. I knew she'd let it rust on rotten tires before she let someone besides Kellen ride it. Still, she kept the chrome polished and changed the oil. Every once in a while, we'd hear the sound of its engine, started and revved a few times in the empty garage before she turned it off. It took her whole body weight to kick start it, but she could do it. Once a year, a mechanic from the local bike shop came to give it a tune-up. Wavy wasn't allowed to pay for that out of her trust fund, so she got an after-school job doing typing.

That, though, that all came after the worst of the circus had ended. The real circus was the lawyers and reporters and total strangers invading our house. Like Wavy and Donal's paternal grandmother, who'd never met them, but wanted them to come live with her in South Carolina.

If it had been up to Dad, he would have let them go. He and Mom fought all the time. About the money spent, about Mom's obsession with the dead-end investigation into Aunt Val's murder, and the endless trips to Powell. About Wavy and her behavior. The sneaking out, the not eating, the not talking, and the strange surprises that made their way into our house, like a baby raccoon living in Wavy's laundry hamper for a month. All the things that had sent Wavy to live with Grandma in the first place, but Grandma wasn't an option anymore.

The whole thing upset Dad's schedule. When Mom was in Powell, he was supposedly making sure we had dinner and went to school. It turned out to be harder than it looked when Mom did it, and we mostly took care of ourselves.

"This is destroying our family," Dad said about once a week.

Mom's response was always, "They are part of our family."

"Look at what it's doing to your daughters and tell me that."

I wasn't sure exactly what it was doing to us, but my grades the first quarter of my sophomore year were awful. Leslie even got a C in Geometry that quarter. Those first few months it was so stressful, sharing space with Donal, who was shell-shocked, and Wavy, who was actively hostile.

At school everyone wanted to know about my aunt and uncle. Were they really drug dealers? Were they murdered? I avoided those questions as much as I could. That was how I made friends with Angela, who had, it seemed like a thousand years ago, come to our house with her sister Jana and read *Forever* out loud. She wasn't in my circle, too pretty and popular, but in the locker room, changing for PE class, when the other girls quizzed me, Angela said, "Leave her alone. It's none of your business." When she saw me alone in the cafeteria, she would gesture for me to sit with her friends.

Whatever it did to Leslie and me, the circus tore Mom and Dad apart. On our neat little suburban street, mine were the first parents I knew to get divorced.

The last thing Dad said to us as a family was, "I can't do this anymore." He should have said, "I don't *want* to do this anymore," because he could have kept doing it. Leslie and I did. It wasn't like he offered to take us with him when he moved out.

Ironically, he left just as the circus was winding down.

Two guys, one in a suit and one with a big black medical case, showed up with legal papers to get a blood sample from Donal. Leslie and I were teenaged and indignant, saying, "They can't do that, can they?"

It turned out they could, because Sean Quinn had filed for custody, claiming he—not Liam—was Donal's father. The evidence had been there the whole time. Aunt Val had always said that Donal's birthday was January 21, but his birth certificate said March 21. Liam couldn't have been his father, because he was in jail when Aunt Val got pregnant.

Some judge we never met decided Donal should be with Sean.

The last night of the circus that was our lives, a lawyer came to pick up Donal, because Sean Quinn was a coward. He wasn't brave enough to face Wavy and watch her hug Donal good-bye. She shook all over, while Donal cried and tried to comfort her.

"I'll come visit. You can send me letters. I'll come for the summer. Uncle Sean says so. That I can come for the summer."

When I started to worry the lawyer would have to pry them apart, Wavy took her hands off Donal and stepped back with a horrible, empty look on her face. While the rest of us went to the door to see Donal off, she crawled into the closet under the stairs.

She stopped eating. Really stopped. She got thinner and paler, walking up and down in her nightgown. Mom threatened to take her to the doctor.

One day I got to the cafeteria at school and opened my lunch box to find half my sandwich gone. Sitting next to me, Angela looked at the half sandwich with one eyebrow up.

"Going on a diet?" she said.

"I think maybe Wavy's going to live," I said.

Wavy did live. She kept eating, secretly, and she went to school. In her dismal white pin-tucked dresses, she looked like a consumptive child from the nineteenth century, transported to the raucous hallways of a public school. She caught up on the course work she'd missed and survived her freshman year of high school. Survived being stared at and whispered about.

Every week she wrote two letters: one to Donal and one to Kellen. Sometimes she got a short note or a postcard from Donal, but nothing from Kellen.

Eventually Mom sat Wavy down at the kitchen table and handed her a stack of letters. Every letter she'd sent to Kellen, all returned from the prison marked UNAUTHORIZED CORRESPONDENCE.

"The judge says you're not allowed to write to him and he's not allowed to write to you. He'll get in trouble if he communicates with you." Mom sounded almost sorry. Wavy gathered up the letters and carried them to her room. She never said a word, and I never saw her write to Kellen again. She usually wrote to Donal after she finished her homework in the evenings, and she always signed the letters, "See you soon. Love, Wavy." See you soon. See you soon.

Donal didn't come for the summer that year. Or any other. Wavy's sophomore year, her last letter to him came back stamped: NOT AT THIS ADDRESS. NO FORWARDING ORDER.

10

DONAL

April 1984

I wasted too much time at the sandwich counter waiting for Sean to come out of the bathroom. The counter guy came by twice and said, "Where'd your dad get to?"

"The bathroom." That's what I said both times.

"He's been gone a while, hasn't he?"

I shrugged, like Wavy, because what was I supposed to do? Sean always took a long time in the bathroom. Sometimes I had to go get him, and he'd be asleep on the toilet with his needle in his arm.

So the counter guy wouldn't ask me again, I got up and walked over to the gas station. That's when I saw the postcards. I ran out to the car and looked for money. We didn't have the Corvette anymore and the new car smelled bad under the seats, like gas and rotten stuff. The carpet was sticky from where somebody spilled a pop. Not me.

I found enough for the postcard, a pretty one of the Grand Canyon that Sean said we didn't have time to see, but I didn't have enough money for the card and a stamp. The lady at the cash register said, "That's okay. I can spot you four cents." She was nice. I was glad I didn't steal the card.

Then I had to borrow a pen, because that was how life was with Sean. I liked it better when I lived with Sandy. I didn't always have to beg or steal things.

I wrote as fast as I could, but I didn't want it to be messy.

Dear Wavy, we had to move and I don't know where yet. I will write to you again when I know where. See you soon. Love, Donal.

"Who're you writing to, sweetie?" the cashier lady said.

"My sister."

"That's nice."

I wished she would be quiet, because it was hard to remember Aunt Brenda's address. Before I could write the zip code, Sean put his hand on my shoulder.

"Whatcha doing, Don?"

"He's such a cutie. He's writing his sister a postcard."

"Come on, buddy. You can finish that in the car," he said.

In the parking lot, he took the postcard and put it in the trash. He squeezed my shoulder hard and said, "Don, didn't we talk about how it's not safe for you to write to your sister?"

"I didn't tell her where we were," I said.

"I don't want you sneaking around behind my back like that again. Do you understand?"

I nodded. Wavy was right. Sometimes you have to nod, even if you don't agree. She was right about a lot of things.

I I

WAVY

1986

After Kellen was UNAUTHORIZED CORRESPONDENCE, and Donal was NO FORWARDING ORDER, I felt dead. I woke up in the mornings surprised my heart was still beating. The food I snuck at night tasted like nothing. I stole a whole red velvet cake from Mrs. NiBlack that was for a charity auction. It tasted like dirt. That was what I imagined it was like being dead. Feeling empty with the taste of dirt in your mouth.

Whatever Val felt now that she was dead, I couldn't think of her as Mama anymore. I wanted to take her flowers like Kellen had done for his mother, but I couldn't stand to go see her now that she was lying next to Liam.

Feeling dead was better than when my heart hurt. Sometimes I thought it might burn through my ribs while I was asleep, and smolder in the sheets until the whole house caught fire. The only thing that made it hurt less was moving my hands. Like Kellen washing dishes, making his head empty. I sliced and knitted and ironed and sanded and hammered and typed, trying to make my heart empty. Home economics class. Typing class. Woodshop class. Homeroom, where I volunteered to make decorations for dances.

The questions never stopped, but in high school, I learned a new way to deal with them. No matter what the question was, I nodded.

Were your parents really murdered? Yes.

Did your boyfriend kill your parents? Yes.

Is it true you were gang-raped by some bikers? Yes.

Aunt Brenda told the story to her book club and they told someone else, who told someone else, and on and on and on, getting less true every time it got told. Even less true than Aunt Brenda's version.

I mostly liked high school. I liked learning things. How numbers worked together to explain the stars. How molecules made the world. All the ugly and wonderful things people had done in the last two thousand years.

I also liked watching people. The girl who was pregnant changed the way she moved to hide it. The boy who looked at people like they were bugs scribbled angry things in his notebook. The teachers kissing desperately in the storage room weren't married to each other. Amy stood too close to the Spanish teacher when she worked the football concession stand. Leaning over, she brushed her arm longingly against Mrs. Ramirez's arm.

Watching and doing made things bearable. Also, time passed, even while I slept. After I turned twenty-one, Aunt Brenda wouldn't be able to frown and say, "I don't think that's an appropriate way to spend your trust fund."

Even before that, I would be eighteen. I could find out things Aunt Brenda didn't want me to know. Where was Donal? How long until Kellen was free?

In the meantime, the things that hurt other people healed me.

At the end of my sophomore year, a girl in my class was raped. Held down and raped by two boys in a bullpen at the city baseball diamond. The rape made other girls nervous, but it reminded me that Kellen loved me. He hadn't raped me. I slipped secret notes in the girl's locker. Notes to say, "You're very good at math," and "Your hair is pretty today."

During my junior year, a boy in Amy's class killed himself. He had terrible acne, purple welts like bee stings all over his face, and he went home from school and hung himself. I could have told him there was no sense in rushing toward being dead. It would find you soon enough, and before it did there were pleasures to make your heart hurt less. If I lay very still in bed at night, I remembered how Grandma's house smelled. The taste of mint ice cream on Kellen's tongue. Donal jumping on the bed to wake me up.

For everyone else, the boy killing himself was scary. It made Aunt Brenda hug Amy harder and tell Leslie it was okay if she wanted to move home from the dorm, where she was lonely, even though the college was only twenty miles away. It made them go to church more, hoping God would comfort them.

I didn't think God could comfort anyone, but I was content to go and sit in the sanctuary. People stared at me sometimes, but they had to follow the rules and I didn't. God made everyone else stand up and sing, sit down and pray, stand up, sit down, pray, sing, pray. God didn't seem to care if I read novels or knitted scarves.

Youth group was harder to get through. Charlotte, the youth pastor, was a hugger. She was big and blond, with an enormous mouth full of teeth to hold her big smiley voice. Once, she visited the house, so she and Aunt Brenda could discuss her concerns about me not being baptized. Swimming in a stock tank under the full moon didn't count.

"I know you'll be discreet," Aunt Brenda told Charlotte. "So I'm

just going to tell you the whole sordid story. To help you understand. So you can be sensitive to Wavy's situation."

Only Aunt Brenda didn't tell the *whole* sordid story. She never
told anyone about the deposition, but especially not Charlotte. As
much as Charlotte loved crying and hugging, she loved to talk about
sex more. Or she loved to talk about how you weren't supposed to
have sex.

"God made your body a temple to honor him and he wants you to
cherish that gift. He doesn't want you to put drugs in it. He doesn't
want you to hurt yourself driving recklessly. And He doesn't want you
to share yourself with just anyone. The gift of your temple is for you to
share with the special person God has chosen for you." Charlotte always looked so happy when she talked like that. Ecstatic.

God also didn't want you to "pollute yourself." Touching yourself
for pleasure wasn't what God designed your temple for, according to
Charlotte. Either God was stupid or Charlotte was confused, because
my temple was clearly designed for that.

"When you get married, the purity of your temple will be a gift
you give not only to your spouse but to God. The gift of honoring
His commandments." Charlotte wasn't married and sometimes I
caught her looking at Kellen's ring on my finger.

I wondered, was Charlotte saving her loud-mouthed temple for
someone?

The girl in front of me had a better question: "But what about
people who aren't virgins when they get married?"

"Our God is a merciful God," Charlotte said. "If a person honestly regrets what they've done—"

"But what if it's not their fault?"

"Yeah, like what if a girl gets raped?" Amy's best friend Angela
said. She sounded mad.

Charlotte's mouth made a big O.

"That's not the same thing," said Marcus. He had a crush on

Amy, but he might as well have been at home polluting his temple as sitting there mooning over her.

"Marcus is right, that's not the same thing." Charlotte's voice went into its pre-cry quaver. "God understands that bad things can happen to good people."

"But it still means you're not a virgin," said the girl in front of me.

"God can make everything right if we trust Him. If we pray, He can take cancer away. He can bring people back to life."

"So God could make you a virgin again?"

People laughed at the girl for asking that, but Charlotte said, "Why is that so funny? God parted the Red Sea and Jesus resurrected Lazarus. He can do anything."

When everybody broke for snacks, I stayed in my corner reading. Sometimes Amy and Angela sat with me, but Leslie was there that night, wanting to run away from college and sneak back into her safe high school life. The three of them were at the refreshment table, when Charlotte walked over to me.

"Can we talk, Wavy?" Without waiting for an answer Charlotte sat down and scooted her chair up as close as she could, so no one else would hear. Like I would want to have a secret with her. "I want you to know that I believe what I said with all my heart. What happened to you, God can heal you of that. Because He knows that in your heart, you're still pure."

Charlotte's hand swooped toward my arm, but stopped short of touching me.

"Will you let me pray with you? Ask God to heal you? To take away what was done to you and make you whole?"

"I don't *want* your god to make me a virgin," I said.

12

AMY

1986–1987

Wavy said it loud enough that everyone in the youth group lounge heard her. Then she walked over to Leslie and held out her hand.

"Car keys?"

"Wavy, she's just trying to help," Leslie said.

Charlotte hurried up to us and gasped, "Will you ask Wavy to come into my office to talk, Leslie?"

Wavy snapped her fingers angrily at Leslie. I could see in Wavy's eyes that she had maybe only ten seconds of calm left. Angela saw it, too, and said, "Jeez, Les, give her the keys."

"They're in my purse."

"Oh, Wavy. Please, let me help you." Charlotte was getting ready to cry.

Wavy turned on her heel, crossed to where Leslie's purse hung over the back of her chair. In one economical movement, she emptied Leslie's purse on the seat and picked up the keys. Five steps to the door and she was gone.

"She doesn't want your help," Angela said.

"God wants to heal her, if only she would open her heart," Charlotte said.

"She's fine." Only as I said it did I realize it was true. Considering everything she'd been through, Wavy was doing pretty well.

"We better go," Leslie said.

One of those rare occasions when Leslie and I agreed. She put her stuff back in her purse and we left. Behind us, Charlotte sniffled.

When we got to the car, Wavy was curled up in the backseat. I got in beside her while Angela rode up front with Leslie.

"What a witch," Angela said. "She's probably not even a virgin. Not that I can imagine anyone having sex with her."

"It's not true." Wavy's voice was flat.

"Charlotte's right. I know you don't like her, but she's right. What happened to you doesn't count," Leslie said. I didn't know if she wanted to reassure Wavy or reassert Charlotte's ecclesiastical authority on renewable virginity.

"I *am* a virgin."

Leslie flicked on the windshield washer. She didn't have the nerve to ask but I couldn't stand not knowing.

"But what about—" I hesitated, because it wasn't a name to be said lightly in our family: "Kellen?"

"He never fucked me."

"Wavy! Watch your mouth." Leslie's perfect impersonation of Mom. I ignored her.

"But the police report. Your deposition—"

"His alibi." Wavy hugged her knees more tightly, her white skirt bunching over her black-stockinged legs. That was the first time I realized that while Leslie and I were growing up, Wavy was staying the same. Staying fourteen. Not even that. Staying thirteen. In three years she hadn't grown at all.

"But your blood on the desk blotter." Why was I arguing? To say, *No, you can't be a virgin*? The police report said so. Kellen pled guilty.

"He broke my hymen with his fingers," Wavy said.

"See? Really, you're still a virgin." Angela leaned over the back-seat, trying to help.

"I wish he had fucked me."

"You don't mean that," Leslie said, half-sad, half-disapproving.

"No one could take that away."

I didn't blame Wavy for feeling that way. The bike and the ring, they were just *things*. Donal and Kellen were all she cared about, and they'd both been taken away from her.

In bed that night, I said, "What was it like?" It makes me sound like a morbid ghoul, but why else had Wavy offered that secret? She wanted to tell someone.

"Wonderful. His hands are big and rough. He slid his ring finger into me. It burned. There was blood, but I wanted to have him in me. He wouldn't."

"But your deposition." I kept coming back to the Gospel. Wavy spoke in Apocrypha.

"He wouldn't. He was scared of hurting me and he wanted to wait until we got married. Rubbing against me made him come. On the desk. Between my legs. Not in me. He never fucked me."

I didn't know what to say, so I lay there and listened to the whisper of covers moving over her flannel nightdress. Tiny sparks leapt like lightning in a petri dish meadow. Wavy sighed and shivered and hic-cupped. After sharing a room with her for three years I was used to the sound of her masturbating. I never got used to the sound of her crying.

———

I lost my own virginity at a party four months later. It involved a nice guy named Marcus, who thought he was in love with me, and too much alcohol. I felt like such a coward about that. Instead of going into it with my eyes open, I lied to myself. I thought if I was drunk it would be this magical thing that just happened.

I'd had a huge fight with Angela, who was going to a different college on a track and field scholarship. She kept saying, "We'll visit each other," but then I found out she was getting back together with her ex-boyfriend, who was going to the same school. Her ex-boyfriend who hated me. I knew we would never visit each other if she was dating him. When I told her she deserved better, she got mad.

"You don't own me," she said.

I felt like my heart had been ripped out, and when Wavy and I got to the party, Marcus was there. I wanted it to be wonderful, like Wavy said, but it was awkward and painful and embarrassing. I was so drunk that after Wavy and I got home, I was sick. We managed to sneak past Mom and into the bathroom, where I vomited my guts up and cried.

"I don't love him," I sobbed. I liked him, but I didn't love him. I wasn't even attracted to him beyond the fact that he had good hygiene. I thought it meant something that he was in love with me, but it only means something if you love the other person. And I loved Angela.

"It's over," Wavy said, as I lay on the floor with a cold washcloth on my forehead. I thought she meant the puking, but she said, "Nothing left to be afraid of."

I'd been afraid of so many things: sex, graduating, college, leaving home, falling in love. Life. Now I'd fallen in love, gotten my heart broken, and had meaningless sex. Those scary things were over. In three months I would leave for college. There would be other things to be afraid of later, but lying there, drunk and hurting all over, I wasn't afraid.

I wondered how it was for Wavy. She'd fallen in love, had her heart broken, almost had sex, and had her whole family taken away from her. Did she still have things to be afraid of?

That Kellen wouldn't love her long enough. The years were adding up. Mom thought Wavy would get over it, but she was wrong. Wavy still loved him, but when he got out of prison, would he still love her?

Wavy made her way as best she could, found ways to fit in on her terms. For instance, she didn't go to her senior prom, but she was the chairperson for the decoration committee. The prom was Valentine's themed: red and pink, with hearts and hundreds of hand-tucked crepe-paper roses with green sisal stems. Things like that always looked effortless in Wavy's hands.

She strung elaborate garlands along the edges of the bleachers, and in the corner where prom pictures would be taken. The garlands were pink and red with bits of gold foil, alternating reversed hearts. Everyone assumed they were hearts, until halfway through the prom, when one of the parent chaperones admired the decorations at just the right angle. That year none of the prom pictures could be used in the yearbook. "Obscene," the school board called them.

Instead of hearts, Wavy had very skillfully alternated between erect penises and curvaceous rumps that narrowed to delicate but well-defined vulvas.

The school board threatened to keep her from graduating, but in the end, Wavy got to walk across the dais in her big boots. She accepted her diploma from the principal's grudgingly outstretched hand, and walked to the other end of the stage. From up in the stands, home from my first year of college, I watched her kiss Kellen's ring.

Four years into a ten-year prison sentence, did he feel the same?

13

KELLEN

June 1987

The hearing room was small, the same gray cinder block as my cell. There was a table for the parole board, another for me and my lawyer, and some folding chairs along the wall for witnesses. I had to wear a leg iron, hooked to an eyebolt in the floor, but at least they didn't cuff me. The room was too warm, close enough quarters I wondered if Wavy would be able to smell me. I'd showered like she might, trimmed my hair, shaved, and tucked my shirt in. Not to impress the board. I didn't figure there was much I could do to make them like me.

Heading into my fifth year, I was tired. I'd spent four years sitting around, reading, lifting weights, and sleeping. Four years thinking about Wavy, because I didn't have enough to do with my hands, especially in solitary. Odds on I was gonna do another year before my next hearing. Another year before I might get a chance to see Wavy again.

After my lawyer, the parole board showed up, then Old Man Cutcheon, who I couldn't hardly believe had come all that way for me after the trouble I'd caused him. Then Brenda Newling walked in. Seeing her looking older, I wondered what Wavy looked like now.

Brenda glared at me like she wanted to burn a hole in me, but it didn't. Wavy hadn't come, and if she wasn't there, I didn't care what happened. I knew the fight was gonna come up and that was the first thing the parole board mentioned.

"I see you had an altercation with a fellow inmate six months ago. A pretty serious one. The man ended up in the infirmary, and you've been in administrative segregation since then? That doesn't exactly suggest you're ready for parole. Would you like to tell us about that?"

I didn't want to, but I had to say something.

"Look, because of my conviction, there's always some guy wanting to mess with me. He came at me with a shiv."

"Did you have some personal issue with him?" the woman on the board said.

"I didn't know him. It's just because of what I pled to. Some guys, they find that out, they have it in for me." I had scars to show for two times I let my guard down.

"Inmates who have sexual convictions involving minors are often targeted by other inmates," my lawyer said. "Mr. Barfoot has worked hard to rehabilitate himself."

"Can you tell us what you've done to prepare yourself for parole?"

"I finished my GED."

"Also Mr. Barfoot completed the court-mandated program for sex offenders," my lawyer said.

I didn't like thinking about that. Three months spending every day in the same room with child molesters and rapists. The whole thing gave me a creeping dread of myself, but I didn't have to lie in the exit interview. *Do you still have sexual fantasies about young girls?*

they asked. No. I never had. I thought about Wavy a hundred times a day, but Wavy was Wavy, not some *young girl*.

Then it was Mr. Cutcheon's turn to talk to the board. It choked me up so that I couldn't look at him. For reasons I still don't get, he took a chance on me when nobody else would.

"Jesse Joe's a good boy," he told the parole board. I was surprised they didn't laugh at him. "I know he's been in some trouble with the law, but the fact is, he loved that girl. He treated her good, took care of her, made sure she went to school. He looked out for her when nobody else did. Not even her, sitting there glaring at me." He cut his eyes over at Brenda. "She wasn't the one taking Wavy to school every day, I tell you what."

I figured that all he meant to do was give me a decent character witness, but then he said, "He'll have a job if he gets paroled. I'd hire him back tomorrow if I could."

After he finished talking, he tried to come over and shake my hand. The guards had to explain to him he wasn't allowed to do that.

"Thanks, Mr. Cutcheon, I really appreciate it," I said. He nodded and kinda waved at me.

"You take care. We'll be seeing you soon. I got this cussed Waverunner I can't hardly figure—"

"Mr. Cutcheon?" the parole board head said.

"Sorry, sorry. I'm going."

He went, and then it was just me and Brenda.

She stood up, and the parole board head said, "You're Brenda Newling? The, uh, victim's aunt?"

"Yes."

"And you've got a statement?"

She unfolded a piece of paper she'd clenched in her fist.

"I'm here today, because Wavy found it too upsetting to come. I'm asking the board to turn down his request for parole, because the damage he's done isn't over. My niece turns eighteen in July and she still hasn't recovered. She was a vulnerable little girl, with no one to protect her from his predations. He presented himself as her friend and groomed her for a sexual relationship. He plied her with presents and seduced her. Betrayed her trust. She used to believe she was in love with him. She felt it was her fault that he assaulted her. That she'd led him on. She's almost eighteen years old and she's never dated. She didn't go to her senior prom. She's never had any kind of normal, healthy relationship with someone her own age and that's his fault.

"Although it happened on her fourteenth birthday, I'd like to point out to the board that she was born on July nineteenth at eight-thirty in the evening. So in fact, when he raped her, technically, she wasn't even fourteen. She was thirteen. And he stole her virginity on a desk in a dirty garage. He robbed her of her innocence and she'll never be able to get that back."

Brenda was crying by the end. So was I. I didn't care what Brenda said, but I loved Wavy and I'd lost her, and I wasn't even allowed to say that. When the parole board head asked, "Mr. Barfoot, would you like to answer Mrs. Newling?" I couldn't even say, "I lost the best thing that ever happened to me." Wasn't that punishment enough?

I said, "I'm really sorry for what I did. I know that doesn't change it, but I really am sorry. I wish I could take it back."

Some days I was sorry. Other days I was only sorry Liam got himself killed. Another few days and Wavy woulda been my wife. Before my parole hearing the two things were about equal, the same number of days feeling each way, but when the door never opened and Wavy never walked in, the scale tipped. If she wouldn't come see me on the one day she could have, I'd done a terrible thing.

PART FIVE

I

RENEE

September 1987

When I walked into my dorm room sophomore year, there was a kid standing on one of the desks, sticking glow-in-the-dark stars on the ceiling. Her hair was in a spiky pixie cut and she wore 20-Eye Doc Martens. She looked about twelve or thirteen.

"Are you Wavy?" I said, thinking *please no please no.*

She nodded.

"I'm Renee."

She waved at me and put another star on the ceiling. Not in random patterns, but actual constellations. Had student housing really stuck me with a child prodigy roommate?

I went to complain to the RA, who said, "What kid?"

It turned out Wavy Quinn was eighteen. She wasn't a child; she was just really small.

And quiet. Oh my god was she quiet.

I talk a lot, so I admit it was several days before I realized Wavy hadn't spoken to me. Not one word. I only noticed because by the end of the first week she still hadn't asked me about Jill Carmody.

It's pathetic, but that was why I'd been looking forward to getting a new roommate. I was waiting for the moment she would ask about the memorial picture of Jill on my bulletin board.

"So, are you mad at me or something?" I said. "Did I do something to piss you off?"

Wavy was sitting at her desk studying. Four days into the semester and she was studying. She shook her head, without even looking up.

"I'm just missing my best friend. Next week is the anniversary of her death." For a second, I thought even that had failed, but Wavy closed her book, and looked over at my shrine to Jill.

"I'm sorry," she said.

I did my spiel. Jill was my best friend. Smart, pretty, All-State volleyball champion. Killed by a drunk driver our senior year. I cried. I'm ashamed when I look back at how I played that game, because I barely knew Jill. I once had a history class with her. When I went to college I made up this story about my best friend dying, because it made me more interesting.

My freshman roommate and I stayed up all night hashing it out, me crying, her comforting me. All Wavy did was give me a sympathetic look and say, "That's sad."

It made me feel like a poseur. I mean, I *was* a poseur, but I'd never felt like one before.

After Parents Weekend, I felt like even more of a fake. By then I was used to what I thought of as Wavy's *weirdness*. I never saw her eat, and in two months I'd heard her speak about a hundred words, mostly things like *yes, no, laundry, library,* and *shut up, I'm sleeping.* The Friday of Parents Weekend, I came back to our room after class and the door was open. I heard someone mutter, "You son of a bitch."

Wow. Another five words out of Wavy, one of them an expletive. Except it wasn't her. It was a middle-aged woman with short brown hair, shoving something back into Wavy's desk drawer.

"Hi. Are you Mrs. Quinn?" I said.

All the color drained out of her face as she closed the desk drawer.

"You must be Renee. I'm Brenda Newling. I'm Wavy's aunt."

"Oh, she's told me all about you . . . That's a joke. You know, because she doesn't talk much?"

Mrs. Newling didn't crack a smile.

"How is she? Really?"

"She's fine," I said. "I wish I could stick to a diet the way she does. Was there anything in particular you were looking for in her desk?"

"No. I just worry about her."

I put down my backpack, wondering what Wavy's aunt was looking for. Condoms? Drugs? Alcohol? Like we wouldn't have the sense to ditch that stuff before our parents visited. With my mom and dad coming on Saturday, there wasn't even aspirin in my desk drawer. I'd even tacked up the campus chapel schedule on my bulletin board.

"Wavy studies a lot," I said.

"She always has. Is she making friends?"

"Friends?" It came out sounding bitchy, but was this woman for real? Mrs. Newling sat on the edge of Wavy's bed with a pleading look on her face. Oh no. I was not doing the mother-roommate confidant routine, so I said, "She's friends with me. Does that count?"

Before Mrs. Newling could answer, Wavy came back to the room with her cousin Amy in tow. After the three of them left, I got down to some overdue snooping of my own. In the back of Wavy's desk drawer was a brass picture frame. I may be self-centered, but I'm not oblivious. I'd asked about the photo Wavy kept on her bulletin board: her little brother, grinning with his two front teeth out. I would have asked about this picture, too, but I'd never seen it.

The photo was of a big guy sitting on a motorcycle in front of an open garage door. He had pitch-black hair that was too long, and his shirt was off, showing tattoos on his arms and chest. He was mostly muscle, but he was carrying some extra weight around the middle. That's my problem, too. It was a sunny day and he was laughing, having fun with the person behind the camera. Who was he?

Right then, I realized I'd been going about things the wrong way. You make people interested in you by keeping secrets, not by passing them out like candy at Halloween.

When Wavy came back from giving her aunt a tour of campus, she sat down to study. On a Friday night. There was no other way, so I said, "When I got home, your aunt was snooping in your desk. Is there anything in there you wouldn't want her to find?"

Nailed it in one. Wavy jerked open the drawer and grabbed the picture. With a crazy pissed off look on her face, she polished the glass with the hem of her skirt.

I stepped closer, pretending I was seeing it for the first time.

"That's a cool motorcycle. Who is that?"

Considering how eager I was to blurt out my fake tragedy, I couldn't believe Wavy didn't want to tell me, but she looked me over, evaluating whether I could be trusted.

"I just wondered, because your aunt seemed pretty upset about finding it. So who is he?"

"Kellen. My fiancé."

She held her hand out so I could look at the ring on her finger. I'd noticed it before, but not thought anything about it.

"You're engaged?"

She nodded.

"Why haven't I met him? Where is he?"

"Prison."

"Are you serious? Why? What did he do?" I said.

"I need to study." Wavy put the picture away and sat down at her desk. Done talking. Poof. I was invisible. She couldn't hear me.

"So are your parents coming to visit this weekend?"

Apparently she could hear me ask that, because she shook her head.

"Why not?"

"They're dead."

"Oh my god, that's so sad. What happened?" That was what people always said when I told them about Jill Carmody.

"They were murdered," Wavy said.

A soon as the words left her mouth I knew I had to take down my fake-ass shrine to Jill. You can't milk a pretend tragedy when your roommate has a real one. It's too pathetic.

I'd told Mrs. Newling that Wavy and I were friends, but it wasn't true. We were just roommates, even after I knew her parents had been murdered and her fiancé was in prison for statutory rape. I saw it as some titillating soap opera.

Wavy and I didn't become friends until our second year together in the dormitory. That was the year I did something so stupid I was too embarrassed to tell anyone. With me, that's saying something. If it'll make people pay attention to me, I'm perfectly willing to humiliate myself.

I slept with my German professor, and not just once, but almost the whole fall semester. It wasn't like I did it for the grade, because I was good at German, but I was so flattered that he was attracted to me in all my chatty, airheaded, you know, fatness.

His wife eventually caught us and there was a huge scene, with the German professor saying, "It was a stupid fling. It meant nothing."

That was me—the stupid fling that meant nothing. The asshole wouldn't even give me a ride home. I cried the whole way, walking across campus from his house to the dorm.

I was an exhausted, hungry wreck. I sat at my desk, sobbing and rummaging in the drawers for anything to eat to make me feel better. Wavy got out of bed in her nightgown, took her student ID card off her desk and motioned for me to follow her. She could be so bossy.

Downstairs, the corridor to the cafeteria was closed at night by a big steel door, which Wavy unlocked in ten seconds of fiddling around with her ID card. She unlocked the door to the kitchen the same way. Inside it was dark except for the emergency exit signs glowing red like Hell, until Wavy opened the giant cooler. In the halo of its blue, misty light, she laid out food for me. Quart boxes of strawberries. A vat of chocolate pudding. An entire tray filled with little squares of lemon cake. A five-gallon bucket of rocky road ice cream and a can of whipped cream.

That's my idea of a friend.

2

WAVY

November 1988

Renee liked to take quizzes out of women's magazines. They were silly, but good for the same thing knitting was good for. The quizzes helped Renee empty her heart, and she filled it so quickly with the wrong things, it was no wonder she needed to empty it. Lying on our beds on Sunday nights, Renee read the quizzes out loud, and I wrote down our answers.

What's Your Romance Style? Renee was the *Bubbly Butterfly*. Flirty but fickle, quick to seal the deal and move on. My score didn't fit any of the categories, so Renee invented a new one: *Wallflower Nymphomaniac*.

"I don't even understand how you could get engaged without having some kind of conversation. Did he just say, 'Do you want to marry me?' and you nodded?"

I nodded and Renee laughed. I looked up at Kellen's picture, which traveled back and forth between my nightstand and my desk drawer, depending on my mood. When my heart hurt too much, I hid it in the drawer. I got out of bed and picked up the picture, intending to put it away.

Renee stopped laughing and took the picture out of my hand.

"That is one seriously beefy hunk of man," she said to tease me.

I snorted and let her put the picture back on my nightstand. Another night before I put it away.

What I missed most about Kellen wasn't riding behind him on the Panhead. I missed watching him eat. Renee ate in darting little bites and without chewing enough. The same way she filled her heart. Too quickly, and with too much talking and not enough feeling.

Our second year as roommates, I went home with Renee at Thanksgiving, and found out why she ate that way. The Dales lived in a neighborhood full of mansions with wrought iron gates and front lawns like public parks. They were rich, but they ate so desperately, they might as well have been stealing food from a stranger's garbage. Even I didn't eat like that anymore.

Mrs. Dale heaped everyone's plate up with turkey, potatoes, stuffing, and gravy. After that, pie and whipped cream. I admired the generosity of all that food. I managed to eat a few bites of turkey and some pieces of buttered dinner roll for the Dales. Small, precise things that I could put in my mouth with people watching. The mashed potatoes were yellow with butter, but they were too complicated. They reminded me of rules I was trying to forget.

"You're not hungry, little girl?" Renee's grandfather said.

"It's okay, Dad." Mrs. Dale gave me a big fake smile. Renee had warned her about me.

"So are you still dating the boy you told us about? Richard?" Mr. Dale said.

"No. Not anymore," Renee muttered. There was no boy. Richard was the German professor who made Renee's heart burn so hot.

"Why didn't you tell me you broke up with him, sweetie?" Mrs. Dale put another slice of pie on Renee's plate and suffocated it in whipped cream.

Renee glared at the pie and pushed a nervous bite of it into her mouth, frowning as she chewed.

"Well, what happened?" Mrs. Dale said.

"You know, Wavy's engaged," Renee said.

"Really? What does your fiancé do? Is he a student, too?" Mr. Dale raised an eyebrow at his wife.

"He's in prison," Renee said.

Mr. Dale almost choked on a bite of pie. In the quiet that came after, I prepared myself to nod, to make the answer I always made. *Whatever you want to be true, it is.*

Renee barked a nervous laugh and said, "God, I'm kidding. I'm kidding! Wavy doesn't have a fiancé in prison."

"Oh, Renee! You and your jokes," Mrs. Dale said. Everyone laughed. "So, are you still going to the gym? How's your diet going?"

The fork fell out of Renee's hand and clattered onto the plate next to the half-eaten pie. Renee looked like she was going to gag, but she swallowed. I felt so angry I had to dig my nails into my hands. All that delicious food spoiled in Renee's stomach. Mrs. Dale was as dangerous as Val. She might as well have put her fingers in Renee's mouth and pulled the pie out. She might as well have shouted, "Don't eat that! That's dirty!"

For Kellen's Christmas letter, I devoted a paragraph to mashed potatoes, and another to the reliable deliciousness of cold pizza. Renee and I always split a pizza on Sunday nights when the cafeteria was closed. She ate her half when it got there, hot enough to burn the roof of her mouth. I ate mine after it was cold, while Renee was asleep.

I wrote to Kellen about how I wanted to cook for him and watch him eat. He approached food the same way he approached kissing:

slowly, thoroughly, and with concentration. Watching him chew and swallow was lovely. Solid muscles working, sending food to fuel all of him.

Since all my letters came back unread, I mostly wrote them for myself. For the pleasure of writing, "Dear Kellen, Tonight was the first night I could see Orion, and I wished you were here, wearing his belt. If we could travel to Alpha Centauri and look at our stars, the Sun would be part of Cassiopeia. From Earth they seem so far apart, but from Alpha Centauri, our Sun is the sixth star, as close as the others."

Kellen and I were like that. At night I thought of him in his cell, two hundred and thirty-seven miles away, according to my car's odometer. Viewed from my bed, he was a distant constellation. From Alpha Centauri, we were twin stars, side by side.

3

RENEE

April 1989

Wavy wrote more letters than anyone I knew. Every week she wrote
to her cousins and her aunt. Twice a month to her high school Spanish
teacher. In Spanish. She also wrote letters to the lawyer who oversaw
her trust fund. Her typewriter was electric, but she pounded on it like
a manual when she wrote to her lawyer, because she and her aunt were
at war over Kellen's money.

Brenda used the trust to control Wavy, and that included forcing
her to live in the dorm. If we wanted to get an apartment together,
Wavy had to convince the trust's lawyer to overrule her aunt. That
required letters. Typing until I thought my ears would bleed from
the sound of it.

The winning letter mentioned "Mrs. Brenda Newling's callous

indifference to my personal comfort." That was how Wavy referred to her aunt in letters to the lawyer. Like she was a cruel stranger. It also made reference to her "special dietary needs and the difficulty of satisfying them in a communal living environment." Another way of saying she had an eating disorder. Mostly she ate in secret and stockpiled food, but when she was really stressed out, like during finals, she ate out of the trash. Like a raccoon. Special dietary needs: other people's discarded pizza.

Wavy also wrote letters to anybody she thought could help locate her brother. She had a huge file box of correspondence from former neighbors, her uncle's old parole officer, teachers at the last school Donal attended. Years of work, starting from the moment she lost him.

Then there were letters to Kellen. She spent days writing them in beautiful penmanship on expensive paper. They all came back opened, taped back closed, and stamped UNAUTHORIZED CORRESPONDENCE.

Those letters seemed so wonderfully tragic to me. Each one a message he would never get. A note in a bottle, bobbing on the ocean. Lost.

4

KELLEN

June 1989

My second parole hearing was almost exactly like the first, except Old Man Cutcheon was laid up in the hospital with a heart attack. The room was too warm and Brenda Newling showed up to read a statement about how I destroyed Wavy's life. I'd nearly convinced myself Brenda kept Wavy away from the last hearing, but now she was over eighteen. If she wanted to see me, she coulda come. She didn't.

When the letter came saying I'd been granted parole, I couldn't hardly believe it, but two weeks later I was free. Or as free as I could be in a halfway house with other ex-cons, checking in with my parole officer every week. I wasn't allowed to live near a school or a daycare, so when I moved out of the halfway house, it was hard to find a place to live. And I had to file my address with the sex offender registry.

Getting a job wasn't easy, either. Old Man Cutcheon ended up closing the shop, and it wasn't like anybody else in Powell was gonna hire me, so I got paroled to Wellburg, which was bigger than Garringer, almost a hundred-thousand people.

The quick lube place was in a strip mall on the other end of town from my apartment, but it had one thing going for it: the manager didn't give me a hard time about my conviction.

Gary was my age, maybe a little older, and bald. He looked at my application and said, "The felony, I have to ask."

"I dated this girl who was fourteen. Her aunt caught us fooling around. I pled guilty, so the girl wouldn't have to testify. I'm not proud of it, but I'm not a child molester. It was this one stupid thing I did. I don't drink. I don't do drugs. I won't steal stuff. I'll show up on time. I'm good with about anything mechanical."

I kept talking, waiting for the hammer to fall, but Gary rubbed his head and said, "Jeez, a felony charge seems like a raw deal if the girl was willing."

"I didn't rape her. I just messed up."

I got the job. It was more like a factory than a garage, just changing the oil in one car after another. Mindless work, which was good.

Four months after my parole, I was living in this damp basement apartment in an old boardinghouse. The sex offender registry, it was only supposed to protect other people from me. While I was living in that apartment, I had the tires on my truck slashed and somebody spray painted PEDAFILE on my door. I moved to a different building, farther away from the nearest school, but spitting distance from the train yard. For a few weeks, there was no trouble, but then somebody put up fliers to let people know a sex offender was living in the building.

A couple nights later, these two young guys stopped me coming up the alley.

"If you showed up dead, I bet the cops wouldn't even care," said the one who hung back behind his friend. He wore a gold cross on a chain.

"They might even give us a medal if we took care of you, you fucking scumbag." The braver one jabbed me in the chest with his finger. No big deal, but eventually somebody was gonna try something serious.

That's what was getting ready to happen the night I met Beth.

I closed the shop some nights, which was more money, but it meant I didn't get home until after dark. Being out wasn't all that different from being in prison. I had to be on my guard all the time, especially since somebody put up those fliers about me.

So I wasn't surprised when those same two douchebags came at me in the alley.

"I don't think you got the message last time," said the one with the cross necklace.

"We don't want your kind around here," the brave one said.

They musta figured two against one gave them an advantage. They didn't know I could take two guys easy when I was sober. Drunk, I could take ten. When they rushed me, I didn't demolish them like when I used to get in bar fights. I coulda put them in the hospital, but I didn't want to end up back in jail, so I took a lot more punches than I gave.

"Hey! Back off, you assholes! I already called the cops!" somebody yelled behind me.

That was enough to send the two douchebags running. As I was leaning up against the side of a trash Dumpster, trying to catch my breath, this woman walked up to me. She kept one hand in her purse, I'm guessing on a can of mace.

"Are you okay?" she said.

"Yeah, thanks. Did you really call the cops?"

"No, not really."

I figured she'd go back the way she'd come, but she stayed there.

"You sure you're alright?" she said.

"Yeah, thanks. Have a good night."

After that, I decided breaking parole was better than getting worked over. So the next day, I bought me a baseball bat.

A couple weeks later, going out to my truck, I passed the woman who saved my ass. I was gonna pretend I didn't recognize her, but she stopped me.

"Hey, Babe Ruth. You have any more trouble with those guys?" she said.

"Not yet."

"Looks like you're ready for them, though. I'm Beth." She held out her hand to shake. I guess she didn't see the fliers.

"Jesse Joe."

"You're a mechanic?" She looked at my uniform shirt with my name embroidered on one side and the name of the shop on the other. "Would you mind giving me a hand with my car?"

I did it, even though it made me twenty minutes late to work. After all, I owed her one. That was my answer when she offered to cook me dinner as payment for fixing her car. We were even.

"No, come over at about seven and I'll feed you."

A month after that first dinner, I moved in with Beth. It made money sense for us to share her apartment. The night I moved in was the first time we had sex. We both got about half drunk, she told me what to do, and I did it. A lot less awkward than me trying to figure out what to do. I guess it made both of us feel less lonely for a while.

Beth was older than me, maybe fifty. Old enough she had a couple grandkids and dyed her hair red to cover up gray. Like my ma, she had a big scar on her belly from a C-section. The one time I touched it, she slapped me.

I knew I'd waited too long to tell Beth about my conviction, because when I finally did, she gave me a dirty look and said, "What is wrong with men? What's the appeal of a fourteen-year-old? Are they just easier to control, is that it? They don't talk back?"

That was hard to take from a woman who bossed me around the same way she did her kids. Same woman who in the middle of sex once said to me, "Damn, Jesse, don't you wear deodorant? You fucking stink. Get off me."

"I loved her. I wanted to marry her," I said.

"Huh, but instead you just had sex with her."

"Do you want me to leave?" I wanted to leave. Sitting on the sofa with her curling her lip up at me was as bad as a parole hearing.

"I don't know. Let me think about it," Beth said.

I slept on the couch that night, and the next morning she said, "It was only the one time? You don't have a thing for little girls?"

"It was the one stupid mistake. She's the only girl I ever dated who was under eighteen." Wavy was the only girl I'd ever really dated.

"Okay," Beth said. I told her what I had to. The plea deal, the sentence, the no contact order, the sex offender registry. Whenever Beth's grandkids visited, I stayed at a motel. Other than that, she never brought it up, but I always felt like she was looking at me and thinking, "What is wrong with men?"

Being with Beth was mostly better than being alone, as long as I got drunk before we had sex. As long as she didn't say, "You need to lose some weight or you're gonna have a heart attack," while I was trying to enjoy my dinner.

Other times being alone woulda been better, especially at night, when I was lying awake next to Beth. She never put her head on my shoulder and definitely never pressed her face into my neck or my armpit and sniffed me. She didn't know the names of any constellations.

Wavy had said, "Stay," and I stayed. She'd said, "Hold on tight," and I held on tight. I knew I oughta let go of her. I couldn't.

5

RENEE

May 1990

In the fall of 1989, Wavy and I got our apartment, this funky place with two bedrooms, a giant bathroom, and a tiny living room. It was part of a big old house, so there were lots of funny things about it, like the pair of faucets that poked out of the living room ceiling right over the couch. We never figured out what they were for.

I spent most of the first year in our apartment trying to convince Wavy that we should throw a party. Wasn't that the point of having our own apartment, being able to do whatever we wanted? Obviously, Wavy wasn't a big fan of parties, but she finally agreed that we should invite some people over to celebrate the end of the spring semester. A little fun before finals week.

I expected I would have to invite all the guests, but Wavy invited some math nerd classmates, and a few co-workers from the hospital, where she did insurance billing. She also cooked a mountain of food, and went around the party encouraging people to eat. That was how she showed affection. When I went through some soul-crushing breakup, she made elaborate meals and desserts for me.

She invited a custodian from the hospital, Darrin, who turned out to be really nice. He said, "I was worried about coming, because she's never said a word to me. But the invitation said there was food, so I figured why not?"

I wondered if Wavy liked him. *Liked* him liked him. He had a baby face and he was nowhere near the size of Kellen, but he was big-boned, so maybe she was thinking of fattening him up.

Except I spent all night talking to Darrin and she didn't seem to mind, even when we went out on the second-floor balcony to smoke a joint and make out. The Bubbly Butterfly strikes again. When I came back inside, Wavy was talking to Joshua from my Philosophy class. I'd invited him because he had a totally hot George Michael five o'clock shadow, but there I was flirting with Darrin, and she was flirting with my date.

Okay, it would be a stretch to describe what Wavy was doing as flirting. She was sitting on the couch, almost close enough to touch Joshua, with a pleasant, "Yes, I'm listening" expression on her face.

I had this proud Mom feeling. She was coming out of her shell! She was blooming!

A couple of days after the party, I was sprawled out on the couch, kind of watching TV and kind of working on my final essay for my Women's Studies class. It was the last assignment I had to turn in for the semester.

Somebody knocked on the front door, and when I answered it, Joshua stood out in the hallway. Finals had cost me enough sleep I thought I might be hallucinating. Perfect five o'clock shadow. Dreamy blue eyes. Cologne. Crisp white button-down shirt.

"Hey, is Wavy home?" he said. He was real.

I stood there like an idiot for a minute, while my brain tried to come up with a reason that Joshua would be standing at our door asking for Wavy. How did he even know her name? Had she actually introduced herself to him at the party?

"Sure. Come in."

I parked him on the couch next to my essay-writing mess, and went to get Wavy. She was in her room, typing, with her Spanish dictionary open on the desk. I think she had a Spanish Lit essay and some kind of Quantum Mechanics final left.

"Joshua's here to see you," I said.

Wavy shook her head and waved her hands at me in baffled horror. Under stress, she still defaulted to silence. While I waited to see what she would do, I had several unkind thoughts. If Joshua was attracted to fragile, ethereal Wavy, I'd never stood a chance with him. The nicest things I've been called are *exuberant* and *earthy*. Anyway, I was the one who invited him to the party. Where did he get off coming around to see my roommate?

"Not here," she finally said.

"Too late. I already told him you were here."

I stood there, enjoying the panicked look on her face, until I really thought about Wavy for a minute. Kellen was serving a ten-year sentence. What was she going to do—wait for him? He was never going to be not too old for her, and now he was a convicted felon. She needed to move on with her life.

"What could it hurt to talk to Joshua?" I said. "He's nice. He's funny. Plus, he's gorgeous. Seriously, have you looked at him? He's like a pre-med Adonis."

Wavy made the face that meant, "Do you know what it's like being me?" I honestly didn't want to know, because she was pretty fucked up. I liked to play at tragedy, but she drank it out of her baby bottle.

"Just go talk to him," I said. "I'll save you if it gets too awkward."

Wavy stood up, and I thought she was going out to the living room. Instead, she walked over and shut her bedroom door in my face.

6

WAVY

I closed the door, but Renee opened it back up. We glared at each other until she said, "You're a coward, Wavonna Lee Quinn."

I didn't fall for that trick in sixth grade. I wasn't going to now. I flipped Renee off and tried to close the door, but she held her ground.

"Pot calling kettle," I said.

"That is such bullshit. Show me one time I was a coward."

Renee thought recklessness was the same thing as bravery. I stepped past her into the hall and walked toward the kitchen. She came after me.

In the front room, we passed Joshua, who looked confused. Not a Kellen kind of confused, where he always worried he'd misunderstood or done or said something wrong. Joshua thought someone else had made a mistake.

I stopped in front of the refrigerator and Renee was under such a head of steam that she bumped into my back. At the party, she had written Darrin's phone number on a napkin and said, "Yeah, I'd love to go out with you." The napkin was still stuck to the fridge. She hadn't called him. He wasn't her type. Not good-looking enough and probably too nice to break her heart.

"Are you seriously going to wait for a guy you haven't seen since you were fourteen? How do you know he even still wants you?" she said.

I jerked Darrin's number off the fridge, sending the magnet flying. When I pinned the napkin to Renee's chest with my forefinger, she made a surprised little O with her mouth.

"Coward," I said.

She smirked.

"Tell you what. I'll call him *after* you talk to Joshua. And you have to try, Wavy. You can't sit there like a stone until he gives up. You have to try or it doesn't count." Renee knew me. When I let go of the napkin, she stuck it back on the fridge.

I walked into the living room, feeling nauseated. Not because I was nervous about talking to Joshua, but because my stomach was full of the poison of Renee saying, "How do you know he even still wants you?" How did I know?

"Is something wrong?" Joshua stood up from the couch.

"No." I took a deep breath and sat down on one end of the couch. Joshua sat down in the middle. Closer than I liked.

"I was in the neighborhood and thought I'd drop by, since I didn't have your phone number," he said.

"Hey, I'm gonna go downstairs and get the mail," Renee said. On her way to the front door, she gave me a warning look.

"So, Wavy. I think your name is so cool. Kind of hippy, but not in a goofy way. Not like Moon Unit," Joshua said, once we were alone.

What was I supposed to say to that? *I'm glad you like my name. The man I love gave it to me.* That probably wasn't what Renee meant when she said I had to try. That was me being *impossible.* Aunt Brenda said that about me. *You're impossible!* Most days I was impossible. Like a unicorn.

"Short for Wavonna," I said.

"Really? I never met anyone with either of those names. So that's pretty cool. I mean, I have a pretty common name, so it's neat to meet people who have unusual names."

Joshua's teeth were perfect. He must have had braces. Renee talked about him like he was a statue. David standing naked in a museum in Italy. I thought he was more like a mannequin in a department store. He smelled like a mannequin, too. Soap, deodorant, cologne, mouthwash. How was I supposed to tell what *he* smelled like under all of that?

"So, what's your major?" he said.

"Astrophysics." I didn't want him to panic, but as soon as I said it, his eyes got bigger.

"Oh, um, wow. So, uh, what do you do with a degree in astrophysics?"

"Become an astrophysicist."

Joshua stared at me. I was being impossible again, saying things he didn't know how to respond to. *Serial conversation killer,* Renee called me.

When she came back with the mail, I expected her to give me an accusatory look, since Joshua and I were sitting there in silence. Instead, she slammed the front door and practically ran across the room to the kitchen.

"Wavy, will you come in here?" she called.

7

RENEE

I went down to get the mail to give Joshua and Wavy a chance to talk in private. She did need to get on with her life. Then I saw what was in the mailbox: a pizza coupon flier and one of those familiar, heartbreaking envelopes. A fancy envelope, addressed to Jesse Joe Barfoot, Jr. Inmate #451197. Stamped UNAUTHORIZED CORRESPONDENCE in big red letters. Except this one wasn't. This envelope had a big red stamp that said RELEASED.

A less romantic person might have taken a more measured approach. Me, I thought, *Screw moving on. This is true love*! Clutching the mail in one hand, and my boobs in the other, I ran up both flights of stairs.

I put the envelope down in the middle of the kitchen table, and when Wavy walked in, I was staring at it in disbelief. She picked up the letter and her hands started to shake. I can only imagine what was going on inside her head, because my brain was lit up like the Vegas strip.

"Does that mean he's been paroled? Don't they have to notify you? If he's out, why hasn't he come to see you?" I said.

Oh, right. If he hadn't been getting her letters, he wouldn't know our address. It wasn't like he could drop by her aunt's house and say, "Hey, where's Wavy?"

How was he going to find her?

He wasn't. We were going to find him. At last, I wasn't just a fat college girl watching a soap opera. I was part of the drama. I was going to rewrite the third act and change it from tragedy to happily ever after.

While Wavy sat there in shock, the envelope pressed between both her hands, I picked up the phone and started making calls, all of them long distance and out of state. I wondered what Mrs. Brenda Newling would say when Wavy's phone bill hit triple digits.

"Hey, what's up?" Joshua said. He stood in the doorway, looking unbelievably sexy.

"Give us a couple minutes, okay?" I was on hold with someone at the office where they kept the records for the state's sex offender registry, a thing I hadn't even known existed until somebody at the Department of Corrections transferred me there.

"Is she okay?" He was looking at Wavy, who seemed a little shaky.

"She's had some news—"

"Ma'am?" Someone came back on the other end of the phone line. "Do you have the offender's full legal name?"

"Jesse Joe Barfoot, Jr. I don't know what the process is—"

"One moment, please."

Wavy looked at me expectantly.

The woman came back on the line and read me a street address, apartment number, and city. Wellburg, which was across the state line, less than three hours away. I wrote it down on the back of the pizza flier, and as soon as Wavy saw it, she jumped up from the table and brushed past Joshua in the doorway. I knew exactly where she was going: to get ready for her reunion with Kellen.

"So, do you think I have a chance with Wavy?" Joshua shot me a panty-melting grin.

For a few seconds, a whole scenario played out in my mind. After I broke the bad news to him about Wavy's fiancé being paroled, I would usher him into my bedroom. Wavy could drive herself to Wellburg. Meanwhile, I would comfort Joshua, listening sympathetically, while I arranged myself on my bed in a flattering pose. I would make him feel sexy and smart and funny.

That's exactly what I was imagining. I would get him in my room and seduce him, thereby accomplishing the whole point of me inviting him to the party in the first place. He really was amazingly good-looking. It wouldn't be a hardship to fall into bed with him, but what kind of lies would I have to tell myself to pretend I wasn't a second choice rebound?

"The thing is," I said. "Wavy has a lot of baggage. Like a nine-piece matched set of hard-sided Samsonite. The girl is so far—"

For the first time in my life, I stopped. It wasn't my story to tell.

"What? Help me here," Joshua said. Even though I wasn't going to kiss his booboo and make it better, I yanked the Band-Aid off.

"Wavy's engaged. She's going to see her fiancé as soon as she gets out of the shower."

I would have needed new clothes and hours to get ready. Wavy showered, fluffed her wispy hair, and put on her favorite dress. It was gray with thin white stripes in it, worn to limp softness. She hadn't seen him in almost seven years and that's what she was wearing.

On the drive, we made a plan. Or I made a plan anyway. I would drop Wavy off at Kellen's house, and then I would go to the library at Wellburg College and work on my Women's Studies essay. That way my evening wouldn't be a total waste, and Wavy could check in with me before I drove home.

By the time we got to Wellburg, it was late afternoon and it had started to rain. We circled Kellen's address and then parked half a block back, where we could see the front door to the apartment building, which was a run-down brick tenement. It faced onto what was basically an alley, with garbage Dumpsters on the sidewalks.

Would Wavy want to live with him in that dismal place? It hadn't occurred to me that I was orchestrating the end of us being roommates. I'd been going along thinking I was Shakespeare, but I'd written myself out of the play. I was staring out at the rain, feeling sorry for myself, when this big old truck drove past and parked at the end of the block.

"Nineteen sixty-nine Ford F-250," Wavy said. She was weird that way. She always knew the years of cars. The man who got out of the truck wore blue work pants and a blue and white striped shirt, like a uniform. Reaching back into the truck cab, he pulled out a baseball bat. He ducked his head against the rain, but he didn't run for cover. Walking up the block slowly, he looked around, but he didn't see us watching him.

8

WAVY

Kellen had lost weight. Of course, they hadn't fed him well in prison, but I could make all his favorite foods and fix that. Seeing him free, my heart jumped in my chest. Not empty, not burning. Alive.

"Oh my God, that's him? That's him," Renee said. "What are you going to do?"

I opened the car door, but she grabbed the sleeve of my raincoat.

"Wait. Should I wait for you? What should I do?"

"I don't know." My heart was moving too far ahead to think about that.

"Well, I'll be at the library. Just let me know everything's okay."

Kellen was already through the apartment building door. I ran across the street, splashing through puddles, and my hand shook on the door handle. I was all the things I'd almost forgotten how to be—nervous, excited, happy. I wanted to run up the stairs, but my legs could only manage one step at a time.

There was no doorbell, no peephole.

I knocked and Kellen answered.

Water dripped out of his starling-wing hair. Embroidered over the pocket of his wet uniform shirt: Jesse Joe. Three buttons undone, showing the tops of the arrows and the calumet on his chest.

"Wavy," he said.

I didn't know what to say. I hadn't thought about that at all. Did I have to say anything? I never had before. I took a step forward, wanting to be in the same room with him. To breathe his air. His eyes weren't soft. They were hot and frightened. He was afraid of me. I was afraid of me.

Sunlight broke through the clouds and rain stopped pounding against the windows. Kellen's breath hitched. Anything could happen. Everything. I pressed against him, smelling him. His sweat.

"Wavy, you can't be here."

I tried to will him to kiss me, the way I used to, but he frowned down at me with his mouth closed. I turned my back on him, and a spiraling hot thing in my chest said, *Leave*. Behind me was the kitchen table. Grabbing the closest chair, I carried it to Kellen and stepped up. Then I was the Giant, towering over him. I took his face in my hands the way he did on the morning I knew he loved me. I lifted his mouth to mine. Would he resist? No.

He opened his lips and I knew Val had been right. People could get into you that way. I was creeping into Kellen. He wanted me to. He kissed me, but he wouldn't touch me, so I took off the raincoat. I unbuttoned the dress myself and dropped it to my feet. The slip, all slippery silk, whispered off me. The panties, which I wanted him to ease down the way he had the first time. The last time. This time my hands did it. My hands for his hands.

Freeing his mouth for a moment, I looked into his eyes, to see if he would come to me.

"Kellen," I said.

"Are you real?"

I nodded. His hands came to rest on my hips, and he lifted me off the chair. I wrapped my legs around him and he carried me to the bedroom. I'd always imagined it on the kitchen table, or the desk at the garage, but a bed was good, too. Everything I needed was there. His shirt off quick, his arms cool with rain and his chest sticky with sweat. I ran my hands over him and found a long puckered scar that split the skin over his ribs. Something they had done to him in prison.

I was eager to rub my tits against his, to show him mine were finally bigger. His hands were all over me. My hands everywhere else. His mouth laughing, even while he tried to kiss every part of me.

"Goddamn, these are *some* boots. How do you get 'em off?" he said.

"Slowly."

He gave up on unlacing when I slid my feet over his shoulders.

His tongue felt good, going into where I was already wet for him. I'd been wet there for him for seven years. His tongue was good but not enough. Pulling him to me, I found less belly to slip my hand past to reach his belt.

"Orion." The same buckle, the one I knew how to open, and he was in my hand. We could go fast now. He shoved his pants down only as far as we needed. That was how much he wanted me, he wasn't even going to take his boots off.

He was so heavy my breath caught in my chest. That was pleasure, being pinned under him, where the air was thin. His cock was as hot as I remembered pressed between my legs.

We could move time. Go back to that day. Undo seven years. I opened my eyes, to let him into me everywhere.

That first moment, when he pushed against me, hardness against softness, was wonderful. The next moment, when he pushed into me, burning pressure and a tearing pain. It hurt more than I thought it would. Kellen was in me everywhere. Inside my nerves. He moaned against my ear.

"Oh, Wavy. I love you all the way."

I pressed my face into his neck and held on, not breathing, thinking the pain would stop, the way it had when he put his fingers into me. I waited for it to go to burning pleasure, because it couldn't go on being unbearable. But it did. The pain cauterized my throat. I thought I might choke until the seal broke open, let out the sob I'd been keeping in.

Kellen stopped. I knew he was looking at me, but I couldn't look back.

"Are you okay?" he said.

I nodded but the tears I'd been holding back escaped. He jerked out of me, as painful as the going in.

"Oh, Jesus, Wavy. You waited for me?"

"Who else?" I said.

"Oh, shit, I'm sorry. I didn't think you'd wait for me. I never thought—after all that mess, I never thought you'd want me. You didn't come to my parole hearings, and I figured I'd ruined everything."

He was pulling away from me, but I dug in, my nails into his shoulders, my heels into his thighs.

"Hold on tight. Don't let go." I learned that from him.

"I'm hurting you, though. And we shouldn't be doing this. You don't under—"

"Yes." I held him tighter, reached between us, found him sticky and still hard. He groaned when I pressed him into me. I only had to guide him there and he stopped arguing. My stomach clenched and my legs shook when he sank into me. Kellen stopped again.

I clawed at his back.

"I don't want to hurt you," he said.

"All the way."

He started again, slowly, and as much as it hurt, I could see how eventually it would stop hurting. The next time and the time after. Given enough time there would be burning pleasure where my softness and his hardness met.

In the end he was pounding into me, panting, saying my name. I was lying on the tracks under a train I was in love with. To not cry, I sank my teeth into his chest. I was a vampire and he had invited me in. He moaned and for a moment all of his weight was on me. Between my legs was an expanse of pain, but my lungs burned with pleasure, breathing him in.

After, his eyes were full of me. I'd imagined he would have so many things to say, but he only lay beside me and looked at me. He was thinking of other ways for me to be his. The ring was on my finger, and I waited for him to see it and remember the one way I already belonged to him.

"Wavy, what are we doing? What am I supposed to do?"

"You love me?" Hearing him say it was like stolen food, to stuff in my mouth when no one was looking. If he said it a hundred times, I would ask him to say it again.

"I love you. I love you with my whole heart." He took my hand, pressed it to his chest, and saw the ring.

The front door opened—click, swoosh—and filled his eyes with other things than me. Anxiety. Obligation. Guilt.

"Jesse? Are you h—" A woman's voice, then a puff of air, surprise. I hadn't just invaded Kellen. I'd invaded his home. As the woman crossed the kitchen floor, he stood and pulled up his pants. I stayed where he left me on the bed. We were that way when the woman walked in.

"I'm sorry, Beth." Kellen fastened his pants while she watched. Orion's belt buckled again. Always someone to walk in on us.

"Do you love her?" I said.

He didn't make me wait for the answer: "No."

Beth's mouth twisted, angry and hurt, but she didn't say, "Liar."

Kellen loved me. Only me. I stood up naked in my boots, some-thing hot running down the inside of my leg. I wasn't embarrassed. I didn't care what anyone but Kellen thought.

"Who the hell are you?" Beth said.

"Wavy." As soon as I said it, I knew he hadn't told the woman about me. She didn't even know who I was.

9

KELLEN

The way her bare shoulders stiffened, I knew what it looked like. There I was living with some woman who didn't even know about Wavy. All I'd meant to do was protect her. It didn't seem fair to say her name to anybody.

"You fucking pedophile," Beth said. "You said it was a mistake. One time, you piece of shit. That's what gets you off? Little girls? I ought to call the cops. I swear. How old is she?"

"Twenty-one," Wavy said.

In a couple months she would be, but seeing her naked in broad daylight for only the second time, I didn't blame Beth for thinking the worst. Wavy was almost as small as she'd been at thirteen. She was all long legs and narrow in the hips. Her tits were perfect, but not even big enough to fill my mouth, let alone my hands. She hadn't hardly grown at all. Did it make me a pervert that I still thought she was the most beautiful thing I'd ever seen? Did it make me less of a pervert that twenty and thirteen looked the same on her? When I had her in my arms, none of that mattered.

"Like hell you're twenty-one," Beth sneered. "Let me give you some advice, little girl. This is his thing. Whatever he told you, he doesn't *love* you. He just wants your little hairless twat."

Wavy laughed. I almost did, too, except Beth glared hard enough to stop me.

"This is her. Wavy's the girl I went up for," I said.

"You did six years for her? God, how old *was* she, you creep? She doesn't look old enough to get a driver's license *now*. You're so goddamn stupid, Jesse. You want to ruin your life, go ahead, but don't think I'll lie to your parole officer for you. Get out."

Beth went back into the kitchen and I pulled my duffel bag out of the closet and shoved clothes into it, with Wavy watching me.

"Get dressed, sweetheart," I said.

"Yeah, get dressed you crazy little bitch." Beth walked back into the bedroom and tossed Wavy's clothes on the bed. "Goddamn, my new sheets, too."

Wavy started putting on her clothes, but she did it like a backwards strip show, smiling at me while she pulled her panties up.

"No cops this time," she said.

I couldn't even manage a smile to answer that, because maybe the cops weren't going to show up, but Beth stood there in the doorway, glaring at us.

"Get out. And I want your key," she said.

While Wavy buttoned up her dress, I took the apartment key off my ring. After I gave it to Beth, Wavy and I went down the stairs and out into the street.

"Where's your car parked?" I said.

"My roommate dropped me off." Her voice just about killed me. Grown up, but still quiet. And happy, the way I'd dreamed about.

When she took my hand, I let her. We walked down the block to my truck, swinging our hands between us. She smiled at me, sure everything was going to be okay, when I knew it wasn't. I held her hand until I had to let go to toss my duffel in the back and open the door for her.

"Nineteen sixty-nine," she said as she stepped up on the running board. I didn't have no secrets from her. She knew exactly why I was driving that truck. For love. For good luck. Because that was the year she was born.

Sitting in the truck, holding her hand again, I thought about all the things I wanted to tell her. I'd spent all those years in a cell thinking about talking to her, but now there was only one thing I needed to say to her.

"Wavy, I can't see you. I'm breaking the conditions of my parole right now, just sitting next to you, talking to you. I can't have any contact with you."

She looked at me hard, not even asking a question. Pissed off and hurt, and I didn't blame her. I deserved that look, but she could be as mad at me as she wanted. It didn't change a damn thing.

"Tell me where to take you and I'll drop you off and—and that has to be that. I can't see you again. Do you understand?"

After that she wouldn't look at me and I couldn't look away. Probably it'd be the last time I got to see her. I'd thought that before, when I was arrested, so seeing her one more time was a gift. I woulda counted the last hour as a gift, too, except this was how it was gonna end. It shoulda been our wedding night, and instead it was just good-bye. She sat up straight, her shoulders square, looking out the windshield. Her hair was cut short, with little curls teasing at her bare neck. Like that birthday night when she'd worn it up.

"My deposition," she said.

"Yeah, I read your deposition. You were brave to do that. To keep me from getting framed for something a lot worse. They really wanted to pin your mama's murder on me." I sometimes wondered if it coulda gone differently. Maybe I coulda pled to a lesser charge, if she'd told the truth.

"It was a message to say I love you." She looked at me and there were tears running down her cheeks. I had to look away.

"My parole says no contact. I can't see you, talk to you, touch you. I'm not supposed to be within a hundred feet of you."

"You were *in* me."

I was skidding on loose gravel, about to wreck my life again. Wreck hers again.

"Wavy, you know I love you—"

"Beth."

"No. Beth ain't nobody to me. We can't do this. I can't do this. I'm always gonna love you, but they won't ever let me have contact with you, because of what I did to you."

For once I was all out of words and that was scary as hell. Wavy nodded. I thought she was ready to say something, but she opened the door and stepped out. I scrambled outta the cab and stopped her before she crossed the street.

"Let me take you home," I said. It was dangerous, but I thought I could know where she lived and be strong enough not to go see her.

She caught my wrist and turned my arm to where there was blank space on the inside. I'd always planned to get her name tattooed there after we got married. Standing there in the street with traffic going by, she reached into her purse and took out a Magic Marker.

She wrote three numbers on my arm, the first part of a phone number.

"Do you remember that, Wavy? Me writing on your arm when I wrecked the bike?" Stupid thing to ask. After all that time, she'd come there and still wanted me. She remembered everything. Before she could write the rest of the number, I pulled away from her. The marker left a long black stripe down my arm.

"I can't," I said. "You know I can't. My parole says no contact."

She let go of me and crossed the street. Didn't even put her marker away, just tossed it on the ground and kept walking. She didn't stop when I called her name, so I went after her and caught her by the arm.

"No, you cannot walk around down here. It's not safe. This neighborhood is full of ex-cons and sex offenders. Folks worse than me."

She jerked her arm away from me, but I grabbed her wrist tight enough she couldn't get loose. For a full minute, we glared at each other, her trying to pull her arm back and me squeezing it hard enough to feel the bones in her wrist.

"I'm not messing around, Wavy. Now tell me where to take you."

"The college library," she said.

It was a fifteen-minute drive over to the university, but we didn't say a word on the way there. As soon as I came to a stop in the library parking lot, Wavy opened the door and swung her legs out.

"Wait. Wait," I said.

With one foot on the ground, one foot on the running board, she looked back at me.

"I'm sorry. I love you—"

Wavy slammed the door right in the middle of what I was trying to say. Maybe I hadn't seen her in seven years, but I still understood her. She might as well have written LIAR on the dash of my truck.

Seeing her walk across the parking lot toward the library's front doors, I knew it had to be over, but I couldn't believe that was how it ended. I wanted to take back everything I'd said, more than I wanted anything else. Being with Wavy would mean going back to prison, because her aunt would find out eventually, but I wondered how long we could have together before I got caught. Long enough to make another four years bearable? Or just long enough to mess up her life again?

10

RENEE

I went to the library with the best intentions, but by the time I got there, the rain had stopped and the sun had come out. The sun and half-a-dozen shirtless college guys playing Frisbee in the grass by the library steps. Instead of going inside, I sat outside and read one of my sources for my essay.

That's what I was doing when Wavy walked up. I let the book on my lap fall closed and lost my place.

"What happened?" I said.

"He finally fucked me."

Finally. Finally? Wavy the chronic masturbator was a virgin? All along I assumed they'd done it, maybe a lot, before they got caught. I'd been so eager to see it as this beautiful romance, that I was willing to overlook Kellen having sex with little thirteen-year-old Wavy, but there she stood, freshly deflowered and looking devastated. Her eyes were red from crying, and she was holding her left arm across her body like it hurt. Her wrist looked swollen.

"Well, looks like he did a bang-up job of it," I said to make her laugh, but her face was empty. "Why are you here? Where's Kellen?"

"Gone. It's over." She used the heel of her right hand to wipe her eyes. I wished I could put my arm around her shoulders and make her feel safe. Seeing her that way was awful.

"Over? What do you mean it's over? I know you love him, but what kind of asshole screws you and then dumps you? Fuck him. You don't need him." I stuffed my book into my bag and stood up to lead Wavy to my car.

I unlocked the passenger's side first so Wavy could get in, but as I was walking around to the driver's side, Kellen's truck rolled to a stop behind my car and boxed it in. He got out of the cab and came around the end of it. Up close, he was a lot bigger than I expected. Not as fat, but taller and more muscular. Built like a bulldozer. Instead of the shaggy hair and the '70s sideburns, he had a crew cut. That picture on Wavy's nightstand had frozen him in my mind at my age, but he was at least thirty.

Over, my ass. Wavy jumped out of the car and ran to him. Hugging and kissing commenced. As much as I wanted to eavesdrop, I got in the car and settled for watching them in the rearview mirror.

Seeing them together as the sun went down and the stars came out, my heart did a little leap of joy. I wanted a fairy tale ending for Wavy, because if she could find happiness, there would be hope for me, too.

II

WAVY

Kellen's hands were shaking, so I squeezed them harder in mine, to tell him it was okay. We hadn't said anything, but he was there.

"The Evening Star." That was the first thing he said. I looked up at it, felt him watching me. Not just watching me, but drinking me up. "You told me before, but I forgot. It's not really a star, is it? It's one of the planets, right?"

"Venus," I said.

"Where I am there's too much light from the city to see the stars. I want to go out and look at the stars with you. I missed that so much. I missed you."

He kissed me before I could say, "Cassiopeia."

When he let me breathe again, I said, "Come home with me. Renee and I have an apartment. Down in Norman."

He closed his eyes, squeezed them tight.

"I can't. It's across state lines. I can't leave the state without my parole officer's say-so."

I kissed him again, thinking we had time to sort that stuff out. We had all the time in the world, now that he was free. It turned out we had too much time. Only a few seconds for me to lift my hand, longing to remind him, to have him kiss my ring the way he used to. A few seconds more for Kellen's eyes to go wet, for his lip to tremble. He didn't kiss the ring. He let go of me and, from the way he leaned against the side of the truck, I knew he was having a hard time standing up. I leaned my head into his chest and held on. Held him up.

"Oh, goddamnit. I can't be with you. If I break parole, they'll send me back to do the rest of my sentence. If I could be with you after, I'd do those four years in a heartbeat. But I go back, and they'll parole me with the same conditions.

"And it's not just my parole. You know, I ruined my whole life. I'm gonna be on the sex offender registry for the next fifteen years. Have to put my conviction on every job application I fill out. Have to ask every landlord how far is the nearest school."

"I was selfish to wish for you," I said. All I'd ever thought about was how much I wanted him. Needed him. I never thought of what it would mean for him.

"You're not selfish, but you're better off without me. I made nothing but trouble for you."

I shook my head against his chest.

"It's true. You were too young and I messed things up for you. It's like your aunt said, you weren't even fourteen really when I raped you."

I reached up and clamped my hand over his mouth hard enough that I felt his teeth through his lips. It wasn't nice, and I didn't care. I wanted to shove those words back down his throat. He pulled my hand away, and his soft eyes said everything was broken. I'd broken him.

"You didn't rape me," I said.

"Okay. Okay, but listen to me. I already ruined my life. I don't want to ruin yours."

"It's not ruined."

I wanted that to be true, but I couldn't imagine what six years in prison would be like. Four years I'd been Aunt Brenda's prisoner, but even when I promised not to sneak out, I went on doing it. That's why it's called sneaking. Kellen had spent six years in a cell. Six years among people who hurt him. Six years without the stars. Looking into his eyes, I knew he would stay with me. He was waiting for me to give him the look that meant *stay*. He wanted me to say, "Stay."

It had been so long since I had the ring resized that I had to spit on my finger to get it off. When it came loose, I put it in his hand.

"No more prison. You're free," I said.

12

RENEE

When Wavy opened the passenger door, I thought she was coming to tell me what she and Kellen were doing. Instead, she got in the car and slammed the door.

"What's up?" I said. She didn't say a word, just sat there in the dark. "Are we leaving?"

"Yes." Her voice was raw from crying. Had he dumped her twice in one day?

I started the car and put it in reverse, but Kellen's truck was still behind me. Jackass. I waited for him to move, but he wasn't even in the cab. I couldn't see him at all.

"Will you tell him to move his truck?" I said.

"I can't." First time I ever heard Wavy admit she couldn't do something.

ALL THE UGLY AND WONDERFUL THINGS   357

"Fine. I will."

I put the car in park and got out. Whatever I thought I was going to find when I walked around the truck, it wasn't Kellen down on his knees. I couldn't tell if he was crying or heaving. Had she gotten her revenge? Dumped him back? I know if I'd been in Wavy's shoes, I would have been salting the earth of that relationship.

"Um, could you move so I can back out?"

He made this choking noise, but he braced a hand against the side of his truck and got to his feet. I could only guess what she'd said to him, because he looked destroyed. It took him a while, but he wiped his face on his shirt sleeve and sort of pulled himself together.

"You her roommate?" he said.

"Yes."

I swear, for a second, I thought he wanted to shake my hand, but he was trying to give me something. When I didn't reach for it, he opened his hand. It was her engagement ring. Oh, yes, she'd dumped him.

"Will you give her this?" he said.

"No offense, but no. You give it to her if you want her to have it." No way was I getting in the middle of that.

He nodded and walked around to the passenger side of my car. Wavy wasn't having any of it. He tried to open her door, but it was locked.

"Goddamnit, Wavy. Please, will you listen to me?" He went on talking in this low, pleading voice, but the only word I could make out was her name.

I couldn't hear whether she answered him, but if she did, it wasn't nice. He came stomping back to the truck and jerked open the driver side door. For about two seconds, I was relieved, thinking he was going to leave. Then he slammed the door closed and kicked it.

The violence of it shocked a squeak out of me.

He took two steps toward me and I took two steps back. I was about to panic when the Frisbee guys came running toward us.

"Hey, is everything okay?" the tallest one said.

"Please, will you just take it?" Kellen said.

"I don't think she wants whatever it is you want to give her."

"Why don't you just walk away, pal?" another Frisbee guy said.

"Why don't you fuck off?" Kellen said.

The Frisbee guys had a conference, and one of them took off running toward the library.

When Kellen took a step toward me, the tall guy said, "Dude, my buddy is going to get campus security."

"I'm just trying to give her this." Kellen held the ring up so the Frisbee guys could see it.

"I don't care, dude. You need to go."

There was shouting up on the library steps and then several people started across the lawn toward us.

"Fucking fuck." Kellen turned around and kicked his door again, twice, hard enough to leave a dent the size of his enormous boot.

"Okay, look," I said.

At that point, I was willing to take the ring, just to make Kellen go away, because he was scaring the shit out of me. Before I could, Wavy got out of my car and came around the truck to Kellen's side.

"He's leaving," Wavy said to the Frisbee guys.

"I'm not leaving," Kellen said.

"You can't get arrested." She held out her hand, and he put the ring in it, folding her fingers over it. He held her hand like that until she pulled it back.

Kellen and I both seemed to think there would be something more, but Wavy walked away and got back in my car. The Frisbee guy came running up and a few steps behind him was a campus cop.

"Sir, why don't you get in your car, and let this lady back out?" the cop said.

Finally, Kellen did.

For part of the drive out of town, we were behind his truck, but when I turned for the highway, he went on straight. I let out a long sigh.

"I know you love him, but what a psycho," I said. "Did he used to do that kind of thing? Kicking in the door like that?"

"Sometimes," Wavy said. She sounded exhausted.

"And your wrist? Did he do that, too? Rough you up?"

"He didn't mean to."

"Right. They never mean to, do they?" I said.

We passed under the last row of streetlights before the highway went to four lanes. I looked over at Wavy, who still had her hand in a fist around the ring.

"Seriously. He's a crazy fucking asshole."

"Don't, Renee." The first time she'd ever said my name.

Because she asked, I didn't say the rest of what I thought, but my rose-colored glasses had been shattered. Kellen wasn't the love of her life. He was a dumb brute with greasy hands and a cheap haircut. A guy with no education and a bad temper. Big enough to kick a dent in the side of his truck, and stupid enough to do it, too.

After almost an hour of total silence, Wavy started making this soft hiccupping noise that I realized was her crying. She had been leaning her head against the window, but she slowly folded over until her head was resting on her knees.

The crying kept getting louder and louder, until it was hard to listen to. You can look up the word *keening* in the dictionary, but you don't know what it means until you hear somebody having her heart ripped out. It went on and on. I was terrified. I didn't think you could cry like that without hurting yourself. I drove faster, ten, then fifteen miles over the speed limit. Then I did something I never imagined doing: I reached out and laid my hand on Wavy's back. I wanted to comfort her, and myself, but feeling her whole body shake made me feel worse, so I put my hand back on the steering wheel.

The last ten miles, I cried, too. I went all-in for histrionic romance crap, but I'd never loved any guy the way she loved him. My heart-breaks lasted a month. I'd eat too much and mope around crying, but I always found a new guy. I was as fickle as those *Cosmo* quizzes said I was. I couldn't imagine being with one guy as long as she'd been with him. I couldn't imagine what it would be like losing him.

When I pulled into the driveway at our apartment, I was almost hysterical. I tried to get her out of the car, but she curled up into a ball and totally ignored me. Even as small as she was, there was no way I could carry her up to our apartment.

For half a second, I thought about driving on to her aunt's house, but just for half a second. That would be traitorous, taking her to a woman she didn't even trust to look at a picture of Kellen.

I left Wavy in the car and ran up to the apartment, trying to think of who I could call to help. Her cousin Amy, but she was at the University of Nebraska. Even if she left right then, she wouldn't be there until the morning, and it was finals week. I was standing in the kitchen, holding the phone and crying, trying to think of who to call, when I saw the napkin with Darrin's phone number. I dialed and he answered. I don't think I made any sense, but when I stopped blubbering, he said, "I can be there in ten minutes."

It was more like five minutes before he rolled into the parking lot in an open Jeep. Watching him jog toward me, where I stood next to my car, I could tell I'd gotten him out of bed. He was wearing sweat-pants, a Marine Corps T-shirt, and tennis shoes with no socks. For a while, we stood there, looking at Wavy curled up in the front seat.

"Are you sure she doesn't need to go to the hospital?" he said.

"She's not sick. She just got her heart broken."

Wavy was so far gone, she didn't even care that Darrin picked her up and carried her to our apartment. He laid her down on her neatly made, virginal twin bed, and she went on sobbing, that god-forsaken ring clutched in her hand.

We left her there and went into the kitchen, where Darrin made us both giant glasses of rum and coke. While we drank, I told him the whole awful thing as far as I knew it. Mostly because I couldn't stand being alone with knowing it, but also because Darrin was a good listener. We had another drink and then another, and talked about everything. My nightmare year in a sorority. His eight years in the Marines. How my father thought I was too stupid to get anything but an MRS degree. How his father was in prison when he was a kid. That was why Darrin joined the Marines right out of high school.

When we went to check on Wavy later, she'd finally worn herself out crying. She was asleep with her arm flung out, the ring next to her hand. I turned off the light and closed the door, but then Darrin and I were standing in the hallway outside my open bedroom door.

"Do you want to stay?" I said.

"I could stay on the couch if you think you'll need me."

"Maybe I need you in here." I felt so stupid, because he looked down, kind of embarrassed. Had I completely misinterpreted his interest in me?

"It's not that I don't want to, because I really would, but in my book this falls under the heading of taking advantage," he said.

He slept on the couch, in case I needed him. I thought about going out to the living room, and seducing him in the safety of darkness. All I did was think about it, though, before I fell asleep.

I woke up to the sound of typing. At first I assumed it must be morning, because what kind of crazy person types a letter in the wee, dark hours, but it was only four o'clock. Under normal circumstances, I would have yelled at Wavy, but considering everything that had happened, I let it go.

Just as I was starting to get used to the peckitty-peck of Wavy typing, this enormous crash brought me bolt upright in bed.

"Wavy?" I shouted, but she didn't answer.

I heard a man's voice in the living room, so I jumped out of bed and ran out there. Darrin stood at our open front door in his bare feet. He pointed out into the hall.

"Wavy just—uh—she came through here carrying a typewriter. I asked if she was—"

Another crash came from the stairwell.

We ran out in the hallway, and I yelled Wavy's name, but she didn't answer. Unless the sound of metal meeting wood that echoed up the stairs was her response. I hurried down the stairs with Darrin right behind me.

Wavy's typewriter was lying at the foot of the stairs, broken into pieces. She stood over it, and right as I got to her, she kicked it and sent the biggest chunk of it skidding across the floor.

"Holy shit," I said. "Are you okay?"

"No." Without saying anything else, she ran down the next flight of stairs, and then I heard the front door to the house slam open and closed.

One of the second floor tenants opened her door and looked out at me.

"Sorry about that. I'll just clean this up," I said.

"What the hell was that?" Darrin said.

"I don't know."

He and I picked up most of the typewriter parts and carried them upstairs. I didn't know what else to do with them, so we took them into Wavy's bedroom, where I could see what had made the crash that woke me up. Wavy had apparently thrown her typewriter across the room and put a big dent in the wall.

"I don't think you're going to get your deposit back." Darrin dumped a pile of typewriter debris onto Wavy's desk and picked up the torn halves of a sheet of paper.

It must have been the letter Wavy was working on. The one that made her murder her typewriter. It was addressed to the lawyer who oversaw her trust.

Dear Mr. Osher:

I'm writing to request that you draft a
letter on my behalf to be sent from your
office to Jesse Joe Barfoot, Jr. As the
conditions of his parole prohibit any
contact with me, I'd like you to communicate
with him regarding a 1956 Harley-Davidson
motorcycle, which has been in my possession
since 1983. It is currently located in the
garage of my guardian, Mrs. Brenda Newling.
I would like Mr. Barfoot to take possession
of the vehicle at his earliest convenience.
It is my wish to sign the motorcycle over to
him as a gift, as it belongs to me
personally, and is not included in my trust.
As it is unlikely that Mr. Barfoot will be
able to receive the motorcycle directly from
Mrs. Brenda Newling, I will of course pay
for any expense related to the delivery of
the item into his possession.

Enclosed, please find the name of a
motorcycle shop in Garringer which can
arrange transportation, as well as the signed
title, and Mr. Barfoot's current address.

Sincere regards,
Miss Wavonna Quinn

I didn't even think about what time it was. To be honest, I didn't
care. I took Wavy's address book out of her desk and called her

cousin Amy. She picked up, sounding groggy and belligerent, but once I identified myself, she got quiet.

"Is everything—is Wavy okay?" she whispered.

"No. I would not say that Wavy is okay."

"What happened?"

"What happened is she just found out that Kellen's been paroled, and under the conditions of his parole, he can't have any contact with her," I said.

"I know. He can't be within a hundred feet of her. Also, no phone contact or letters. She knows that."

"She did not know that! Do you think she would have gone to see him if she'd known it could get him thrown back in jail?" Wavy kept a lot of secrets from me, but there was no way she'd have gone to see Kellen knowing that. It certainly explained why their happy reunion had crashed and burned.

"She went to see him? Why?" Amy said.

"Why? Because she loves him! And how did you know he'd been paroled when Wavy didn't even know?"

"My mom told me. Like a year ago, when he was paroled."

"Your mom? How does she know? He got paroled last year? Wavy didn't even know he'd been paroled until yesterday." I knew I was screeching, but I wanted to reach through the phone and slap Amy until she said something that made sense. Darrin sat down on the couch next to me with a concerned look on his face. I was so glad he was getting to see me at my screamiest.

"How could she not know? They sent a letter to say he was up for parole. Oh, crap." Amy went totally silent, so I knew she was figuring out what I'd just realized. "The letters went to my mom's house and she never told Wavy."

"But you knew! And you never thought to mention that in any of your letters?" I said. My opinion of Kellen changed about every five minutes, but Wavy loved him, and her aunt had no right to keep that kind of secret from her. Neither did Amy.

"We don't write those kinds of letters. She—she writes to me about NASA launches and medieval urban planning. Besides, we don't talk about Kellen in my family. We just don't, okay? You don't know what it was like when all of that happened."

"I thought you were on her side."

"I am. But Mom thinks she's doing the right thing," Amy said. "What would you do if you thought somebody molested your thirteen-year-old niece?"

"She's not thirteen anymore, and you don't know what this is doing her. She thought they were going to be together! She still loves him!" Normally, I would have been crying by that point, but I was full of righteous anger, so when Amy started sniveling into the phone, I did not feel sympathetic.

"Is she okay?" Amy said.

"No, she spent about five hours crying her heart out, and then she went tearing out of here at four a.m., going God knows where. I don't know where she is or when she's coming home. I guess, if you hear from her, let me know."

I didn't wait to hear what Amy said. I just hung up.

"Do you want me to go look for her?" Darrin said. He squeezed my hand, which surprised me, because I wasn't sure at what point we'd started holding hands.

"No, if she's mobile, she'll be alright. You wouldn't believe some of the crazy shit she's survived."

"Do you want me to leave, so you can get some sleep?"

"I'm too awake to go to back to sleep," I said.

Darrin's hair was mussed from sleeping on the couch, and that early in the morning, his beard stubble was coming in. I'd thought he was so baby faced when I met him, but without the close shave, he looked kind of rugged. When I scooted closer, he put his arm around me.

"Yeah, I don't think I could sleep either," he said.

Thinking about how close I'd come to sacrificing my dignity on the altar of Joshua's good looks, I took a thorough accounting of Darrin. He was single, in school, and gainfully employed. He had come through for me out of the blue, and he was still there. If I wanted to stop getting my heart broken, it wasn't enough to stop being self-absorbed. I needed to stop chasing after guys as self-absorbed as I was. I leaned in so that my mouth was in kissing range.

"Maybe we'd both get some sleep if you got in bed with me," I said. If he'd pulled the *taking advantage* number again, I don't think I could have forgiven him, but lo and behold, he kissed me.

Of course, we didn't go to sleep until dawn. I had finally drifted off, with Darrin's arm around me, when I heard the front door open. I thought about getting up to see what Wavy was doing, but I was naked and comfortable, so I stayed in bed. Then there was a thumping sound, and the front door opened and closed. A few minutes later the door opened and there was more thumping.

I got dressed and went out to the living room, where a pile of large library books was forming next to the coffee table. I picked up a blue, leather-bound volume marked "State Penal Code, 1981 to Present, Volume XXIV." On the spine was a sticker that said "LAW REF Non-Circ."

While I was trying to decide what it meant, Wavy came through the door carrying more books, stacked up almost to her chin. She dropped them next to the other books, and went down the hallway to her bedroom.

"Are these reference books from the law library?" I yelled. "You can't check these out, can you?"

"The janitor smokes."

"You went to the law library, snuck past the janitor on his smoke break, and stole books?"

I could almost hear her shrug.

She came back with a spiral notebook and a pen, picked up the top book, and hauled it to the kitchen table. From there it looked like any other homework assignment. She ran her finger down the index, thumbed into the book, and started reading. Every once in a while, she would stop and copy something into her notebook.

I left her to it, and went back to bed.

When Darrin and I finally got up, she was still working. It was the kitchen table, after all, so I cooked brunch around her. I was worried it would be awkward, but she said, "Hi," to Darrin, and shifted some of the books, so there was a place to eat. Honestly, I was the only one who seemed uneasy, but that's because I was trying to figure out what was going on with Wavy. She'd gone from destroyed to driven overnight, but driven by what? She hadn't put her ring back on, and there was a gap of paler skin on her hand where it usually was.

When she took a bathroom break, I reached across the table and grabbed her notebook. "No Contact Order" was the header on the first page. Below that was a series of bullet points. Expiration of civil orders. Automatic NCO in cases of DV. Imposed by parole board. Imposed by parole agency. Imposed by sentencing judge.

The header on the next page was "Process for removing NCO imposed by parole board." The pages after that had headers for different scenarios, waiting for Wavy's notes.

13

WAVY

June 1990

For a few days afterwards, I could press my fingers up into myself and find the raw spot Kellen had left. The swelling in my wrist went down after a few days, and left a bruise in the shape of his fingers. Then that faded, too.

I put the ring away in the velvet box the lady in the jewelry store had given me, because I couldn't wear it anymore. Kellen had made me keep the ring, but he hadn't put it back on my finger. That meant it wasn't my wedding ring. When I pressed it to my mouth it was just a rock. The difference between a meteor falling through the atmosphere and a meteorite lying in the dirt.

I didn't regret kicking my electric typewriter down the stairs. Aunt Brenda had given it to me for my high school graduation, and whether she intended it or not, gifts take up space in your heart. I needed that space now. I finished my Spanish essay on a computer on campus. For the letters I needed to write, I had the manual Underwood that Grandma taught me to type on. It was Army green and weighed almost thirteen pounds. It worked fine, and Grandma didn't take up any more room in my heart than a floor takes up space in a house.

When Renee wasn't complaining about the sound of me typing, she was hovering anxiously. I don't know what she thought I would do if she left me alone too long. Get high on correction fluid? Or maybe she thought I would do what I did: write a letter a day to Kellen's parole officer until his supervisor wrote me back.

```
Dear Miss Quinn,


I apologize for the delay in responding to
your letters. To answer your questions: the
conditions of Jesse Joe Barfoot's parole
were not set by this office. Therefore, we
are unable to alter the no contact order.
The conditions of his parole were set by the
sentencing judge. To have them changed, you
would need to file a formal appeal in the
district court where he was sentenced.


Sincerely,
James Teeter
```

"What happens now?" Renee said.

"Formal appeal in district court."

I opened my accordion file folder, put the letter in one slot, and pulled out a Form J-319-7. Modification to Orders of Protection and No Contact. I put it in the old Underwood and rolled it up.

"Wow, there's a form for that?" Renee said.

I'd requested the form, even before I knew I would need it, just like I'd requested copies of Kellen's final judgment from the district court. I took those out, too, to be sure I got everything correct on the form.

It made me sick to see him listed there by the name he never wanted: Jesse Joe Barfoot, Jr. They'd taken away his identity, pressed him back into his father's mold. Kellen wasn't the only one who had his identity stripped away in those records. Every place I appeared, I was *the minor victim*, identified only as WLQ. To protect me, of course, even if I didn't want to be protected. That was what I put in the very small space provided on the form for me to justify my request to have the no contact order rescinded. *I do not wish to be protected by the court's order, as the defendant presents no danger to me.*

"Have you considered becoming a lawyer?" Renee said, while I typed.

"Never." I thought of all the lawyers who'd passed through my life, and I didn't envy any of them the part they'd played.

I drove up to Garringer by myself to file the form and pay the fifty dollar filing fee. After that, I waited. Just like I'd been waiting for years. Renee talked about how electronic mail was going to be the next big thing, but the dented mailbox in the front hall of our apartment building was still my god. Every day I prayed that it would deliver up a letter from Donal or from someone who knew where he was. I prayed for it to bring me an answer from the district court.

I wondered if that was what it was like for Kellen, after he'd written Liam's phone number on my arm. When he was sitting alone and bleeding, waiting for me to come back, had it seemed like a month to him? Had it seemed longer? Had it seemed hopeless?

14

KELLEN

July 1990

That first week, I slept at the same dive hotel where I'd stayed when Beth's grandkids came to visit. Most of June, when the weather was good, I stayed at a campground in a tent I picked up from an Army surplus store. Reminded me of sleeping out in the meadow with Wavy, and it was that memory as much as the summer heat that made me give it up. After a couple more nights in a motel, I moved in with Craig, one of the guys at the shop. Him and his wife was expecting a baby, though, and she didn't like me being there when he was out.

By the middle of August, I was back to another crappy motel, and working as many hours as I could, so I wouldn't have to be at the motel except to sleep.

I had my head up under the hood of a Toyota when somebody

said, "Jesse," behind me. There was Beth, with her hair dyed this new dark color of red, holding my baseball bat. Wouldn't have surprised me if she'd swung it at me, but she said, "You forgot this. Thought you might want it. And your winter coat."

The employee lounge was just a closet with lockers and chairs, but it was kind of private, so I took her in there. I stuck the bat and coat in my locker and counted three hundred dollars out of my wallet.

"Thanks for bringing my stuff. This here's for May's rent and electric," I said.

"You were only there for a week."

"Yeah, well, I still owe you the rent."

She took the money and put it in her purse. Then she just looked at me, so I knew she was waiting for me to say something.

"Look, I'm sorry about what happened. I know that was a lousy thing to do to you. If I'd been thinking—"

"Is it over? Are you still breaking your parole?" Beth said.

"No. I haven't seen her again."

"If it's over, you could come back. I won't put up with you breaking your parole, but if you promise it's over, we could try again." I guess I didn't answer soon enough, because she stood up and put her purse over her shoulder. "Jesus Christ. I can't believe I came here thinking you might be interested in a second chance."

"I can't come back, because I can't promise anything. If Wavy showed up tomorrow, I'd do it all over again. I loved her the first time I saw her and I still do."

"Love at first sight, huh?" Beth snorted. "How old was she?"

"Eight."

"That's creepy."

She said a bunch of other shitty things, too. "You should've stayed in prison if that's how you're going to live," and, "Nothing like flushing the rest of your life down the toilet over some girl you're never going to be with." Like I didn't wish I was dead most of the time. Like I hadn't spent some time thinking about where I could buy a gun and solve it. Almost as much time as I'd spent thinking about breaking my parole and seeing Wavy.

After Beth got that out of her system, she asked me to move back in with her. I said yes, but only as roommates. She needed help with the rent, and I needed some place to stay that wasn't gonna get me in trouble with my parole officer.

It woulda been nicer to live alone, but at least now Beth couldn't lay there at night and talk me half to death when I wanted some quiet. She didn't have any business complaining about my deodorant or my haircut or my tattoos. She still did, but I didn't have to pay attention.

The real difference was that Beth couldn't put her hand on my dick and say, "Turn off the TV and let's go in the bedroom," whether I wanted to or not. I don't think I could have stomached that. Not when I had Wavy burned in my brain. Some nights, when I came home from work and walked into the kitchen, all I could think of was the way she'd stood on the chair and stripped down to her boots. How she'd run her hands over me. No woman had ever looked at me the way she did, or touched me that way. Like she wanted me, like I was worth wanting.

Most times all I could think of was how she'd come there and given herself to me. I didn't even have the decency to tell her we couldn't be together until after. Just desperate to be with her. I was still the same guy who let her give me a hand job when she was all of thirteen.

15

RENEE

August 1990

It got to where Wavy wouldn't even let me check the mailbox. If I went to get the mail, she practically tackled me when I came back, and yanked it out of my hands.

"Good thing I'm not expecting any love letters," I said, while she rifled through the fliers and bills.

"You don't need love letters." She thumped her hand on the kitchen table half-a-dozen times to mimic the sound of my headboard knocking against my bedroom wall, but I knew she didn't begrudge me the fun I was having with Darrin.

Three weeks later, Wavy's answer came. Or rather an answer. It was a copy of the form she submitted, with the bottom half filled out by hand. The box next to *This matter was not set for hearing* had been

ALL THE UGLY AND WONDERFUL THINGS   375

checked. Below that, where the form said, "After review of the file and evidence, the court orders that the above referenced Protection or No Contact Order, entered on September 9, 1983, shall be modified as follows," someone had written *NO modification. Order remains in force.* That same person had signed the form. Judge C. J. Maber.

"The judge said no? He said no? What a fucking asshole!" I was so pissed off, I couldn't imagine how angry Wavy must have been. It wouldn't have surprised me if she had torn the form up or thrown her typewriter down the stairs, but she didn't. She spent maybe a minute glaring at the form and grinding her teeth. Then she sat down, stuck a piece of paper in the typewriter and started typing: *Dear Judge Maber.*

Contrary to Wavy's usual habits, it was short and polite, just a request to meet with the judge. When she didn't get an answer, though, the letters multiplied exponentially. The sheer quantity of them started to worry me, because at what point did it become harassment to send a letter a day to a judge? At least if the cops showed up, Wavy had returned all the illicitly borrowed law books to the library.

I wasn't home when the letter came, but I knew something big had happened by the way Wavy was tearing around the apartment when I got home from my first class of the semester. She had half the clothes in her closet strewn out on the couch, and as soon as I walked in, she put the letter in my hand. It wasn't even from the judge. It was from his clerk, and it just said, *Judge Maber is available to meet with you on Wednesday, August 15th at 8:00 am. The judge's court session begins at 9:00 a.m., so please be prompt.*

We had less than thirty-six hours to get Wavy ready for her meeting with the judge and the girl owned a closet full of plain-Jane smocks, four pairs of shoes, two pairs of boots, shower shoes, and a pair of tennis shoes for her phys ed requirement that I know for a fact she bought in the children's department. If I was going to help Wavy look like an adult, we had to start from scratch.

I don't know if Wavy slept that night, but the next morning, we drove into the city early enough to be there when the stores opened. Within an hour, we had to give up on a business suit. They didn't make them in Wavy's size. We settled on a school uniform skirt in navy wool, but there was nothing else in the girls section at Macy's that didn't look like it was for little girls. The cashier there suggested what she called a "luxury ladies store" that carried small sizes. The sort of chichi place my mother loved to shop at. Wavy had turned twenty-one in July, so she could write checks off her trust without getting permission from anyone. Otherwise, I could imagine her aunt's response to Wavy dropping almost four hundred dollars on a silk blouse in an extra-small petite, and a pair of Italian snakeskin slingback pumps in a size four-and-a-half. My mother once described Wavy as "two steps away from the trailer park," so I couldn't wait to tell her they had the same taste in dress shoes.

Back at the apartment, Wavy washed the styling gel out of her hair and I gave her waves instead of spikes. I showed her how to shave her legs, even though she didn't need it. You couldn't even see the hairs on her legs.

"On principle," she said. If adults shaved their legs, Wavy would shave hers.

Then we took the only trial run we were going to get. Skirt, blouse, bra, pantyhose, and shoes. I taught her how to walk in the heels, and once she could manage the stairs and a trip around the block, I officially declared her a grown-up.

In the dark hours of Wednesday morning, we made three attempts at her makeup. The first time, she was nervous about me touching her face. The second failure was a product of how disturbing Wavy looked in full makeup. Like a child prostitute. In the end, we went minimalist: lipstick, eye shadow. By the time she left for Garringer, the sun was coming up, and Wavy looked, if not exactly like an adult, then adultlike.

16

JUDGE
C. J. MABER

I remembered the case, although it never went to trial. It didn't hurt that I'd had Barfoot in my courtroom before on two separate assault charges. He left an impression. A giant of a man with a vicious temper, who still managed to look sheepish in court. I didn't bother to pull the file before I declined to rescind the no contact order.

When the letters started coming, I looked at the file to refresh my memory. I still wasn't inclined to meet with Miss Quinn, but I knew from long experience that some people cannot be put off. Some of them will persist until I agree to meet with them.

Miss Quinn arrived at my chambers right on time, and I was glad to see she was a serious young woman. I had no patience with the weepers and the screamers. That kind of woman makes me ashamed of my own sex. Miss Quinn was poised and well-dressed, but I couldn't have guessed her age if I hadn't already known it. Because Barfoot pled out, I'd never laid eyes on the girl, never seen how small and delicate she was. Honestly, if I had, I would have sentenced Barfoot to more than ten years.

She took the chair I pointed her to and set down a briefcase, which invariably held a photo album, containing pictures meant to tug at my heartstrings.

"Miss Quinn, may I call you Wavonna?"

"Wavy," she said.

"Wavy, then. May I ask you some questions?" I liked to get at the things it didn't occur to them to tell me. Most of all, I liked to let them know that they were important to me. To let them know they had value that wasn't connected to the man they loved. Some of them got impatient, wanting to get to the real matter, but for many of them, I was possibly the first person in authority who had ever really expressed interest in them. Wavy was neither impatient nor starved for attention. I asked her about whether she was in school or employed. Both.

"Astrophysics," she said, when I asked what she was studying. A smart girl, then.

"I know you've come here today to try to convince me to rescind the no contact order I put in place at Mr. Barfoot's sentencing, but your presence here is proof to me that it was the right thing then and is still the right thing."

"It isn't fair." She didn't quite interrupt me, but she snuck in those three words while I was taking a breath. "Keeping him away from me was supposed to protect me, but I don't want to be protected. I love him and I'm being punished even though I didn't do anything wrong."

I was struck silent for a moment, not by her words, which I'd heard hundreds of times from hundreds of other women, but by the quality of her voice. Husky and incredibly quiet, but not shy. I could have cut her off at any moment, because that little speech took her half a dozen breaths.

She was quiet for a moment, uncrossing her legs and reaching for her briefcase. As I'd known she would, she sprang her heartbreaking photo album on me. Or at any rate, her heartbreaking photo. It was a picture of Mr. Barfoot, Wavy, and a little blond boy of five or six years. All three were smiling. Mr. Barfoot had taken the picture, holding the camera out in front of them. They looked happy, of course. Familial. That was the point of those pictures.

"This is my family. My little brother, Donal. Kellen. Not Barfoot. My real family. You can help put it back together," Wavy said.

"I somehow expected more from a girl as bright as you obviously are."

Her eyes narrowed, so that I could see I hadn't rattled her so much as I had angered her.

"I cannot even begin to tell you how many women I see like you, Wavy. Women who have fallen in love and think that gives a man the right to do anything to them. Most of them are victims of domestic violence, which I realize was not the case for you. What Mr. Barfoot did to you, however, was equally as harmful, if not more so. These women come to me, sometimes after waiting for years for their husbands, boyfriends, fiancés, the fathers of their children, to get out of prison.

"They come to me and beg me to reunite them with this man they love. This man who has slapped them and punched them and kicked them and sometimes raped them. They blame his terrible childhood, or the drugs, or the alcohol, or another woman, or the war. They come to me with a photo album, just as you have, to show me pictures of happier times, and they ask me to make their family whole again. I am telling you this, because I want you to understand how many times I see this, because I think you're smart enough to see the rationale behind my decision. To see that I did the right thing by protecting you. And not just when you were a child, but by protecting you from making a mistake now."

"Were you there when my father did this?" She laid her finger to her bottom lip, where she had an old white scar.

"Of course, no, I wasn't there to protect you from any injuries your father might have inflicted on you. That doesn't negate—"

"Kellen protected me," she said. They always had a story about some kind or generous thing he'd done for them.

"Look at you. You're in your senior year of college, with the opportunity for a good, successful life ahead of you. If you return to Mr. Barfoot, who not only was willing to exploit you as a child, but who is a high school dropout with a criminal record full of assaults, what do you think will become of that opportunity?"

"He took me to school. For six years. Paid my school fees. Dropped me off. Picked me up. Six years. No one else cared. His money pays my tuition now. He gave me this opportunity," she said.

"Miss Quinn, I need to get ready for court. I truly wish you the best. Even for Mr. Barfoot. But you would both be better served by focusing on your respective futures, rather than dwelling on the past." Getting them to leave was always the hardest part. They didn't want to give up. They wanted to fight. Maybe they thought that was what I wanted to see: proof of how much they loved this man who had hurt them. Wavy, however, stood and picked up her briefcase. As she was about to retrieve the photo she'd laid on my desk, she hesitated.

"Your family?" she said. Before I could stop her, she reached across my desk and picked up the framed picture that I always kept facing myself. It was an old photo, from when my children were small, and my husband and I were both thinner and less gray.

"Yes."

She shifted her gaze from the photo to me. I was discomfited by the intensity of that look, and I saw it for what it was: an accusation.

"Your family is real, but mine isn't? Real people with real feelings, but my family isn't—" She ran out of air and took a gulp. "—real to you. You think. I'm a character. A story. Those women you talk about. Not real people to you. Stupid women. Stupid photo albums. But you. You're smart. You make smarter choices. For us."

She was almost panting and, seeing the way the picture trembled in her hand, I rolled my chair back from the desk. Although there had been a few close calls, I'd never actually had a physical altercation with anyone. I always kept the door open so that if things got heated the bailiffs could hear, but Wavy's anger was so hushed no one had noticed.

"Please don't upset yourself. I really do have to go to court." I stood up and walked around the desk. Although she was still holding my family photo, she didn't try to stop me, so I poked my head out into the hallway and gestured for the bailiff. "Edward, would you please escort Miss Quinn out?"

She put the picture frame down and went with Edward, but as she walked away, she raised her voice.

"I'm real. I'm as real as you are. My family is real like your family," she said.

17

WAVY

I needed to get back to Norman in time for my afternoon class, but when I passed the exit for the old quarry where we raced the Barracuda, the rotation of the Earth seemed to slow. The sun hovered at a standstill in the sky while I turned the car around and drove back through Garringer. I used to think of it as a big city, but now it was gone in a blink, and I was on the road to Powell.

Driving down Main Street, I felt like I was in a ghost story, but I didn't know who was the ghost—me or all of Powell County. Downtown wasn't much different than I remembered, maybe a few more storefronts were empty, but the hardware store had the same tools in the window, and the Shop 'n Save had hail damage to their front sign. Off Main Street, Cutcheon's Small Engine had a yellowed sheet of notebook paper taped in the window. "Closed till further notice," it said in Mr. Cutcheon's handwriting.

Kellen's house was occupied, but rundown. Nobody had painted it since we did, and the carport looked like it was about to fall down. Two dogs chained up in the front yard barked at me as I walked past.

On the drive out to the meadow, I turned off the air-conditioning and opened the windows. The heat and the dust rolled into the car, but the wind in my face was the closest I could get to riding on a motorcycle.

There was a new double-wide parked where Sandy's trailer used to be, but I think the people living there were actually farming, because there were tractors parked by the barns. Cattle grazed in the meadow, and they turned their heads and watched me with soft brown eyes as I drove past. The driveway to the farmhouse was so washed out, I had to park on the road and walk up, getting gravel in my fancy shoes.

The honeysuckle vines had crawled up over the front porch and collapsed the trellis below the attic window. The screen door flapped in the breeze, and the kitchen door stood partway open. When I lived there, we'd never had a key to the kitchen door, so the police must have simply pulled the door closed. Anyone who wanted to walk in, could, including me.

I hadn't been inside the house since Donal and I left that July to go visit Aunt Brenda. She never allowed us to come back. The kitchen floor was stained brown from Val's blood, and grayed over with the dust of strangers walking through. Vandals must have used the table and chairs to build fires in the front room's fireplace. They'd left behind beer bottles and spray painted the dining room walls. Upstairs in my room, Aunt Brenda had only taken the quilt Grandma made. She took that to Tulsa and packed it away, because it was an heirloom, too valuable to use. She'd left the little black and white TV, and someone had broken out its screen. I could see from the dirty sleeping bag and the condom wrappers that strangers had used the bed where Kellen and I spent so many nights lying next to each other.

I came back down to the kitchen and stood at the spot where Val had died. Just a few feet away from where Kellen kissed me for the first time. I pulled the kitchen door closed as I went out, and the porch floor creaked as I crossed to the steps. Walking back to my car, I followed the overgrown path to the limestone steps, where Kellen had sat after his wreck.

I'd been wrong about the Earth's rotation slowing. It went on as steadily as always, and the afternoon was long gone. To the west, Venus and Jupiter held court with the setting sun. A few days before, the Magellan spacecraft had reached Venus, and started sending back pictures. Below the horizon lay Orion, resting until autumn, when he would rise over the meadow with only the cows to see him.

I thought then of Voyager 1 and 2, so far away. They were launched the same year I met Kellen, and now they had reached the end of our solar system. Although their programs were being powered down one by one, they traveled on. NASA said that in another twenty-five years, they would exit our heliosphere and cross into interstellar space. In another three hundred thousand years, Voyager 2 might reach as far as the star Sirius, but it would never come home.

That was how I felt, as I walked down the driveway to my car. I was moving forward into space, but I would never come home again.

Hours later, walking up the stairs to the apartment, I still felt like a satellite untethered from gravity. Above me, Renee opened our apartment door.

"Wavy! Oh my god, where have you been?" she shouted.

When I reached her, she was a star, pulling me into her orbit.

"Judge Maber called. She said, 'Tell Miss Quinn that she was right. She is just as real as I am.'"

18

KELLEN

September 1990

Beth could nag at me all she wanted about my cholesterol, but I went back to eating bacon and eggs and pancakes with real butter like Wavy used to cook. That's what I had for breakfast before my weekly meeting with my parole officer. Beth was at the counter packing her lunch while I ate, but she kept looking over her shoulder at me. Made me real self-conscious.

"What?" I said.

"Did you see the mail yesterday?" she said.

"No." I figured somebody had stuck another flier about me in the mailbox. People still did that, even though I was careful. I never talked to kids, not for nothing. Far as I was concerned, kids didn't exist. Which left me feeling like shit any time I saw some kid's busted down bike. I coulda fixed it, but people mighta thought the wrong thing.

Beth pitched a letter on the table in front of me. The only mail I ever got was official stuff from the Department of Corrections, only this one wasn't. It'd been years since I got a letter in that handwriting, but I knew it from back when Wavy used to send me Christmas cards from her aunt's house.

"I won't tell you again," Beth said. "If you break your parole, you can't live here."

She went back to fixing her lunch, and I tried to finish my breakfast, but that letter had thrown me for a loop.

First, it meant Wavy knew I was living with Beth again. All she had to do was call the Department of Corrections and they'd give her my current address off the sex offender registry. I had to figure she thought the worst of me, because what else was she gonna think? I'd made her keep the ring, and went back to living with Beth, like the ring didn't mean a thing to me.

Second, it meant Wavy had something to say to me, but what?

"Are you going to open it or read it through the envelope?" Beth said. It was the same voice she used to say all the mean things she said when I came back.

"Neither. Just throw it away. That's what you were gonna do anyway, isn't it?"

She didn't hardly wait for me to get the words out of my mouth before she picked it up and tossed it in the trash can. After that I couldn't get the food down my throat, and it was time to go. When I went to scrape my plate off into the trash, there was the letter staring up at me. I dumped what was left of my breakfast in on top of it.

My parole officer was a good guy, but busy, so I was usually in and out in under ten minutes. It started out like all the other meetings. How are you doing? How's work? Having any troubles? Then all the sudden, he said, "Have you been in contact with Wavonna Quinn?"

"No. Hell, no." First outright lie I ever told him. I broke out in a cold sweat and I couldn't figure which made me seem guiltier: looking him in the eye or looking away. I gave him a good long stare and said, "No way. Why would you think that?"

"Just curious," he said. *Just curious*, my ass. I thought about that letter and about how Beth was still pissed off at me. Made me wonder if she hadn't called him. He didn't push me on the subject, and two minutes later I was out of there.

I shoulda gone to work, but I didn't.

I drove home, went into the apartment, and first thing, yanked the lid off the trash can. Inside was a new trash bag. It was my job to take the trash out, but Beth had done it, just so she could throw Wavy's letter away.

That's how I ended up in the garbage Dumpster, sifting through bags of trash. The day was warming up and that Dumpster stank like hell. I musta opened a dozen bags before I found Wavy's letter, sticky with syrup. I crawled out of the Dumpster and sat down on the curb next to it. My stomach was right up under my throat, when I opened the envelope.

Dear Kellen,

I thought you would come to me after you got the letter from the court, but you didn't. I can imagine a thousand reasons you wouldn't come and only one reason you would, but I hoped that reason would be enough. I won't bother you again. I'm only writing because I have something I need to return to you. Because of its size, it would be best if you could come get it. Will you meet me at my aunt's house over Labor Day weekend? Sunday at 4? If you prefer not to see me, you can come after 5 pm. I'll be gone by then.

See you soon.

Love,
Wavy

I never got any letter from the court, but there'd been a few weeks when I was moving around so much I didn't know where I was gonna sleep, let alone where to tell my parole officer I was living. Then again, maybe it came and Beth threw it away.

Not knowing what was in that missing letter scared the hell outta me, because I couldn't afford to go getting my hopes up. Whatever was in it, I had two choices. I either had to throw the letter back in the Dumpster and go to work, or I had to go upstairs and pack my stuff. There wasn't no middle ground.

19

AMY

I hadn't planned to go home for Labor Day, until Mom told me Wavy was coming.

"That's what her letter said. The first one I've had from her in months," Mom said.

Wavy hadn't written to me since May, either, and now that she was twenty-one, I'd started to wonder if we would ever see her again. Hearing that she intended to visit was a relief, until I considered that she might be planning a showdown with my mother. The question was whether I wanted to witness it.

Mom threw the same Labor Day party every year: a Sunday lunch of daiquiris and burgers on the back patio with a few of her book club friends. Wavy didn't show for lunch, and by four o'clock, everyone else had gone home. Mom and I were in the living room, when Wavy walked in the front door, carrying a couple of manila envelopes. She looked weary.

"You're too late for lunch, but I'm glad you came!" Mom said.

I didn't know what to say. *Sorry I was an unwitting accomplice to my mother's betrayal?*

"Did you come down by yourself or did you bring Renee?" I was hoping for somebody else to be a buffer between Wavy and Mom.

"Meeting her boyfriend's parents," Wavy said.

"Oh, so she's getting serious with a new boyfriend?" Mom said.

We managed small talk for twenty or thirty minutes, but just as I started to relax, the doorbell rang. Wavy glanced at her watch and, for a few seconds, weariness transformed into grief. Then she stood up and went to answer the door.

"What in the world?" Mom said it like she expected a pleasant surprise. When she and I got to the door, Wavy was signing something on a clipboard held by a skinny guy in a baseball cap. Behind him, a flatbed truck stood parked at the curb.

"Did you have car trouble?" I said.

"Or did you finally decide to sell that old motorcycle?" Mom's look of triumph was wasted on Wavy, who was already backtracking through the house to open the garage door. The motorcycle stood in the corner with a bed sheet thrown over it to keep off the dust, in between visits from the mechanic.

As Wavy pulled the sheet away, the envelopes slipped out from under her arm. I bent to pick them up and found one addressed to my mother and one addressed to Kellen. His contained something small and square. A ring box. I held them out to her, but she had her hands over her eyes.

"You son of a bitch!" my mother screamed from the front yard. "You just broke the conditions of your parole! I'll see you back in jail!"

Wavy grabbed the envelopes out of my hand and we both ran out of the garage.

Kellen stood out in the street next to an old dented pickup truck. He looked terrified, and who could blame him, with my mother shouting like that? I ran toward Mom, and I expected Wavy to go to Kellen, but she came after me.

We caught up with Mom on the front porch, as she was opening the storm door, probably going inside to call the police. Wavy reached past her and slammed the door closed.

"You lied to the parole board and you lied to me," Wavy said through clenched teeth. She looked both angry and like she might cry.

"I was only trying—"

Before Mom could explain herself, Wavy flattened one of the manila envelopes against Mom's chest with her open palm. "This is from the judge, to change Kellen's parole."

Kellen squinted up at the porch, at the three of us watching him. It dawned on me that he didn't know why he was there. He was risking going back to jail on nothing more than Wavy's word. He didn't know it was the happiest day of his life.

I understood then why the reunion was happening there instead of someplace else. Not to throw it in my mother's face, but because Mom's house was the place where Wavy had drawn a line. The day she stood in our driveway and screamed, "Mine!" she wasn't talking about the motorcycle.

As Mom opened the manila envelope, Wavy started down the sidewalk. Kellen crossed the street and stepped up on our curb. I expected a joyful, over-the-top romantic movie reunion, but they walked toward each slowly. They met about halfway, and she handed him the other envelope. He felt the bottom of it, where the ring box was, and shook his head. It was easy to make out the word *no*, but I don't know what else he said. When Wavy spoke, I could guess what she was telling him. His answer made Wavy throw her head back and laugh.

Kellen opened the envelope and stuck his hand in. He pulled out the ring box, just as Wavy jumped up and threw her arms around his neck. The force of it staggered him back half a step, but when they kissed each other, it *was* a romantic movie. The sequel to that good-bye in Kellen's shop.

I think they would have gone on kissing for a long time, but Mom stepped off the porch and shouted, "Get off my property, you bastard, or I'll have you arrested for trespassing!"

Blushing and frowning, Kellen lowered Wavy to her feet. She took his hand and led him toward the driveway.

"If he steps foot on my property, I'll call the police!" Mom knew Wavy couldn't move the motorcycle by herself, and the tow truck driver seemed to take the trespassing remarks to heart. He stood by the cab of his truck watching us warily.

"I'll help you," I said.

Together, Wavy and I pushed the bike down the driveway. A few times I thought we were going to drop it, but we made it to the curb. Ignoring my mother's glared threat, Kellen took it from us and rolled it into the street with a stunned look on his face.

"I wonder if it'll even start," he said, as he swung his leg over the bike.

I just knew it would start the first time and it did. When he twisted the throttle, the whole street echoed with the engine. Kellen grinned at Wavy, and then he seemed to remember something. He stood up and pulled the ring box out of his pocket. The ring wouldn't go up over her middle knuckle until he ducked his head and licked her finger. He laughed as he slid the ring up.

"We gotta get that resized," he said. He raised her hand to his mouth again and kissed the ring. I'd taken a few steps back, feeling awkward about intruding on them, but Kellen looked at me and said, "Do you really think your mom's gonna call the cops? 'Cause technically, I am breaking my parole. I'm not supposed to cross state lines without my parole officer's permission."

"I don't know," I said. We all three turned to look at Mom, who came across the front lawn toward us, glowering. "But now might be a good time to leave."

"Where should we have him take the bike?" Wavy gestured to the tow truck driver.

"To hell with that, sweetheart," Kellen said. "Get on and let's ride this thing."

"Give me your keys and I'll have him take your car home," I said.

Practically glowing, Wavy handed me the keys. She hugged me so fast and hard, I didn't even manage to hug her back.

Then she hiked her skirt up and got on the back of the bike. Laying her cheek against Kellen's shoulder, she wrapped her arms as far around him as they would go. He gunned the bike and they rode away, leaving Mom, me, and a confused tow truck driver standing in the street.

"I want that pickup truck towed," Mom said.

20

KELLEN

December 1990

We were quiet for most of the drive, with Wavy staring out the window, but when we saw the first sign for Tulsa, her shoulders tensed up.

"We don't have to do this," I said.

For the first time in almost two hours, Wavy looked at me. Glared at me. Times like that I was glad she didn't talk much, because that hot look woulda come with a mean mouth.

"I just thought maybe you'd changed your mind."

"I didn't." She went back to looking out the window.

I sure hadn't changed my mind. I didn't want to do it when she first suggested it, and I still didn't.

The closer we got, the more nervous I got.

"I love you," I said. I couldn't always get a free pass with that, but she laid her hand on my leg. I put my hand on top of hers and wiggled the diamond under my thumb. A few miles later, she leaned over and rested her cheek on my arm. Her stomach growled.

"Did you eat anything?" These days she could actually sit down and eat at the table, but last night, she couldn't get any dinner down. No breakfast either, that I saw.

"Too nervous," she said.

But she still wanted to do it. The harder a thing was, the more likely she'd be able to do it. I couldn't hardly believe what she'd done to get me back.

With her holding my hand, I coulda gone on driving forever, but then there was the exit. A couple more turns, a minute waiting at the last stoplight, and we were there in less than three blocks. After I parked at the curb, I took the flask of bourbon out of the glove compartment and drained it.

"Liquid courage," I said.

I expected Wavy to frown at me, but she leaned over and kissed my cheek. Then she reached into the backseat and shook Donal awake. He sat up and rubbed his eyes, still half asleep and surly. I felt for the kid. He wanted to be there about as much as I did.

Following Wavy up the sidewalk with the flowers in my right hand and the bottle of wine in my left, I felt like an asshole making her go first. She rang the bell and stood in front of me like a shield. Donal stood behind us like he wasn't even involved. He was still working out how he fit in.

When the door swung open, it was somebody I didn't know. A young guy with a ponytail and a pink polo shirt. He didn't know us, either, but he let us in.

"Merry Christmas! I'm Brice Standish. I'm Leslie's husband," he said.

"Who is it, Bri—?" Leslie came into the hallway and stared. I hadn't seen her since she was a teenager, but grown up, she was narrower in the face, more like Val than Brenda.

"Hey, Leslie," I said.

Then Amy walked in and said, "You came."

She headed straight to me and I thought she was just going to take the wine, but after she had it out of my hand, she put her arms around me. Surprised the hell out of me. I knew Amy didn't hate my guts the way Brenda did, but I hadn't figured any of the Newlings would be *happy* to see me. Wavy had her fingers hooked into my belt loop, and she didn't let go when Amy added her to the hug, so it was the three of us holding onto each other, which was weird but good. That's how we were when the storm door opened behind us.

Where my hand was on Amy's back, I knew the second she saw Donal. She shivered and took a step back from me and Wavy. Then one of her hands came up over her mouth.

"Donal," she said. "It's so good to see you."

"Donal." That was Leslie, and she looked like she was gonna cry.

Amy tried to hug him, but he was all bristly teenager, crossing his arms over his chest and ducking his head. He wouldn't even say hello.

"Is everything okay, Leslie?" Brice said.

"It's fine. These are my cousins, Wavy and Donal Quinn. And this is, uh . . ."

"Jesse Joe Kellen," I said.

Still smiling, Brice stuck his hand out to me. I shifted the flowers and we shook.

"Not Barfoot?" Leslie said.

"Nope. The judge changed it. It's Kellen. Now, Brice, you better step back," I said, as I let go of his hand.

"Why's that?"

"You don't wanna be standing too close to me when your mother-in-law realizes I'm here. Maybe she'll just call the cops, but there's a good chance she'll try to kill me. Either way, you don't wanna get caught in the crossfire." Like always, my nerves kept me talking.

Brice laughed like it was a good joke, but Leslie gave me a nervous smile.

"The flowers are gorgeous. Let's put them in the dining room in the good crystal vases," she said.

Vah-zes. Turned out they were fancy glass, and too small for the flowers, so I used my pocket knife to cut down the stems.

"It's like Hell's Angels Floral Arrangements," Brice said, staring at the tattoos on my arms while I messed with the flowers.

A mistake, wearing a T-shirt, except that Wavy liked to see her name running down the inside of my forearm in three-inch letters.

"I wasn't ever in a gang. I pretty much managed to get into trouble all on my own," I said.

"Who was at the door?" Brenda Newling walked into the dining room, drying her hands on her apron. Behind her was a tall redheaded woman I didn't know. Right when I needed it, the bourbon kicked in.

"Hey, Brenda. It being Christmas and all, will you at least give me a head start before you call the cops?"

21

AMY

He actually called my mother Brenda. I waited for Armageddon, while Mom gaped at her prodigal niece and the much-maligned and long-reviled Jesse Joe Kellen. A flush crept up his cheeks, as he folded his knife and put it in his pocket. We were all holding our breaths, expecting a scene, but then Mom saw Donal.

I sympathized with the shock in her face. At fourteen, he was taller than Wavy and even thinner. Everything about him was defensive, his shoulders hunched inside a gray hooded sweatshirt, and his hands jammed in the pockets. He may have been Sean's son, but he looked so much like Liam I felt like I'd been punched in the stomach. I can only imagine what Wavy felt when she looked at him. Like seeing a hybrid of someone you love and someone you hate.

In the awkward silence, I could see Mom trying to feel a bunch of things at once—anger, annoyance, relief, and then—when she looked at Donal—love and guilt. However he'd been brought back to us, we were all at fault for how he was lost.

Mom came around the table and tried to hug him, but he backpedaled, scowling. I think he might have escaped out the front door, except that Kellen laid a hand on his shoulder and kept him there.

"You're just in time! Dinner's ready!" Trisha said. She stood there looking beautiful and welcoming. I was so glad I'd invited her.

"I'll put more place settings out," Leslie said.

She added three more places to the table, while Trisha and I got kitchen chairs to make up enough seats at the dining room table. Then we started carrying in the food. When I brought out the ham, Trisha was shaking Kellen's hand.

"Hey, Trisha. Good to meet you," he said.

"I'm Amy's roommate," she said.

My *roommate*. Hearing that stopped me cold, because I remembered that drunken night in high school when Wavy had tried to comfort me. "Nothing left to be afraid of," she'd said. Even if that wasn't true, I wanted to live like it was. I wished that I had introduced Trisha properly to Mom and Leslie, but all I could do was correct the mistake.

"Actually," I said. "Trisha is my girlfriend."

Trisha's mouth dropped open for a second, and Leslie snapped her head around to look at me. Like a reward for my bravery, Wavy reached out and shook Trisha's hand.

In an act of diplomatic caution, Leslie put as much distance as she could between Kellen and Mom, but the result was that they sat at opposite ends of the table, facing each other. Still, it probably wasn't much worse than most family holiday dinners. Mom was torn between glaring at Kellen and smiling tearily at Donal, who sat next to him. The rest of us tried to keep the conversation going with as much harmless chatter as we could muster. We talked a lot about the weather, and Leslie and Brice's honeymoon to Mazatlán.

Wavy seemed different but I couldn't tell why. She managed to eat half a dinner roll and a bite of ham that took her almost five minutes to chew and swallow. Kellen ate slowly and methodically, clearing his plate, while Donal picked at his food.

"How are you, Donal?" Mom asked over dessert. She'd asked that a couple of different ways during dinner, but all she got were mumbled responses.

"Where did you find him?" Leslie said, like it was a scavenger hunt.

I tried, "How did you find each other?" Because that was the question nagging at all of us. After seven years, how had Donal come to be sitting at our table for Christmas dinner?

"My parole officer knows this private detective," Kellen said. "Got him to look through juvenile records in a couple states. He found Donal out in California."

"What about Sean? Where is he?" Mom looked at Wavy when she said it, even though the answer was likely going to come from Kellen.

At the mention of Sean, Donal stood up from the table, sending his fork and his napkin tumbling onto the floor. He shoved his chair back and stomped out into the entry. A moment later the front door slammed.

Kellen picked up the fork and napkin, while Wavy whispered something to him. He and Mom stood up at the same time. He followed Donal out the door, while she headed toward the front windows. Part of me wanted to give them some privacy, but it wasn't the strongest part. I peeked out the edge of the curtain.

Donal and Kellen stood on the front walk, just about where Wavy and Kellen had been reunited earlier in the year. Donal was hunkered down against the cold, while Kellen leaned over him, talking. Donal nodded. Kellen took out his wallet and handed Donal some money. Then he pulled something out of his front pocket and palmed it to Donal, while giving him a rough pat on the shoulder. As Kellen came back up the sidewalk to the house, Donal got into their car, started it, and drove away.

I tensed, waiting for the inevitable explosion. As soon as Kellen stepped into the dining room, my mother said, "What are you thinking? He's not old enough to drive!"

"Yeah, well, he's not old enough for a lot of the shit he's been through," Kellen said.

"You cannot be serious. You cannot be serious," Mom said, even though he obviously was. "And what if he gets pulled over? What then?"

"He won't get pulled over. He's a decent driver, and dollars to donuts he's just gonna go up the road to the gas station and buy a pop or something."

"We have some pop here," Leslie said.

"He don't need anything to drink. He needs to get some fresh air."

"He is only fourteen!" Mom said.

Kellen clenched his jaw, and I could see that under all his jokes about my mother's anger, he was carrying a grudge. I imagine six years in prison will do that.

"What do you want from the kid? What the hell do you want? You think this is easy for him? Coming back here after all these years and seeing his family and not knowing what to say or how to act. It's fucking hard, okay? It's hard for him."

That shut Mom up for a few minutes. Kellen dropped back into his chair with a thud. He snapped his napkin across his lap and picked up his fork. We were all quiet while he chewed an enormous bite of pie.

"So is Donal living with you?" I said.

Wavy nodded.

"Since November," Kellen said. It looked to me like it wasn't easy for him, either.

"What happened? I mean with his uncle—your uncle? Sean?" The whole conversation was a minefield.

"He's dead," Wavy said. Kellen looked at her and she shrugged.

"He died of a heroin overdose, more than two years ago. Donal went into foster care after that and then ended up in juvie."

"Juvie?" Leslie said. "Like jail?"

Kellen sighed and set his fork down. "Yeah. He had some trouble on a breaking and entering charge. Nothing serious. The kinda shit kids get into at that age. We hired a lawyer to get us through family court. Good guy, did okay by us. You know, I had to have my parole transferred down here, and then I can't live with anybody under sixteen because of the sex offender thing. But the lawyer got us an exception for Donal, since he's my brother-in-law."

"Wow," I said. It was like getting important news from a telegram: Sean dead, Donal in jail, Kellen and Wavy married. Stop.

"That's great that he could come live with you," Trisha said. She and Brice were both trying not to look stunned by their crash course in Wavy's life.

"Yeah, it's really great." Leslie jumped in late, but she made up for the delay by nodding vigorously. "So how is he?"

"He's doing better. But like I said, it's hard for him."

I waited for Mom to say something that would show she was happy, but she sat there looking like she'd been slapped. Despite all her efforts to keep them apart, Wavy and Kellen were together. I felt sorry for Wavy, because we were the only family she had. Kellen and Donal and us. She hadn't come to rub my mother's nose in it. She'd come to make up with Mom.

"So when did you get married?" I said.

"She didn't tell you?" The heavy crease between Kellen's eyes smoothed out and he smiled. "I thought you told her, sweetheart. Day after we got the bike, we rode down to Vegas and got married. Her roommate, Renee, and her boyfriend followed us down in the car, in case we had any troubles with the bike, but everything was dandy."

"The postcard. I didn't realize that was—congratulations!" I'd received a postcard of the Las Vegas strip, but all she'd written on the back was "Thank you," signed with a W and a heart.

"Was that fun?" Leslie said.

"It was a whole lot of noise and people, and we were tired when we got there, but you know, we had a great ride, and we didn't have to wait three days for a marriage license."

"Impatient." Wavy gave Kellen a sly look that made him grin.

"Hell, we was engaged for eight years. I'd say I was plenty patient."

Wavy laughed. Mom scowled at her plate.

"We talked about eloping, but Leslie wanted to do the big ceremony," Brice said.

"What was it like? You didn't have an Elvis impersonator, did you?" Leslie said.

Mom stood up, like you would at a wedding reception to make a toast, and I thought she would finally say something to make Wavy feel welcome. All she did was put her salad and dessert plates on top of her dinner plate and gather up her silverware.

"You cooked it, Brenda. We can clear it off," Kellen said.

She let him take the plates out of her hands. While he carried her dishes to the kitchen, the conversation was dead. Mom sat down, but without a plate to glare at, she finally looked at Wavy.

I wondered if she was doing the same thing I was doing, trying to figure out what was different about Wavy. There was something different. Not just that when Kellen came back to the table and ran his finger across his pie plate, Wavy opened her mouth and let him stick the whipped cream in. Something passed between them and he frowned.

"Oh, sweetheart, are you sure you wanna do this right now?" he said.

"Before Donal comes back."

"Fair enough."

Wavy took a deep breath and said, "Sean killed Val and Liam."

Aunt Val had been dead for seven years, but finding out who killed her turned it into a fresh wound. Leslie cried. I cried. Mom fell apart. Everyone else sat there quietly, waiting for it to be over.

Finally, Leslie wiped her eyes and said, "Do the police know?"

Kellen reached for his wallet, chain rattling, and pulled out a folded sheet of notebook paper. With a worried look on his face he smoothed the paper on the table.

"No, we haven't told the police nothing. I don't think Donal's ready for that. He hasn't exactly been making friends with the cops lately. He wrote this to Wavy, while he was still in juvie, right after we found out where he was. They sent a whole lot of letters while we were trying to get the custody stuff figured out. The first half is about Sean, about the situation. Look, I don't wanna say nothing rude. I don't know if I—"

"Just say it," Mom said.

"The first part is just about, you know, Sean being Donal's father."

Kellen wasn't a fast reader, and he seemed worried about saying the wrong thing. I thought of offering to read it, but it was Wavy's letter and she'd given it to him.

"That day, when you dropped Donal off at the ranch, he says he went up to the farmhouse and Liam's bike was there and Val's car. Donal says, 'I could hear him yelling.' Sean, he means. '*You said you loved me. You promised, you bitch.*' Sorry."

"It's okay," I said.

"'And Mama was screaming, *You killed him!* She was crying and I was too scared to go in, because they were yelling the way Liam did. You know, how he would get crazy. I wanted to run away, but I was scared to leave Mama there.'"

Wavy stared through the dining room wall, but the rest of us watched Kellen, who put his hand over his eyes for a moment. When he went back to reading, his voice was raw.

" 'Mama was saying, *No! No!* And then I heard the gun. After that, it was quiet for a while. So I opened the door and saw Mama. She was on the floor with the gun in her hand, but Sean was standing over her. He told me what to say to the cops. To tell them I was alone, that nobody else was there. He made me say it over and over, so I wouldn't screw it up. Sean said if I told anybody he was there, something bad would happen to you. That's why I went back to the house after Sean left and took the gun. I went—"

Kellen stopped. Mom was crying again. Wavy squeezed Kellen's arm and he said, "I don't wanna read that part."

"Yes," Wavy said.

"No, sweetheart, I really don't."

"Please."

After almost every sentence, I thought Kellen would cry, but he made it to the end of the letter.

"Donal says, 'I went to the garage and I saw you and Kellen together. I'm sorry about spying on you, but I was so scared. I needed to know you were okay. If you were with Kellen, I knew you were safe. Except the cops said . . . he—he raped you. Maybe that was my fault, because I told the cops that I saw you on the desk in the office with him. And then after Kellen got arrested, it wasn't safe to tell anybody. Sean always said something bad could happen to you. I didn't know what he might do, if Kellen wasn't there to protect you. Now that Sean's dead, I guess I can tell you. I hope you're really coming to visit me like your letter says. Since you're my sister, they say I can have a contact visit with you. See you soon. Love, Donal.'"

Kellen picked up his napkin and blew his nose. He sat with his head down, until Wavy stood up and leaned over him. When he raised his head, she held his face in her hands and kissed him.

She glanced at Mom and, for a good minute, all they did was look at each other. Mom had tears running down her face, but Wavy was smiling.

"You wanted to protect me. I know. We're going to be okay."

"I'm glad," Mom whispered. She actually sounded it.

The front door snapped open and Donal skulked into the dining room holding a Styrofoam cup. Fumbling in one of his sweatshirt pockets, he pulled out a handful of crumpled bills and the car keys. When he laid them on the table next to Kellen's plate, a few coins rolled loose and fell on the floor.

"Oh jeez," he said, seeing us all looking weepy.

"It's okay. I think we're done crying," I said.

Donal reached out and laid his hand on the back of Wavy's neck.

"Icy paws," she said and swatted him away. For a second he cracked a smile.

Then she picked up her plate and carried it out to the kitchen. Kellen followed her with the ham platter, and Donal trailed after them.

When I took what was left of the pie into the kitchen, the three of them were standing at the sink. Donal and Wavy were both eating off her plate and Kellen was washing dishes. Seeing them next to each other, I figured out what was different about Wavy. The top of her head almost reached Kellen's armpit. She had grown.

ACKNOWLEDGMENTS

I want to offer my thanks to the following people:

Jess Regel, who set all this in motion and who has been there every step of the way.

Liberty Greenwood and Robert Ozier, for wrecking my house, putting it back together, walking the dogs, and rescuing me on a regular basis.

Gary Clift, Doc Fedder, and Ben Nyberg, who first suggested that writing books wasn't the worst thing I could do with my life.

All the wonderful people at St. Martin's Press and Thomas Dunne Books: Laurie Chittenden, Melanie Fried, Tom Dunne, Pete Wolverton, Laura Clark, Katie Bassel, Lauren Friedlander, Anna Gorovoy, Olga Grlic, Jeremy Pink, and Joy Gannon.

This book's early readers and cheerleaders: Renee Perelmutter, Jessica Brockmole, Lisa Brackmann, Dana Fredsti, G. J. Berger, Sarah W., Norma Johnson, Laura Anglin, Erica Greenwood, Kari Stewart, Sue Laybourn, Teri Kanefield, Shveta Thakrar, Jenna Nelson, Michelle Muto, Jan O'Hara, Jennifer Donahue, Stacy Testa, Susan Ginsburg, and Gretchen McNeil, BAMF.

Sarah Kanning and Leslie Soden, in whose guest rooms I wrote the first draft.

All of my writing friends: Purgatorians, Lurkers, Pitizens, and the indomitable YNots.

My beloved Vox peeps: Amy Heisler, LeendaDLL, Terry Snyder, Laurie Channer, Lurkertype, Lauri Schooltz, Katrine, RobbieDobbie, madtante, Jaypo, Ms. Pants, and many more.

Clovia Shaw, for her limitless curiosity, her righteous Google-fu, and her 24/7 free consultations.

Reading Group Gold

ALL THE UGLY AND WONDERFUL THINGS
by Bryn Greenwood

About the Author
- A Conversation with Bryn Greenwood

Behind the Novel
- A Note to Readers

Keep on Reading
- Recommended Reading
- Reading Group Questions

A
Reading
Group Gold
Selection

For more reading group suggestions
visit www.readinggroupgold.com.

 ST. MARTIN'S GRIFFIN

What was the inspiration for this novel?

I was driving through rural Kansas at sunset, and I saw a guy riding a motorcycle down a dirt road through a hay field. My curiosity was immediately piqued. Who was he and where was he going? In that instant, I just knew there was a little girl hiding in the hay. The first scene I wrote was Wavy and Kellen meeting at the edge of that meadow beside a wrecked motorcycle. I didn't know who they were, but it was obvious to me that they needed each other. Kellen was injured. Wavy was hungry. They were both terribly alone. I felt sure it had been weeks, if not months, since anyone had looked at either of them and acknowledged their humanity. After that, I worked backwards to figure out who Wavy was, who Kellen was, what their story was.

"My personal experiences definitely informed some of the details in the book."

Your biography mentions that you're the daughter of a "mostly reformed drug dealer." How much of the story is inspired by your own childhood?

My personal experiences definitely informed some of the details in the book. When I was a kid, my father was a meth dealer, and he lived on an armed compound in the country. As a result of his career choices, I witnessed a lot of wild things and met some unusual people. The other part of my life that I drew heavily on for this book was my habit of getting involved with much older men. Like Wavy, at the age of thirteen, I fell in love with and dated a man more than twice my age. To an outsider, that relationship probably looked inappropriate (and it was certainly illegal), but I have fond memories of my time with him. We had a loving, consensual romance that nurtured me more than a lot of my adult relationships have. That experience gave me insight into Wavy's motivations, and probably made me more inclined to deal sympathetically with Wavy and Kellen's situation.

Was it your intention to write a story where conventional ideas of right and wrong are turned upside down?

It's less about wanting to turn right and wrong upside down, and more about wanting to demonstrate how blurred the line between right and wrong can be. When it comes to *All the Ugly and Wonderful Things*, the line disappears altogether at some points in the book. Instead of offering moral guideposts, I'm asking readers to suspend their everyday perceptions of morality and sympathize with flawed characters. Often those characters are good people who make bad decisions. Things like poverty, addiction, and abuse lead a lot of people to make decisions that look immoral from the outside, but that make a kind of sense when you're in that situation. We may be horrified by Kellen's plans to marry teenaged Wavy, but it's the only solution he sees for rescuing her from her parents. There are other options open to Aunt Brenda, but she chooses not to exercise them until a crisis forces her hand. Personally, I sympathize with characters who are trying to figure out the least bad thing they can do. Characters in bad situations with limited options are always more compelling to me than characters who have clear boundaries and make neat, practical choices.

Why did you decide to use so many narrators to this story, and how did you choose them?

When I first learned to write short fiction, I was taught to reverse the roles of antagonist and protagonist, and write both versions. The goal was to understand all my characters, even the ones I might not naturally sympathize with. That continues to be part of my creative process. In terms of Wavy's story, I knew I couldn't rely on the central characters to give a complete view of her relationship with Kellen, so I went further afield than I usually do. Because I wanted to know what things looked like from all angles, I investigated the story through a lot of peripheral characters, which makes it feel almost like a documentary.

Although I ended up with sixteen narrators in the book, I actually wrote a lot more than that, including scenes from the points of view of Val, Liam, and Aunt Brenda. Wavy's parents didn't make the cut, because they were so focused on themselves that their narratives derailed the story I wanted to tell. Although Aunt Brenda is the natural antagonist to Wavy, her narrative turned out to be redundant. Aunt Brenda doesn't need to speak, because the average reader knows exactly what she's thinking. It's what we would be thinking if we were in her shoes.

What do you hope readers will take away from this story?

Above all, I hope my book makes people think seriously about the nature of consent and a child's right to bodily sovereignty. So often, when we speak about consent, we're talking about sex, but it's not the only kind of consent that matters. In

grappling with the issue of underage sex, people often overlook Liam forcing Wavy to eat, Brenda forcibly restraining Wavy, and all the other non-sexual ways in which Wavy's consent is violated in the course of the book. Kellen is the only one who regularly seeks her explicit permission for any kind of physical contact. The question of what rights children have is incredibly complicated and there are no easy answers. The subject haunts me, because I worry that a child who has no power to say yes also has no power to say no. Children are regularly abused, because our society fails to listen to them. Even when we do listen, we often don't believe children. That's the environment that allows predators in positions of authority to flourish.

Secondarily, I hope that readers will spend some time thinking about the nature of family. When our own families let us down, how do we deal with that? How do we constitute new families? How well do we do at accepting the families that people choose, as opposed to the ones they're born into?

I often hear from readers who find Wavy and Kellen's early interactions sweet, but who are deeply troubled by how the relationship evolves. *Why can't their relationship stay platonic?* those readers ask.

When I'm writing, my characters frequently do what they want, without regard for what I think should happen. This was very true for Wavy and Kellen. For obvious reasons, I tried repeatedly to keep their relationship platonic until she was older. I threw women at Kellen. I tried to give Wavy other friends. I tried to motivate Aunt Brenda or Miss DeGrassi to get involved. None of it worked, because no one was willing to make the sacrifices Kellen made for Wavy, and there were too many external factors pushing them together.

Even as a child, Wavy is absorbing messages about how to survive in the world as a female. The primary lesson she learns from Val, Sandy, Dee, and even Aunt Brenda is simple: get a man. If you get a man, he'll take care of you. This is a pressing issue for Wavy, because her parents are failing so spectacularly to provide for her and Donal. As Kellen is the only adult regularly caring for her, it's hardly surprising that she decides to make him "her man." Of course, Wavy is at a disadvantage when it comes to securing Kellen. As most of us have experienced, when our friends get into a new relationship, they tend to wander away from us. The whiff of a woman's perfume on Kellen's coat does more than make Wavy jealous, it threatens her central position in his life. She can't afford to lose him, and the obvious way to keep him is to prove to him that she's a viable sexual partner.

Take Wavy's entry into puberty and awakening sexuality, her love for Kellen, and her need to keep him attached to her. Mix those all together and it's easy to understand how, at thirteen years old, she arrives at the night of Kellen's twenty-sixth birthday, prepared to offer him a sexual relationship.

How Kellen ends up there is also linked to his childhood. As much as we would like his feelings for Wavy to be paternal, they're not. *Paternal* for people like Wavy and Kellen is nothing good. In their world, a father is at best someone who neglects you, at worst someone who beats you. Kellen is trying to be better than the father he had, better than the father Wavy has. He's trying to be her friend. What starts out as an act of kindness to a neglected little girl becomes the closest friendship he's ever had. Kellen has had a lifetime of being an outsider, and Wavy is not just the first girl he's ever loved, she's the first person to love him since his mother died.

Of course, Kellen is also a young man who wants what most young men want: love, companionship, and sex. Wavy offers him the first two for many years, and when she offers him the third, maybe it seems like a natural development. She has become the center of his world, their relationship the only solid one in his life. On the night of his birthday, he's drunk and she's dressed up as a reasonable facsimile of a woman. His mistake is almost inevitable, if not entirely forgivable.

Afterwards, what happens follows the same set of guiding stars. When Kellen carries a naked and shivering Wavy up to her bedroom, he concludes that he has three options. I left it to the reader's imagination to decide which of these options he thinks is "terrible" and which is "too awful to consider."

Kellen can cross a line that is clearly marked, even in his mind, as wrong. Wavy has offered him a relationship that includes sex, and there is no one in her life to protect her from that kind of predation, except Kellen.

The second option is for him to walk away. He can acknowledge that his feelings for Wavy are inappropriate and that her feelings for him make him a fox guarding a henhouse. Perhaps this would be the most moral choice for him, but if we imagine Kellen exiting Wavy's life to avoid crossing that line, we must consider the consequences. He ensures that she gets an education, that she eats, that she has clothes and shoes, that her home is clean, that she's protected from the dangerous people her father's business has introduced into her life. If Kellen walks away, he leaves an enormous void in Wavy's life. One that will either go unfilled, or will soon be occupied by a man with fewer scruples than Kellen.

There remains then the third choice: to slow the advance of Wavy's overtures. Kellen can't simply push Wavy away without reinforcing a deeply damaging message she has absorbed from her mother. Wavy believes she is dirty, and for Kellen to completely rebuff her would be devastating to her. His explanation that she is "too young" holds no water with Wavy, because she already has an adult's responsibilities, and the women in her life are already giving her lessons on how to navigate a relationship with a man. Sandy gives her a makeover to make her more sexually attractive. Val

lectures her about the importance of birth control, on the assumption that she is already in a sexual relationship with Kellen. In Wavy's world, she is not too young to take this next step.

More importantly, Val's lessons remind Wavy that the world is ugly. Men only want one thing. Women only have one function. Therefore, the only reason Kellen wouldn't be open to an adult relationship with her is that she's undesirable or "dirty."

Ultimately, the responsibility for what happens rests on Kellen's shoulders. Someone with a less dysfunctional upbringing might have found more solutions than he does, but like many adult children of abuse, he is constantly operating under crisis conditions and he has terrible decision making skills. In the moment, seeing the awful thing that he's allowed to happen, he simply looks for the choice that will cause the least harm. From his perspective, that is to deploy the same methods of negotiation he's used with Wavy for as long as he's known her. To delineate and define boundaries and to seek mutual respect. The end result is not one we would wish for any young girl, but what part of Wavy's life is?

—Bryn Greenwood

Recommended Reading

The Heart Is a Lonely Hunter
Carson McCullers

I recommend this with the caveat that this book broke my heart. At its center is a young girl from a large, poor family, and a deaf-mute who loses his lifelong companion. It's about small-town poverty and loneliness, and the desperate need people have for love and companionship.

The Little Friend
Donna Tartt

While Harriet is growing up in a very different environment than Wavy, this book spoke to me about the difficulties of being a child in a family that is disintegrating around tragedy. The Quinns' family tragedy is meth and abuse, while the Dufresnes' is the murder of Harriet's older brother.

The Great Gilly Hopkins
Katherine Paterson

A throwback to my own childhood reading, this is a story about a wounded girl who's hard to love. Gilly has been passed from foster home to foster home, until love and family seem like dangerous propositions.

Methamphetamine: A Love Story
Rashi K. Shukla

This is a very compassionate inquiry into the lives of people who use, manufacture, and sell crystal methamphetamine. It's not easy reading, but it's honest and it provides real insight into how people end up making and using meth.

Winter's Bone
Daniel Woodrell

A bleak, brutal story about the complications of
family and meth. Sometimes when I think of Ree
Dolly, I imagine an alternate reality in which there
was no one to protect or buffer Wavy from her
parents' lifestyle. It's a short read, like a punch to
the face.

Lolita
Vladimir Nabokov

I recommend this not because it's similar to my
book, but because it is dissimilar. Nabokov's prose
is gorgeous, but the story itself is a reminder
of how easy it is for adults to take advantage
of unprotected children. Despite being the
titular character, Lolita is an afterthought whose
happiness is of little interest to the narcissistic
narrator.

Reading Group Questions

1. From the first moment we meet Wavy, her life is filled with rules. Most are her mother's rules, but some are hers. What rules are holding Wavy back and which ones does she use to construct a sense of safety? How do the rules change as she grows up?

2. Wavy's fears and her efforts to resist fear are major themes in the story. How does the refrain "nothing left to be afraid of" guide Wavy's life?

3. More than once, it's remarked that the kitchen door of the farmhouse is unlocked, and Wavy points out that there isn't even a key to that door. On a practical level, what does it say about Wavy and the people around her that this door is never locked? As a metaphor, what does it tell us?

4. Kellen is a murderer and Wavy knows this from an early point in her relationship with him. How is she able to know this while still considering him a good person? What things in her life have prepared her to accept two seemingly contradictory ideas? How do you feel about this paradox?

5. The book provides multiple points of view of Wavy and Kellen, including their own. How are your impressions of them altered by a narrator's biases? Who seems like the most reliable narrator? Who seems the least reliable? How do you decide whose opinion to trust?

6. Aunt Brenda's perspective is the one that most clearly correlates to our current social attitudes toward relationships like Wavy and Kellen's, but is she the hero of this story? To what degree do you sympathize with her?

7. Compared to Wavy, her cousins and her college roommate are ostensibly the product of "normal" upbringings. In what ways are they more emotionally healthy than Wavy? In what ways do they have similar emotional issues?

8. Until 2006, the state of Kansas had no law requiring a minimum age for marriage, as long as the underage bride or groom had parental or judicial consent. On occasion this produced child brides far younger than Wavy would have been. The law now sets the minimum age at fifteen, a year younger than the age of consent. How does marriage change our views of what would otherwise be statutory rape? What if Kellen's wish had come true, and he and Wavy had married after her fourteenth birthday? How would we view that relationship once it was sealed by law?

9. When we talk about "consent" we have a bad habit of restricting it to the question of sex, but what other types of consent are at play in the story? Stress is placed on Wavy's capacity to consent to a sexual relationship with Kellen, but what about her capacity to consent or refuse consent to other things?

10. Of the female role models in Wavy's life, which has the greatest effect on her? How do these role models color her views about herself and her relationships?

11. As much as we may wish for Wavy and Kellen's relationship to remain platonic, what do you feel contributes to its steady shift toward becoming first romantic and then sexual? What might have happened if it had remained platonic?

12. Amy narrates a large portion of Wavy's life, while only revealing parts of her own. How does she choose what to reveal and what to hide? And why might she prefer to tell Wavy's story over her own?

13. What is the dynamic between Wavy and Kellen as husband and wife at the end? Who do you see as the decision maker? The moral compass? What other roles have they taken on, and how comfortable are they in those roles? Considering their backgrounds, how likely are they to succeed in creating a healthy relationship and a "normal" family?